Simon stopped for a mom
He didn't seem to notice tha
the body of his dead assi

Somehow, Simon managed to keep a straight face after that.

"Okay."

"If I could kill you without causing problems with the Round Table, I would have done it last year," Simon said. "But you're marginally more useful than annoying, and your Valkyrie's ... Sig's ... ability to talk to the dead is an even bigger asset here. Miss Newman wasn't affected by that thing's power word either, and I find that very interesting. She might be more useful trying to exorcise these things than our own priests."

"Sucks to be Choo," Choo muttered.

I didn't like Simon's tone. "We're not chess pieces."

Simon did look down at his assistant then. Maybe he was making a point. "We're all chess pieces."

Praise for the Pax Arcana series:

"The Pax Arcana books are seriously good reads. Action, humor, and heart with unexpected twists and turns. If you are (like me) waiting for the next Butcher or Hearne—pick up Elliott James. Then you can bite your nails waiting for the next James, too."

—*New York Times* bestselling author Patricia Briggs

"Loved it! *Charming* is a giant gift basket of mythology and lore delivered by a brilliant new voice in urban fantasy. Elliott James tells stories that are action-packed, often amusing, and always entertaining."

—*New York Times* bestselling author Kevin Hearne

"I loved this book from start to finish. Exciting and innovative, *Charming* is a great introduction to a world I look forward to spending a lot more time in."

—*New York Times* bestselling author Seanan McGuire

"With each new chapter in his outstanding Pax Arcana series, James ups his game in both excellent character development and world expansion. If you love wisecracks in the face of ultimate danger, then John Charming is definitely your man!"

—*RT Book Reviews* (Top Pick)

"In a saturated literary realm, James's tale stands out for the gritty, believable world he builds.... This is masculine urban fantasy in the vein of Jim Butcher and Mark del Franco."

—*Booklist*

LEGEND HAS IT

PAX ARCANA: BOOK 5

ELLIOTT JAMES

www.orbitbooks.net

Copyright © 2017 by Elliott James LLC
Excerpt from *Strange Practice* copyright © 2017 by Vivian Shaw

Cover design by Wendy Chan
Cover images © Trevillion
Cover copyright © 2017 by Hachette Book Group, Inc.

Orbit
Hachette Book Group
1290 Avenue of the Americas
New York, NY 10104
orbitbooks.net

First Edition: April 2017

Orbit is an imprint of Hachette Book Group.
The Orbit name and logo are trademarks of Little, Brown Book Group Limited.

The publisher is not responsible for websites (or their content) that are not owned by the publisher.

The Hachette Speakers Bureau provides a wide range of authors for speaking events. To find out more, go to www.hachettespeakersbureau.com or call (866) 376-6591.

Library of Congress Cataloging-in-Publication Data
Names: James, Elliott, author.
Title: Legend has it / Elliott James.
Description: New York, NY : Orbit, 2017. | Series: Pax Arcana ; 5
Identifiers: LCCN 2016050469| ISBN 9780316302371 (paperback) |
    ISBN 9780316302364 (ebook)
Subjects: | BISAC: FICTION / Fantasy / Contemporary. | FICTION / Fantasy /
    Urban Life. | FICTION / Action & Adventure. | FICTION / Fantasy /
    Paranormal. | GSAFD: Fantasy fiction.
Classification: LCC PS3610.A4334 L44 2017 | DDC 813/.6—dc23 LC record
available at https://lccn.loc.gov/2016050469

ISBNs: 978-0-316-30237-1 (paperback), 978-0-316-30236-4 (ebook)

Printed in the United States of America

LSC-C

10 9 8 7 6 5 4 3 2 1

To Kim. We're as different as the moon and the sun, but we always come around, and we always have each other's backs. Love you always.

Faustus is gone. Regard his hellish fall,
Whose fiendful fortune may exhort the wise
Only to wonder at unlawful things,
Whose deepness doth entice such forward wits,
To practise more than heavenly power permits.
—Christopher Marlowe, *Dr. Faustus*

Remember
First to possess his books, for without them
He's but a sot, as I am, nor hath not
One spirit to command: they all do hate him
As rootedly as I. Burn but his books.
—William Shakespeare, *The Tempest*

WHAT AN INTERVIEW WITH BARBARA WALTERS MIGHT LOOK LIKE

WALTERS: So... you claim that your last name is Charming.

ME: Well, with a capital *C*, yes. My name is John Charming.

WALTERS: And you're the descendant of the original Prince Charming.

ME: There was no original Prince Charming. Have you ever heard of a Charming dynasty anywhere? Some of my ancestors became involved in some [CENSORED]-up events that got distorted over time and passed down as fairy tales. None of them were royalty.

WALTERS: They weren't?

ME: No, they were not.

WALTERS: So, why call them Princes?

ME: If you were a storyteller in the Dark Ages, you didn't tell stories about violent heroic commoners, Barbara. The nobles didn't want the riffraff getting any ideas. Working-class peasants getting visited by elves or fairy godmothers? Sure. Joe Schmoe picking up an axe and carving up a powerful monster who lived in a castle full of treasure? That was a little too close to home.

WALTERS: So, your ancestors were really commoners.

ME: My ancestors were Gaulish soldiers who became crypt robbers after Rome conquered Gaul. Learning how to deal with undead monsters and magical curses was part of the job. Then eventually one of them figured out that monsters who live a long time tend to accumulate lots of legally seizable wealth, so my family stopped being criminals and became monster hunters full-time.

WALTERS: So, they weren't exactly peasants, either.

ME: It took a few generations, but my family eventually became rich and later became titled and crossed over to England during the Norman invasion. But hunting monsters is how we got our name.

WALTERS: I don't understand.

ME: Regular folk were named after their occupation back then. It's why we still have last names like Miller and Smith and Hooker and Dungburner.

WALTERS: But how is grave-robbing charming?

ME: Okay, I know I'm imagining this interview, but this really isn't how I imagined this interview.

WALTERS: Have you ever seen one of my interviews?

ME: Just clips. You always look very earnest in them. Like everything the person is saying is the most important thing you've ever heard, and you're taking everything very seriously.

WALTERS: Is that a problem for you? You present yourself as something of a smartass. Do you want to be taken seriously?

ME:—

WALTERS: John?

ME: To go back to your original question, part of being a monster hunter was being a witchfinder. And part of being a witchfinder was selling charms and breaking enchantments and showing people how to set up wards. That's how we got the name Charming.

WALTERS: But wouldn't that make you John Charmer? There are Millers, not Millings. Carpenters, not Carpentering.

ME: Wow. You're tougher than I thought.

WALTERS: As you pointed out, you're imagining me right now. Are you tough on yourself?

ME: You're not going to make me cry, Barbara. [CENSORED] off.

WALTERS: We'll get back to that. You haven't explained why your name wouldn't be Charmer.

ME: If you're really interested, a lot of people's names ended with *-ing* before Alexander Pope started formalizing verb tenses. You still get the occasional Hunting and Manning and Dunning and Redding and so on.

WALTERS: It turns out I'm not really interested.

ME: Okay.

WALTERS: So. John Charming. You hunt monsters.

ME: Yes.

WALTERS: You must be very good at it. I've never seen one.

ME: You probably have. Remember Sleeping Beauty, where the fairies put a whole kingdom under a sleeping spell?

WALTERS: Yes.

ME: Well, the fae put most of the world under a spell. It keeps people from noticing any supernatural event that isn't a direct threat to their existence.

WALTERS: So, the supernatural is invisible?

ME: Some beings maybe, but not as a general rule.

WALTERS: I don't understand.

ME: What did the third person who passed your car this morning look like?

WALTERS: I have no idea.

ME: Was he or she invisible?

WALTERS: According to you, they might have been.

ME: Hah. Maybe they were. But probably not. You just didn't notice them. That's how the Pax Arcana works. A zombie could be doing interpretive dance behind you right now, and you just wouldn't register it as anything worth questioning or remembering.

WALTERS: Is there a zombie doing interpretive dance behind me right now?

ME: No.

WALTERS: So. This spell. You called it the Pax Arcana?

ME: That's what we call the whole magical truce that the spell helps maintain.

WALTERS: A truce? That sounds like there was a war.

ME: There was. It was called the Dark Ages. Mankind and magickind almost wiped each other out.

WALTERS: Are you talking about inquisitions and witch trials?

ME: Not just them. There are thousands of recorded references to supernatural beings and how to kill them. We just look at those written scraps as proof of how barbaric and irrational ancient people were instead of treating them as actual historical documents. Like we're so much more intelligent than our ancestors because we have smartphones and espresso machines.

WALTERS: Are you still talking about fairy tales?

ME: I'm talking about diaries, letters, and court transcripts. Pliny the Elder. Paracelsus. The Book of Kells. And that's only the cases that were written about in a time when most people were illiterate and there were no printing presses or phones or televisions. Figure there must have been thousands of events for every one that got written down. Then figure that for every document that survived the ravages of time, Saxon invasions, and church bonfires, there must have been hundreds of—

WALTERS: You've made your point. So we almost destroyed magical beings. How did they almost destroy us? Wouldn't that have made the history books?

ME: Did you ever hear of the Black Death?

WALTERS:—

ME: That wasn't just a plague. It was a magical curse. That's what forced us to agree to the Pax Arcana. Two thirds of the Western world died.

WALTERS: Who is this "us" you keep referring to?

ME: The Knights Templar.

WALTERS: [Laughing] So, your family didn't just become knights; they became Illuminati.

ME: We don't use the *I* word. And there are other secret societies in other cultures who help keep mankind and magickind apart too.

WALTERS: If no one notices these monsters all around us, why bother?

ME: I said no one notices monsters who aren't a direct threat to their existence. Some are direct threats.

WALTERS: So, some monsters are still…monstrous?

ME: Yes. And knights still take care of them.

WALTERS: You mean you kill them.

ME: If they're not already dead, yes.

WALTERS: But only the monsters who draw attention to themselves.

ME: Yes. That's the Pax Arcana in a nuthouse. I mean, nutshell.

WALTERS: I find all of this very disturbing.

ME: Well, my name could have just as easily been John Disturbing. I guess I lucked out.

WALTERS: John Disturbing might be more appropriate. You don't seem very charming, if you don't mind me saying so.

ME: No one likes to be stereotyped, Barbara.

WALTERS: But aren't knights supposed to be chivalrous?

ME: First of all, I'm no longer a knight. Secondly, knightly honor is a load of horse[CENSORED]. Most knights considered raping commoners a right of birth. They rode around on trained warhorses and wrapped themselves in plate mail and mostly killed unarmored men on foot who were armed with axes and pitchforks. If a knight got captured in battle, he usually wasn't killed, because he was worth a lot of money. He gave his word not to escape—his parole—and sat out the rest of the war, drinking wine and listening to minstrels and flirting with the ladies in his host's castle until his family ransomed him. Do you know why the Magna Carta got signed?

WALTERS: [Laughing again] Because of magic?

ME: No. Because English peasants came up with a longbow that could punch an armored knight off his horse at ninety yards. As soon as [CENSORED] got real, knights got more reasonable.

WALTERS: You seem angry about knights. Why aren't you one any longer?

ME: I became a werewolf.

WALTERS: A werewolf.

ME: Yes. A werewolf.

WALTERS: Can you change into a wolf right now?

ME: I said I was a werewolf. I didn't say I was good at it.

WALTERS: Well, maybe I'll see you on a full moon.

ME: Let's hope not.

WALTERS: So. You hunted monsters. Then you became a monster.

ME: Yep. Nietzsche called that one.

WALTERS: And you were surrounded by monster hunters.

ME: Yes. It was socially awkward.

WALTERS: So you left.

ME: Actually, I ran for my life and spent several decades hiding.

WALTERS: Decades? You don't look older than thirty.

ME: My body heals from most damage really quickly. Age is a kind of damage.

WALTERS: Wow. [Laughing] Sign me up.

ME: Hardly anybody younger than thirteen and older than forty survives being bitten by a werewolf, Barbara, and then only if they're in really good shape. Most people's hearts give out during their first change, before the fast healing kicks all the way in. Then they can't have kids. A fetus can't take that kind of punishment either.

WALTERS: Still...

ME: Then there's the emotional side. Becoming a werewolf means having a lot of foreign instincts and really primal impulses hardwired into your brain. It's like spot-welding a refrigerator to a dishwashing machine. Sometimes, you wind up trying to wash dishes in the freezer compartment. A lot of people can't handle it.

WALTERS: But you handled it.

ME: It's like being an alcoholic. It never stops being a struggle. And werewolves live a long time.

WALTERS: Is that why you seem so angry when you talk about knights?

ME:—

WALTERS: John?

ME: I hid among normal humans for a long time. I got lonely. I fell in love. A knight found me and killed the woman I loved while he was trying to get to me. And it was my fault. That's why I'm still angry when I talk about knights.

WALTERS: This woman...

ME: No.

WALTERS: No?

ME: I've said all I'm going to say about that.

WALTERS: So, that's still a struggle too.

ME: Are we done here?

WALTERS: Why this interview? Aren't you still being hunted?

ME: No. A while back, some werewolves organized into a really big pack and started giving the knights a hard time. The knights agreed to stop hunting me after I helped them broker a peace treaty with the wolves.

WALTERS: Really.

ME: Really. The new leader of the wolves is a friend of mine. He changed the name of the pack to the Round Table and agreed to help the knights with some of the worst supernatural incidents.

WALTERS: [Laughing] The Round Table? Like King Arthur's Round Table?

ME: Yeah. But more like the Native American tradition of round tables. He's Chippewa and has a weird sense of humor.

WALTERS: So, you have friends.

ME: Yes. And there's someone in my life again.

WALTERS: Another werewolf?

ME: She's a Valkyrie, actually.

WALTERS: A Valkyrie.

ME: Yep. Her name is Sig.

WALTERS: We're talking Wagner here. Big horned helmet. Huge singing voice.

ME: We're talking someone who can shot-put a prize pig and sees dead people. That's actually how Sig and I met.

WALTERS: Shot-putting prize pigs?

ME: No. The ghost of the woman I loved sort of rented some space in Sig's brain for a little while.

WALTERS: That must have been complicated.

ME: I also killed Sig's former lover.

WALTERS: Was he a monster?

ME: Yes, but the human kind.

WALTERS: So, it was *very* complicated.

ME: Sig and I both had a lot of issues we hadn't dealt with, and they sort of all came together in a perfect storm.

WALTERS: This really is starting to sound Wagnerian.

ME: I wouldn't know. I don't actually like opera. It's the way people sing conversations. It freaks me out.

WALTERS: *That's* what freaks you out?

ME: Everything's relative.

WALTERS: Let's get back to Sig.

ME: Okay.

WALTERS: You're in love, however you got there. You have friends. Are you happy now?

ME: I am. That's freaking me out a little too.

WALTERS: I'm sure it is. From what you've said, you were orphaned, then condemned by the people who raised you. You were alone for decades. Then the one person who accepted you for who you were was killed, and you blame yourself for it. Do you ever talk to her through this Sig?

ME: No. Alison and I said good-bye.

WALTERS: Her name was Alison? If you could say anything to Alison, right now, what would you say?

ME:—

WALTERS: [Leaning in like a compassionate vulture] John?

ME: [Tearing up] Dammit, Barbara.

WALTERS: What would you say?

ME: [Whispering] Thank you.

WALTERS: Thank you?

ME: Thank you for teaching me how to love.

WALTERS: [Leaning back with an air of self-satisfaction] So. What's next for John Charming?

ME: [Wiping moisture from corners of eyes] Well, I'm going to try really hard not to make fun of you for asking me to refer to myself in the third person.

WALTERS: And after that?

ME: It turns out that the Knights Templar aren't the only Western secret society that knows about the Pax Arcana. I recently found out about some organization called the School of Night.

WALTERS: The School of Night.

ME: It's an occult group that goes all the way back to Shakespeare's time.

WALTERS: Is this School of Night a friend or an enemy?

ME: Definitely an enemy. It took them a long time, but they actually managed to infiltrate the Knights Templar. They grafted a fake branch onto the Templars' family tree. We had a whole family of traitors in our ranks going back three or four generations.

WALTERS: You mean *they*.

ME: What?

WALTERS: The knights. You said *we*.

ME: Oh. Yeah. It happens.

WALTERS: Isn't this School of Night enforcing your Pax Arcana too?

ME: I'm not sure. Ultimately, I think they want to destroy it. They definitely want to destroy the Knights Templar.

WALTERS: What would happen if they did?

ME: I have no idea.

PART THE FIRST

Four Vettings and a Funeral

Prologue Two: Electric Boogaloo

CLEANUP IN AISLE NINE

New York City

Seniority had its perks, and working aisle nine was one of them. Fred (Freda) Byrd was on the short side—five feet two—and most of the stuff in the baby-food aisle was light and easy to pack. The baby-food jars almost went together like Lego pieces, and the diapers were fluffy and big and acted like padding for the breakable goods when Fred had to put overstock back on the storage pallet. Win-win-win. Plus, Fred got to look at pictures of smiling babies all night long, which wasn't bad for her mood now that both of her chicks had left the nest. There were worse ways to get out of the house. Greg's back had finally forced him to quit driving his fuel truck, and Fred guessed she loved him, but having him around all the time after twenty-eight years getting used to having time to herself was seriously getting on her nerves.

As a general rule, Fred took her time facing up the aisle. Wayne Lehardy wasn't too bad as stock-crew bosses went—he and Fred had worked together at the old store on Oceanside ten years before—but Wayne would still make Fred's life miserable if he thought he could get more work out of her. But tonight, Fred was pushing it a little so that she could go help the new girl out over on the canned-vegetable aisle.

Robin Hanks was cute, and Randy Prutko had been finishing up on aisle five early so that he could go "help her out." It wasn't any of Fred's business, not really, but Robin wasn't some pretty little thing shaking her rear end to get the dumbass males to do her work for her—Fred had seen a few of those in her time. Robin was quiet and a hard worker. The girl was working a night job because it went along with her waitressing hours and her community college classes, and she didn't want any part of any Randy Prutko, but Robin didn't know how to handle him.

Fred didn't really know how to handle Randy Prutko either, but Fred wasn't a cute young girl, and she could at least put herself between them. There was something wrong about that shitheel. It wasn't just that Randy was big and knew it, wearing tight T-shirts that showed off his arms even if they made his stomach stick out like a basketball. It was something hiding in the back of those flat, shiny eyes. Something growling in the back of his throat when Randy talked about how nobody could make any money working for somebody else, or complained about stuck-up college bitches. Wayne made the stock crew take breaks together—he said it was to help them be a team, but they all knew it was so he could make sure nobody took too much time off—so Fred got to hear plenty of Randy Prutko's views on life.

Fred got to watch Randy sit too close to Robin, too. Got to watch him make little comments that were supposed to be funny, speculating on what a wild party girl Robin probably was off the clock, or asking the girl fake-friendly questions that any fool could see she didn't want to answer. Nothing too out of line, but enough to bring out Fred's maternal instincts.

"I don't mean you. You ain't one of them stuck-up college bitches, Robin," Randy had said two nights before, while Wayne was taking a bathroom break. His voice had been so sugary, it made Fred feel like her teeth were getting drilled at the dentist's office. All of the other men on the night crew had shifted in their chairs a little uncomfortably, but none of them wanted any trouble. They just wanted to do their jobs and get home.

"Yeah, she is." Fred had stepped in before Robin had to respond. "So take your sorry ass somewhere else."

The rest of the guys had laughed at that, and Randy'd had to pretend to laugh with them because he couldn't punch Fred, and any other reaction would have cost him his job or some serious respect. But he'd shot Fred a brooding look, and Robin had given her a grateful one, and now Fred was in some stupid race trying to straighten up the baby jars so she could get over to Robin's aisle before Randy could toss up those dog food bags.

Fred was almost ready to start wheeling her last pallet jack back to the storage area when the lights began flickering, and then the store went completely dark. "JUST WAIT FOR THE EMERGENCY LIGHTS," Wayne called out calmly from aisle ten. "THEY'LL BE ON IN A SECOND."

But that second went, and it took a few other seconds with it on the way out. August Vaughn said something over in the frozen-food section that made Fred hope there weren't any customers in the store. Fred was fifty-five years old, so she didn't already have her cell phone in her hand, but when it finally occurred to her to use the device as a light source, the screen wouldn't light up. Fred kept tapping it dumbly. Why would a blackout affect her phone's batter…oh, hell. Fred was from a generation that grew up half-expecting to die in a nuclear war at any minute, and she remembered something about how pulses from nuclear bombs would wipe out all the electricity.

As soon as Fred had that thought, a dozen more crowded through her head, too many to fit through the door all at once. What would she do if this was for real? Should she try to get home to her basement? Should she load up her car with canned goods and water? Would her car work? Was this some kind of Korean or Russian attack? A terrorist thing? Why wasn't she freaking out more? Where were Tyler and Savannah right now? How was she going to get in touch with her kids if the phones weren't working?

An animal sound derailed that last train of thought, a scream that echoed loudly off the walls and ceiling as if the dark grocery store were the size of a private bathroom. Fred had never heard any noise like it before. The growl had a human's messed-upness rumbling around in something that didn't sound like a human's chest. Too full of itself and hating it to be an animal. Too loud to be anything else. Maybe it was only because Fred had just been thinking about him, but an image of Randy Prutko's creepy eyes flashed through her head, followed by a thought that shook her so hard that it seemed like knowledge from some distant memory. A memory Fred hadn't known she'd had until that very second. That sound was Randy Prutko. That sound was Randy's creepy insides turned inside out.

Even though that was crazy.

There was another loud sound, a huge crash followed by another and then another, glass shattering and metal clattering and people yelling, and then packages of diapers were cascading all around Fred, cushioning her as the heavy weight of a store shelf pushed her farther down to the ground. Fred wasn't sure how long it went on. She grabbed a huge pack of diapers and curled herself around it on the floor like she was hugging a teddy bear, closing her eyes even though it was dark. She stayed still long after the floor stopped shaking and scattered voices started yelling.

Pretty soon, there was a faint orange light. Fred forced her head up through a bunch of diaper packs and hit her head against something metal. She didn't have a very clear view, but she could see Wayne Lehardy's legs and the glow from one of those yard torches that were supposed to keep insects away. The long line of shelves on Fred's aisle had been knocked over, the ones on her left catching on her pallet jack and tilting it over before halting. It left a slanting tunnel about three feet high, mostly filled with spilled baby goods.

"Wayne!" Fred yelled, and it was as if her voice was a signal. The store was filled with another scream that was loud and human and also not human in a way that just wasn't natural. Like a human scream but bigger. There was the sound of metal clanking, and then Fred saw a black-armored leg come down into her field of view. Something lashed out and cut Wayne Lehardy almost in half; he folded in a spray of blood and exposed bone and . . . and Fred threw up. No gagging, just spewing. Fred was a spray can, and someone had pushed down on the top of her head. At the end of the aisle, a big black armored hand reached down and grabbed the torch that was still lit, lying in the middle of a small spreading pool of igniting citronella oil.

It was crazy. Crazy, crazy, crazy. Fred's mind shut off while that thought kept coming back and getting stuck. But when the thing picked up the torch and lumbered off, Fred knew where it was going. To the canned-vegetable aisle. Robin's aisle.

∿1∿

NO STALKING IN THE LIBRARY

Clayburg, Virginia

Once Upon a Time, I was being stalked. It wasn't a mercilessly hot afternoon in the twisty stinking backstreets of Calcutta, and I wasn't hurriedly making my way through the dimly lit compartments of a rollicking train headed for Istanbul—it was actually a quite pleasant summer evening in Clayburg, Virginia, on the campus of Stillwater University. The grass was freshly cut, the warm air was cooling, and the sun was a soft lingering glance...and I was being stalked anyhow. It seemed a little unfair. I didn't see or smell whoever (or whatever) was trailing me, but you know that feeling you get when you feel someone's eyes on you, and when you turn around, you catch someone staring at you? I didn't turn around, but it wasn't because I dismissed the feeling—it was because I trusted it completely.

Casually reaching into my pocket, I took out that week's burner phone and stared at it for a while as if I were getting a message instead of making one. Then I texted Molly Newman that I wasn't going to be meeting her in forty minutes after all. Molly was the holy person in my Monster-Hunters-R-Us club, and a while back, she had gotten badly burned while performing an impromptu exorcism. She was off her pain meds, but Molly still wasn't driving a lot because it made her tense, and having to lift her shoulders and keep them in the same position while steering hurt. I was spending a lot of time in libraries, trying to find out what kind of fingerprints an occult society called the School of Night had left on the pages of history, so I didn't mind chauffeuring Molly around.

At the moment, I was supposed to be picking Molly up from some kind of philosophy class whose title was a full sentence and contained a lot of suffixes. I had once snuck into the last bit of the class out of curiosity, and after a few minutes had leaned over and whispered to Molly that this was no time to stop taking pain medication. She had just shushed me and kept taking notes.

Somebody's watching me, I texted. *Have Choo pick you up and tell Sig I'm heading for the library.*

Molly couldn't have been too into the class because she responded immediately. *By the texting of your thumb, something wicked this way comes?*

I smiled in spite of the situation, but I couldn't think of an appropriate Macbeth quote to mangle in response, so I tapped out *Unsure* and put my cell away. Molly would text me if she couldn't get in touch with Sig or Choo, so, in a way, I had just killed two birds with one phone.

There weren't a lot of students on Stillwater's campus in July, and the commons had a lot of wide-open space for Frisbee-throwing and outdoor graduation ceremonies and such, so I didn't pull any of that overt pretending-to-tie-my-shoe-so-I-can-look-behind-me nonsense. The likelihood that my stalker didn't know I was onto them was the only advantage I had. I just kept heading for the university library.

The library's lobby had metal detectors that had been installed after the Virginia Tech shooting not too many miles or years before, and I had a silver steel knife in my knapsack. Well, it was more like I had a knapsack around my silver steel knife, but either way, it could be a problem. There were small wooden cubicles against the wall where students could put their possessions before passing into the library proper, but I decided to just put my knapsack on the small wooden table next to the metal detectors, then put my keys and phone in the small wicker basket set on it.

As soon as I passed through the metal detectors, I reached around and grabbed the knapsack again. There was no campus security guard around to call me on it—I'm guessing the university cut the funding for that about three months after the devices were installed. The bored student on some kind of work program behind the front desk hadn't looked up from his texting when I came in, and the only other two people in the lobby smelled like adjunct faculty (coffee, beer, pizza, and desperation).

The two were sitting in the plush comfy chairs in the west corner having an animated discussion about the upcoming parking issues that would arrive with the fall semester. From what I could tell, the specific topic was that the university should become a walking campus for everyone except faculty. The general theme was that Americans needed more exercise and that the university administration was greedy, shortsighted, and incompetent. I thought the walking campus was a good idea myself, but somehow I suspected the two were including themselves in with the tenured faculty that would still have car privileges in their vision of a parking Utopia.

I decided to hang out in the front lobby for a little while. If I was being followed by a single competent individual, he, she, or it would come in after me quickly to make sure I wasn't threading through the library to find another exit. A team would send someone after me too, but they could afford to give me a little more lead time while they spread out around the building, and whoever they sent would have to remove any earbuds or concealed weapons before going through the metal detector. That was a show that I wanted to see. Either way, staying still for a few moments would tell me something, so I grabbed some book called *The Devil's Grin* by an A. Wendeberg and sat down at a wooden table facing the entrance. When I set my backpack down by my chair, I unzipped the top.

The first few pages of the book seemed pretty interesting.

My stalker walked in before too long. The library took a deep breath when she opened the door, and I caught a whiff of dhampir. That just meant that whatever ceremony had tried to turn her into a vampire had been bungled somehow, and she still retained some humanity, at the very least enough to walk around in faint daylight. Her face wasn't classically beautiful— her cheekbones were a little too pronounced, her eyes a little too big, her nose a tad small—but she carried herself with an absolute confidence that made her quirks seem like a distinct brand of attractiveness. Her build was slim and feminine and athletic, and I could tell from the way she moved that she had martial arts training. A lot of it. It was the way she kept her weight centered and feet balanced so automatically that it seemed natural. Her skin was pale but not waxy, and her red hair so dark that it was almost brown. She wore both her hair and her dress short. The latter was black and high on her upper thighs, tight but comfortable-looking as it hung around almost a foot above knee-high boots. A purse on very long straps was slung casually by her right hip at about the same place that a gun would be holstered, and her hand was resting against it. If she'd had outlandishly sized breasts, she would have looked like she was auditioning for a video game.

Intent eyes narrowed in on me immediately, then took in the metal detector. Her slender and very red lips quirked, but she walked over to the wooden storage rack and somehow managed to crouch elegantly in that short dress. I'm pretty sure she transferred something that wouldn't fit in her purse from her right boot to the back of one of the small cubicles, using her body as a screen.

She didn't waste any time coming over to my table, moving her purse around the metal detector the same way I'd negotiated my knapsack. This time, everyone in the library was watching, but no one protested. When she got closer, she greeted me in a low voice that sounded like she had smoked a lot before her body stopped getting damaged by such things. "You are not as stupid as you dress."

I was wearing running shoes, faded jeans, and a dark green T-shirt. "This isn't a big city university," I said. "I look like I belong here. You fit in about as well as a porcupine in a petting zoo. What do you want?"

Somehow, she didn't flash anything but a tight smile as she drew a chair and sat across from me in one smooth motion. She was sex on legs. Long legs, though I studied them dispassionately. "I am just satisfying my curiosity. I heard Stanislav Dvornik was dead. I wanted to see who finally killed the old bastard."

So, that's what the lack of contractions and the flat place where an accent should be was all about. She was probably

Eastern European. Stanislav Dvornik had been a kresnik—a member of an Eastern European society of vampire hunters—and kresniks aren't as uptight about working with werewolves and dhampirs and cunning folk as knights traditionally are. Stanislav Dvornik had also been a homicidal shitheel, and I was in a relationship with his former girlfriend. "Are you disappointed that I beat you to it, or looking for revenge?" I asked.

Her eyes were hazel and sharp and had seen a lot of people die. "I do not know."

"I've had relationships like that," I admitted. "Are you going to let me know when you figure it out?"

That slender mouth made another slash of a grin. "Now, where would the fun in that be?"

"Ah," I said. "You're one of those."

"One of what?" She didn't sound like she cared too much.

"I'm not sure there's a word for it," I said. "But it's like ennui with sharp teeth. In my experience, very few things are as dangerous as predators who have long life-spans and get bored easily."

She laughed softly, but the laughter had a dark undercurrent. "Do *you* get bored easily?"

"I'm pretty sure I don't," I said. "I've tried really hard to find out, but people like you keep showing up and ruining the experiment."

"Ah," she mocked. "You are one of those."

I played along. "One of what?"

"In *my* experience, very few things are as sad as killers who do not want to admit they are killers."

"Oh, I'm a killer, all right." There was no point denying it; I've killed more things than I can count or pronounce. "But I make a distinction between killing and murder, if that's what you mean."

"That is part of it," she agreed. "The hypocrisy."

24

"Everybody's a hypocrite sometimes," I said. "It's the reasons we need to be a hypocrite that define us."

"Maybe you should be the one taking a philosophy class instead of your friend," she observed.

At the mention of Molly, my body released some pheromone with fear and rage and more than a hint of homicide seasoning it. My stalker inhaled slightly through her nose as if smelling the bouquet of a delicate wine and smiled faintly. "Did I just make an enemy?"

"I haven't decided yet," I echoed her. "But if I remove your head from your shoulders now, I won't consider it murder."

"Good," she told me. "You should keep that kind of thing clear-cut."

"It will be," I promised. "So, how did you know good old Stan?"

Maybe she kept her smiles so tight because of sharp incisors. Whatever the reason, the next grin she flicked my way was almost gone before I saw it, and she ignored my question. "He must have really hated you."

"It was loathe at first sight," I confirmed before trying again. "How did he react when he met you?"

"He wanted me." She said it without a trace of self-consciousness. "Stanislav was a hypocrite too. He was terrified of getting old, so any woman who represented immortality threatened and attracted him at the same time. Any male who did not age just pissed him off."

"That made him a d-bag," I said. "It didn't make him a hypocrite."

"He was a hypocrite because he slept with the things he hated," she explained. "And killed the things he wanted to be."

That sounded about right. "You're Kasia," I guessed. I had only heard the name on two occasions, once while Sig and Stanislav were arguing in the back of Choo's van, and once in a truck stop, but I have a good memory for such things. For most things, actually.

She smiled that smile again, so small that it almost wasn't, but she wasn't faking it. "Sigourney mentioned me?"

Sig hates being called Sigourney, and I suspected Kasia knew it. "Briefly," I said. "I don't think Sig likes talking about you."

"Guilty consciences will do that."

"Are you sure you're here about Stanislav?" I asked.

She made an amused sound and ignored my question again. "How did he die?"

"The same way he lived," I said. "A complete asshat."

She waited.

"He tried to kill me," I elaborated. "I won't say it was unprovoked, but it was definitely an overreaction. A betrayal, too. We were supposed to be on the same side."

"So, it was over Sigourney." She didn't sound like she was guessing.

"It was never about Sig," I said. "He just made her his excuse for a lot of things. That's what self-destructive shitheads do. They have this idea of what they need, and they try to force other people to fit into that idea like it's a cookie-cutter mold. And when a person doesn't or can't, the asshats blame them for it."

She nodded. It was a small motion, and I don't think she realized that she was doing it. "You are not what I expected."

"That's the other way Stanislav died," I said.

"I believe it." She switched topics abruptly. "You smell like you are attracted to me. Do you want to have sex?"

"Sure," I said. "I'm into bondage, though. I like to tie up my partners and put them in a shark cage first. Is that okay?"

Kasia laughed. "I could be up for it, but somehow you do not seem like the type." She rose up from her chair then, scooping her purse off the floor by the top of its straps so that I wouldn't be alarmed, and smoothly shifting it onto her shoulder.

"Leaving so soon?" I asked.

"I am guessing Sigourney will be here shortly," she explained. "I do not think it would be a good idea to be around both of you at the same time yet."

"It probably wouldn't be," I agreed. I didn't like the sound of that *yet*. "Speaking of bad ideas, something needs to be said."

She waited.

"I'm a wolf," I told her. "This is my territory."

"That was much better," she said approvingly.

"You sound like a coach or an ice-skating judge."

"All existence is a competition." Kasia mimed holding a scorecard over her head. "I give that a seven point five."

"After all that training and hard work," I said. "It comes down to politics."

"I think you might almost be funny." She studied me for a moment, then announced: "I have decided to tell you something."

"Okay," I said.

"The Knights Templar are going to be contacting you soon."

"Because of something you've done?" I asked carefully.

She dismissed that suggestion with a small puff of breath. I caught a waft of nicotine so faint that it was almost a rumor. "That is possible. I brought your friend Simon a message from the kresniks recently."

I wouldn't call Simon Travers my friend. I respect his competence, and we're roughly on the same side, but at best he and I kind of cordially hate each other. I say *kind of* because sometimes it's not so *cordially*. Sometimes it's not so *hate each other*. As part of the Grandmaster's ongoing efforts to gracefully transition Simon into an administrative role, Simon had recently become a turcopolier, which meant that he dealt with outsiders. That could mean coordinating between different chapters of knights or communicating with other secret societies or recruiting non-geas-born to the cause or hiring mercenaries for special tasks. The position is a tradition that goes all the way back to the Crusades, and it's become one of the stepping-stones to Grandmaster.

But all I said was: "What kind of message?"

"A message from the kresniks."

Right. "So, why tell me anything if it's none of my business?"

She gave me that look that a certain type of teacher reserves for particularly slow students. "We might wind up working together. I wanted to meet you before that happened."

"So you could kill me if you didn't like the idea."

"Perhaps I wanted *the opportunity* to kill you before that happened. I am a strong believer in snap judgments." She mimed breaking something in two, and for some reason, I pictured a spine.

"I'm a strong believer in trying to figure out what the hell is going on."

"Put your ear to the ground," she said, "and you will hear the tremors."

"Tremors," I repeated. "So, it's really big. Whatever it is."

"Somewhere between the Titanic and the apocalypse," she agreed.

"Which one of the four horsemen would that make you?" I wondered.

She gave me one more of those enigmatic smiles for the road. "I think you already know the answer to that."

"You are awful pale."

The smile disappeared. "Careful."

"It's a little late for that," I told her.

"Hmmn," she said thoughtfully. "Maybe even an eight." I didn't respond, and she turned to leave then. "By the way, I am driving a red Audi, but it is not mine. I can give you the license plate if you do not want to bother following me to the parking lot."

I waved that off. "It's no bother."

∾2∾

YOU'D BETTER SMILE WHEN
YOU DON'T HAVE A FACE

New York City

Shalaya Copeland had a definite strategy for moving through
the city. She set the volume on her music low so she could hear
something if she really had to, but when some fool yelled out,
"Damn, girl, you got a walk," she just kept moving like she
didn't hear it. The kind of music Shalaya listened to kept her
moving fast too. Not running and not shuffling, because running made you a target, and slowing down was an invitation
for people to pitch something or grab something or beg for
something. Some tourist might even try to be friendly.

So, it took a while for Shalaya to notice the man without a
face. New York City was full of faceless people after all; they
just usually had noses and ears and mouths. But Shalaya was
a dental hygienist and spent enough time looking at mouths
and noses anyway, especially during allergy seasons. It was
why Shalaya liked to walk outside during her lunch break. She
had grown up in a house full of yelling and got tired standing

around in one place getting fat and old and talking about TV shows just to be saying something. The white boy from UPS who was always trying to get her to talk to him called her an introvert.

"Better than being a pervert," Shalaya had shot back.

"You sure about that?" he'd asked with a slow smile that wasn't too bad, but Shalaya just kept walking. He made those tight brown shorts look good, but Shalaya knew a dog when she saw one. And that dog got a lot of bones. She'd rather go home and snuggle up to her circulating fan and some Japanese cartoons until she met somebody real.

What was all that noise up ahead? It took a while to get through because Shalaya was listening to some Colonel Loud song about California and mostly feeling it. But the noise was loud and growing louder.

Shalaya almost stopped in the middle of the sidewalk, but it was lunch hour. She was in the heart of the city, and people got nasty if you clogged up its arteries. Shalaya moved to the side and put her back against the window of a beauty parlor. Up ahead of her, the sidewalk crowd was parting in a weird way, like it was giving birth. But what emerged wasn't any baby. Some man without a face was walking in Shalaya's direction, people scrambling to get out of his way. He wasn't lurching or anything. He was wearing a pretty sharp suit and carrying a briefcase like there was nothing unusual going on. Shalaya didn't see as many briefcases now that everybody was keeping their business up in a clou— WHY DIDN'T HE HAVE A FACE?!?

Shalaya wasn't the only one trying to figure that out. Other people with the same question were crowding around her. Some shaggy guy who looked like a grown-ass narc trying to go undercover in a high school was leaning against her patch of wall, talking loudly though Shalaya didn't know who the fool was talking to. The phone he was holding up was dead. "It's gotta be some kind of advertising stunt."

Some tourists—two well-fed retirees in white baseball caps and sunglasses—turned around with those "Gosh, isn't New York somethin'?" looks on their faces. "Advertising what?" the woman asked. She was having trouble with her phone too.

"Maybe there's a new Magritte exhibit at the Met," the know-it-all replied. Shalaya almost told him that the picture he was thinking of wasn't faceless, that the painting was of a guy hiding behind an apple, just to let him know that everybody wasn't as stupid as he was acting. But other voices began chiming in as the faceless guy got closer.

"...latex..."

"...gonna get sued..."

"...creepy..."

"...no signal..."

Finally, the faceless guy walked past, but the opening he left behind filled up with rushing crowd before Shalaya could shoulder her way through the clot of people around her and make a move. And she wanted to move. If it was some kind of publicity stunt, Shalaya didn't want anything to do with it. And if it wasn't a publicity stunt...she really didn't want anything to do with it. Probably was a publicity stunt, though. Some new horror movie or protest group or fools trying to go all viral.

The sound of car horns was getting louder, and when she took her eyes off Mr. Faceless, Shalaya saw why. A traffic light was flickering on and off, and the cars weren't playing nice while they tried to work out who went through the intersection next. And that was just too much weirdness right there. Shalaya started angling her body to go back to the subway and saw some big white guy with receding hair in a T-shirt and shorts making his way toward the freak, yelling angrily.

Despite herself, Shalaya settled back against the window.

The faceless man wasn't slowing down, and the beefy loudmouth—you could tell it just by listening and looking at him—grabbed the faceless man by the shoulder and spun him around. What happened next made every part of Shalaya's body weak at once, like she was going to just collapse into a puddle. The faceless man's head cracked open, like one of those plastic eggs that people put jelly beans in for Easter baskets. A pale seam appeared where a mouth ought to be, and then the whole head tilted back and revealed teeth way longer and sharper than any set of teeth had a right. A crazy long tongue was flicking around in that mouth like a snake.

The beefy guy backed away, but it was too late. The freak didn't even slow down. It reached out casually and made a swiping motion like it was parting a beaded curtain, only the nails it had been keeping clenched in a fist were extended now. The loud-mouthed guy reeled away screaming. His face was covered in blood. He reached up and wiped at the blood with his palm, and it was like he was wiping a chalkboard clean. The blood was smearing and disappearing, and so were his eyes and nose. Other people were yelling too, but Shalaya barely heard them. She had managed to clear herself an opening, and Shalaya turned and staggered away on legs that suddenly felt like stilts. Lurched like a stork until she got her balance and didn't look back. Shalaya just kept on walking.

∾3∾

HOW DO YOU SOLVE A PROBLEM LIKE KASIA?

Clayburg, Virginia

We didn't exactly look like a crack team of professional monster hunters. We looked like we belonged in a series of pictures beneath the caption: *Which one of these best illustrates the word MOTLEY?* At six feet even with broad shoulders, toned muscles, and too much heft to ever be a model, though it was all taut and serviceable, Sig had spent the night experimenting with making indelible runes and wards with a blowtorch. Her efforts had left her distinctly sweaty and smudgy in a sleeveless white tank top and thin green cotton pants. Her long and recently pale white hair was bound behind her head in a tight knot.

Molly, on the other hand, was short, thick-spectacled, unruly-haired, and wearing a T-shirt with a picture of a cartoon girl on it. Said girl was wearing a crazed expression and a tie-on fuzzy cap with long pink bunny ears.

Normally Choo dresses like he lost a fight with an Army

Surplus store, but Choo had been Skyping with his not-quite-ex, or his ex-ex (Chantelle had moved to Charlottesville recently and was hinting that Choo might want to do the same, a fact he'd grumpily managed to work into the conversation at least three times). He was dressed somewhere between casual and oh-I-just-happen-to-have-Barry-White-on-in-the-background. His long-sleeved shirt was a warm shade of red and looked soft. His short dreadlocks had a slight sheen to them that suggested some kind of hair product, and a thin gold necklace was around his throat, the first time I'd ever seen him wear such a thing. His belly had gotten a little smaller and his burly chest more defined since he'd started trying to win his divorced wife back.

"What did this Kasia look like?" Sig demanded.

I proceeded to reel off a laundry list of details, including approximate height, weight, small scars, balance, the hint of cigarettes in her voice and scent, her coloring or lack thereof, the shape of her face, and style of her mannerisms. I was talking about the blunt but polished fingernails, which were the only thing about my stalker that had been unfashionable, when Choo cut me off. "Damn, did you stick a thermometer up her ass, too?"

"That's not until the third date," I explained. "I'm a gentleman."

Sig sighed. "Whatever. That's Kasia."

The four of us were at a wooden bench beside a hiking trail in Mankin's Park. Sig had been keeping an eye on the area because—as Sig put it—there was a ghostly presence there who wasn't quite ready to quit flirting yet. A lot of homeless people in southwest Virginia like to camp out in wooded areas on the edge of towns during the warmer seasons—not because they're the mutant inbred cannibals and rapists who comprise Appalachia in Hollywood productions, but because they're trying to hold on to their dignity and independence while struggling with whatever combination of factors led them there. I've spent time doing that myself. The bad vibe produced by Sig's polterguest encouraged wood wanderers to move a little farther down the trail. As an added bonus, there was also just enough mojo in the air to mess with any electronic surveillance.

Molly—whose short frame was jammed between Sig and Choo on the bench so that the three of them almost made an *H* shape—asked the obvious question: "So, who is this Kasia? And what is her deal, exactly?"

Sig sighed again. "I don't think there is an *exactly* with Kasia."

"So, what's her deal, not-exactly?" Choo rumbled.

"She was Stanislav's partner when I met him. Met them." Sig snapped each word off. It was a time in her life that Sig kept trying to put behind her, and it kept biting her on the ass.

"Then she's like me," I said. "A monster who's a monster hunter. Was Kasia Stanislav's partner or Stanislav's *partner*?" I made air quotes around *partner* on the second repetition. It was better than pumping my hips and yelling, "Ka-ching!"

"They were having sex," Sig said. "I don't know how much that meant to her, though. Kasia treated lovers like fast food, but she could also get sentimental about the oddest things. She was crazy unpredictable."

I had figured that much out for myself. "She seems to enjoy putting people off-balance."

"Did she offer to have sex with you?" Sig asked.

"Yeah," I said. "But I didn't take it personally."

"Let's get to the important stuff, Sig," Molly said gently but firmly. "How crazy and unpredictable does this Kasia get? John said she mentioned me specifically. Do I have to worry about coming home to find my puppy boiling in a pot on the stove?"

"And what about that stuff she told John about big trouble coming?" Choo added. "Is it bullshit?"

"Why do you think I know?" Sig asked irritably. "I was a complete mess when I knew her."

Choo made a rude noise. "Aint none of us what I'd call well-adjusted."

"I'm just saying, I had no idea what I was back then." Sig sounded a little bit more than just exasperated. "I was still drinking. My entire family was dead. It's not like I was in a good rational place, okay? If I were, I never would have gotten involved with Stanislav...the way I got involved with him."

"How *did* you go from apprentice to sticky with Dvornik?" I had never really pressed for specifics before. "Was it over Kasia's half-dead body?"

Sig's face turned a dark shade of crimson. "Stanislav and I had sex for the first time while she and he were still doing whatever they were doing. I guess you could say we cheated on her."

Every time I pictured Sig and Stanislav naked, I wanted to clutch my forehead and start screaming, "My mind's eye! My mind's eye!" But somehow, I doubted this would be helpful.

"What would Kasia say about it?" Molly asked gently.

"She put me in a coma," Sig said. "She probably thought I was dead or she would have finished the job. Stanislav had to pull me out of it by projecting himself astrally into my dreams."

Molly made a small face. "So she's really mature and well-adjusted about the way she handles conflict resolution."

"I don't remember much of it," Sig admitted. "Like I said, real glamorous stuff. And just because Kasia attacked me, it doesn't mean she loved Stanislav. She and he had some weird always-fighting grudge-sex thing going on, and she never claimed to be monogamous. But she was a bit like a cat, you know? She might not like something, but that didn't mean she wanted anyone else playing with it."

None of us said anything. The signs Sig was putting up all read: HANDLE CAREFULLY. HIGHLY EXPLOSIVE MATERIAL WITHIN.

"Being an alcoholic doesn't make for pretty stories." Sig was staring at the ground with such ferocious focus, someone in China was probably rubbing the back of his neck and looking around confusedly. "If anybody wants to judge me for messed-up things I've done, I've got a million of them."

Molly patted Sig's knee. "We all have stuff like that."

"Not me," I said. "My past is so clean and shiny, I have to put on shades just to read my diary."

That drew a snort out of Sig, and Choo played along with it: "Put on some safety goggles, maybe."

Molly kept it simple and sincere. "All you can do is try to be the best person you can be right now, Sig. That's all anybody can do."

"Just take it one day at a time." It was hard to tell if Sig was saying that sarcastically because she'd heard it at so many AA meetings, or repeating the words like a mantra.

"Break it down into smaller pieces," Choo put in. "Did you and this lady get along before all this went down?"

"Kasia hated me," Sig said instantly. "And the feeling was mutual. Kasia was the one who taught me how to really fight, and she was a complete bitch about it. I can't tell you how many times she knocked me out. If I were a normal human, I'd probably be brain-damaged."

"You sure you're not?" Choo indicated me with a head yank. The implication was clear. *Look who you're dating.*

That was taking the acting-stupid-to-cheer-Sig-up thing a little too far in my opinion, but Sig just rolled her eyes, so I asked, "Do you think Kasia's evil?"

Sig had a hard time parsing that one out. "Kasia only hunted things that were worse than her, but she was completely ruthless about accomplishing a goal. And if she felt justified at all, she could be vindictive to the point of crazy. She seemed to enjoy it."

I could see that. For some people, anger is the only emotion that doesn't make them feel vulnerable, so it becomes their only way of expressing any kind of passion. "Let's just assume Kasia still has intense but messed-up feelings about Stanislav," I said. "I'll bet she had severe daddy issues."

"Why does everything with women have to be daddy issues?" Molly groused. I've never heard Molly talk about her parents in any detail. All I really know about them is that they're lifelong Baptist missionaries who broke off any real contact with Molly when she told them she was a lesbian. As Molly once put it, they're still waiting for Molly to come to her senses.

"Call it what you want, but I'll bet Stanislav was Kasia's mentor and safety net before he became her lover," I said. "If becoming a monster was easy, they'd call it something else. And as messed-up as he was, Stanislav was probably something to hold on to when Kasia was scared or feeling bad about herself."

"Kasia told you all of that?" Sig asked skeptically.

"You did," I said. "That's how Stanislav pulled you in, right?"

Sig looked at me for a long moment. "I don't know if I want to throw something at you or drag you behind a tree and tear your clothes off."

"Enough with the icky," Molly chided. "It sounds like trying to hunt this Kasia down might be the worst thing we could do. She might be looking for an excuse to go off on a vendetta."

"You might be right," Sig conceded reluctantly. Very reluctantly. I could smell how badly she wanted to kick this Kasia's ass, and I was picking up a little fear and shame mixed in there for good measure. The Sig I know doesn't scare easily, but the past is a funny thing; she was remembering a Sig I didn't know.

I took her hand and squeezed. "It's not all dark, you know."

She squeezed back so hard it hurt a little.

"I'm not sitting still, doing nothing," Choo declared. "You don't win any games playing defense."

"You don't win by attacking blindly either," I said. "We need to learn more about Kasia and this big trouble she told me about."

"There might still be some kresniks who will talk to me," Sig said. "And I'll ask Parth to look into her."

Parth is a naga, a kind of Indian were-serpent. Immortality has rendered Parth a bit detached from the concerns of everyday humans rushing to make sense out of their existence, but he keeps immortal life fresh by constantly trying to learn new things. It's how he evolved into a hacker in the 1980s and then a software mogul in the new millennium.

"Sure," I said. "And I'll talk to Simon. Might as well hear it straight from the horse's ass."

Sig frowned. "You're going to try to get a straight answer out of Simon? That's like trying to slice bread with a corkscrew."

"Not just Simon. The Grandmaster of the Templars told Ben that there has been an increase of magical incidents in New York City. Emil asked Ben to send in reinforcements from a lot of surrounding areas." The Round Table and the Knights Templar were actually doing a little better at working together, but in a tentative, grudging kind of way that only illustrated how badly they'd been working together before. The two groups had come close to renewing hostilities a few months back, and the revelation that both the Round Table and the Knights Templar had been played by a third party who wanted them to destroy each other had left everyone involved half ashamed and half surly. Werewolves and knights were both willing to unite against a common enemy and tear this so-called School of Night a new classhole, but the organization had turned to smoke.

Choo finally addressed the knight thing: "I don't like you talking to this Simon. You get kind of crazy when knights are around."

"I anticipate crazy when knights are around." In fact, I was already running over possible hidden motives for Kasia's appearance in my head. It was possible that Kasia wanted me to contact Simon because getting me involved with whatever chaos was going on would also pull in Sig. Or it was possible Simon had told Kasia to give me a hint of trouble because he would rather have me come to him. It would be a way of circumventing my authority issues and avoid drawing attention to the fact that I don't directly work for Simon, a fact that he hates. Or maybe it was Simon who wanted Sig involved because her whole walking/talking Ouija board thing is pretty useful. And I had a feeling that trying to map those possibilities out loud would just help make Choo's point. Still, just because it was complicated and twisted didn't mean it wasn't true.

"Choo's right. Every time you work with knights, you get super protective and paranoid and kind of dark. You cut him and me out, too," Molly said. "That's not happening this time."

I had, in fact, been about to suggest leaving them out of the picture. "You don't want any part of knight business, Molly," I warned her. "That world is cold and crazy."

She smiled sunnily. "Let's burn that bridge when we come to it."

"Yeah," Choo said. If Choo got a hint of something hidden, something that even had the potential to be a threat, he had to know about it. Even if he didn't want to, he had to. It was the quality that made him a good exterminator and a lousy sleeper. Choo also had to complain and be a pain in the ass the whole time, but that was what it was. I know a little bit about that kind of venting system myself, and I'd rather have somebody like Choo on my side than someone who said all the right things and flaked when things got hairy. Choo elaborated a bit: "If something's coming that's as big and bad as this Kasia says it is, it might be everybody's business."

"It'll suck like nobody's business," I said. "Do you really want to cut to the front of the line for something like that?"

His reply was short, eloquent, and filthy.

❧4❧

HONK IF YOU'RE HORNY

New York City

Maybe New York City wasn't so bad. Zach Owens was a high school art teacher in Buffalo, and he'd always kind of resented the Big Apple. In fact, Zach always called it the Big Crapple. He hated the way people on TV always meant the city when they said "New York," as if the entire surrounding state didn't exist. He hated the way most New Yorkers—which only meant people from the city, there was no point fighting it—came through Buffalo like they were on their way to or back to some place more important, and how they seemed to spend most of their time appalled at how many things Buffalo didn't offer. Loudly appalled.

Mostly though, Zach hated that so many of his friends had moved to the Big Crapple after graduation. Zach came from a big, tight family; he wasn't going anywhere. That wasn't the same thing as going nowhere. Zach also hated the way his friends referred to Buffalo as Cow Town or the Big Cow Patty when they came back to visit their families. Neil goddamned

Blevins was a twenty-eight-year-old waiter, and Neil still acted like Zach was stuck in some peasant village because Neil had been an extra in some movie.

Then Zach had met a woman named Carleigh, only she had crossed out the "eigh" on her laminated name tag with a black sharpie and replaced it with an *I*. It was while Zach was in the Big Crapple for a four-day weekend at the latest educational seminar. Ironically, the seminar on how social media was changing public education had to be conducted in person. Zach and Carleigh-with-an-I had wound up sitting next to each other in a small group where they were examining how social media could lead to unprofessional behavior or misunderstandings. And somehow, Zach and Carleigh-with-an-I fit together. Zach had almost heard the click.

Zach had been pretty smooth about getting Carleigh-with-an-I's phone number too, and he wasn't usually smooth. He'd casually taken his phone out and asked for her number as if he wanted to prove something about the texts-gone-wrong exercise they were doing, and Carleigh-with-an-I had smiled when she gave it to him because she knew he was going to text her later and ask her if she knew about any good places to eat or something, and then she would say that she knew a place so good that she wanted to go there herself, and he had, and she had.

And Carleigh-with-an-I was from New York. The city. She was also in Zach's hotel room. In Zach's bed. And Zach was flat on his back in a postcoital state of shell shock, wondering if maybe moving away from Buffalo was so unthinkable after all.

That's when Zach heard the flute outside. The sound was shrill and reedy, playing a kind of music Zach had never heard before, if it was music at all. The notes veered wildly, cheerful one moment, then violently lurching off to someplace spine-jarring. Zach would have yelled at whoever was making those sounds to shut up, except Zach knew way down in the sewers of his subconscious that he did not want to meet that person. Not ever.

Carli (Zach was an old-fashioned guy, and it seemed like they should be on a real-name basis now that he'd come inside her) didn't seem to share Zach's instinct. After she and Zach had finished making love—and Zach thought that maybe that's what they'd really been doing—Carli had pulled the bedsheet up to her chin while giggling at her sudden shyness. That shyness, pretend or otherwise, disappeared when the music started playing. Carli let the sheet drop without a thought, listening so intently that it seemed like her entire body was some kind of tuning fork.

The hotel room lights began flickering as the music got louder, and then the lights went out entirely. The sounds of a television set coming through the walls of the room next door stopped. The digital clock facing Zach turned off. Only the moonlight outlining the closed curtains of the long hotel window remained to alleviate the darkness.

Then a smell pervaded the room, sour and thick. No, more than one smell. There was wine mixed up in it, so heavy in the air that it almost felt like Zach might get drunk smelling it. And the musk of sex. Lots of sex. The smell that he and Carli were giving off, distilled down to its essence. Despite the bolt of fear paralyzing him, Zach realized he had an erection.

Carli ripped the bedsheet off, bolting for the door. Zach gave a loud startled grunt of denial, but the only thing that slowed Carli down was that she couldn't seem to figure out the door's backup lock. Naked, she tugged frantically at the door handle while the flute got louder.

Part of Zach wanted to run for the bathroom and huddle in the tub with the shower curtain drawn, and part of him wanted to run over there and knock Carli out of the way and slam his body against that hotel door to bar it. Instead of doing either, he crept toward the doorway tentatively, grabbing his shirt off the floor and holding it over his waist with one hand and reaching the other hand out toward Carli like she might pop. Zach tried to say something, but he was too scared to yell over the sound of the flute. It was irrational, considering all of the noise Carli was making, but as long as somebody was playing that flute, they weren't doing anything else.

Zach could hear other sounds crashing through the melody in staccato bursts of violence: glass windows breaking, male voices cursing, the sound of floors and concrete walkways vibrating beneath frantic feet. When Zach finally made it to Carli, her scrabbling fingers managed to twist the locking latch by accident, and she yanked the door open an inch, shrieking while she savagely tugged it back and forth against the security lock at the top of the door frame, one of those contraptions where a ball bearing slides into the tip of a metal triangle that folds over it.

For a moment, the lights of some passing vehicle briefly lit the crevasse where Carli had forced the door partially open, and Zach caught a glimpse of a thick, squat hairy back passing by, a flute bobbing up and down from its profile. But Zach didn't really see the flute or the strange half human/half goat legs carrying the thing. All Zach saw were the stubby horns coming out of the flutist's head. The weight of every Sunday-school class and sermon Zach had ever attended came crashing down on his imagination. Then the headlight beams and the figure were both gone, but the shrill music and the parade of half-clothed or naked women following it went on.

Zach cautiously put his fingertips on Carli's shoulder, and Carli whirled on him, screaming. Carli didn't have very long fingernails, but she had a kind of manic strength that made them long enough. Zach felt something tear and burn at the side of his throat.

He stumbled backward, his hand over his neck, and Carli turned back to the door, already forgetting Zach existed. Panicked, Zach tried to check the hotel room mirror in the faint light. Was he dying? Had Carli torn an artery? Zach didn't want to take his fingers off his throat in case they were the only thing holding it together, but he did. A loose, bloody flap of skin flopped down, and Zach almost passed out. His knees hit the floor hard, and he bit his tongue half off at the same moment.

He also saw his open overnight bag. If there was a God, and Zach believed there was even if Zach had just spent the evening in a way his preacher wouldn't have approved of, maybe it was God who put Zach's face right next to his MP3 player. The MP3 player that still had Zach's earbuds plugged into it.

A draft of cold air on his exposed genitals shocked Zach back into action, if grabbing an MP3 player and crawling on the floor can be called action. Zach made his way over to the door on one hand and his knees, his left hand clutching his throat again. There was blood against his hand but no spurting. No spurting. No spurting. No spurting. When Zach reached Carli, he fumbled around with the MP3 player in a horribly unfunny slapstick comedy. He put an earbud in each hand, and the MP3 player fell and yanked the cord free of the connecting terminal. Then Zach managed to put the MP3 player in his teeth, got the earbuds in each hand, and realized he'd forgotten to turn the player on. The only saving grace was that Carli was completely ignoring Zach as long as he wasn't actively trying to restrain her. As small as she was, she had almost yanked out the metal bolts attaching the security bar to the wall.

Zach finally lurched up and body-slammed Carli into the

door, shutting it, putting her off-balance long enough to plug the earbuds into her ears. Carli threw an elbow into the soft spot right below Zach's breastbone, but the Kings of Leon were blasting in her ears full volume, and she stiffened, a confused look coming over her face. Zach doubled over and then fell sideways on his hip, trying to bring more air back into his body than his shallow breaths would allow. Then Carli was down on the floor beside him, wrapping her arms around his neck, her hot tears on his cheek, and they huddled there and waited for the nightmare to go away.

∽5∽

A FEW MOMENTS OF QUIET DEFLECTION

Simon refused to answer any questions about big things or horizons unless it was face-to-face, which was unfortunate because he was currently in New York City. I'm sure big cities are fine for some people, but they're not the best place for introverts with anger management issues and really good hearing and a finely honed sense of smell. It's like being in a house where every room has a TV turned all the way up to a different channel. Plus, New York and I kind of have a thing going on. Not a "Me and Mrs. Jones" kind of thing either. More like a Hatfield and McCoy kind of thing. I keep swearing I'll never go back, but you know what they say: Necessity is an inventive mother, or something like that.

Sig and I got up at the crack ass of dawn. She pulled on a short white bathrobe while I pulled on some boxers, and we trudged tiredly down Sig's narrow apartment stairwell. Sig likes to wrap around me while she sleeps—she calls me the heater—and normally she's soft and cool and still, but the night before, she'd been all elbows and knees and grunts. It was like trying to sleep next to a wheat thresher, but whenever I tried to roll away, Sig clung to me like she was drowning in her dreams.

Sometimes, Sig acts like she needs some time to think when she's stuck in a bad place and really needs to talk to somebody, and sometimes, Sig really needs some time to think, and the boundaries she's drawing are protected by hidden landmines and trip wires and tiger pits. I'm not complaining. I'm just as bad about that kind of thing, if not worse, and God only knows how I'd handle it if Sig told me that someone from my past had shown up and talked to her. "Hey, John, I met the sister of your dead lover today," or "The son of your old Templar partner, Nick Arbiter, showed up and says he blames you for his dad's death." I suspect I might be a tad preoccupied myself. The only difference is, when Sig errs, it's on the side of pushing me to talk about stuff before I'm ready, and when I mess up, it's on the side of leaving her alone longer than I should. We don't mean anything by it; we're both just giving the other person what we'd want in their place. But as far as I could tell, Sig really did still need to simmer for a bit.

I made breakfast—nothing fancy, just some bacon-and-egg sandwiches and steel-cut oatmeal with lots of fruit—and Sig and I sat next to each other on her sofa, mostly silent, our hips pressing while we ate. Sig likes to listen to NPR in the mornings. I'm fine with that so long as her radio alarm doesn't wake me up to their foreign news segment. I try to stay reasonably informed on bombings, genocide, natural disasters, riots, and assassinations, but I like to have my coffee first.

"You know, if this stuff with Kasia is that emotionally booby-trapped, I wouldn't hold it against you if you wanted to sit this one out," I offered.

Sig didn't act offended, which meant she'd seriously been considering it. "Can *you* stay out of it?"

"I don't think so," I said. "The knights and the Round Table are being forced to work together with all of this stuff going down in New York right now, and Ben wants someone to work closer with Simon on this thing. Someone who understands how knights think."

"Someone who speaks paranoid and devious."

"Exactly," I said. "Ben didn't order me to do this, but he asked me, in his own way. And I owe Ben a lot."

Sig laughed a little, not entirely amused. "Ben doesn't trust Simon either."

I shrugged. Knights and werewolves had come a long way, but only because they'd started out trying to kill each other.

"I owe the Round Table a lot too, John."

I didn't deny it. "You're not obligated to take on anything that would be bad for you."

"Hello, pot? This is kettle. Shut up."

I set my oatmeal down and pressed myself against her side, rubbing my chest slowly up and down against her shoulder and moaning, "Oh yeah, tell me to shut up, baby. That's good. Now punch me in the arm and call me an idiot."

Sig laughed and pushed me off her. "Like you have room to talk about social skills either. What is this, National Hypocrite Day?" Then she punched me on the arm, not hard, and said, "Idiot." I grabbed her hand and kissed it, then settled down and went back to my oatmeal.

We ate in silence for a bit, and then Sig sighed. "There's no such thing as a fresh start, is there?" The question didn't exactly come out of the blue, but it didn't come with a set of instructions, either.

I chewed on a strawberry to give myself a little time to think. "I tried to avoid my past for a long time. Every time I moved to a new place, I had a different name, sometimes a different look. And I always got into the same old trouble eventually."

"Do you think it ever gets better for people like us?"

"Probably not. But I think people like us can get better at it. What I have with you is new to me. All kidding aside, I like it."

Sig considered this silently, then took the bowl out of my hands and set it on the coffee table. She gave me a deep, long kiss, then shifted so that her back was to the armrest of the couch and she was facing me, one foot on the floor, the other planted on the couch cushion. Sig undid the bathrobe and let it fall open.

I always give myself a lot of lead time before I go on a trip. I'd never been so glad about that.

Eventually though, Choo and Molly did arrive in Choo's van, and we formed a little convoy, me driving Sig in my car, Choo following. The last time we'd been to New York, having only one vehicle had been a problem. This time, Sig spent most of the trip on her phone, trying to get in touch with people overseas who didn't want to talk to her.

"I think someone has put some kind of word out on me," she said at one point.

"Probably the kresniks," I offered.

Sig's lips tightened. "Right." Then she went back to not accomplishing much.

Simon's directions led us to some kind of building in Queens that looked like a warehouse, except the bottom floor had a lobby front whose main windows were impenetrably dark tinted glass, and yellow letters advertised that it was a social media relations crèche, whatever that meant. The side parking lot was surrounded by a chainmesh fence, and the guy manning the tollbooth didn't look like a retiree padding out his pension. Not unless he'd retired from eating small children. "Wow," Sig said. "Friendly-looking."

"I'm having second thoughts about just walking in there like this," I said. "Maybe we should go to Plan B."

"What's Plan B?"

"I haven't worked out all of the details yet, but it involves finding you a Girl Scout uniform and a box of cookies."

Sig gave me an "uh-huh" look. "If that's a strategy, it needs work. If it's some kind of fetish, you and I are officially over."

"Officially? What, you give out certificates?"

Sig got serious. "If we're going to do this, let's do it."

There was no way I was driving my car into that parking lot; the knights would probably take the vehicle apart and put it back together again with all kinds of surveillance and tracking devices while I was talking to Simon. I finally found a parking space about a mile away that I liked, and said, "I'd still feel better if you guys stayed out of this part. I don't like that Simon agreed to let Molly and Choo walk into this place so easily."

Sig reached over and stroked the back of my neck. "You listened to Molly, right? If you get in trouble…when you get in trouble…you're not cutting any of us out this time."

I leaned over and she turned her head so that I could kiss her briefly. "I listened."

Sig kissed me again on the tip of my nose. "Simon's a manipulative prick. He's going to try to control you, and he'll use your concern for us to do it whether we're with you or not. But if we are with you, it might actually make it harder for him."

I kissed her again and, behind us, Choo honked his horn.

Getting out of the car, I ran face-first into a wall of heat so thick it felt like a solid thing. We lived further south, but Virginia mountains run cool, and New York City in the summer doesn't make for a dry heat. Too many rivers, too many people, too much trash, too many big buildings trapping the too much hot air coming off the too much concrete.

We weren't dressed for the weather either. I had on a T-shirt and jeans, and I was carrying the guitar case that holds a lot of my odds and ends in a false compartment. Choo was wearing a light windbreaker over a tee, and he was holding a gym bag as if he'd just come from working out. Sig looked somewhere between functional and fashionable, toting a backpack and wearing combat boots, green cargo pants, and a black tank top whose straps crossed over her neck and left her strong shoulders bare. Molly was the only one in shorts and relatively baggage-free, a large silver cross around her neck.

"Before we go back home, I want to see that play, *Hamilton*," Molly announced.

Choo grunted. "I want to get some grenades."

Which pretty much said it all. Most of us weren't in the mood for small talk, but Molly gave it a try. "You know, I've never seen you play that guitar, John."

"That's because I don't *play* my guitar," I told her. "I *am* my guitar."

"Really?"

"I can't play unless I get to that place where I can feel the song with my whole body, mind, and soul."

"How long does that take?"

"About twenty-six years," I said. "So far."

Molly nodded seriously. "That's too bad. It just occurred to me that Choo plays the piano, I play a clarinet, and Sig has a nice singing voice. Plus, we drive around in a van. We could be a mystery-solving musical group."

"There's one small problem with that," I said. "I can't see you ever being in hell, and I can't picture myself doing that kind of thing anywhere else."

"You artists are so temperamental."

Somewhere along the way, I got a phone call. I thought it would be a little pain-in-the-ass reminder from Simon, but when I checked the number, I saw that the call was from Sarah White, which was unusual, and not just because I was using a burner phone. Sarah's a cunning woman who I occasionally consult about the odd curse or creature or coma. I contact Sarah sparingly because Sarah doesn't charge money; she trades favors. We've become friends anyway, I think, but Sarah and I don't send each other Christmas cards. "What's up?" I asked.

"That's what I want to know." Sarah sounded tense. "Where are you? What are you doing?"

"Is there someone holding a knife to your throat or something?" I asked.

"What?!?" Sarah seemed genuinely shocked. She's not naïve, not at all, but I'm pretty sure she grew up in an environment where love was unconditional and feelings were honored. "No!"

"Are you at the bakery?" Sarah has built herself a mostly quiet life around a small bakery in Bonaparte, New York. It's another reason she and I aren't better friends. I've tried to be quiet life material, but I guess I haven't tried hard enough.

"Yes."

"Let me talk to one of your employees real quick, Sarah. Preferably one I've talked to before."

Sarah sighed. "Hold on." There was a pause, and then a voice I recognized came on. "Hello?" Leanne Collins sounded tentative.

"Is everything at the bakery okay?" I asked. "Has anybody strange come by the shop or anything?"

Leanne laughed. "Just Kevin." I heard Kevin Kichida complain good-naturedly in the background. Kevin is Sarah's apprentice and the sperm donor for Leanne's child, though they're not romantically involved. It's complicated. Kevin had recently quit college and was looking for a place in Bonaparte.

I smiled. "Good enough. Thanks. Could you give the phone back to Sarah?"

"I forget how paranoid you get," Sarah said when she came back on.

"I'm not paranoid," I said. "A vast secret global conspiracy keeps trying to ruin my life."

Sarah made a rueful noise. "I guess it does at that. Should we have a code word so you'll know when I'm not being held hostage?"

"Sure. If you're ever talking to me on the phone under duress, try to work this phrase into the conversation naturally: *neon red enema tango.*"

She laughed. "I don't think we have the same kinds of conversations."

"Seriously, if we decide on something like that, we should do it in person." We were getting close enough to the Templar front that I wanted to get the conversation over with. "Why do you want to know what I'm doing?"

"I just had a dream about you," Sarah told me.

I almost asked what I'd been wearing, but Sig was right next to me, and that would have been too flirty from a man in a committed relationship. Especially a man in a committed relationship with a woman who could throw a spear through the hole of a rolling doughnut at fifty paces. "I thought you were at work."

"I wasn't asleep when I had the dream."

That didn't sound good. "So, it was a vision."

"Yes."

I hate prophecy crap. "Why do I have a feeling we weren't braiding each other's hair in a sunny meadow full of unicorns?"

"You and your friends were in New York City," Sarah said quietly. "And you were trying to get away because the streets and buildings were swelling up, getting bigger and bigger as if they were going to explode. Cracks were opening up in the ground and the buildings were popping stitches."

"Stitches?" I repeated.

"It was a dream, John. And things were peering out of the dark cracks that were opening in our world."

I cleared my throat. "And you got something bad out of that?"

"I guess I'm just a fretter. Where are you?"

"Me and my friends are in New York City," I said. "We're about to see some people I don't want to see because someone told us that something really big and bad is happening."

"Oh, good," Sarah said. "So, I really was worried for nothing."

I'm more of a chuckle-wryly-on-the-inside kind of a guy, but that surprised a small laugh out of me. Sarah is usually a serious and dignified person. I got back to business again quickly, though. "You shouldn't be able to have any prophetic dreams about me. I'm geas-bound."

"I know that. But it didn't feel like just a dream. Maybe I was having a precognitive dream about the city and Sig, and my subconscious put some things together and imagined you into it."

"Prophecies can Photoshop?"

"Or maybe the vision was just that powerful." Sarah's voice got a little tighter. "The last time I had one as intense as that was when my father died."

The good news just kept on coming. "Okay, thanks for the

heads-up. Do you want me to call you if I find out anything specific?"

It was a serious question, and she took it as such. "Yes. No. Oh, poop."

Poop? I waited.

"Yes," she said finally.

"Okay," I said. The word was more a small prayer than a statement of fact. The warehouse-like building was coming into view and I wanted to wrap the conversation up.

"Kevin and I are coming to New York," Sarah decided.

That was fast. "Are you sure?"

"It was one of those dreams that I have to do something about." Sarah didn't sound too happy about that. "I was hoping I just had to warn you, but the feeling that I'm supposed to do something isn't going away, and I didn't really tell you anything you didn't already know."

Well, if that made sense to her, I wasn't going to argue. Sarah is useful to have around. We made a few arrangements about getting into contact with each other and said good-bye, and I gave the others a very brief rundown of the conversation while we made our way to the building that I was mentally referring to as Asshaven.

"This is your last chance to back out," I told the others. Being caught between different worlds sucked, but I was used to it. I wasn't used to the way my separate worlds kept moving closer together, though, and it made me antsy.

"We're your friends, John," Molly said.

"Exactly." There was a point somewhere in there, and I wasn't sure which one of us wasn't getting it.

～6～

ASSUME THE EXPOSITION

Someone opened those black tinted doors and let us into a lobby where three guards in red suit jackets waited. They looked like a cross between movie ushers and Navy SEALs. There was also a receptionist and a custodian visible, both of them suspiciously fit-looking. One of the guards was a werewolf from the Round Table too, which I guess was progress. Whether it was or not, we had to leave our weapons behind while we went through a five-foot-long checkpoint that involved an x-ray scanner, a metal detector, a black light, some covert holy symbols, and a test involving a little cup the size of a thimble with a tiny needle at its base. This had become a standard security precaution once the knights learned that some kind of skinwalker cult was working with or for the School of Night. Skinwalkers can imitate anyone by making a magical suit out of the victim's peeled skin, but the magical suits also function as a kind of armor. They don't bleed easily, if at all.

"Just don't prick the middle finger," I said as the guard obligingly put the cup over the tip of my pinky. "I may be using it soon."

The last step was a thorough frisking by a very large man who smelled hostile. His little plastic nameplate had a brass-looking sticker on it that said MARK. His groping was both impersonal and a little too personal, but at least it wasn't a first date. I had seen Mark once before, carrying a golf bag for Simon at a Templar-owned country club in Boston. Mark was much more convincing as a security type than as a caddy; he looked like he used to play throwback for Charles Darwin.

"I'd better get some flowers after this," I said as the frisking continued a little longer than seemed necessary.

Mark didn't respond.

"Has something made you guys step up the security?" Sig was being searched just as thoroughly, though by a woman.

Still no comment. These people had a non-answer for everything. I gave up and stared at the doors beyond the receptionist's desk while "Mark" went through my guitar case. The Knights Templar usually prefer to spread lone members of the blood around in a wide number of legit enterprises, but sometimes the Order likes to staff and run an entire business so that nobody has to tiptoe around the bullshit. The receptionist could probably fire on us with a rocket launcher, and no one would say anything except, "Herb! Get the pressure hose."

When Mark gave me a temporary ID, I noticed that the knuckles on his right hand had been skinned recently. Probably from dragging on the ground so much. "Does this mean you'll answer our questions now?" I asked.

"It means I might tell you to stop before I shoot," Mark rumbled. We didn't get our weapons back, but Mark led us past the lobby to a large warehouse floor full of rows and rows of office types working side by side on computers with no cubicles to hide their screens from each other. The segmented line of white plastic monitors created a giant spine where uniform rows of people made small motions and constant clacking noises. It reminded me of insects stripping a corpse clean.

"What are they doing?" Sig asked me in a low voice.

"How would I know?" I whispered back. "The last time I was a knight, Pong hadn't been invented yet." Maybe these Templars were doing whatever legit job was their front, or maybe they were busy inundating the Internet with outlandish conspiracy theories and wacked-out claims that made the supernatural seem ridiculous. Or maybe they were posting articles and blogs claiming to prove that real supernatural events were hoaxes, or even planting viruses or posting objectionable material that would get real sites taken down. Maybe they were scanning for real warning flags of supernatural events, looking for grains of sand in the digital desert that they were helping to create. Can you say *Sisyphus*?

"We call this place the hack factory," Mark contributed, then shut up as if afraid we might ask him to do it again.

We eventually reached the back section of the room where a series of small offices made mostly of glass were located. Simon Travers was in one of them, watching our approach with his implacable brown eyes, and Kasia was sitting in a rolling chair next to him. Simon made some minor adjustments to make sure no one could see the weapons beneath his expensive beige suit and stepped out to meet us. At middle age, Simon is what you'd get if some mad scientist spliced Brad Pitt and Jude Law together, but even though he's smooth and creamy on top, you can see where the veneer is starting to wear away from hard use. The skin beneath Simon's eyes is ever so faintly scarred, and his nose is oh so slightly imperfect from being broken and expertly reset more than once. Simon still manages to make the imperfections look rakish, though. Like the minor flaws give him character and set him apart from all of the perfect, pretty male actors in Hollywood who can't understand why their action roles keep getting stolen by Australians. He smells like an odd combination of skin moisturizer and hair dye and excess testosterone.

Simon's greeting wasn't as urbane as usual. "I expected you half an hour ago." Just for the record, we were ten minutes early.

I held my arms open. "What, no hug?"

Behind us, the man who might have been named Mark made a sound like he was choking on something, probably the hot blood of an enemy.

Simon gave Sig a curt nod. "Miss Norresdotter. Lovely as usual. I'm hoping you can be helpful again."

Sig was staring at Kasia. "You'll have to tell us what's going on first."

"That's the very first order of business," Simon promised.

Molly stepped forward and held her hand out to Simon. "Hi. I'm Molly Newman."

Simon finally remembered to turn on the charm. He flashed a smile that should have had a kilowatt ranking and took Molly's hand. "Simon Travers. Delighted to finally meet the rest of Team Charming."

"If you call us that again, I might just punch you," Sig advised. "I'm not saying I will. I just can't promise I won't."

Simon seemed amused. "Team Norresdotter doesn't have much of a ring to it. What would you rather I call you?"

"A cab," I said. Oh, Groucho. I miss you.

"How about the Mollifiers?" Molly suggested.

"Not happening," Choo said curtly.

Simon returned his attention to Molly. "Please ignore anything John has told you and make up your own mind about me."

"I never ignore anything John says." Molly had a pretty

bright smile of her own. "And I try to make up my own mind about everyone."

"And I love Molly," I told Simon. "So remove that manicured claw and stay ten feet away from her at all times, you oozing suckhole." Except I said it with a look, not actual words, and I reluctantly took Molly's cue and introduced Simon to Choo. Choo took Simon's hand warily. Both men said a few words and neither said they were pleased to meet the other.

At some point, Kasia had followed Simon out of the office. "Sigourney."

"Kasia." Sig might have moved her head a fraction of an inch. I can't swear to it. "I'd introduce you to Molly and Choo, but apparently you've already been spying on my friends."

Kasia sliced off a smile so thin that her mouth barely moved. "Does anyone really know who *your* friends are, Sigourney?"

Oh, good. There wasn't going to be any weird tension after all.

"The kresniks sent Kasia here as a courtesy when they started having visions about this city all the way across the ocean," Simon explained. "They chose her because some of the visions had you and Kasia in them, Sig, and you two used to work together."

"We never worked together," Sig corrected.

Kasia was in complete agreement: "We briefly worked with Stanislav Dvornik at the same time."

"Can you be more specific about this vision?" I asked.

Simon grimaced. "Not really. Sig and Kasia were in some sort of tower surrounded by pale white statues. It was dark, and there was a feeling of great significance."

"A dark tower," I repeated. "Were there any French knights or novelists from Maine involved?"

"No, but we're trying to discreetly check out every skyscraper in New York."

Sig and Kasia were continuing to have their own conversation as if no one else was in the room. "What was up with Clayburg?" Sig asked. "Were you trying to warn me away or get me involved or just messing with me?"

Kasia regarded her with a strange blend of amusement and hostility and indifference. "The last thing I owe you is any explanations for my behavior."

"If you wanted to let me know you were around, you could have just sent me a text," Sig said. "Or even arranged to meet me for coffee. Why turn this into some big dramatic fucked-up thing?"

Kasia's lips showed a little more range of motion by twisting. "When I knew you, your whole life was some big dramatic fucked-up thing. Has that changed?"

"I've changed," Sig said.

"I have not."

"Kasia's a professional." Simon mentioned this as if he was reminding Kasia of that fact. "I wouldn't have let her in on this, kresniks or no kresniks, if she didn't have a reputation for getting the job done. She's been very useful hypnotizing eyewitnesses into forgetting what they've seen recently, too."

Kasia wasn't the type to sigh, but her eyes took on a brooding simmer. "I am willing to work beside you, Sigourney, since Ladislaw seems to think it is important that I do so."

That never got explained fully, but Ladislaw was apparently some kresnik psychic whose word meant something to Sig. Did I mention that I hate prophecy crap? Sig nodded reluctantly, and I addressed Kasia. "Let's cut to the chase. If some butt-uglies with spells coming out of their who-knows-whats attacked us right now, would you have Sig's back?"

Kasia gave me a look that suggested I was being tiresome.

"It happens all the time," I assured her. "Hell, that's where I get my mail."

"That's true," Simon said. "It's why I call John when I want to flush out an enemy who's proving hard to find. Charming has a real talent for making people want to kill him."

"I always do what I say I am going to do," Kasia said. "Sigourney will tell you that much."

Sig still hadn't taken her eyes off Kasia. "Kasia sticks to the letter of her agreements even if she doesn't always honor the spirit of them."

"And I can always kill you later if you piss me off too much," Kasia added.

Simon didn't waste any more time on unpleasantries: That's one of the few things I like about him. He just started walking briskly away. "Come on." Mark started to follow us, but Simon called back without turning his head: "You can stay, Mark."

"I think you're supposed to throw him a banana when you say things like that," I suggested helpfully, and Sig gave me a light punch in the arm, though her lips finally twitched. Simon didn't respond. Instead, he led us to a set of stairs that had one door leading to a basement level and another metal panel door, the security kind that is slightly recessed into a wall and usually leads to janitors' closets with lots of toxic chemicals. Simon unlocked the latter.

It looked like a normal storage niche to me. It was dark and full of mops and brooms and buckets and rolls of brown paper towels and various containers of disinfectants, but Simon went on in and said, "Close the door behind us." We did, and when Simon reached a fuse box on the back wall, his hands did something with the switches. There was a pneumatic hiss, and the section of floor we were standing on slowly dropped with a tired sigh.

"No way," Choo muttered, but the floor descended anyhow. We traveled maybe twenty feet, and suddenly we were facing another small room about the size of a storage closet, but this one led to an iron spiral staircase going down. Everything was faintly lit by light from below.

"Thank God," I said.

Simon looked at me warily. "What?"

"I was afraid there was going to be a set of Batman and Robin costumes waiting for us."

"That's not as funny as you think." Simon didn't elaborate. When we moved forward, the section of floor we had ridden down began to rise again. I could see that it was basically a concrete platform on a thick segmented metal pole like they have beneath barber chairs. The platform could probably be jacked up manually by some kind of hydraulic lever in a pinch. Knights spend a lot of time around power outages.

We went down through service tunnels full of wide halls, thick walls, and heavy metal doors. There were guards in Templar field armor, a weave of Kevlar and spider silk that looks like something between a B-grade science fiction movie and an S&M fetishist's wet dream. Small dense plates made out of space-age plastics covered vital organs and nerve clusters to provide additional protection against impact and sharp edges, and the riot helmets had visors of dark glass with an infrared option. The guards were armed with pump-action shotguns and cattle prods that could probably kill a human and shock a buffalo into unconsciousness.

We reached a vault door that had a combination lock as well as several keyholes. There were no doorknobs, unless you counted the two guards on either side of the entrance. Simon turned to me. "Just remember: You asked to involve your friends."

That was still a bit of a sore spot, and Sig interceded before I could say whatever I was going to say. "We were told you were about to contact John, anyhow."

"I was considering it," Simon admitted grudgingly. "Charming is good at moving through supernatural communities where normal knights can't tread lightly, and this case is unusual."

"Maybe you should consider keeping me a little better informed in general," I said. "It seems like whenever we get involved in something, we're running around trying to deal with all kinds of crazy stuff breaking out and having to piece together the story behind it as we go along. It'd be nice to be more than one step ahead of an avalanche for a change."

Choo grunted agreement, but Simon didn't quite see it that way. "You don't get to spend most of your life hiding out in the middle of nowhere and then complain because you're not on top of things. That's by choice."

Huh. That had an uncomfortable ring of truth to it. On the other hand, it's also true that Simon desperately needs to spend a few days in some comfortable pajamas, watching bad television and eating things that aren't good for him until he finally breaks down and starts sobbing inconsolably.

Simon couldn't quite stop there. "You don't get involved with anything from our world except your Valkyrie unless it finds you first or you run smack bump into it."

"My name is Sig," Sig reminded him. "You said this case was unusual. How unusual?"

"It will save time if I just show you." Simon went through the laborious process of opening the door, and we wound up in a hallway leading between rows of observation cells. There was a stationary guard on the other side of the door and two roving ones.

One of the roving guards approached and became our escort as we walked down the corridor. Each cell had steel walls and a door made of thick security glass. Said glass was molded around metal bars about the size you'd expect to see in a rhino cage. Some of the prisoners were manacled to the walls, some wore chains that sank into holes in the floor, and some wore collars with digital readouts that wouldn't work if there was a massive magical surge.

One extremely attractive woman in a hospital gown was trying to form words around a tongue that had obviously been mutilated, and maybe with a larynx that had been removed too. Another prisoner was a satyr out of legend. Not that I had ever seen a satyr, but he was a burly man with goat horns whose hooved legs were completely covered in fur. Unlike most cartoons and illustrations I'd seen, this satyr had a large and way-too-visible penis. He seemed very fond of it.

Something that looked humanish but on a large scale was sleeping on the adjacent cell floor instead of a cot, swaddled in the kind of chains that anchor aircraft carriers. Another cell was full of mist, and the next had an occupant whose faceless skull was completely hairless and egg-shaped. One of the roving guards joined us along the way, and we all wound up standing in front of a cell that had little brown bubbles visible where the glass door had been caramelized. I moved forward to peer at the bubbles more closely. Simon explained: "That thing in there can generate fire out of a third eye."

That "thing" appeared to be a normal man in a T-shirt and boxers. He was either in his forties or his thirties and not aging well. A beefy guy, Caucasian, unshaven, just a little over six feet tall, with big shoulders, a potbelly, and thick arms that suggested he still liked to bench press or curl iron or did some job that involved a lot of lifting. Something about his skin tone was screaming for vitamins, and his eyes were exhausted sinkholes. His hair was brown with patches of grey, cut cheaply and short over a flat slab of a head. He looked mean and stupid but not particularly noteworthy.

"I don't see any third eye," Sig said. "Do you mean the psychic kind?"

"Just wait."

The man seemed to notice us. His expression became alert and completely impersonal at the same time, his head slowly swiveling toward us as if on gears. That already-sallow skin began to lose color, leaching into an ashen grey. Sagging flesh didn't disappear but tightened, as if someone were pumping air into him. The pupils and irises in his eyes turned red, and folds of flesh in his forehead parted to reveal an opening the size of a golf ball. The eye behind that opening was entirely red, and it spit a small sphere of fire. The spark enlarged rapidly until it exploded against the cell door in a bright, hissing fireworks display.

"The hardest part is keeping the oxygen level in his cell consistent." Simon almost made the remark sound conversational.

"Pyrokinesis?" I wondered. It's not like that red eye had tubes or nozzles.

"Who the hell knows?" Simon's lapse into mild profanity was another bad sign. If I got any more, I was going to have to start counting them on my toes.

"Does *he* know?" Molly asked. "Is this some weird kind of possession?"

"We think so, but traditional exorcism techniques don't seem to have any effect." Simon gestured vaguely. "Before it started changing, that thing used to be Randy Prutko. He worked the night shift stocking a grocery store. He's single, divorced, has two DUIs and several marks on his record that involve violence."

"What kind of violence?" Choo wanted to know.

"Bar fights, domestic abuse, and you can throw ignoring a restraining order and resisting arrest in there too," Simon answered. "Randy's the one who went crazy in a grocery store and kidnapped a female stock clerk after setting the place on fire."

Molly gave Simon a sharp look at that, but I stuck to the facts. "This girl Randy kidnapped. Was she a pretty young virgin?"

"I don't know if she's a virgin, but she's young and pretty. A knight managed to intercept Randy in a back alley while he was carrying the young lady to his apartment. Randy killed the knight, but fortunately, this is New York."

"Why is that good?" This from Choo.

I answered absently. "In big cities, knights are as thick as a Brooklyn accent." I was about to ask another question of my own, but then, for a brief flash of a second, it looked like the prisoner was wearing black armor. Not Kevlar. Black medieval armor. But as soon as I tried to study it, the armor blinked out. Everyone else was staring directly at the prisoner too, but they didn't seem to see anything. That kind of thing has happened a few times since I took a trip to the Dreamtime with Sarah White, and every time it does, I pretend it didn't. The man opened his mouth, and what came out was a sense of impact rather than a sound. I know that doesn't make sense, but the lights dimmed briefly before coming back on, and the air pressure changed. My ears popped even though I didn't see the cell door shake.

Sig and Choo and Kasia reacted more visibly and staggered backward. Choo leaned groggily against the wall for support. "What was that?!?"

Simon had the grace to seem mildly embarrassed. "*That* was a word of power. I didn't think it worked through soundproof glass."

"You did not test that first?" Kasia snapped. Whatever her

liaison status, she wasn't armed any more than I was, and Simon apparently hadn't brought her down there before.

"How was I supposed to test it? Whatever it is, the power word doesn't work on knights because we're all protected by a geas." Simon glanced at Molly, who seemed unaffected. "It doesn't seem to work on Miss Newman, either."

Sig gestured at the prisoner. "What is that thing?"

"As far as we can tell, he's a maladin." We must have looked confused, because Simon added, "A maladin is a paladin that's gone bad. It's basically a rip-off of an anti-paladin or a death knight or a doom knight. Randy was dressed in a full set of black armor when we found him."

"I've never heard of any of those things." I sounded a little accusing. How had I not heard of any of those things?

Molly seemed more fascinated than alarmed. She was staring into the cage as if there were a leprechaun there instead of a fat freak in boxer shorts. "They're from video games."

"Old-fashioned role-playing games too," Simon added. "The kind involving dice and tables. But the point is, they're modern fictional creatures, not mythical."

I just stared at him.

"They don't really exist," Simon clarified. "They never did."

I turned and focused my stare back on the prisoner. He looked real enough to me.

"You see my problem," Simon said.

❧ 7 ❧

SNAKES ON A PLAYGROUND

New York City

Cristian Ortiz liked taking his niece to this particular playground because it made him forget he was in a city for a while. Not that Cristian had ever lived anywhere else; he just liked the idea of it, living someplace with a lot of trees. These trees were tall enough to block the sight of big buildings in the background, and the nearest parking lot was at least a quarter-mile away, which kept a lot of people from coming there. No, that wasn't right. A lot of people came there. But a lot of people didn't. Cristian spoke and thought in English more than Spanish, but that didn't mean English always made sense to him.

Most of the adults who showed up were white women, and some of them wore the kind of clothes that advertised that they did yoga or Zumba or some other thing that probably ended with an "uh." Cristian was all right with that. He couldn't afford to take his eyes off Noemi for too long, though. The playground was covered with little pebbles, and if Cristian wasn't careful, his niece would pick one up and put it in her mouth. A few days ago, his sister-in-law had called Cristian over while she was changing Noemi's diaper. "What's this?" And when Cristian had looked down, he'd seen three little poop-covered rocks in Noemi's diaper.

Still, watching Noemi wasn't too bad. Cristian's older brother, Marco, was stationed somewhere in sand land getting engineering training for when soldier time was over, and Moncerrat was trying to get a nursing degree. Those classes were kicking Moncerrat's ass a little, and she and Cristian were both staying with Cristian's folks, so Cristian didn't mind helping out with Noemi when he wasn't driving around, stocking vending machines. If Noemi had been Cristian's kid, he'd be catching it from his friends for being Moncerrat's mujer, but watching his niece just made Cristian a good uncle. Didn't really figure, but not many things did if you thought about them too much. You just had to roll with it.

"Your daughter is adorable." Cristian had seen the woman who'd spoken around the playground a few times before. Maybe that's why she was talking to him. She looked to be getting up there but not too old yet, younger than most of those blancas who wait to have a career before having a kid. She looked serious, but maybe that was just the papers she was grading. Or the glasses. Or the careful way she was talking, like she was in a movie. Or the way she smiled, nervous and quick, like she wasn't used to it. She looked pretty tight in those slacks and that white buttoned shirt, but Cristian just nodded and gave her his no-hablo-ingles smile. Somebody had waved a magic wand and made Cristian a legal citizen after his big brother joined the army, but he'd spent his whole life knowing that talking to white women with money was a good way to get into trouble.

The woman didn't go back to her grading, though. Those

must have been some bad papers. "My two boys are the ones on the monkey bars. Rafe and Jude. They're pretending the ground is full of snakes. They're trying to make it from one end of the playground to the other without touching the ground."

That did sound like fun. Cristian and Marco used to play a game kind of like that when they were kids. They'd pretend a soccer ball was a bomb, and they had to keep it from hitting the ground or they'd all explode. But Cristian carefully didn't look over at the area that the woman was talking about. He just smiled blankly some more and returned his attention to Noemi. No hablo ingles.

"My ex-husband taught them that game." The woman's voice was sad for a second, and then it got angrier. "He was very in touch with being a child."

"This is why people like you have therapists," Cristian told her in Spanish. "So you don't have to talk to strangers in the park." *Or your families,* he thought, but Cristian didn't say that last part out loud. It seemed too mean to put into words, even in a language the woman didn't understand.

But the woman wasn't listening to Cristian, anyway. She was staring out at the playground, the skin on her face pulling tight and going pale as her mouth kept opening soundlessly. Gun. It was Cristian's first thought as he tracked her stare, but it wasn't some crazy person with a gun. Some pebbles on the playground were shifting in a bad way. Like something was going to come shooting out, like water or oil or lava in one of those old cartoons. But what came out was alive.

The thing was purplish and looked like pictures Cristian had seen of tapeworms in that high school science class that he'd mostly slept through, except it was big, python big, and ended in a round opening that was almost as wide as its body, the mouth full of sharp teeth. Some little kid, a boy, maybe two years old, started waddling over toward the thing, head up in an attitude of wow, and some woman screamed his name and started running after him.

The worm thing swiveled its mouth toward the woman—it didn't have eyes, so it must have been tracking by sound—and then the monster spit some pale yellow stuff right into the woman's face from almost twenty feet away. The woman went down flat on her back, making noises out of a melting face that Cristian wasn't ever going to forget. Not the noises. Not the face. Not ever.

Then everybody was screaming, and maybe that was good, because it seemed to confuse the thing for a minute. Cristian bolted off his bench and headed for Noemi, but he still stopped to pick up the toddling boy who had turned around to stare at his mom. Bending to swoop the kid up saved Cristian's life. The worm thing spit some of that acid stuff Cristian's way, but it only caught the outer meat on Cristian's left shoulder as he dipped down. It probably hurt, but Cristian had bigger problems. He swerved around the worm thing and then swerved again as another patch of gravel started shifting.

Noemi. She was crying when Cristian picked her up with one arm. He almost dropped the other kid, but they were close to some big pyramid-looking stone thing with wide slides on two sides and big steps on the other two. Actually, the thing was shaped like a small ziggurat, and Cristian knew that because his pops had gotten into that Aztec stuff for a while. It was another reason why Cristian liked this place, but he didn't care about that at the moment. He scooped Noemi up in his other arm and stumbled toward the big metal slide. He tried to run up the sloped surface, but even though the slide wasn't very steep, the kids in his arms were squirming and screaming and Cristian slipped and fell about six feet up. He started to slide back down. Back to the bottom, where another of the worm things had come out of the ground and was swiveling its head around like a periscope.

Cristian yelled, then wished he hadn't. The snake thing swiveled in Cristian's direction, and he rolled sideways on the big base of the slide, tumbling over the two crying kids in his arms. Acid splatted in the spot where Cristian had been, and at least the weight of the thrashing kids kind of anchored him and kept him from sliding down any farther. Cristian reached the edge of the slide, and then he pushed the kids over the slight rise between the slide and the stone stairs on the other side of the ziggurat.

Something sharp bit into Cristian's ankle, and he screamed and kicked and thrashed until he tore his foot free, leaving a hunk of skin behind. It burned like hell. If that thing was poisonous, Cristian was dead, but not dead yet. Cristian rolled onto the stone stairs of the ziggurat and picked those kids up and staggered all the way up to the top of the concrete playground attraction with only a little bit of a limp.

Then Cristian collapsed at the top of the ziggurat and pinned Noemi and the other kid there, on the solid square stone area between the two opposite slides, about ten feet wide. The kids were still crying, but Cristian had it in the back of his head that even if he died, his body could still protect Noemi this way. But Cristian didn't die. At least not right then. His ankle still burned, but it kept him awake while he lay there holding on to the kids and listening to the screams.

~8~

DOWN THE RABID HOLE

Simon gave us a while to realize that we'd never heard of anything remotely like what he'd just described. Or wait... maybe I had. I gestured at Prutko. "Is this guy a tulpa?" Tulpas are dream creatures come to life. They absorb the psychic essence of concentrated mass belief and somehow use it to form a material body. Opinion is divided as to whether tulpas are ghosts whose self-esteem is so low that they latch onto all of that stray wishful thinking out there and let it define them, or if tulpas are just some kind of random suck-ass phenomenon that doesn't have any logical justification for existing, like black holes or ATM fees. What matters is that if enough people spend a lot of time believing really hard in a clown with a giant crab claw called Dr. Plucky, a crab-clawed clown named Dr. Plucky might appear one day. Tulpas are why the current urban legends about a video game creation called the Slender Man becoming real are so scary.

"What we're dealing with may be some kind of tulpa variation." Simon didn't take his eyes off the whatever-it-was. "But these aren't cases of something manifesting out of nowhere.

The incidents have involved actual people or animals transforming into something else."

"How many incidents?" I asked.

"Eight that we know of," Simon said moodily. "But they seem to be increasing in rate and frequency. The first two were months ago. Then another three popped up weeks ago. And now three more have happened within the last two days."

"You must be charting the locations where they appeared," I said. "Have you found an epicenter?"

Simon gave me an approving look for what may have been the first time ever in the history of ever. "There's no useful pattern as far as we can tell, except that all of the incidents have been within New York City."

"Why did you say *useful* like that?" I asked. "Are there non-useful patterns?"

"We're plugging data into computers that… Well, let's just say that we have people in both the NSA and NASA. They gave us so many far-fetched and useless correlations that we wasted more time than we saved."

"Is that guy in there really obsessive about video or role-playing games?" Sig interjected.

What she was really asking was whether his transformation was some kind of manifestation of his inner self.

Simon didn't answer because a small shower of paint flakes fell from the ceiling. The corridor we were in was soundproof, and the foundation beneath our feet was solid, but something somewhere had caused a big impact.

Simon and I looked at each other. "You should probably give us some weapons now," I said conversationally.

The lights went off, and it turned out that the walls of the prison corridor were covered from top to bottom with holy symbols, sigils, and wards drawn in luminescent paint. This became evident when the symbols started providing enough illumination to see by even if they did make the hallway look like a rave party. Simon wordlessly handed me a silver steel knife while taking a M9A1 out of his jacket. The guard who was with us handed Choo another knife, and while he was doing so, Sig removed another M9A1 out of his hip holster and Kasia took the cattle prod strapped to his other leg. The guard was still armored up and carrying a shotgun, after all.

The other roving guard was moving to join the sentry at the entryway when the heavy vault door tore out of its framing wall and knocked the stationary guard off his feet. I don't know any way to make this sound believable, so I'm just going to say it: In the crude, newly opened passage was a huge freaking floating eyeball. It was about the size of a wrecking ball with big, thick open lids and long eyelashes, floating maybe three feet off the floor. I've met a lot of scary-ass things, but they were undeniably real and had a certain evolutionary logic; I could usually figure out how they ate or went to the bathroom or made little monster juniors. This thing's creepy absurdity was an indifferent insult to everything I knew about existence.

The eyeball blinked, and the approaching guard went flying backward through the air, bouncing off the wall and skidding across the floor. The guard who had taken point in front of us opened fire with his shotgun, but the loads stopped dispersing and hung there suspended in midair. The way the metal pellets weren't dropping to the floor gave me a bad feeling, and I slammed Molly against the wall so that I was between her and the eye thing. I wasn't being chivalrous. I heal fast. Simon crouched and positioned himself behind the foremost guard while Sig and Kasia and Choo flattened themselves against opposite walls.

It was a good call. The eye blinked, the floating ammo

disappeared from view, and the guard who had fired the shotgun was hurled off his feet as the metal grains flew backward too fast to see, smashing into his weapon and body armor. Simon stepped aside like a matador as the guard's body flew past him, not seeming to notice the bits of blood spraying off him as several pellets grazed his shoulder. I charged the eye, yelling, "It blinks when it uses magic!"

I wasn't looking forward to getting smashed by that thing, but again, I regenerated and the others didn't, and if Sig blasted it while its eyelids were closed, it would be worth it. But the half-assed plan didn't work. The next wave of force the eyeball generated was less powerful but wider. The glass doors containing mist and a naked sleeping male respectively both shattered into large rounded fragments, just the way security glass is designed to.

I was ripped off my feet but not thrown very far. Sig and Kasia managed to stay upright while everyone else went sprawling, but Sig's aim was fouled. I was rolling into a crouch when Simon's bodyguard, Mark, appeared in the doorway behind the eyeball. Mark had grabbed a shotgun from somewhere and began firing into that pulpy flesh. Something cold and jellylike hit my face from all the way down the corridor, and the eyeball dropped to the floor with a disgusting wet impact that I heard even with my ears ringing from the shotgun blasts.

Unfortunately, the mist that the eye had freed from a cell turned out to be alive. It also turned out to be acidic. The mist poured through the now-open spaces of the bars and engulfed Mark in a loud, screaming, skin-peeling hiss. Mark tried to reel back, but the mist traveled with him, swirling around him while he fired a pointless shotgun round into the ceiling. Mark didn't have eyes or an epidermis by this point, and the mist was inside his throat, cutting off his protests.

I didn't even have time to feel helpless. A long blue tongue came whipping out at an angle between the bars on my right and snared my knife hand. It was insane and probably against at least a few laws of physics, but when that tongue retracted, it did so with enough force to pull me toward the cell door. I was drawn closer to the egg-headed humanoid that had been staring at me without eyes earlier, but now it had a mouth that didn't stop where a mouth should. The maw was gaping so wide that I couldn't see the face that wasn't behind it. There seemed to be a lot more teeth than I was comfortable with too, and they hadn't gotten a lot of dental attention.

I braced a foot against one of the cell bars and turned. The motion let me switch the knife to my free hand. I didn't have the leverage to hack the tongue in two, so I stabbed through the narrowest part and tore sideways. The rest of the tongue ripped free, and I ran for my life. The mist that had consumed Mark was coming at us, its gassy body narrowing into a tendril.

Whatever else that mist was, it was indiscriminate; it poured through the bars of the cell I'd left behind, toward the closer prey. I could hear the guy who'd used too much tongue shrieking in agony behind me.

An alarm went off, and as I ran toward the others, I saw why. At some point during all this, Choo had pulled a fire alarm. Water came pouring from the ceiling somewhere between a sprinkle and a torrent. At first, I thought the water was just diluting the acidity of the mist thing, or even dispersing it, but I heard a high-pitched squeal behind me like air being forced through the rupture of a very large balloon. It wasn't a human noise. It wasn't even a humanoid noise. The wisps of that living mist emerged back into the hallway, dissipating in a way that suggested thrashes and jerks.

When the mist thing was gone and the fire alarm had been turned off, I heard Choo ask, "What the hell?"

"This is a knight facility." I could barely hear Simon's words with the alarm still echoing in my ears. "The sprinklers are full of holy water."

Normally, I would have asked Simon why he wasn't dissolving too, but it didn't seem like the right time. The knight who had caught bullets on his body armor was back on his feet, if obviously hurting. Even the knight who had been ping-ponged off a wall had managed to pull himself up and was checking on the one who had been knocked down by the vault door, but what was left of Simon's assistant, Mark, was never going to move again. The guy had given his life protecting me even if I doubted that this was his primary goal, so I just stayed quiet while Simon signed for the remaining knights to summon a cleanup crew and take a head count of the civilians on the level.

"Civilians?" I asked when Simon was done delegating.

Simon pointed at the corpse of the giant eye thing. "If it's like the others, that monster didn't just pop out of nowhere. We've been holding a few of the people who actually saw these things transform."

"Please don't tell me that thing was an eyewitness."

"We don't have time to be cute," Simon snapped. "This changes things."

How could it not? But what I said was: "Changes things how?"

"I have to take care of a few things first. You've seen what you needed to see here. Let's get some dry clothes and find something to eat." Simon began walking down the hall, and, given the alternatives, we followed him.

"Why are you being so accommodating?" I couldn't help asking.

Simon stopped for a moment and faced me again. He didn't seem to notice that this put him right next to the body of his dead assistant. "Let's be honest."

Somehow Simon managed to keep a straight face after he said that.

"Okay."

"If I could kill you without causing problems with the Round Table, I would have done it last year," Simon said. "But you're marginally more useful than annoying, and your Valkyrie's... Sig's... ability to talk to the dead is an even bigger asset here. Miss Newman wasn't affected by that thing's power word either, and I find that very interesting. She might be more useful trying to exorcise these things than our own priests."

"Sucks to be Choo," Choo muttered.

I didn't like Simon's tone. "We're not chess pieces."

Simon did look down at his assistant then. Maybe he was making a point. "We're all chess pieces."

PART THE SECOND

Mission Implausible

~9~

MYTHING THE POINT

Something was off. Again. Still.

Simon's idea of getting something to eat meant leaving the knight facility altogether.

He said that he wanted Sig to check out places where the manifestations had occurred in case the spirits of any of the victims were still hanging around, and that the place we were going to eat at was on the way to the first location, but still, our stopping for anything other than a PowerBar didn't exactly go with the whole laws-of-our-universe-being-suspended thing. I'd seen Simon in emergency mode before, and this wasn't it.

It didn't help that I was actively looking for a catch. If working with Simon didn't wind up exposing unpleasant surprises at some point, I'd rush out and buy a lottery ticket just in case miracles were contagious.

It also didn't help that I was physically uncomfortable. I had wound up wearing a spare set of Simon's clothes, which included a cool wisp of a green pullover thing that was theoretically a shirt. It felt like a big silk handkerchief with sleeves. The ensemble was completed by tannish pants that were like skinny jeans except they weren't. It felt like someone had Saran-Wrapped my ass.

I wasn't used to the smell either. Simon's shirt had more feminine scents pressed indelibly into the sheer fabric than I could easily count, and whatever cologne he used off the clock used patchouli to mask the smell of artificially infused sexual attraction pheromones. Thank God my underwear had stayed reasonably dry. After smelling Simon's shirt, I wouldn't have gotten near his briefs unless I was aiming a flamethrower at them.

It didn't take long before we pulled into the parking lot of what used to be a Chinese restaurant. Now it was just for sale or rent. "Was the food bad?" I asked Simon idly as we got out of our respective vehicles. Not that I was really anywhere near as nonchalant as all that. I've always had good posturing.

"The food was supposedly excellent." Simon removed a briefcase out of the trunk of his car. I hadn't seen him put it in there. "The ventilation system broke down, and the owners decided it would be cheaper to declare bankruptcy than try to fix it."

Simon probably knew this because the Knights Templar own a lot of real estate agencies. The loose structure of those kinds of operations makes it an easy way for knights to come and go on their own terms with a legal excuse for income. The practice is useful in other ways, too. It was a good bet that Simon used a lot of buildings whose ownership was in transition as temporary meeting places and drop-off points and safe houses and temporary prisons. If any observers came back and investigated this place in a few months, for example, all they'd find was a legit restaurant being operated by clueless civilians.

"We're keeping our weapons with us from now on." Sig was talking to Simon as much as she was telling the others. Me, I was already taking my guitar case out of the back of Choo's van, so maybe she was being polite. No one seemed to think this was a bad idea, not even Simon.

Kasia, however, made a point out of asking me: "Do you always do what Sig tells you to do?"

"Absolutely," I said. Sig snorted.

Kasia returned her attention to Sig. "So, you still have that strange power to turn dangerous men into weak, dependent assholes."

"Stanislav and I were codependent." Sig smelled angrier than she should have been. "And he wasn't a man. He was a disease that grew a penis, you half-dead skank."

"Kasia's also half-alive," I told Sig. "Let's try to focus on the positive." It was an attempt to lighten the tension, and I might as well have been bailing water out of a sinking lifeboat with a thimble. There was an entire silent conversation going on between Kasia and Sig, and I had no idea what they weren't saying.

"I am not positive about a lot of things." Kasia decided that was the last word and followed Simon inside the restaurant.

Choo cleared his throat and nodded at the restaurant. "I'd let it go, if you can, Sig. We got bigger problems. This thing's as bad as she told John it was."

"It is," I admitted. "It's freaking insane."

"So, we know we're going to work with them." Choo was still talking to Sig. "Let's just get on with it."

Sig agreed, if reluctantly. "Pretending to be the grown-up sucks."

I usually pretend in the other direction. "I'll take your word for it."

She gave me a smile. It was a little strained, but it was a smile. "Hush."

"Okay," I said. "But only because I'm your sex-addled love slave."

Sig gave my bottom a little smack. "And don't you forget it."

I made some excuse about needing to go find the little were-wolf's room and checked the restaurant for potential exits, defensible areas, weapons, killer clowns, crazed ninja hordes, the other giant eye that went with the first one we'd shot up...that kind of thing. I still eventually wound up in a large back room with Chinese tourist porn painted all over the walls in loud, bright, warm colors. The paintings portrayed lots of dragons and bamboo houses and bridges and people with white-painted faces. Sculptures made out of bronze-tinted papier-mâché were everywhere too. The long rectangular table had a small spread on it. There was orange, apple, and pomegranate juice to drink, and apple slices and bananas and grapes to nibble on if the gazpacho soup and crepes weren't filling enough.

I raised an eyebrow at Simon. "No coffee or meat?"

"Some of us remember our knight training." Which was petty. I was trained in the 1940s and '50s, and even if I wasn't, my body heals damage faster than any pizza slice can cause it. Simon poured some water into Kasia's glass from a pitcher, and she nodded as if she expected no less. "There is no why in coffee."

It took me a moment: *why* as in the letter *Y*, because coffee is spelled with two *E*s, and why as in no reason why anyone should drink it. "No, but there's an *organ* in *organic*," I replied. "And I'm pretty sure I know which one."

"Hey," Molly objected mildly. She's a vegetarian.

Sig gave my thigh a squeeze. "If I can work with Kasia, you can work with Simon."

She was right, and Simon laid his briefcase on the table and took out a bunch of books that looked like graphic novels or workbooks. I could see one clearly while Simon held it up and flipped through it. The glossy cover had a picture of some kind of yellow-skinned demonic-looking creature in a baldric and thong. It was distinctly male, overly muscled and veiny to the point of parody. The creature was also holding up a big sign that said THE MALE WHO DREW ME HAS ISSUES ABOUT THE SIZE OF HIS PENIS. Well, actually, it was holding up a ridiculously oversized sword that had lots of impractical chains dangling from it, two metal balls hanging at the end of the links. The title was *A Guide to Monsters and Mayhem for the Nightcrawlers' Guild.* The bottom of the cover mentioned something about a "dice twenty system."

When Simon found what he was looking for, he spread the book out and laid it on the table. On page twenty-three was a big floating eyeball. The heading said that it was called an "Eye Witness." And I thought I'd just been making a bad pun.

"Eye Witness?" Sig packed a lot into that simple repetition: Disbelief. Mild pain at the sheer cheesiness. White-knuckled what-the-hell-is-going-on-here tension.

"Just read it," Simon said, and Molly pulled the book closer and read the words out loud for the people in the cheap seats. According to the book, Eye Witnesses were thought to be the eyes of mysterious cosmic voyeurs taking an interest in mortal affairs for reasons known only to them. The eyes were the only parts visible as these beings peeked into our dimension from their own plane. Mostly passive, the eyes could harness great telekinetic powers if anyone attempted to interfere with their viewing pleasure.

"That's kind of clever," I said as Molly slid the book back toward Simon. "And creepy. And a complete crock."

"That mist you saw was also created for this game," Simon said. "It's called an Acist."

"As in acid mist?" Molly asked.

Simon looked like he wanted to pat her head and give her a biscuit. Instead, he proceeded to flip through the books he'd pulled out and showed us illustrations that resembled all of the creatures we'd seen back at Asshaven. Some of them were completely made up, and some were variations of the myths inspired by actual creatures.

I was having a hard time processing. "What is this Nightcrawlers' Guild?"

Simon snapped the book shut. "You've all heard of *Dungeons & Dragons*, right?"

I'd never checked that stuff out, either from a lack of friends or because imagining I'm hunting monsters isn't really my idea of escapism. But we all nodded, and Molly said, "I played it while I was at Sweet Briar College."

"The Nightcrawlers' Guild was basically one of many *Dungeons & Dragons*–inspired companies making products that were interchangeable with other game-playing systems."

"So, this eyeball thing came to life from a game," Choo repeated. Maybe he thought it would make sense if he kept saying it. "We're dealing with monsters who came to life from a game."

"Is anybody else thinking of that scene from the original *Ghostbusters*?" Molly asked.

"I am now," I said. One of the pleasures of knowing Molly is that she will watch any movie that catches her fancy an indeterminate number of times, even a bad one if it's the right kind of bad, and she has spent a lot of time catching me up on movies that I missed while I was traveling outside the United States. Now we speak our own movie language. "The big fight at the end?"

"Yes!" Molly looked at the others. "You know, the scene where if they think of something, a demon will take their thought and make it real? So they wind up fighting a giant Stay Puft Marsh-mallow Man?"

I turned toward Simon and tried to channel Molly's comment a little. "Is it possible that this Nightcrawlers' Guild is actually a cult? Could they have built in some kind of ritual so that every time a certain number of people play one of their games, it becomes a kind of summoning ceremony for tulpas?"

Simon sighed. If he wasn't careful, he was going to turn into a real boy. "It's something we're looking into, but not all of the transformed people turned into something out of these books. Let me walk you through it."

He began to methodically display a series of beige folders. Maybe reading from an actual folder sounds quaint, but knights don't like to make information Internet-accessible. The papers and photos Simon was removing had sigils watermarked beneath the writing. The symbols didn't channel a lot of magic, but anybody who tried to take a picture of the papers would find the image blurred. Anyone who tried to copy them would wind up causing copier breakdowns.

Simon went on to briefly describe the people who had transformed into monsters that were half make-believe and half familiar. Jenny Starkey was a shut-in with a basement apartment who changed into a troglodyte. Not a real troglodyte—a caveman urban legend dating back to a time when Cro-Magnons and Neanderthals still coexisted—this one had scaly skin and a rank smell.

Andrew Martin was a low-level drug dealer who mostly sold drugs on the side to supplement his income as a groundskeeper for several hotels. He became a made-up monster called a Sleech. Basically, a normal man except there were pale membranous tentacles coming out of his torso, and they could inject

a narcotic agent into bloodstreams that made the victims listless and cattlelike.

Don Sheridan was a construction worker who had become
the overly muscled slag of a humanoid I'd seen chained up in
the complex beneath the corporate building. As far as anybody
could guess, he'd become some kind of ogre.

Mitzi Unger had become a siren, and she was a bit of a
puzzler. The original Mitzi didn't look anything like the
almost-too-beautiful woman I'd seen in the cell, the one whose
throat had been operated on. She was a short, stout woman
with a dour expression on her face, and her attitude didn't seem
particularly sensual. The picture showed a tired woman who
hadn't spent a lot of time primping, and according to Simon,
Mitzi had spent most of her time trying to keep the pizza place
her husband owned from going under while raising their two
sons almost single-handedly.

Mitzi's first official act as a siren had been to use her hyp-
notic song to have her two teenaged sons beat her husband to
death.

Choo found Mitzi particularly disturbing. He had recently
had a chunk of ear torn out by a real siren and undergone several sessions of otoplasty. Now both of his ears are smaller as
part of the fix, and the injured one still isn't working at peak
efficiency. "That ain't a siren. Sirens have bird legs."

Simon gave Choo a bored get-with-the-program look. "Again,
it's a combination of the real thing and the popular version presented in video and table games."

"Give us a little slack, Simon," I said. "We're used to fighting
the real monsters that inspired media versions. We're not used
to fighting the media versions inspired by real monsters."

Simon's lip curl was a reluctant form of agreement.

"Was this Mitzi Unger seductive in real life?" Molly asked.

"Not as far as we've been able to tell, but who knows what her inner life was like." Simon went on with his presentation. The next picture showed the egghead that had tried to greet me with a little too much tongue. Gus Gordon was an accountant, even if his official job title said something different. According to Simon, he had become a jobombi, a type of zombie made from the kind of person who is anonymous and always fading into the background. Jobombies get absorbed into some soul-crushing job until their individual identity is consumed. The jobombi then goes through the routines of its former existence on autopilot until someone notices it and challenges it, at which point it reacts violently.

"Why did someone notice it so soon?" I wondered. "Why didn't the Pax kick in and make people ignore it?"

Simon glared at me as if the answer was my fault. "That's the worst part. It might be that with all of the cosplayers and attention-seekers and publicity stunts in New York City, people didn't realize that there was actually something supernatural going on, even subconsciously, so the Pax didn't kick in. Or it might be that this increase in magic incidents has severely weakened the Pax in this area, and it's not operating as effectively now that we need it the most."

Peachy.

The next photos were of the goat man I'd seen. Alex Holden had played a flute in his high school band. Ten years later, he'd become a waiter making over a hundred thousand dollars a year. Alex seemed to get a lot of gifts from older women that he met during his job. He had been in a motel with a married woman who wasn't his wife when he changed into a satyr and started playing a magical flute that drove women insane. Apparently, he was trying to start a supernatural orgy.

"How did you contain that?" Sig asked curiously.

"We didn't, not entirely. Fortunately, everyone who heard the music forgot what happened shortly after we put a stop to it. Hopefully, that includes the people who got away."

"Yeah," Choo said. "But..."

"If you hear a story about some unknown person dosing water with LSD, freezing it, and putting it in the ice machine of a motel, you'll know why."

"And you really think that will fly?" Sig asked skeptically.

"We drugged the survivors with LSD," Simon told her. "We really dosed water with LSD too, and froze it and put it in the ice machine. The police are already doing the rest."

The last pictures were of Randy Prutko, the shelf stocker who had become some kind of black knight. He was supposed to be a violent moron, but hardly a dark prince of power.

"My people are still putting together files on the last two manifestations." Simon closed Randy's folder. "The person who became that floating eye was a woman named Bailey Semones. She was the one who called the police when Mitzi Unger became a siren and had her sons kill their father."

"There must have been more to her than that," I argued. "Why did you take her into custody?"

"Because we could," Simon said. "Bailey is old and lives alone and seems to spend most of her time spying on her neighbors. The knight who questioned her realized that Bailey had no friends and spent a lot of time watching the Ungers, so he thought she might be a good information source."

"And that makes..." I paused to tally it up. Black knight. Satyr. Faceless thing. Big Honking Eyeball. The death worms that were apparently still a cover-up in progress. "Five incidents in the last twenty-four hours. The frequency really is increasing."

Simon gave me a tired thanks-for-rubbing-it-in glare. "I have two plans for putting an end to this fast. One of them involves

Sig talking to any spirits left behind by these manifestations. They might tell us how the School of Night is doing this and who we have to kill to make it stop."

Sig ignored that for the moment. "The School of Night? You think those nutcases are behind this?"

"I do." Simon looked at Molly and Choo. "Have John and Sig told you about them?"

The answer was no. Simon looked pleasantly surprised. Choo and Molly did not. "The School of Night is a secret occult society. No one knows much about it, but the few known references to the group begin in England around the Elizabethan era. Some of its founding members were John Dee, Walter Raleigh, and Christopher Marlowe. We thought we killed them out a long time ago, but recently the organization popped up again."

"The same John Dee who claimed to talk to angels?" Molly's voice noticeably tensed.

"Yes. Most people think Marlowe's play, *Doctor Faustus*, was based on John Dee."

"That's the play about the guy who makes a deal with the devil, right?" Choo said.

"Right. A bookish scholar makes a bargain for power and doesn't realize that he's being manipulated and used by evil forces way beyond his control."

Choo looked around the table. "Is it too late to change my mind about getting involved with this?"

Simon's smile wasn't. "Yes."

I tamped down an *I told you so* until it lodged somewhere in my upper chest muscles. Instead, I asked, "But why do you think the School of Night is involved?"

"Because like people from every age, the original School of Night was convinced that the world was on the brink of destruction. What made them different was that John Dee wanted to guide the process. He wanted to help bring about the end of the world so that he could fashion a new one in its place."

"Sort of like a controlled burn," I said.

"That's not a bad comparison."

It might have been a compliment if it weren't for the amount of surprise that Simon had managed to pack into the statement. Choo didn't care about any of that. "What kind of new world did this dude want to start?"

Simon's expression went flat. "Dee wanted to bring about a new age of magic. I don't think it's a coincidence that uncontrolled magical incidents are breaking out at the same time that the School of Night has been exposed and we're trying to hunt down every last one of their members. I think we've forced them to speed up their timetable."

"Fine, I'm sold," Sig said. "Where would these ghosts I'm supposed to look for most likely be hanging out?"

Simon was still formulating a response when his cell phone vibrated. He took it out, listened, then announced, "I'm going to have to take a break and make some calls while I still can. The attackers are here."

Let me just repeat that. He said the attackers were there. Casually. It was the first time he'd mentioned it.

It looked like I wouldn't be buying any lottery tickets anytime soon.

✥10✥

SIMON SAYS

What attackers?" Sig didn't direct the question at Simon. True to his word, Simon had moved away from the table and was making a phone call, ignoring us. Sig spoke in a low voice to Kasia.

For all their tension, Kasia skipped being pissy now that a tangible threat was on the horizon. "This School of Night has made several attempts to abduct Simon, and they don't know that Simon knows that this restaurant has been compromised. He came here hoping to draw them out."

"He brought my friends here," I said.

Simon actually paused and answered me, speaking up. "I'm the bait. Not you." Right. Because that changed everything. Then Simon went back to the phone.

I focused on Kasia. "This wouldn't be the other plan Simon has to try to wrap this whole thing up quickly, would it?"

Kasia just smirked. The expression looked natural on her.

Choo tilted his head at Simon. "I really don't want to work with this guy anymore."

"I was wondering why Simon was being so considerate about

lunch." Sig sounded resigned. "I guess he wasn't wasting time at all. He was multitasking."

"None of you even have to get up," Simon said. "We have this covered."

I wasn't about to punch him or waste time throwing a hissy fit if an attack was imminent. The bastard had probably counted on that when he planned this. It was why he'd waited until now to tell us. But what I did say was: "I'm not staying out of this while my friends are in the middle of it." He had probably counted on that, too. I turned my attention back to my friends. I'd been listening in on the other end of Simon's phone conversation and was already opening my guitar case and unlatching the false bottom. "There are at least eight people moving across nearby rooftops. There's also a green van circling around. The guy talking to Simon figures it's coming down the back alley as soon as the teams on the roofs are in position." I looked at Kasia. "Are these people trying to kill Simon, or do they want something from him?"

"They want something from him. He said that they have had opportunities to kill him from a distance when I talked to him this morning."

"Good." I fastened on my katana and wakizashi. "If they want to capture Simon, they're probably not going to just blow this place up except as a last resort."

"You have the oddest way of comforting people," Molly said.

I looked over at Simon. "What's the best way for us to pitch in without getting in the way?"

He held the phone away from his mouth again. "Help guard the back alley. We emptied the adjacent buildings with a story about fumigating, and we're watching all their entrances. If you see any people in the recessed stairways or a box truck, they're ours. The hand sign is Epsilon Beta. Kasia, you should back up our people on the roofs." She left without a word.

"What about the rest of us?" Sig opened the plastic tube she'd been carting around and removed a new weapon that Choo had designed for her. Modern tent poles are made of three parts whose sections are linked by an elastic string, so that the poles can be disconnected and their parts held side by side for easy packing. Choo had made Sig several sectional throwing spears based on the same principle, though the sections were heavier and the binding stronger. Their shafts were hollow and the spears were still too light to use like bladed quarterstaffs, but they had exorcism runes burned into their hafts and were good for throwing and slashing. Sig grasped the center section of one as she removed the disconnected spear, and the rest of the weapon snapped into place in a series of blurs and clicks.

"I assumed you would all stick together," Simon said.

"You assumed wrong." Sig looked at Molly. "You should stay in here, Molly. These don't sound like supernatural threats."

Molly held out her hands. "I'm not arguing." Then she looked at Simon. "I've made up my own mind about you, by the way."

"And I'm not waiting here." Choo's surprisingly deft meat-hook hands had already assembled the basic parts of an AS50 sniper rifle from his carry bag. Not too long before, Choo had gotten some sniper training from a professional while hanging out with a man named Jerry Kichida. Choo probably wasn't a real sniper yet, but he'd gone from being a good shot to an excellent one. "But we need to have a talk later. I came here to hunt monsters, not kill humans I don't even know."

Yeah, well, I'd advised Choo and Molly to stay out of it. I didn't stick around to make that point, though. My senses make me the best scout, and my fast healing makes me the logical point man, so I strode off and Sig followed close behind. Kasia was already just a scent trail. One of the knights I'd smelled in the kitchen was standing beside the back entrance, holding an MP5 at ready. I addressed him like I had every right. "Are the adjoining roofs still secure?"

They were.

There was an *L*-shaped counter that spanned two walls and long wide windows on both sides of the red back door. Choo didn't have to sweep anything aside, because the room was completely devoid of any furniture and knickknacks anyway. He just opened the window and began setting up a small tripod rest for his rifle. I think he was planning to lie on the counter facing the back alley. I never actually saw because a dark green van turned and came down the alley in reverse.

It was a pop and drop. Open the back doors. Fire out of them. Then either jump out or hang on depending on how things go from there. But things didn't go according to plan.

First, a box truck that had been parked on the street outside the alley reversed in behind the van and stopped, almost filling the entrance entirely. At the same time, a lot of things began generating cover noise. Somewhere on some nearby street, a very loud car alarm went off, and several other very loud car alarms joined in as if forming a chorus. Somewhere else, a pedestrian started playing very loud gangsta rap with a lot of discordant sounds in its background, some of them sirens and gunfire and car crashes.

In the alley itself, a metal strip knocked over some cardboard boxes as a thin cable pulled it snakelike over the alley. When the metal strip was stretched tight, it became clear that it was being pulled between two recessed stairways that led to boiler rooms. It was a spike strip, the kind cops use to halt vehicles, and it wound up in a diagonal position because the stairways weren't exactly parallel. The van still backed over the strip. First one rear wheel and then the other popped violently, causing the vehicle to skid left then right before braking too late to save the front tires.

For my part, I was already moving toward the van, and moving fast. The van's back doors flew open before I reached it—probably so I wouldn't reach it—and I got a brief glimpse of four men in ski masks and body armor. They were standing behind some kind of swiveling chain gun like the kind used in helicopters. I swerved left so that the gunners behind it would have to move the barrel away from the restaurant to track me.

I needn't have bothered. A spear had already flown down the alley, and it traveled into the barrel of the gun, the spearhead warping and scraping its way down the metal tube until it was lodged some four inches deep. One of the gunners lurched forward to try to grab the haft of the spear where it was sticking out of the gun's barrel, and I moved so that he was between me and his partners, drawing my wakizashi in the same motion. He tried to back out of the way, but it was too late.

Kevlar does a lot better against impact than it does sharp edges. Not too long ago, a company proudly gave a demonstration of their new groundbreaking knife-proof vest, and the reporter who'd volunteered to wear the vest for the demo wound up getting stabbed. The lower curve of my wakizashi sliced through the armor, but instead of cutting all the way through, the sword's point kept sliding into the breach. Blood began spurting out of the side of the man's torso, and I let go of the snared blade and stepped up onto the back platform of the van, hurling myself onto the van's roof, flopping sideways and turning over and over like a rolling pin.

Somewhere below me, three men were shoving a gurgling and thrashing body out of their way and stumbling around the belt feed of a huge, inoperative mounted gun while they tried to figure out who was going to fire at the people in the restaurant and who was going to fire up through the roof at me. They wouldn't take as long as normal men either, so I somersaulted into a crouch and unsheathed my katana, bringing it over my shoulder, reversing it, and driving it down through the roof above the driver's seat with both hands. The metal parted like tin lips in a kiss, and I could see that the driver and the man in the passenger seat weren't wearing masks or body armor. My blade anchored in the left side of the driver's face, and I leaned downward to finish driving the sword through the driver's brain, then let go of the sword hilt and rolled to the side. Bullets started tearing through the roof from below, and a few of them took pieces off my right thigh.

The passenger's door slammed open, and I dropped off the side of the van, managing to grab the barrel of an emerging pistol and push it away before it began firing. The man holding the handgun didn't try to fight me for it. He let my body pass and threw himself down on top of me so that I couldn't land on my feet. I managed to exhale before my back hit the ground, but the oxygen still took its sweet time coming back. At least the force of the impact tore the gun out of the man's hand.

I turned, but the bastard used my own momentum to keep us rolling, and he wound up straddling me, drawing a large knife from behind his back while my limbs were flailing around. I didn't have the leverage to hurl him off me, but I bucked my hips and kicked my leg up and managed to get my knee behind the edge of the open van door. The door swung hard so that its edge scraped the side of the man's temple and knocked his knife wrist sideways. I caught the wrist of his knife hand with only a minor slice on my left palm and rammed the heel of my right hand into the bridge of his nose. There was none of that driving-fragments-of-bone-into-his-brain bullshit, but I did manage to snap his head back violently enough to knock him out.

He went limp as the side door of the van slid open and another man with an HK416 jumped out. I don't know if he was planning to bring his gun to bear on me or if he was just trying to get out of a van where Sig was bouncing his remaining comrades around like billiard balls. The reason I don't know is because the new attacker dropped as a bullet went through his head. Based on how little of the head was left, Choo had gotten his AS50 set up after all.

I took the time to draw in a few deep breaths before dragging my ass off the ground. My right leg was okay to walk on, even if it did burn like hell. I shoved the man Choo had killed all the way back into the van, where Sig was stacking bodies like cordwood, then picked up the fallen weapons and pulled the man I'd knocked out after me, closing the van door behind us.

Then I paused. Now that I had time to register it, I smelled plastic explosive. C-4 has a faint smell, but it's a distinctive one, and I was picking up a lot of it. Shit. I traced a vague sigil in the air for Sig, and she got it immediately and began scratching some sigils into the inner paneling of the van. It was a pretty simple ward, meant to keep spirits away, but its magic was strong enough to interfere with wireless signals, and we sometimes used it to make sure that no one was spying on us electronically. The sigils ought to be equally effective at keeping any detonator signals from reaching the van. Or at least I hoped so.

I went outside and stood guard while Sig did her thing. The sounds of violence were distant, scattered, and tapering off. When Sig was finished, I used some of my returning breath to say, "Yikes."

"Yikes?" Sig echoed. "Since when do you say *yikes*?"

"Unless my nose is off, this van is packed with explosives."

"Oh." Sig went quiet for a moment. "Yikes."

"Told you."

"I thought this van was what they were going to take Simon away in."

"Whoever planned this must be a sore loser." I looked around. "We were lucky. This van must have some listening devices in it, or somebody's watching it from a distance. They probably wanted to wait until more people were around to blow this thing up."

Sig didn't have any trouble following that logic. "Get more bucks for their bang, you mean."

"Yeah."

"Maybe the bomb is just on a very long timer."

"I can think of at least three good reasons why it's probably not," I said. "But how about I get my swords and we get the hell out of here anyway?"

Getting on top of the van was a little harder with a wounded leg, but I didn't take a lot of time, anyhow. I was pulling my katana out of the driver when I heard a soft hum that I didn't recognize, somewhere between the sounds made by a wasp and a handheld vacuum cleaner. And the noise seemed to be getting louder.

"Something's coming!" I drew my Ruger Blackhawk while cries of alarm came from the restaurant roof. A moment later, a grey drone came flying into view. It looked like a machine insect, a monster Frisbee with four separate propellers extending from its side. There was a circular dome on its top and a narrow cylinder on its bottom. I didn't get a very good look because the cylinder began firing bullets as soon as the drone came into view.

Hell's own hailstones began tearing down the alley toward the van, but then the drone veered off as bullets fired by at least three different sets of high-caliber rifles began tearing into its propellers and center. When the drone tilted, it went down fast, slicing through the air and smashing into the restaurant's roof. The damn thing had probably been monitoring the battle from a distance, and when the wireless communication from the van was cut, whoever was operating the drone had tried to detonate the C-4 the hard way.

I ran to explain the situation to whoever was in the box truck. Somebody had to get that van someplace safe, even if that meant driving it into a river, and I wasn't leaving my friends behind.

It didn't take too long for someone to drive the van away, but by the same token, every second it took was too long. Eventually, Simon came out of the restaurant while Sig and Kasia and I were helping transfer bodies from the roof to the back of the box truck. He was trailed by two men in police uniforms, and the officers were carrying a normally dressed man between them as if helping a drunk navigate. Our attackers must have made a run at the front of the restaurant too, maybe had some reinforcements disguised as pedestrians come up the sidewalks. It made sense that Simon would want some real cops with Templar blood on hand to divert crowds and help contain the situation if things didn't go as planned.

"Live bodies in the box truck" was all Simon said as he passed. "Dead bodies in the furnace room."

"I need thirty seconds," I said.

"I don't have thirty seconds." But Simon paused anyhow.

"You just put my friends in harm's way because your day planner is full."

"They knew the risks," Simon said.

"That's the thing," I said. "They didn't. If they die fighting, they die fighting, but if anything happens to them because of some lie you told them, or some truth you didn't tell them, I'll hold you responsible." Normally, I would have said a lot more, or said it differently, but I didn't trust myself.

Simon's eyes seemed brighter than usual, and not in a good way. "There can't be more than one person in charge, and that person is me. You ought to remember enough about being a knight to understand that."

"I remember a lot of things about being a knight that you don't want me to go into." I gestured vaguely, trying to encompass the whole city around us. "Ben asked me to be a liaison with you again, but let's get this straight: You're going to have to try to contain these magical incidents whether we're here or not, and we don't need you if we decide to look around on our own. Don't assume my geas will keep me here if leaving is the only way to protect my friends."

Now Simon's face didn't show any emotion whatsoever. It wasn't even threatening in that way that lack of emotion often is. He was like a computer processing information. "You think I wouldn't rather hold you or kill you than have you running around loose?"

"You walk my friends into an attack without telling them again, we're going to find out."

"Are you done?" Simon asked.

"That's it," I said.

Simon walked off without a word.

Sig had never stopped stripping one of the prisoners. "Wow. Is that how knights argue?"

I bent down to help her. "In the field, yeah. That was a full-blown soap opera."

"You needed to say that." Sig took a knife out and cut through the laces of some combat boots rather than trying to undo them. "Do you think Simon's gone nuts?"

"Hell, yes," I said. "I told all of you that before you volunteered for this mess."

Sig slowed so she could stare me down. "I mean more nuts than usual."

"No. This is what he wanted." Maybe Simon hadn't anticipated that giant magic eyeball, but he'd planned the rest of this to keep us off-balance and limit our options as much as possible. He'd known I wouldn't buck the chain of command right before a fight, and we'd barely had time to think or object or ask Simon anything since we'd gotten enough information to ask some intelligent questions. Like, did Simon really have no clue how the School of Night was pulling off these transformations? And why did the School of Night want Simon alive? And did the knights have any emergency backup plans if everything went pear-shaped? I knew for a fact that the knights had done some seriously messed-up things that had killed thousands of people when there was no other way to conceal evidence of massive magical incidents. The Great Chicago Fire. The Great Molasses Flood in Boston. Blowing up the levee in New Orleans during Katrina. I was pretty sure they'd started at least one wildfire in California recently, too. God only knew what kind of final resorts Simon had cooking in the back of his brain if things in New York went south, and he probably didn't want me speculating about them.

Even Kasia's inclusion made more sense if I assumed that Simon was trying to keep us too distracted to look at things closely. Odds were, Simon was going to claim that we had to hurry and move on to the next stage as soon as we were done tying up the loose ends here, and the worst of it was, if magical incidents really were breaking out like brushfires, the prick would be telling the truth.

"And you think that's not going nuts?" Sig wondered.

I didn't respond immediately. The way Simon's and my working relationship was evolving wasn't a simple thing. "It is nuts, but he's not going that way. He's been that way all along. I knew who I was dealing with when I called him."

Sig looked at me curiously. "You still don't seem as upset as I would have expected."

"I'm pissed, but I try not to indulge that kind of thing right after a fight." I kept my voice calm. "Too much adrenaline and emotional bullshit going on under my skin."

"You're not a robot." Her words came out a bit tart. I'm not sure why. She was dealing with her own stuff.

"It's not the emotional part that bothers me," I said. "It's the bullshit."

"That's—" Sig started. Then she paused and stopped. A reluctant smile twitched across her face, and she leaned forward and briefly kissed me on the cheek. "Okay."

I wasn't exactly sure what the *okay* meant, but that was… okay.

Kasia came up and threw another corpse down the stairwell to an old-fashioned furnace room. "This is all very vomit-inducing, but have either of you noticed that these men are all South American?"

"I noticed," I said. The Knights Templar have a lot of Latino members, but the family of impersonators who had managed to insert themselves into the Templar power structure were of Celtic descent. I took out the knife my attacker had used and showed it to Kasia and Sig. It was a distinctive weapon, big with an elaborately decorated hilt, and part of the blade was edged on two sides, but only part. "I don't think the School of Night fell for Simon's trap after all. I'm pretty sure this is a South American knife. A facón."

Sig directed a one-word question my way. "Mercenaries?"

Military contractors are one of those awkward truths that most people know exist but don't really think about too much. They're basically armies without nations that can get their hands on anything from tanks to combat copters to antiaircraft missiles, and they can do it semi-legally because they often work for corporations or governments. I know for a fact that the Templars own and run at least one of the ten biggest military contractors, though not all of its mercenaries are of the blood. It's an easy way for the Templars to get advanced weaponry that no governments are going to want to look at too closely for fear of stumbling down a long, tangled path of black ops and self-incriminating evidence.

And many of the dirtiest and cheapest military contractors come from South America, outfits that are constantly disbanding and reforming under new names. That country's history of civil wars without restraint has left a lot of unemployed killers running around without a home they can go back to.

Simon said the Order had been hunting down the clan of false Templars nonstop, and there hadn't been that many of them to begin with. Was the School of Night hiring mercenaries to bolster their dwindling number of soldiers? South American mercs might be ideal for that purpose; a lot of them wouldn't be in the databases of any American law enforcement agencies, and they wouldn't know anything because they were paid not to ask questions.

Or had the School of Night hired mercenaries because they were disposable? If the person calling the shots on the other side was as twisty and crafty as Simon was, I wasn't too crazy about the idea of getting caught between them.

～11～

DIGRESSION IS THE BETTER PART OF VALOR

As part of his ongoing campaign to make us more manageable, Simon wanted to split up my group. "I've given you some names related to the transformees to check out, Charming. You and Kasia and Mr. Childers can start doing whatever it is you think you can do that normal knights can't. I want to take Sig and the holy woman with me."

Hard, swift-moving men in nondescript clothing had finished securing prisoners into the box truck. It looked like the inside of the truck bay had side rails with manacles looped around them, with some items hanging on the walls that belonged in a hardware store or an S&M parlor. An interrogation room on wheels. Did I mention that I don't like Simon?

Several young males—maybe squires—dressed like tag artists were covering blood spatters on the pavement and walls by spray-painting over them. Sometime in the next day or two, another team of Templars would come in and use the graffiti as an excuse to sandblast the pavement and walls. One of the spike strips was hissing and winding over the pavement while someone in a boiler room reeled it in. It was time to get out of there.

Sig is more used to working with others than I am, and she said, "I don't like it either, John, but I really do think Simon wants to get this over with as fast as he can, and me checking things out with my gift makes sense. Separating Kasia and me and you and Simon does too. You wasting time hanging around just to protect me and Molly doesn't."

As if to rub salt in my suspicions, Simon was exaggeratedly polite when he added, "This isn't a conspiracy, John. Molly is an exorcist. Sig is a medium. You and Kasia are hunters. I'm just trying to utilize each of you the way that you're best suited for."

The problem was, *utilize* is just a polite way of saying *use*. Sig had her own reservations. I think she didn't want Kasia running around unsupervised, and she didn't like me partnering with Kasia, and she didn't trust anyone else to handle her. At any rate, Sig tilted her chin at Kasia: "Kasia has a kind of honor, John. But if her job is to screw you over for Simon, she'll lie, cheat, steal, torture, and kill to do it."

Neither Simon nor Kasia seemed offended by this warning. In fact, Kasia gave a half-nod.

"Good to know," I told Sig. "Meet me by seven at the contact point we had the last time we were in New York. Or at least let me know why you can't."

Sig held out a fist for me to bump, and I obliged. "I won't tell you to be careful," she said. "But keep surviving."

"Sounds like an '80s song," I said.

"For God's sake, don't sing."

When my group got to the van, I held the front passenger door open for Kasia. She accepted the courtesy with a tilt of her chin and a faint smirk. Maybe she realized that it was my way of making sure she didn't try to sit behind me.

The inside of the van was a little too heated in more ways than one. The thin pants I had borrowed from Simon didn't offer much insulation from the hot plastic seat cover, and I felt as if I were getting the backs of my thighs grilled. The mood was a bit uncomfortable too. Maybe it was because there were only three of us now, or maybe it was because the adrenaline was wearing off, or maybe it was because we were back in a familiar environment and it made the crazy stand out, but it was suddenly obvious how odd and awkward Kasia's presence was. Choo turned on the AC and his police scanner.

I called Sarah White. "I want to see you, but I've got a dhampir who works for the kresniks with me, and I can't guarantee she won't tell the Templars about you."

Sarah wasn't thrilled by this information. "What's going on?"

I told her some of the basics.

"Goddess," Sarah said.

I guess that about summed it up. "She's not a psychic, if that helps. The dhampir, I mean."

"Go ahead and bring her along." And then Sarah told me how to find her. It was a little complicated.

"Are we going to check out the names on Simon's list?" Kasia asked.

"I want to make a stop first."

"You seem to think you are in charge of our little trio here." Kasia drummed her nails on the dashboard. Maybe it wasn't a coincidence that this positioned her to lash out with her elbow. "I did not agree to that."

Meaning part of her job was to keep me coloring inside the lines.

"Are you working for the kresniks or Simon?" I asked.

"The kresniks do not give me rules." Kasia sounded amused at the thought. "They give me money and objectives, in that order."

"So, what's your objective?"

"To keep whatever is happening here from getting worse. That means working with Simon. It might even mean working with Sigourney. It does not mean letting male egos and alpha-male bullshit slow me down."

"Fair enough," I said. "But sometimes, you have to take time to save time."

"That is true," Kasia agreed. "But only because you said *sometimes*. I will need something less vague, or we can stop the van and settle this outside."

That sounded pretty tempting after watching her mess with Sig, and I knew Kasia could smell the desire to fight coming off me, but we weren't wolves establishing dominance. I doubted Kasia would handle losing well, and I knew I wouldn't. And one of us would have to lose. Even if I killed her, I'd just wind up on the kresniks' shit list again. The only reason they hadn't come after me after I killed Stanislav Dvornik was that the knights were taking care of it at the time.

So I strung together an argument. "The assumptions we make at the beginning of a search do more than anything else to define its outcome. There are probably a thousand knights running around this city right now, and they're all working on the same basic set of assumptions that Simon just gave us. The person I want to see might be able to give us a different perspective on what's happening and how it's happening."

"He's saying it's a party, and everybody is bringing lasagna and Jell-O," Choo put in. "We want to get some banana pudding."

"Yes, thank you for explaining that to me." Kasia put her

elbow away and things went awkward and quiet again, which was okay by me. Silences are a good way to get people talking, and I wanted Kasia to show some more of her cards. Unfortunately, she didn't mind the silence either.

It was Choo who finally asked Kasia, "So, you're still holding a grudge against Sig after all this time, huh?"

"Do not be so dramatic." Kasia settled back into her seat without explaining what that meant.

"I hadn't been surrounded by dudes with guns and bad attitudes back there, you'd have seen dramatic," Choo grumbled.

I put it mildly: "I didn't like the way things went down back there either."

Choo's laugh was bitter. "Yeah, but at least you got an invitation to that party I was talking about."

Huh. "What do you mean?"

"This Simon only wants me along so he can get his hands on the rest of you," Choo said. "I don't like being a token."

"I don't think it's about ethnicity with Simon," I said.

Choo smiled without humor. "It's not always a black thing." Then Choo looked at Kasia. "Even if I am stuck here driving Miss Crazy."

"Simon uses people like tools," I said. "He probably doesn't think you can do anything for him that his knights can't do better."

"Isn't that true?" Kasia drawled, again not putting much emphasis into it.

Choo gave her a glare, but it was only mildly hot, not extra spicy. Kasia was baiting him, and Choo's not stupid.

"Maybe for Simon," I said. "Simon already has access to all the weapons he needs. But Choo isn't just a weapon supplier. He's an innovator. He's also someone I trust."

"Ah," Kasia said dismissively. Maybe she saw trust as a liability.

"John keeps me from being outnumbered by the women too," Choo commented.

I wasn't sure why Choo felt a need to say that. Trying to make sense out of another man's behavior when his pride has been stung is problematic at best. Trying to make sense of his behavior around an attractive woman assumes that there's sense to be made. Trying to figure out his behavior under both those conditions? Forget about it.

Kasia took the comment as sexist, at any rate. "Men talk about being logical and unemotional, but even the softest woman has to make decisions every day that would shrivel a man's testicles."

"It's true," I told Choo. "Would you say I'm a spring or an autumn?"

Kasia directed a scornful glance at me over her shoulder. "It is too late to act stupid. I have been listening to you."

"That was your first mistake," I said.

"Yeah, and it's a doozy," Choo chipped in. "I made it too, and I've had to listen to him ever since."

Kasia made a scoffing sound. "Words, words, words." Was that a Hamlet reference or a coincidence? "You act like a fool, but I think you are more like a doctor, tapping and poking away at people's reflexes and tender points to see where they kick and twitch." She took her index finger and jabbed it at the dashboard of the van several times. "Poke. Poke. Poke. You will have to do better than that to sound me out." Then she smirked. "Or try to poke me with something bigger."

Yeah, right. Like her "penis flytrap" routine wasn't at least half an act too. I looked at Kasia and thought about how she wanted to hurt Sig, and the idea of it traveled through my entire body like ice water. "Just so we're clear, I'm not interested in being your revenge sex."

Kasia aimed a flawlessly plucked eyebrow at me, then returned her eyes to the road. "Never is a long time for people like us."

Choo intervened. "I thought you were pissed off about Stanislav."

Kasia shrugged one bare, sleek shoulder. "*Pissed off* is not the right way to put it."

"You seem to speak English pretty well," I nudged. "Put it another way."

This time she didn't smile, ironically or otherwise. "I speak English better than most Americans, but it does not have enough words for complicated emotions. The Brits think those are best left unspoken, and you Americans like to pretend everything is simple."

"All right, all right," Choo said. "But you didn't go to Clayburg to check out Sig because you were in a good mood."

Kasia smiled faintly. "That is true. It does not mean I am one of your cartoon supervillains."

"Are you sure about that?" I challenged. "You wanted to have the obligatory pointless fight scene a moment ago."

Kasia moved that shoulder again. It was a nice shoulder, and I didn't want to notice stuff like that. "Fighting is how I poke."

I leaned forward in my seat. "How about we take an am-I-a-supervillain quiz? True or false: I got superhuman strength from a lab accident or brush with the supernatural."

This time Kasia didn't bother to look at me. "Ha-ha."

"We'll count that as true," I said. "True or false: My idea of anger management is making sure that everyone who ever laughed at me writhes in unspeakable torment for the rest of their pathetic little lives."

Choo cracked up in his mouth a little bit, and Kasia finally decided that talking was better than listening to me. "There are not many things that I still have strong feelings about, bad or good. Stanislav is one of them."

"And the feelings are bad *and* good?"

"Most of my strong feelings are," she said. "I want to know why Stanislav died. I want to know why Sig is sleeping with the man who killed him. I want to know if I am obligated to kill any of you for old times' sake when this is all over."

Choo grunted. "I can tell you that."

Kasia disagreed. "It is not something anyone can tell someone else. I will figure it out."

"I never did nothing to the man, and he tried to feed me to vampires just for knowing Sig," Choo said. "Figure that out while you're at it."

"We are going in circles." I don't think Kasia meant just the conversation.

"That's what my friend said to do," I told her. "Maybe she's making sure that we're not being followed." I didn't think so, though. Sarah's driving instructions had been very precise about how many times we were supposed to cross a *Y*-shaped intersection, and I had a feeling that our route was sketching out some kind of sigil or symbol on the canvas of the New York City streets.

Choo finally came to a stop. "I'm dropping you two off. Whoever attacked that Chinese restaurant staked it out first. This van has a target painted on it now, and I want to get a new ride, or at least some new plates and a paint job. Some more burner phones, too." Choo still has a lot of contacts from his days as an army supply sergeant, and his contacts have contacts.

"Try to get an ice cream truck. It's the perfect cover." I leaned forward to look at Kasia. "You don't mind dressing up like a clown, do you?"

Kasia gave me a look of almost lazy contempt. "Or you can just dress the way you usually do." The look she gave Choo was considerably harder. "If you try to run, you will not get very far."

"He knows that," I said.

Choo didn't need my help. He ignored Kasia just fine on his own. "You going to be all right for wheels?"

I waved him off. "We'll figure something out."

Sometimes, I think I should have those words made into a coat of arms.

~12~

ARE YOU INN OR OUT?

The building we were supposed to meet Sarah at was in the top fork of the crossroads, the first in a long row of old but serviceable brownstone tenements. "Tell me more about this cunning woman," Kasia said as we approached it.

"All you need to know is that she's a powerful psychic and has a knowledge base and way of looking at things that we don't."

"It is more than that," Kasia said. "You like her."

Sig had said something similar the first time she'd heard me talk to Sarah on a phone. "I don't want to sleep with her or be her, if that's what you mean. But she's one of the few actual grown-ups I know."

Kasia seemed to find this amusing. "You do not think Simon is a grown-up?"

"I think Simon is a grown-down," I said.

"And I think you are a grown-sideways." I didn't ask her what that meant, but she explained anyhow. "At times you seem like a wise old soul, and other times you seem like you have not grown up yet."

We stopped in front of the building. "Feel free to go do your own thing."

She gave that slight smile. "I did not say it was entirely unappealing. Men like you can be fun in bed."

"Sig and I don't have an open relationship."

Kasia studied me. "Neither did Sig and Stanislav. And yet you two cheated on him."

I probably shouldn't have responded, but I did. "We didn't sleep together until long after Stanislav was dead. I told Sig how I felt. Hell, I told him how I felt. Sig decided to break up with Stanislav because they had a messed-up relationship. He proved she was right by flipping out and trying to kill us. Maybe we didn't handle it right, but we did the best we could at the time."

She gave me a you're-full-of-shit look but didn't push it. "Sigourney and Stanislav cheated on me."

I was skeptical about it being that cut-and-dried, but even if it was true, so what? Sig had said she was still drinking and dealing with her parents' deaths back then. She wasn't lying about what she'd done. She wasn't proud of it. It's not like I haven't done things I'm ashamed of. "So, you're here for revenge after all?"

When Kasia raised her face again, her mouth had a bitter twist. "I already got it. Later, Stanislav and I cheated on her."

That took a moment to process. "So, whatever your deal with Sig is, it really isn't about right or wrong."

Kasia rolled her eyes. "You might convince me that some choices are better than others. You will never convince me that there is such a thing as right or wrong. We feel what we feel. We do what we do."

That was true. Or it was the biggest lie the devil ever told. I'm still working on that. "So, have you figured out how you feel yet?" I asked.

She shrugged.

The building had a sliding steel panel door instead of a glass one, and its windows were made of thick green tinted glass the color of old Coke bottles. There was no buzzer. On either side of the door were community bulletin boards advertising different kinds of classes, bands, rental opportunities, missing pets, and people looking for travel companions. On the left side, there was an ad for an art class that had a Chinese man in some kind of ceremonial dress facing right. On the opposite side of the door, the same ad had the same Chinese man facing left. I stared at the ads for a moment before stepping forward. The door had four different locks, but none of them were...locked. I had the distinct feeling that if I hadn't followed Sarah's route, they would have been. The heavy-looking door slid open so easily that it almost felt like it was opening itself.

Yay.

Kasia and I walked into a lobby that took up about half the first floor of the three-story building. Square wooden tables and chairs were spread about the room and had place settings, though all were currently unoccupied. The walls were murals, painted to create the illusion that I was looking out on a vast plain beneath a velvet purplish sky whose clouds were traveling forward. The sense of motion was rendered so realistically that I almost expected the clouds to start moving again at any moment. The floor was covered with grass. Real grass, and not mowed either, though it hadn't grown out of hand. It probably didn't dare. The ceiling was supported by columns made of stones—real stonemasonry too, not that cheap and easy architecture where ill-fitting rocks are fused together with tons of Kwik-Crete.

Behind the old-fashioned wood counter that dominated the back of the lobby were three identical women—possibly similarly dressed triplets with the same smile. The women's coloring was vaguely Mediterranean, and each was dressed in a frilly light blue blouse that had an open neck and bared shoulders. I noted with an emotion somewhere between amused, disturbed, and mildly hysterical that the woman on the left was writing something on a pad with her left hand. The woman on the right was writing something with her right, and the woman in the middle had both hands held behind her back, so that it looked like the women on either side of her were appendages. All three were tall and appeared to be somewhere in their fifties, with big-boned bodies and what the writers I grew up with used to call magnificent bosoms. They exuded an earthy sexuality. There were kegs and bottles of wine mounted on racks behind them, and mugs, and room keys. An open door seemed to lead into a kitchen area.

"You must be John and his guest," the middle woman said with a surprisingly deep but alluring contralto. I was just glad she was the only one speaking. If all three women had addressed me in unison, I might have run out of there shrieking, and that wouldn't have been good for anyone's dignity. "Sarah told us you were coming."

As soon as the woman spoke, dogs began trotting into the lobby. A collie came padding in from an open hallway to the side. A Rottweiler popped its head up from where it had been lying at the speaker's feet and braced its paws on the counter. Several mutts led by a German shepherd came trotting down the stairs from an open stairwell. I'd smelled them, of course, but I hadn't known they were unleashed. Unlike most packs smelling a werewolf, the dogs merely sniffed and looked at me curiously.

Kasia murmured in a low voice, "I think your friend sent you to a dog hotel."

The spokeswoman's face became contemplative in a way that made my scalp tighten. She smelled like a human, but the glance she gave Kasia suggested that she hadn't had any problem overhearing the dhampir, and her expression was mirrored on the faces of her subordinates, if that's what they were. I addressed our hostess politely. "That's me. Has Sarah gotten here yet?"

"She's waiting for you in room 2D." The woman on the left shoved a sign-in sheet attached to a clipboard across the counter. "But you'll have to sign in. *With your living blood!*"

No, just kidding. I took the ink pen the middle woman handed me, and looked at the sign-in sheet thoughtfully. There was a bronze plaque built into the counter next to it, with a staff that had two snakes twined around it etched into the metal. The middle hostess followed my gaze. "This inn was a clinic in the 1940s," she said blandly.

Sure it was. While I studied the register, memorizing the other names and looking for small print, a handsome young-looking brown-haired man wandered downstairs from the stairwell. He was wearing nothing but a pair of blue bikini briefs and a beard that had been carefully trimmed to look scruffy without being unattractive. The body on display could have been a professional swimmer's, and a light coating of hair dusted his chest. There were no visible scars or blemishes anywhere on him.

It was early afternoon, but the man's movements were indolent and sensual and self-satisfied, giving every impression of having just crawled out of bed. He probably always looked like he had just crawled out of somebody's bed. He smelled like an incubus, a male succubus who absorbed life energy through sexual interaction.

The man gave the receptionists a lazy half-wave and wandered over to where mailboxes were built into the west wall, camouflaged by the paint job. Everyone in the lobby paused to observe him, even the dogs. I was watching because he was a monster, and I was trying to figure out what the hell was going on. That's probably why the females were staring at him so intently too. Taking his time, seemingly unaware of all the attention, the incubus casually sorted through some old-fashioned mail. At a guess, he was a lot older than he looked. Then he closed the box and sauntered back across the lobby and up the stairs.

I cleared my throat. "So, is this place a boardinghouse or a bar or a brothel?"

"I told you. It's an inn," the middle...I guess I should call her an innkeeper...said.

I tried to focus on the essentials. "And Sarah is your friend?"

All three nodded gravely.

"Did she tell you my full name?" I asked.

"We wouldn't be talking to someone of the knights' bloodline if she hadn't told us a little bit about you," the middle woman said warmly, finally placing both hands on the counter. "Anyone who got the Templars to accept werewolves is welcome here, Mr. Charming. We take in all kinds of strays."

"Really?" I went ahead and signed my real name. They already knew it, and any binding spells would slide off me anyhow. "It doesn't appear very busy here. Not enough to require three receptionists."

"I love the word *appears*," the woman on the right said, still smiling pleasantly. "It rolls right off the tongue."

Yeah, well, so did the word *bilge*. I didn't say that out loud, though. Sarah had vouched for me. I could at least *try* not to make her look bad.

Kasia signed in, and I thanked our hostesses and went upstairs. Two of the dogs followed us.

"I used my real name," Kasia murmured.

I looked over. Was her face paler than usual? "That's your choice."

"You do not understand," she said. "I picked up that pen and tried to write an alias. And I signed my real name."

I can't say I was surprised.

~13~

A STATUE OF LIMITATIONS

Scaly, winged, vaguely humanoid, the two shapes soared serenely around the skyscraper, and Janine had a moment. But knights must be knights, so all Janine said to her partner, Ed Morgan, dry-like, was: "I think I may know what's disrupting the wireless signals around here."

Because it had been a lack of carrier signals, not gargoyle statues come to life, that had brought them there. A lot of Templars by blood who weren't suited for combat worked for phone companies, notifying the Order of strange wireless issues. Personally, Janine would rather risk her life on rooftops. There were different kinds of dying, and a nine-to-five job pretending to care about IRAs and quotas and self-evaluation forms seemed a particularly slow and horrendous one.

Dressed in the coveralls of repair personnel, Janine and Ed had talked their way up to the top of the neighboring skyscraper with dire-sounding warnings about an overdue elevator maintenance check. Janine never had problems convincing people that she worked any kind of blue-collar job, no matter their gender or sexuality or class bracket. Janine was hard and fit and scarred, her black hair shaved down to a mossy surface, her body moving with absolute physical confidence.

Male eyes boldly followed Janine wherever she went, but the men themselves generally didn't, not often, or if they did flirt, it was with an overconfidence that came from wealth or hours spent in a gym, a proprietary assumption that Janine was a fellow predator and that they should just go ahead and do this thing. Women flirted with Janine more frequently and more indirectly than she was comfortable with. Her eyes were more prone to probing stares than warm glances, and her lips made a flat line more often than a smile, and women often seemed to assume that Janine was trying to discourage males. Janine wasn't *trying* to do anything. She looked the way she looked.

Ed wasn't as intense as Janine, a fact which he attributed to being more laid-back and which Janine figured was because he didn't fully grasp situations as quickly as she did. "Have you ever hunted gargoyles before, Janine?"

Ed in twenty seconds or less: At twenty-six, he was eight years younger than Janine, more than a hundred and thirty pounds heavier, blond, square-chinned, with the bright, perfect smile of someone who had gotten over having his real teeth knocked out. A classically handsome man, only bigger. Wider-faced. Larger-assed. Hammier-handed. Thicker and broader.

"No one has hunted these things before, Ed," Janine said, wondering for the seven hundred and eighty-third time how Ed had ever made it past squire training. "Gargoyle statues don't look like the earth elementals they're based on."

Ed, accepting it, was unfazed. Not dumb, just content to let Janine do the remembering or finding out for him. Another victim of growing up Google. "So let's tell them they shouldn't exist. I bet I can be *real* convincing."

"Maybe." Janine considered the office workers in the surrounding windows, blithely going about their businesses, unaware of anything unusual, while pedestrians surged on the streets below. The Pax. Still working. People below would notice if it began raining heavy scaled bodies, though, or if the gargoyles became hungry. Imaginary teeth or not, those large, sharp, meat-tearing fangs didn't belong to herbivores. Janine reached down beneath her shirt and pulled out a small silver St. Francis medallion, kissing it for good luck. "We're going to have to lure them over here onto our roof and kill them close up. Quietly."

The Pax only made people screen out unnatural noises. Distant gunshots were all too familiar.

Ed squinted, grunted unhappily. "Those hides look tough. Maybe too tough for subsonic ammunition."

"Then I suppose it's lucky you're a big strong lummox and I brought a crossbow." Janine was already pulling out the disassembled weapon from her canvas bag, her nimble, callused fingers flying over the bits like a surgeon's. There was rappelling gear to assemble too—Janine wasn't fighting things that flew without being anchored to the rooftop first.

"What am I supposed to fight them with? This?" Ed brandished his knife.

There went seven hundred and eighty-four. Maybe Janine would get a prize when she wondered how Ed made it past squire training for the thousandth time. Nothing fancy. A new partner would be nice. "I saw a fire axe on our way up here. Why don't you go get it?"

At least Ed didn't ask what floor the fire axe had been on. Janine removed her signal mirror carefully, carefuller, carefullest. Flying things like shiny objects. Slowly, keeping her eyes on those changing flight paths, Janine began signaling the nearest fire team to send reinforcements.

Sniper teams had spread out and settled among rooftops all over the city, dandelion spores with rifle bores, covering New York in an insecurity blanket. A thousand yards away, Vic Lotz was on the top floor of a high rise. Lotz, who swore he could shoot the testicles off a pigeon a mile away. Janine hoped he was right. Lotz usually was, at least about shooting. It was the only way he got away with being such a jackass.

Ed grumbled off to get the axe.

~14~

THIS IS HOW THE WORLD BENDS

Kevin Kichida opened the door to Sarah's rented quarters. He was twenty now, but in the short time that I'd known Kevin, he had lost a father, killed a grandfather, found out he had a child of his own, inherited a fortune he couldn't legally declare, quit college, and become a cunning woman's apprentice. Any one of those things could age someone a decade, and Kevin's slender frame had gained weight, both in muscle mass and emotional presence. He'd lost his orthodontia and his hipster hair, but more than that, he'd lost some of his twinkle, and he didn't have that much outward sparkle to begin with. The light summer suit he was wearing over a black shirt was an expensive-looking turquoise.

"Hey, Kevin. Why are you all dressed up?" I asked by way of hello.

"I don't know yet." He offered a hand for me to shake. "This suit put me on this morning."

You have to expect statements like that if you hang around cunning folk. It's why I don't. I could hear Sarah making clanking and scraping sounds somewhere west of us—she's an aleuromancer, which means she can sometimes see the future in sifting flour. It also means that she bakes a lot, even at the most inappropriate times. Especially at the most inappropriate times. I stepped through the doorway and introduced Kasia.

The room didn't exactly seem like a sentry post for Armageddon. The quarters were modestly decorated with furniture that looked comfortable but old and secondhand, the kind of place you'd expect to rent furnished from an elderly widow. The living room opened into one narrow hallway that had an opening where the kitchen sounds and smells were coming from.

Sarah came out with a plate of fresh, hot scones, and we gravitated toward a coffee table surrounded by chairs in the middle of the living room. I found a red-cushioned armchair that smelled like pipe smoke, and Sarah sent Kevin to get some blackberry tea. When we were all settled in, I asked Sarah, "What kind of madhouse have you checked yourself in to? Is this place an inn or a shrine?"

Sarah smiled. She had a nice smile, and her long black hair framed clear skin and soft curves. "The two used to be synonymous. That was a good thing."

"Uh-huh."

"I'm serious. This place is a shelter for outcasts and travelers." Sarah sipped her tea. "All you have to do to be welcome here is not belong anywhere else. You and your friends can probably stay here too, if you want."

"I'm afraid I might die horribly," I said. "And I don't want to be rude."

"The sooner we get on with this, the sooner we can leave," Kasia told me with all the subtlety of a bulldozer. She was giving off a growing sense of impatience like a coal giving off heat.

"Tell me how I can help," Sarah said.

"I know what's happening, but I need a better understanding of how it's happening," I said. "And who might be able to do it, and why."

I guess I can't blame Sarah for being skeptical. "So, you finally want to learn more about magic?"

I've never had an objection to learning enough about magic to stop anyone who abuses it. I've just never wanted to mess with the stuff myself. As far as I'm concerned, magic is a bucket full of unstable explosives covered with rusty nails smeared in feces. And the bucket is sitting on a rotting plank suspended over a dark bottomless pit. "You bet," I said.

It's possible that I wasn't entirely convincing. Sarah's smile was a little crooked as she looked at Kevin. "Why don't you tell him the basics, apprentice?"

Kevin looked at me, didn't look at Kasia, and cleared his throat again before launching straight into lecture mode. "All right. The first thing you need to understand is that all physical reality is made up of three things: varying wavelengths of thought, sound, and light—"

"Hold up." I made the time-out sign with my hands. "Physical reality is made of thought?"

"Quantum physicists have proven that the very act of observing molecules changes the way they interact," Kevin responded. "They only have theories as to why."

There was something self-serious and a little too earnest and formal about Kevin. It almost seemed pompous, but I didn't get that vibe, not really. Kevin's father had died trying to save Kevin not too long before. Maybe Kevin was dealing with it by trying a little too hard to make his life count.

Sarah decided to help her apprentice out. "You were raised Catholic, John. In the first chapter of Genesis, God says that there is light, then there is light. Then God sees that it is good.

First God imagines light, which is thought. Then God says that there is light, which is sound. Then God sees that there is light, which is light. Thought, sound, light. That's the basis of the time-space continuum, all three reinforcing each other. Things like mass and motion and gravity are the byproduct of those creations moving through time and space."

I didn't bother wondering what an actual physicist would say about all this. "Okay."

Kevin picked up the thread again. "Sound is a medium through which thought perceives time. When we speak or listen, it is in a series of beats proceeding one after another in chronological order."

"I'm with you," I said.

"Light is a medium through which thought perceives space," Kevin said. "Without light, there is no sight."

"Still with you," I said.

"The mind experiences physical reality through time and space, but the mind is not bound by either," Kevin said.

I didn't tell him I was still with him.

"I know you're not psychic—" Kevin began.

"He says he's not psychic," Sarah corrected.

"But have you ever been in a car and suddenly known exactly what song is going to come on next?" Kevin asked. "Have you ever had a feeling about someone who was far away, and when you called that person, you discovered that your feeling about them was accurate? Have you ever realized that you're living through a moment that you've dreamed before? Have you ever literally felt someone staring at you?"

"John's experienced all of those things." Sarah stated it like a fact.

Kasia was looking at me now, but she spoke to Sarah. "What if I have not?"

"Close your eyes." Sarah waited until Kasia reluctantly did so. "Now hold your hand in front of your head and picture it there, in front of your closed eyes. Can you do that?"

Kasia humored her and put her hand in front of her closed eyes. "Yes."

"You just made a picture inside your head that is bigger than the inside of your head," Sarah pointed out. "How is that possible?"

"Why should I care?"

"I'll get to that." Kevin sounded a tad peevish. "If you'll let me finish. As far as manipulating reality goes, what you have to realize is that things look solid, but all matter is actually a moving current of atoms and molecules. In seven years, all of the cells in our body will have been replaced by new ones."

"True," Kasia granted.

"Good." Kevin gestured at the apartment around us. "Reality is a liquid, not a solid. The only thing binding the constant flow of atoms and molecules in specific patterns is electrons, or electromagnetic connections. Shift enough electrons around and you begin to change one element to another, one shape to another."

"So, something is shifting a lot of electrons." Kasia sounded bored. "This helps us how?"

Despite my reservations about Kevin's new air of seriousness, I had to admire his composure. He kept going despite the hecklers in the crowd. "Our thoughts are basically electrical impulses. That's why observing something affects the way its molecules interact. When you cut right down to an object's atomic structure, our thoughts are made of the same energy that binds molecules in the specific patterns that we call reality."

"That's why symbolism is so important to magic," Sarah cut in. "We deny it instinctively because we're terrified of losing our individuality, but we are all connected physically and mentally. Some of the atoms that are you might be me soon. And all of our minds can go to places outside our physical bodies where other minds travel and meet."

Kasia sneered. "Are you saying we are all one?"

"Don't ruin this for me," I told her. "We're almost to the part where I get a lightsaber."

"You asked us to talk to you," Sarah reminded me.

"You're right," I admitted. "Sorry."

"The most powerful types of magic, like the Pax Arcana, tap into a place where all minds can travel," Kevin said. "It's like an ocean made up of drops of water that all think they're individuals. Think of making magic like building dams and channels and water wheels to harness the power of mass minds to shift reality. The water drops don't know what they're doing—they're all still just moving and traveling along—but the current they are a part of is producing power all the same."

"I get why a bunch of people believing the same thing would be so important for this kind of magic," I said. "Getting thoughts to move in the same direction, so to speak. But I'm not seeing your point about symbolism."

"Symbolism naturally channels thought," Sarah said. "All symbols condense complicated truths into visual or verbal representations that have strong emotional charges. We call symbols that do this consciously art. We call symbols that do this unconsciously archetypes."

"I've heard of them," I admitted.

"Symbolism is like mental spackling," Sarah said. "It makes instant connections between perception and reality and emotion that might not hold together if someone stopped and questioned them too intently. It goes straight to a part of the brain that we don't consciously access."

I read a lot, and not just my complete *Calvin and Hobbes* collection. These were not new concepts. Jung called the place where all minds are united the collective unconscious. At least some types of Eastern religions believe that physical reality is a shared dream created and maintained by our minds, and Nirvana is where the shackles of our material bodies are thrown off and all physical reality melts away. A lot of modern physicists think we're living in a simulation. Medieval Christians believed that a cavern angel put a finger on the lips of all newborn babes and told them not to tell anyone where they had just come from, and that this is why lips have clefts and why souls can't remember being joined all together in heaven. At least some pagans believe that every living soul is a part of God, that we are the vehicles through which God experiences the world. Plato believed that our reality is but one in a series of reflections and shadows corresponding to perfect truths that we sense but cannot consciously recall. Modern Christians believe in intercessory prayer, believe that if enough minds focus their sincere thoughts on asking for something to happen, God might listen and change their reality.

Sarah's mind went down a similar track. "I personally believe that the reason everything is all connected...thought, time, and space...is because before our reality was our reality, everything...all of us...existed as a thought in the imagination of one being. For lack of a better word, we call that being God."

"I do not believe in God," Kasia said flatly.

Sarah's brief smile was genuine. "I did say that was personal."

I had a moment of silent struggle. I didn't realize it at the time, but the fate of the entire world hung on that moment, or at least the fate of my world as I knew it. I almost didn't tell Sarah the rest of it. She didn't need to know, and between my geas, my training, and my own cynicism, the instinct to isolate, compartmentalize, and ration information is so deep that it might as well be in my DNA. But Sig had recently taken me to task for that tendency, and Ted Cahill had died playing that game and almost taken the rest of us with him, and I was pissed off at Simon for playing that game with me. Not only that, but Sarah and Kevin weren't tools for me to use. They had come here into the eye of a storm and talked to me freely, with no strings, because they trusted me.

"This involves John Dee," I began, and stopped because Sarah did something. I don't know exactly what she did, but suddenly the world seemed to narrow to a point between the two of us. I could feel her concentration so intensely that I wouldn't have been surprised if the chair I was sitting on had been dragged toward her. "What's wrong, Sarah?"

Sarah didn't answer. Her voice was a power wire stripped of insulation, and she smelled like fear. "How does this involve John Dee?"

"It's likely some associates or followers of his are causing these weird incidents," I said cautiously. "Some new incarnation of the School of Night, if that means anything to you."

It meant something to her, all right. Sarah swore. Me, I view most profanity like any other kind of vocabulary, but Sarah... she's not the swearing kind.

Kasia sensed this. "Say what you need to say."

Sarah took another sip of tea, and her hand was trembling slightly. "John Dee claimed to talk with angels."

Kasia scowled. "If I do not believe in God, I certainly do not believe in angels."

"Then treat it like a metaphor!" The skin over Sarah's face seemed to be drawing tighter. "Or assume he talked to powerful beings pretending to be angels. The Fae or djinn, perhaps. He published several books based on those conversations."

There was something in Sarah's inflection...so slight that if it weren't for my enhanced hearing, I'm not sure I would have caught it. "You put a little extra sauce on the word *published*," I accused, "and most people would have said that he wrote those books, not published them. Either you think Dee didn't really write them, or there were unpublished ones, too."

"There is a rumor, no, more like a whisper of a rumor, of an unpublished book with a strange power over reality." Sarah's voice was soft. "A very, very bad book."

"Was it *Fifty Shades of Grey*?" I asked. "This explains everything!"

Sarah smiled reluctantly. It was better than what her face had been doing. "It's called the Book of Am."

If she was waiting for some sign of shocked recognition, she was disappointed. Kevin sounded half-accusing: "I've never heard of it."

"Very few people have," Sarah said. "And even fewer believe what they hear, for which we should be very, very thankful."

I took a guess: "The book of half-God or almost-God?"

"Very good," Sarah said. Kasia and Kevin gave me odd looks.

"In Hebrew, God's name, Yahweh, means *I am*," I explained. What? I said I read a lot.

"The Book of Am was about developing the powers of creation and destruction," Sarah said. "But it was a horrible perversion of how reading is supposed to work. The book had a living will. People didn't read the book so much as the book read them."

"If the book reads people, what does it do when it is through with them?" Kasia asked. "Somehow, I do not think it throws them away or puts them on a shelf."

I saw where she was going with that. Kasia was wondering if the people who were transformed had read the book, but I didn't buy that. Randy Prutko hadn't been a reader, and nobody who'd changed into a giant freaking eyeball in the middle of a knight holding cell had smuggled a copy of a book in with them.

"I'm not explaining this well," Sarah said. "When someone reads a book, they take an author's ideas and filter them through their own experience and needs and circumstances. That's why no two people ever read the same book, and why no one ever completely agrees about a book with anyone else. The effect of the book's words is changed as it moves through the filter of the person reading it. Reading is an interaction. But the Book of Am changes all of its readers to make them fit its needs."

"And what are its needs?" Kasia asked.

"The book transforms the reader into a kind of puppet god," Sarah said. "It uses the reader's imagination and will to create a literal world where magic lives and breathes openly."

"So, basically, it's like *Genesis for Dummies*," I said.

Startled, Sarah laughed, then put a hand over her mouth as if ashamed of herself. "You really don't have a reverent bone in your body, do you?"

"It's okay," I said. "Maybe I'll have one in seven years."

Kasia stayed focused like a cobra. "What happened to this book? Where is it?"

Sarah's eyes slid toward me oddly. "People who have even heard a rumor of it say that the book was taken by the Knights Templar back in the Elizabethan era."

Uh-huh. I really had been researching the School of Night, and a couple of random facts I'd stumbled across didn't seem quite so random anymore. Simon had said that the knights shut down the School of Night back during the Elizabethan era, and not long after that, a book called the Voynich manuscript had surfaced, a mysterious tome that a lot of people associated with

John Dee. In a long-ago lore class, that book had once been mentioned as an example of how knights work—Templars had stolen the book and replaced it with a counterfeit full of an entirely fabricated language. The original Voynich manuscript had gotten its name from the person who held it for a time— could it have been the Book of Am? If the knights had a book like that, they would keep the book in their central archives, and the archives had been breached earlier that year. Breached by members of the School of Night. It was how we'd found out about them. And one of the School of Night's founders was John Dee. There was no way all of that was a coincidence, and Simon hadn't mentioned any of it.

~15~

EAST SIDE STORY

I tried to call Sig, but phones didn't work in the Inn of Weirdness. Of course they didn't. The place was using gas lamps.

"You smell like you are going to kill someone," Kasia observed as I put my phone away.

I gave her a stare with some varnish on it.

Kasia seemed amused for the first time since coming to the inn. "I did not say I minded. But are you certain that you should tell anyone else about this Book of Am? Simon has his reasons for not talking about it. If it becomes common knowledge that something that powerful is real and out there..." She didn't have to finish the thought. All kinds of major supernatural players and predators would come out of the woodwork and add to the chaos of the situation, whether messing with the book was a good idea or not. Dealing with nuclear bombs and bioweapons is insane too, and that hasn't stopped anybody.

"If Simon wants to keep the book a secret that badly, I wouldn't put it past him to eliminate us or contain us for real. And that includes you, Kasia," I said. "The knights aren't kresniks. They don't like working with dhampirs."

"Really?" she said dryly. "I never noticed. But has it occurred to you that Simon did not tell you everything because he was afraid that you would do exactly what you are trying to do now? Or that you feel justified in doing what you are doing now because he did not tell you everything?"

"Are you trying to be my and Simon's couple's counselor?"

"Hardly."

"Whatever. This is why Ben Lafontaine wanted me involved. Spreading the secret out a bit more will make us less vulnerable," I said. "And keeping this kind of thing from allies can be as big a risk as being open with them. Every terrorist incident and every school shooting, you always find out that there were warning signs, but the different people holding the pieces never communicated and put them together."

Again, Kasia ignored the subject of trust altogether. "We are looking for the person behind these incidents, anyhow," she argued. "Does mentioning this book specifically change anything?"

"It changes everything," I said.

"How?" Kasia demanded.

"Let's start looking up some of those people on Simon's list," I said. "And I'll show you. Do you want to come along, Sarah?"

"I don't think so." She didn't sound all that regretful. "If the book is tapping into a place where all minds connect, I should contact some people who are very sensitive to that sort of thing."

"Just admit that you want to call the Psychic Hotline," I said. "I won't judge."

I should really start categorizing looks to save time. The one Sarah gave me was look #43, the Remind-me-why-I-never-turned-you-into-a-frog special.

"If you're going to do your own thing, can we borrow Kevin?" I asked.

"I'm not a cup of sugar," he said irritably.

Kasia puckered her lips at him. "Are you sure about that?" Her mood really had lightened up. For all her naysaying, Simon's spiel had probably left Kasia with a lot of little unanswered questions and contradictions nagging at her, too.

Sarah seemed to regard Kevin and Kasia's interaction with both amusement and mild alarm. "Do you promise to keep Kevin safe, John?"

"Absolutely not," I said.

Even outside the inn, I couldn't get in touch with Sig or Molly.

"Simon has not done anything to them," Kasia scolded when she smelled my frustration and worry. "They are probably just communicating with dead spirits."

It's odd, the things you can find comforting in my line of work.

I almost called Simon, but that conversation was going to take a little more thought and a lot more cool. Every time I pictured him, my fingertips itched and all I could see was Simon's throat. I'm pretty sure that was the wolf stalking. I mean, talking. I did get in touch with Choo and Ben Lafontaine, though, and I gave them the *Reader's Digest* Condensed Version of what I'd learned. My pack leader was pretty pissed at being kept out of the loop too, but mostly he focused on what he should tell the wolves he'd been sending to New York and whether or not he should keep sending them. I asked him to give me a little more time so I could give him a bit more perspective on that decision, and he agreed.

As far as getting perspective went, despite my promise to show Kasia how knowing about the Book of Am changed everything, the house belonging to Randy Prutko's ex-wife was surrounded by reporters. I suppose it had been naïve to expect otherwise. As far as anyone knew, Randy was still on the loose after killing a bunch of his coworkers and setting his grocery store on fire.

So we got back in Kevin's car and made our way to the fringes of the Lower East Side. I don't know if that put us in the lower Lower East Side or the upper Lower East Side and don't really give a damn. Randy Prutko's grandfather lived there, and that was good enough for me. The area was borderline middle-class, maybe a little over half Caucasian and a little bit of everything else, full of working-class immigrants, retirees, and some artistic types who were slowly being driven out by encroaching gentrification. The last time I had been through there, the gentrification had been slowed down by abandoned construction projects, but it looked like the economic heart attack had been a seizure rather than a full-blown stroke. Things seemed to be picking up a bit, at least to my outsider's eyes.

After we parked, we decided that if anyone asked, Kevin would pretend to be a young hotshot representing a Japanese corporation that had recently bought out my bounty-hunting agency. Kasia and I would be bounty hunters, and Kevin would pretend to be monitoring us in the field to see how we operated. Whether anyone believed that the three of us were representing a legal enterprise or not really wasn't the point. The story worked just as well if people believed we were hiding something more threatening.

"Sure," Kevin said. "Play to the American fear of Japanese investors or Yakuza."

"You're too young to be a Fed and too well dressed to be a cop," I said. "You're the one who decided to put on a thousand-dollar suit and carry a black beechwood cane around."

"Sarah's teaching me to cast fire with it."

I had to admit, that was a hell of a selling point.

"How about I be the mysterious badass martial arts specialist brought in to be intimidating?" Kevin asked.

"Wouldn't that be a stereotype too?"

"Yes," Kevin admitted. "But it would be a cool one."

I think Kevin wanted to impress Kasia. He might have been an Obi-Wan Kenobi in training, but he was also young and male.

Kasia didn't try to hold her amusement in. "I think John and I can be intimidating more believably." Which was probably true. Kevin's parents had made him start training in aikido and kenjutsu early and intensely because he grew up under the shadow of a powerful and homicidal grandfather, and Kevin had later killed the man, but deep down, Kevin still didn't want to hurt anyone unless he absolutely had to. I'm not saying that like it's a bad thing. Kevin is an empath who spent most of his short life being home-schooled by a mother who loved him, and his attitude is a natural reflection of that. His personality only comes out in glints and whiffs, but his distaste for violence shows in his too-earnest eyes and body language. That didn't keep Kevin from looking at Kasia and the way she was dressed in a doubtful way that could only spell trouble, though. We were making our way through a large parking garage, and there weren't a lot of people around us, but I could hear some on different levels, and cars passed by every few minutes.

"You think—" Kevin started.

"Don't say—" I began.

"—that you can lo—" Kevin paused because Kasia's palm had suddenly appeared right in front of his face. At first, I just thought that she was showing restraint because she didn't want to get his outfit bloody, but then Kasia held the pose longer than was dignified. Her muscles were taut, straining as if something inside of her might snap.

"Kasia?" I asked.

Kevin carefully stepped backward, away from her palm.

"I was just going to dump him on his ass, not hurt him." Kasia kept trying to push forward. She looked like a mime struggling in a windstorm. "Why can't I touch him?"

"Probably because Sarah put some kind of spell on you," I said. Kevin was still in shock. "Or that inn did."

Sweat was beading down Kasia's face, and dhampirs run cool. "Did you know this would happen?"

I saw where that was going. If she'd been playing around a moment before, Kasia really wanted to hit somebody now, and I was the next-closest target. "No, but I wouldn't have taken you to see Sarah if she couldn't protect herself. You probably can't tell the knights about her either."

"You set me up." When I didn't respond, Kasia's fangs came out. "You told your friend I was a dhampir, not a kresnik, over the phone. That part where you assured her I was not a psychic. Did you do that so she would know I was not protected by a geas?"

"I did that so that she'd—" Ever stare out from a moving amusement-park ride and watch things blur past? Kasia came at me like that. I barely shifted to the right in time to push her punch away at the wrist, letting her arm drive her fist past me. She was stronger than me. Maybe stronger than Sig. Kasia tried to continue forward with the motion and stomp on my ankle, but I dropped into a swivel that whirled one foot away and brought the other behind her shoe while it was off the ground.

Kasia was tilted backward, but she arched her back and caught her fall with her hands and cartwheeled heels over head to her feet again. It was like something out of a martial arts movie, and very few actual fights are. I would have shown her why, but I wasn't really trying to hurt her. Yet. So instead of pursuing her, I put the knife that had appeared in my hand away and tried again. "I w—"

She charged. I would have knocked her off her feet if she'd kept at it, but Kasia was sneakier than that; she caught my lunge punch at the wrist and used her greater strength to pull my body sideways, exposing my ribs and limiting my attacks. Shit! I kept turning with the motion and brought all of my body weight down on her thumb. She wasn't *that* much stronger than me; I broke free and deflected the blow she sent toward me with an elbow strike. Her fist slid up my arm and glanced off my shoulder.

It felt like that shoulder had been shot by an elephant gun.

I began an open left-handed slap while she was partially turned by her own attack, just to swish some air around, knowing her enhanced hearing would pick up on it. Kasia moved to block, but instead of following through, I pivoted into a right hook. I was aiming for her temple, but Kasia yanked her head back and I broke three fingers on her forehead. Strong or not, though, Kasia only weighed so much, and I knocked that weight around. She still somehow snapped off a short side kick while she was falling back.

The kick shouldn't have had much power—her body weight was going in the opposite direction—but when I turned slightly to catch it on my right thigh, raising my leg like I was marching in place, I slipped. I didn't slip much, but my pivot foot was on concrete that was smooth and slightly slanted and slick with grease where car emissions had gone to die, and I was slightly off-balance at just the wrong moment in just the wrong way. I reeled backward into the hood of some kind of family sedan, and its car alarm went off.

We stood there, Kasia and me, staring at each other while the alarm brought the rest of the world back into focus, and then we reached some kind of silent accord. Our shoulders and spines relaxed.

"This discussion isn't over," she told me.

"Sure," I said. "Good start, though. Way to use your feeling words."

Kevin, who hadn't moved the entire time, spoke up. "You're not enslaved or anything, Kasia. That kind of binding works both ways. It means Sarah and I can't hurt you without a good reason either."

"I do not want to live in a world where someone cannot hurt me for no reason." Kasia studied Kevin as if memorizing his acne scars. "Where is the fun in that?" Then she turned and stalked off in the direction we'd been walking.

"She's the muscle," I told Kevin.

This time, he didn't argue.

We wound up in a place that smelled like strong coffee, good borscht, and potato pancakes. Stewed and jellied fruit was on sale in brown glass jars that lined the windows, and I'm pretty sure the owner was selling some kind of cheap, homemade, pungent alcohol that smelled like leftover potatoes and fruit from behind the counter, at least to his trusted customers. Said owner was Alek Prutko, Randy Prutko's grandfather.

Alek was sitting at a table, talking to some other men who didn't fall into the eighteen-to-forty-nine demographic valued by advertisers, wearing an apron that declared he was just taking a break. First, our entrance raised a thick white eyebrow, and then it raised Alek himself. He was a big man, and he got up with a grunt like the seventy-something-year-old he was and shuffled toward us. "You're here about Randy. You're not reporters or police, though."

"So, what are we?" Kevin asked softly while he really should have been shutting the hell up and watching. The irony was, Kevin didn't want to get rough, and he was making it more likely that we'd have to. Giving up the initiative and encouraging the old man to think was no way to avoid escalating to threats or force.

Alek jerked his head at Kasia. "She's a killer dressed up like a hootchie girl. He's an ex-soldier. You're an I-don't-know-what."

This sharp old buzzard had grown up somewhere a lot harsher than the East Side. Some place where assessing people was an absolutely crucial survival skill. He'd killed people too, in his day. It's a myth that you can always tell, but sometimes you can't miss it. I stepped in. "We have some questions about Randy."

"What if I told you I don't care?" he countered.

Kasia said something in an Eastern European language that I didn't know. Whatever it was, it sounded very matter-of-fact and took some of the starch out of one Alek Prutko. For a moment, he looked queasy, and his big shoulders sagged. But the old man was made of stern stuff. He rallied, shrugged, and said, "Let's sit down. I'll answer your questions. You won't tell me any lies or things I don't really want to know. And then you can get the hell out."

"Sounds good," I said agreeably. We sat at a square table that was old but clean, and a slender young blond girl came and brought us glasses and water. It was really just an excuse for her to eavesdrop and glance at Alek questioningly. He ignored her. He didn't want Kasia to see how much he cared about the girl, or guess that she was some kind of family. It was a pointless gesture—both the old man and the girl were saturated in the same smells from living under the same roof, none of them sexual—but I liked him more for making it.

We talked for a time. I focused on asking Alek about Randy

Prutko's social life, and it turned out that Randy had never had much of one. Alek said that Randy had stopped coming by or calling after Alek stopped giving his grandson money, and that had been a long time before. I believed him. I believed Alek when he said that Randy had always been a mean little shit too, that Alek had tried to love Randy but never liked him. I was beginning to think I was wasting my time when Alek said, "The only thing Randy was ever really proud of was being a Knight."

My pulse did a drumroll. "A knight?"

"That's what they called his high school football team." Alek sounded dismissive, another sign that he hadn't grown up in America. The United States is the only country in the world that thinks American football is interesting.

I had to make absolutely sure. "The team was called the Knights?"

"Yeah. Randy was only on the team for two years, but one of those was the year they won a state championship. He was still wearing that team jacket the last time I saw him, and that was ten years after he graduated."

I went along like I was just making idle conversation. "I think I know the team you're talking about. The Knights' uniforms were..." I squinted like I was having a hard time remembering.

"Black," Alek said.

∽16∽

SLIME AND PUNISHMENT

Commander?"

Chris Fry hated being called commander—he had paid for college by going into the navy, and he worked for the sheriff's department, not on another goddamned submarine. But there wasn't much about running a county jail that he did like. He'd only taken the job because it was essentially an administrative position. Fry had thought, mistakenly, that the lower personal risk and better pay might be good for his blood pressure and let him spend more quality time with his family.

Right now, though, the prisoners they'd evacuated from the holding area were handcuffed to anything that would hold them down—radiators, desks, benches, tables—and Fry's men weren't being too gentle about shutting their screaming charges the hell up. Fry's title was the least of his worries. "What is it, Deputy?"

"You need to see something." Deputy Tingle—and Jesus, did she ever get teased for that name—was normally a tough customer, a solid, stocky, no-nonsense officer. Eyes like flint but a soft voice and a calm manner that were good for soothing people no matter what side of the law they were on. But right now, Jackie was showing some cracks. Hell, everybody was losing it. Fry had already had to lock Billings and Alley away in the visitation room because they were scaring everybody with their freaked-out bullshit about some kind of blob thing eating that child molester. His dispatcher, Betty Jean, had snuck out of the building and fled right after relaying the message that they were under quarantine and that the CDC was on their way. Fry was one meltdown away from having a mutiny on his hands. If Tingle wanted to keep something disturbing private, he should probably be commending her good sense.

So Fry just said, "All right," and followed her.

Fry couldn't help taking one last nervous look at the holding-area door whose edges were sealed off with duct tape—all those radiation and biohazard drills they'd had to go through after 9/11, and it still came down to duct tape. A memory of that blue Jell-O-like shit oozing between the bars and over the floor shuddered through him again. The image kept coming back, and it felt like a violation each time, like it was pouring through a toxic leak in Fry's own head. Goddamn if it hadn't looked like that stuff was moving with intent.

"Some of the guys are saying the government is jamming our cell phones," Tingle said softly. "To keep us from calling our families and getting word out. They say somebody is trying to avoid a panic."

That had occurred to Fry too. He'd even thought about nuclear strikes and EMP in the atmosphere, but the lights were still on. "Crazy rumors always start in situations like this." The words rattled around in his mouth like dried peas. Situations like this? When had Fry ever been in a situation like this? When had anybody? But what was he supposed to say?

"I'm not sure this is what we think it is," Tingle murmured cryptically as she unlocked the door to the impound room.

Fry followed Tingle in and shut the door behind him softly. There were only three storage racks and a few cabinets in the area—they were a small county—and she led him around a storage rack to where a bunch of spare blankets were bundled on the floor. Tingle went over to the blankets and pulled several of them off... Betty Jean Brown. The dispatcher who'd fled the station. Except she hadn't, obviously. Fry could see where somebody— Tingle probably—had cut off the restraints that had been binding Betty Jean, but she still wasn't moving. Breathing, though. Drugged, probably. Or hit really, really hard.

Fry's hand went to his gun.

Tingle'd had a little more time to think. "Did you actually hear Betty Jean say that we were under quarantine?"

What? No, he hadn't. That had been... who had that been? Deputy Caldwell. And by the time Fry had gone back to verify it, Betty Jean was gone, and the radio wasn't working anymore. But Jesus, there had been some kind of goddamn flesh-eating bacteria in the holding area, or hallucination-causing shit in the air, or a toxic waste leak from hell. Sealing off the building made sense. If somebody else hadn't said the CDC was on the way, Fry would have called them himself.

Wait... that draft...

That was the last conscious thought Fry had until he woke up on the floor, staring at Tingle's slack face. He tried to move and plastic chafed his wrists and ankles. He tried to scream and realized why his jaw hurt so much. Something was stuffed in his mouth.

Fry's thoughts didn't immediately turn to escape. His first thoughts weren't even about trying to figure out what had happened to him. What Fry woke up to was a wave of despair. He should have given up his badge when he first started realizing that he was feeling too much contempt for the people he had to deal with on the job. When he started becoming more protective and more distant from his family at the same time, like one of the people he had to protect his family from was the person he was becoming. He loved Mary so much. He'd never cheated on her, not once. Their youngest, Gabrielle, would be in college in five more years, and Fry would be up for retirement in six, and he'd just been playing a waiting game, telling himself that he and Mary would reconnect, that it would all be worth it.

That was the first thought that came to him: He'd waited too long.

"Sorry, Commander." It was Mason Caldwell's voice. The son of a bitch even had the balls to sound like he meant it. Fry craned his neck and saw Caldwell's large form crouching above him. Mason was probably Fry's toughest deputy. Before this, Fry would have said that Mason was also his most dependable. "There really are people on the way to take control of the situation."

What people? What situation? What the fuck?

~17~

X MARKS THE PLOT

That was your big payoff?" Kasia demanded as we walked out of the store and/or restaurant. "The stitching that holds this world together is coming undone, and all we get is that Randy Prutko's high school football team was called the Knights? So what? We already knew Randy Prutko had some reason for thinking of himself as a black knight. How does this help us?"

"You're not getting it," I said. "Sarah and Kevin said this Book of Am focuses its reader's mind to change reality. Not Randy Prutko's mind. Not Mitzi Unger's. Not Jenny Starkey's. What determines how a person transforms isn't their inner character. They change to fit the way they appear to whoever is reading the book."

"Exactly!" Kevin said. It wasn't even close to *exactly*, but I suppose saying "Vaguely!" wouldn't have had the same impact. "And not just that, the monsters from these role-playing games came around long after John Dee wrote the book. If our Reader X is making them real, it means that his imagination isn't just a battery or a power source for the book like Sarah said . . . He's a filter." Kevin faltered. "She was talking about rumors, but Sarah's not usually wrong."

Reader X. I liked that.

Kasia did not. "I ignored that witch babble the first time."

"That's why you're still not getting it," I told her. "We've been looking for connections between what these people became and who or what they were. But if we want to find this Reader X, we should be looking at how these people *seemed* and what kind of person they would seem that way to. That's what will lead us to the Book of Am and its reader."

"Uhmmm...John?" Kevin said in a way that meant trouble.

"What?" I asked.

"I think we're being watched."

I didn't halt; motion means options. But mentally, I went from neutral to high gear with a lurch. I focused on my sense of smell. I listened. I scanned the area and glanced in reflective surfaces. Nothing alarming. No pings on my internal radar. "Who?"

"Don't laugh," Kevin said.

"I'm on your side, Kevin," I said. "Whether I laugh or not. Who?"

"The ravens."

I took more notice of the birds gliding above us. Four of them landed on the roof of a boutique ahead and lined up on its edge like dominoes. Three more continued to circle high in the air, shadows outlined by the dying sun.

I hate ravens. Forget the romantic-sounding name—ravens are just crows with pretentious attitudes. "Are there even supposed to be ravens in New York?"

"They've been coming in for the last few years," Kevin said. "There are huge nests of them in Queens."

I didn't ask why he knew that. "If you're right, they're going to be tough to shake."

Kasia scowled. "I suppose people would notice if we started shooting them."

"These are New Yorkers," I said. "They only ignore cries for help."

"I've got this." Kevin didn't sound completely confident, but he completely sounded like he wanted to be confident. "Just follow my lead."

So we did. Not that it was all that hard. Kevin didn't start running, and he didn't dart down any sudden alleys or into any buildings. We just kept walking. Which would have been fine, but we were getting closer to Kevin's car. After a while, I said, "Aren't you going to slam that cane on the ground and yell *You shall not pass!* or something?"

"I'll know when it's time." A year ago my comment would have lightened Kevin up, but I heard the tautness in his voice and let it go. What was up with him?

Kasia picked the conversation back up from where we'd dropped it. "You are saying you want to use these transformees like living Rorschach blots."

"That's right," I said. "Now that we know Reader X strongly identifies Randy Prutko with his high school football team, it makes it a little more likely that Reader X was in high school with Randy Prutko. That alone cuts the number of people we want to start with from twenty million to a couple of thousand."

"If you are correct."

Thinking about something else *did* seem to help Kevin relax. "When did you say the role-playing game these monsters are based on came out again?"

I rummaged around my memory and found the information, but it was Kasia who answered first: "It was around the same time that Randy Prutko was playing football."

"If Reader X was a gamer in high school back then, he was probably a white male," Kevin said. "Statistically. And since Randy Prutko was turned into something dark and powerful, Reader X probably saw Prutko as strong and threatening. Do you see what I mean? You talk about this Prutko like he's a loser, but to this Reader X, Randy Prutko was He Who Must Not Be Named."

"I see what you mean. That does make it more likely that Reader X knew Randy in high school, doesn't it?" I said. "High school is the only time when assholes like Randy have any real social power."

"A high school male who played role-playing games and saw a mean, stupid football player as a threat," Kevin said. "We're really reaching here."

Kasia surprised me again. "Assuming something is not true because it is a stereotype is just as foolish as assuming it is. It is not as if this Prutko was one of your high school football heroes. He got kicked off the team, yes?"

"I didn't have any high school football heroes. I was home-schooled." Kevin suddenly swerved and led us to some kind of huge apartment building with three parallel entrances. There was a code key lock, but Kevin held his palm on it for a moment, concentrating, and then his fingers punched out a number. The door clicked open.

We entered a stairwell, and Kevin led us down to the base-ment level of the apartment complex. There were no out-raged bird cries or sounds of flying bodies hurtling against the entranceway behind us. The bottom landing led to a long concrete hall with storage cages made of thick wire—it seemed to run under and join all three stairwells of the building. The light bulbs sticking out of the ceiling were faint, far apart, and uncovered, but the shadows they cast weren't impenetrable. As we trudged through the murk, Kevin abruptly stopped and turned in front of a storage unit full of costumes hanging in plastic sleeves from long rolling clothes racks. There were ballerina outfits, cowboy costumes, police uniforms that looked like something out of the early nineteen hundreds, and a lot of clothing that could have conveyed anything from Colonial America to Victorian London equally unconvincingly.

"Somebody's a community theater director," I commented.

Kasia smirked her smirk. "Perhaps they have strange taste in bedroom games."

Kevin seemed a little disappointed that we weren't more excited or impressed. "Come on. Let's change how we look from overhead."

Kasia reached out to the padlock and hinges and twisted. Hasps popped before the lock did, and she hadn't even put any body weight into it. The show-off. She entered the storage area without ceremony and quickly located a new purse, a tight green shirt that barely covered her navel, a white skirt with a floral print, and a straw summer hat. Kasia disrobed without any sign of discomfort, and in that first surprised glance, I definitely didn't notice that her body was toned and small-breasted, her legs long and her hips slightly curved and her shoulders sleek.

That's my story, and I'm sticking to it.

Speaking of stereotypes and truth, it was the men who took the longest time to find an outfit and get dressed. Kevin forced himself to stop gawking at Kasia and looked at his cane instead. "What am I going to do with this?"

I almost asked him what the cane thought about it, but I was taking it easy on Kevin. Looking around, I spotted a carry bag full of baseball bats amid a pile of gloves and some baseball uniforms. After some thought, I stuffed Kevin's cane into the bag, then tossed him a baseball uniform. "How about you be a baseball player, and Kasia can be your girlfriend walking with you to practice?"

Kasia frowned. "You are not coming with us?"

"I'll meet you at the car. We don't know if these birds can count or not." Then I looked at Kevin. "Do we?"

He shook his head.

"You and I should stay together." Kasia didn't explain why. "I think you are taking your shy-virgin act too far."

"That's not what this is." Kevin sounded a little pissed. "John wants you to protect me while he makes sure no one follows us."

I really was trying to tread carefully around Kevin, but I wasn't going to lie about that. "I told Sarah we'd look out for you."

Kevin didn't like that one bit. "I thought you told her you wouldn't."

"I told her I couldn't make any promises. She knew what I meant."

"You don't get to decide if I get protected or not anymore!" Kevin's voice rose. "If I die, I die. Nobody else dies protecting me!"

Like his father had, he meant. Huh. I'd wanted to know what was up with Kevin, but that wasn't a can of worms. That was a deep dark pit full of snakes. "We should talk," I said. "Seriously. But now's not the time, okay?"

"I have not agreed to this arrangement either," Kasia reminded me.

"I'm not trying to ditch you two," I said. "Promise. The psychic should lead. The muscle should protect him. The tracker should follow. That's just good tactics."

Surprisingly, Kasia accepted that. I found a black suit that was about my size and might look expensive from a distance, under stage lights, and I began stripping down. The shirt was a little tight around the shoulders, and I wouldn't be able to conceal both my Ruger and my knife under the jacket, so the gun went in Kevin's baseball bag. There was no way I was putting on a tie. In a fight, those things are like a noose around your neck.

Kevin and Kasia headed for a different stairwell from the one we'd come in, and I tried to call Sig again while I gave them their head start. No connection. I hate leaving messages on answering services—you never know who might wind up listening to them—but I made an exception. If we wound up dying, somebody ought to know to look out for ravens.

When I judged it was time to go, I found a utility exit that led out onto a back alley. It didn't take long to orient myself around Kevin and Kasia since I knew where they were going, and I took an alternate route that let me glimpse them intermittently. The two of them were holding hands. I was pretty sure that was either part of their cover or Kasia messing with Kevin or both, but wouldn't that be something to have to explain to Sarah later? More importantly, I didn't see any ravens following them, and I stepped under some awnings along the way and checked my own trail discreetly.

It kind of bothered me that Kasia had decided to trust me. We were letting our guard down around each other a little, united by a common purpose and threat. It wasn't anything outwardly noticeable—not something either of us said or did—but we were treating each other as partners and equals. I had to be careful about that. I had been operating under the assumption that Stanislav Dvornik had seduced Kasia, but maybe this was how she had gradually seduced him. Not all seductions are sexual.

I was thinking of new ways to proceed with the hunt for Reader X when I got to the multistory car park. There wasn't a raven in sight, but the sun was almost done for, and they were dark birds. It was past rush hour, and the traffic inside the car park was sporadic. There's something about almost completely empty large structures, a quality that hangs suspended between reverent and sinister. Definitely a slight tilt toward sinister in this case. The wide winding concrete ramps of the car park were stained black from the smokers' coughs of all the cars that had passed over them through the years, and the yellow lighting made the concrete pillars and ceiling seem jaundiced. I went up a stairwell to floor D and found Kasia waiting for me. Kevin was there too, but he had stepped aside and was talking to Sarah on his phone, which meant she'd already left the inn. He seemed to be interested in redefining the terms of his apprenticeship with her. Good luck with that. I'm a pretty mean hand at poker, and every time I try to negotiate with Sarah, I wind up owing her a favor way more dangerous than anything I asked her to do for me.

"I need to call the turcopolier," Kasia told me.

"Even though he didn't tell you about this Book of Am?"

"He was under no obligation to do so," Kasia replied. "And telling him where we are and what we have put together definitely falls under my agreement with him."

So, Kasia *had* needed to negotiate with Simon to be included. And she seemed to want to stick close to me. Put that together, and Kasia was keeping an eye on me for Simon while Simon kept an eye on Sig for her. I actually respected that. "It's almost time to meet Sig. Tell Simon that playing games to keep that from happening wouldn't be smart."

Kasia smiled her crooked smile and left to call a crooked man who walked a crooked mile. She used some sexy-older-woman magic to get Kevin's keys from him without an argument and got in his car, turning the engine on and the radio up so that her conversation was covered by some guy with a whiny falsetto sing-ing about letting his girlfriend leave a toothbrush at his place. Well, that was fine. That Kasia wanted privacy, I mean, not the guy with the falsetto. Two could play the private-conversation game. I found a pillar to lean against and took my own burner phone out, and this time I managed to get in touch with Sig. It turned out she hadn't heard my message yet.

"You don't sound out of breath," she said. "Does that mean you're not running for your life or having sex with Kasia?"

Sig was in a weird mood. Danger, Will Robinson, danger.

"That's what it means," I agreed.

"Good," Sig said.

"Is Simon with you?"

"He just stepped away to take a phone call," Sig said.

Okay. "How are you?"

"Surprisingly bored." That actually sounded like a complaint. When Sig is dealing with tension, her go-to response is to con-vert the stress into some kind of direct action. "Whatever's going on, I think these magical transformations use the same kind of energy to manifest that spirits do, until there's none left over. I'm picking up on zero ghost activity around these things. What about you? Simon looks like he's about to piss thumbtacks."

"About that. I figured out something that might be a game-changer." And I told her the rumors about a Book of Am and our theories about a Reader X.

When I was done, Sig said, "I guess killing Simon wouldn't be a good idea."

"Probably not."

Sig's not the kind to give up easily. "Maybe it's so stupid, it's brilliant?"

"I think it's just so stupid, it's stupid," I said regretfully. "You'd better invite Simon to dinner with us."

"All right." Sig paused. "Did you call me so that you wouldn't have to talk to him yet?"

"I called you because I wanted to hear your voice," I said.

"You're learning," Sig observed. "You didn't miss a beat there."

"Buy toothpaste."

"What?" Sig asked.

"Oops, sorry," I said. "I read off the wrong note card."

She laughed. "Shut up."

"I love you," I said.

"I love you too."

I don't know if that was the best or the worst place for the phone to cut off. Somewhere beneath the music that was beginning to come and go in intervals, I heard the distinct chink of a baseball bat smacking against another, the rasping hiss of something hard sliding across canvas.

"John?" I was really starting to hate it when Kevin turned my name into a question. I shoved my phone back into the pocket of my suit at the same time that I turned around, not rushing it, straining my senses for any vibrations under my feet or sounds of objects passing rapidly through the air. Kevin was holding a baseball bat in his hands. Twenty feet away from him, seven ravens were sitting on the edge of the concrete balcony of floor D.

∽18∽

NEVERMORE THIS, BITCH

It wasn't like a werewolf's transformation. One moment, the ravens were hunched there, motionless. The next, seven full-grown men were crouched on the edge of the half-wall surrounding floor D. They were bald, gaunt, shirtless, and black eyed, wearing identical dark trench coats and pants. Their bare feet and hands had long, gnarled yellow nails, and all of them wore the same expression of remote, uncaring, alien intent. Strangely—not that any of it was what I'd call normal—the concrete wall, which had been smooth beneath them, was now jagged and pocked with missing hunks of mass.

I shed the jacket I was wearing as if I were dropping an act, and I guess I was. No more pretending to be a civilized person.

Kevin had been trained for this sort of thing too, in his own way. His voice was steady. "What do you want?"

Not to talk, apparently. The seven ravenlings—I refuse to call them men—hurled themselves off the balcony, their trench coats flapping beneath and behind them, their bodies going much farther than gravity-bound bodies should.

Kevin's bat ignited with a sound like a giant indrawn breath, and so did the ravenling that he lashed out at. Screeching a bird's caw, the ravenling tore the bat out of Kevin's hand before crumpling in on its own burning body, going down in flames, and not metaphorically. Another ravenling came bounding over both of them, its body horizontal to the ground. The move looked like the beginning of a dive that was taking its own sweet time. Kevin stumbled backward over the bag full of baseball bats, and it saved his life. He fell back, and the clawed hand that would have torn his face off just knocked his baseball hat off instead. Kevin didn't roll with his tumble, but the ravenling didn't drop behind him right away either.

Another ravenling was half-leaping, half-flying my way, but the left top of the ravenling's forehead suddenly sprayed blood. Kasia must have already had a suppressor on her pistol. The ravenling didn't die, but somehow it changed course in midair—which should have been impossible. The birdman veered off anyhow, stagger-skipping over the concrete like a plane trying to touch down. It finally fell to the ground and began convulsing.

I charged the ravenling that was regaining its feet behind Kevin, hurtling into it from the side like it was a tackling dummy. The creature was lighter than a human would have been, but there was something odd about its trench coat. I could feel the fabric—if that's what it was—rippling and sliding beneath my skin, not so much one substance as a bunch of greasy serrated layers overlapping. Somehow, the ravenling put up more wind resistance than it should have, too. Instead of smashing its body through the trunk window of a red hatchback, I wound up bouncing us both off the car.

As I held on to the thing's torso, I was whirled around and almost pulled off my feet. My knife was in my right hand—don't ask me how it got there; it just did—and I stabbed the ravenling three times fast between its ribs. I would have kept stabbing, but another ravenling came hurtling at me five feet off the ground.

I pushed off the ravenling I'd been stabbing and made an awkward backhanded slash with the knife, more to keep the next attacker off than to seriously damage it. A clawed foot severed a tendon in my wrist and the knife went flying. I dropped down and one ravenling passed above me while another some fifteen feet away changed direction in midbound and touched down facing me. The ravenling I'd stabbed dropped to a knee between two parked cars and took a breather. It was chaos. I was bleeding from more surface slashes on my upper arms and ribs than I could feel, but that wasn't a priority—the scattered baseball bat rolling on the concrete floor in a lazy half-spiral was. I lunged forward, scrambling, half-crouching, and grabbed the baseball bat with my good hand while the nearest ravenling came bounding.

It wasn't a fully powered swing, not one-handed, but I managed to pop up and put my body into a turn that broke the bat against the ravenling's forehead. I pivoted aside like a drunk dancer and the stunned ravenling nosedived past me, tumbling to the ground. A flapping disruption of air and claws skittering over concrete warned me—the ravenling who'd torn my wrist was coming back for more, behind me. I leaned away and a slash that would have severed the top of my spinal column drew blood from the back of my neck instead. I couldn't even make a fist with my impaired hand, but I could still drive my right elbow into the ravenling's face, and I did.

That ravenling fell back, and the one I'd stabbed came hurtling at me from the side, its arms outstretched. What did it take to put these things down? I started to step away, realized at the absolute last second that I was about to put my head in the arc of its claws, and stepped back toward the ravenling instead, inside its reach. Our bodies came together, but it was lighter than it looked—maybe hollow-boned like a bird—and I headbutted the ravenling in its bony nose before it could finish wrapping its arms around my neck. The ravenling was stunned for a moment, and I jammed the broken-off handle of the baseball bat up beneath the ravenling's breastbone and ripped.

The bat handle split in my hand, but it did the job. The ravenling dissolved into a cloud of mildly warm steam and drifting black feathers that smelled burnt. A small broken bird was left impaled on my improvised stake. Then the ravenling I'd elbowed off me came back, and I threw both the bat handle and the dead bird in its face to slow it down; it only made the ravenling falter for half a second, but half a second was enough. I had a measure of their strength now, and I caught a slashing claw by the wrist with my left hand, stopped the arm cold, and leaned into the hold to keep the ravenling's body from moving forward. Halted, the ravenling began to settle back down on its heels, and I shifted my grip on its wrist before it got its leverage back, pivoted so that the ravenling's arm was hyperflexed by my body weight, and broke its elbow with a forearm hammer.

The ravenling made a bird's shriek. I drove a knee into it and broke several of the ravenling's ribs. It flew off me, veering ten or twelve feet to the side, if unevenly. The ravenling I'd smacked with a baseball bat picked itself off the floor and came at me, but this time, it was staggering instead of doing some Peter Pan impersonation.

Kevin came to my aid then. Fire is easy for cunning folk to summon and hard for them to control; air is the opposite. Winds are hard to gather because air is everywhere and nowhere at the same time, but once air has a visible and slightly more dense form, like smoke, mist, or fog, air is easy to manipulate. Kevin breathed in some of the smoke coming from the burning bird he'd killed, held the smoke in his mouth without taking it down his wind-pipe, then blew outward. A surprising amount of smoke gath-ered from floor D and released in the same direction, impacting against the ravenling before me and mushrooming around it in a black cloud. The ravenling was already a bit groggy, and now it was blinded and choking.

I stepped in, blocked two almost desultory slashes at the fore-arms, and drove my left fist into the ravenling's sternum. When it hunched forward, I brought a knee upward and snapped its neck.

Somehow, there was only one ravenling left, the one whose ribs and elbow I'd broken. Kasia darted around its almost com-pletely useless left side, put the ravenling in a choke hold, then yanked the ravenling half off its feet and broke its neck with a sharp twist and some unforgiving downward pressure from her shoulder. The ravenling dissolved into that weird mist, and a dead bird dropped at Kasia's feet.

I looked past her. The ravenling who had been convulsing had apparently been in death throes, and there were two more bro-ken birds I'd never accounted for lying on the concrete beyond it. They must have flanked my part of the fight and come at Kasia from different sides, for all the good it had done them.

Blood was trickling down Kevin's face from a scalp wound, and he pressed the sleeve of his uniform against it. "What was that?"

"That," I said disgustedly, though I don't know what I was disgusted at, "was seven raven brothers."

Stepping forward, Kasia examined my face carefully. "What does that mean?"

"Seven raven brothers are in an old fairy tale called 'Seven Brothers,'" I said.

"I know that one." Kevin's voice was a wince somehow.

"That's the one where a girl cuts off her finger and uses it as a key."

"That's it."

A blue Toyota Prius came slowly rolling around the bend from Floor E, maybe driving cautiously because the noise we'd been making had carried several levels above us. There were seven very visible dead ravens scattered about, though at least the one Kevin had killed wasn't smoldering any longer. The splintered remains of the baseball bat I'd used were lying on the ground, and two other baseball bats had come loose when Kevin kicked the carrying bag, which was still lying in the middle of the thoroughfare. Kevin stepped between two cars and hid his face by pretending to fiddle with a lock, and I hurriedly picked my jacket off the ground and pulled it on. My forearms were a bloody mess, though the wounds had already begun healing. There was no position I could assume that would hide the bloodstains on my pants, though. Kasia appeared uninjured, but at that moment, I registered that she was no longer wearing a floral print skirt. All she had covering her lower half were skimpy black panties that would wad up into something smaller than a golf ball.

The Prius came on, if cautiously, and I could clearly see a man and a woman, comfortably middle-aged and upper middle class. The driver's face was fleshy, but his eyes were still noticeably wide as he slowed down even more, almost stopped, then swerved to avoid Kasia and slowly drove past us and over the carry bag. The woman in the passenger seat turned to look at us over her shoulder, her mouth open as the car slowly made its way down to Floor C, but she wasn't reaching for a cell phone, and I didn't hear the car speed up as it went down the next two levels.

New York City.

We got down to the business of trying to figure out what the hell had just happened.

❧19❧

KEEPING IT UNREAL

A small rectangle with the words SPEED RACER COMIN ROUND THE TRACK flashed in all caps across Jojo Huffman's monitor screen and kept flashing. He barely had time to delete the warning before his supervisor came hurtling down his row, the ex-knight's Popeye forearms making the wheels on his wheelchair spin like a washing machine. The code monkeys at the hack factory had started pinging Anson Brown out of self-defense. Being so low to the ground made him hard to spot as he tooled around on the smooth concrete floor, mostly silent except for the soft sucks of rubber compressing and unpeeling from cement. It had been Anson's idea to remove all the cubicles and stack the code monkeys next to each other so that the buttsuck had a racetrack to zip around on. It was to maximize space and foster team effort, he'd said. They were all Templars, there to keep secrets from other people, not each other, he'd said.

The bag-biter said a lot. Like, right now, Anson was saying, "Hurry up and finish what you're doing, people!" Calling it over Jojo's shoulder, already come and gone. "There's some weird shit happening with birds on the Lower East Side, and I need someone on it!"

"There's weird shit happening everywhere, dumb-ass," Jojo said in his dreams. Any fool could see that the city's mainframe was crashing and all kinds of magical malware was getting in. Code monkeys had started grabbing sanity naps on cots set up in the corners. Jojo himself was on his too many-ieth power drink, and he hadn't had a good bowel movement since yesterday. His eyes were poached, his teeth hurt, and his tongue was wearing a fuzzy condom.

"Yeah, Mojo," Sam "Samwise" Stevens muttered on Jojo's right. "Do that thing where you push that button to finish that stuff."

Jesse "Hackerman" Ackerman snickered on Jojo's left. It was gospel among the workers in the hack factory that Anson didn't really know how to code. The ex-knight had learned to push a few keys around, but calling that penile wart a programmer was like calling someone who painted by numbers an artist.

Jojo was the artist. Jojo was laying some line mines, trying to get a blogger to download a virus that would open up all his cyber secrets to Jojo's prying little eyes. The blogger kept trying to post the same feed about a fire being started by a small man who turned into flame. Normally, Jojo wouldn't have sweated it—bloogle like that actually made Jojo's job breezy—but this blog clog had gotten all aggro when he twigged on to the fact that the fire truck responding to the fire was from a fire station much farther away than it should have been—and who noticed things like that, anyhow? The town scryer was riding all over the Internet, yelling questions nobody wanted asked.

Some way, some play, Jojo was going to get some leverage on that dicksicle.

∾20∾

PICTURE THIS

As soon as our phones were working again, I found several missed calls, voice messages, and texts from Sig, none of which said anything different. She hadn't liked it when we got cut off, and the messages were sort of the cell phone equivalent of someone mashing an elevator button several times to make things go faster. She called me again while I was still listening to one of the voice messages. The conversation was pretty focused on essentials, with the end result being that Kevin dropped Kasia and I off at my car. Choo was parked behind it in a new van, a blue family job with more seating and less storage, sitting quietly behind the steering wheel in the dark. No lights, no music, no cell phone, no AC running, just Choo sitting there with a rolled-down window.

That didn't seem like a good sign. Me being me, I approached Choo cautiously. We were beneath an overhead bypass that spiraled above on a curving bridge supported by huge, thick columns of stone. I had parked my car there because the area was blocked from view and only accessible by a relatively low-use utility road.

"I hear you got attacked by birds," Choo greeted me.

"We did," I agreed. "That's why you shouldn't be sitting here in the dark all alone. Why aren't you meeting up with Sig and Molly already?"

"We got to talk," Choo said.

"Okay."

He'd apparently been waiting to say something, but now that it was time, Choo hesitated. His elbow was resting on the window frame, and he tapped the top of the van with the palm of his hand absentmindedly before finally saying, "Most of my life, I've been doing stupid things because I was pushing back against something."

So, we were taking the long way around. "Me too."

"My momma was a college professor, and she wanted me to be her showpiece. She wanted me to get straight As and learn to talk her talk and wear nice clothes and be refined so she could show me off to her friends. Or at least it felt that way at the time. Felt like she was trying to get me killed in high school."

Kasia wasn't much for the scenic route. "Do we really have time for this?"

"I know this guy," I told her. "He wouldn't be taking so long if it wasn't hard to say, and he wouldn't be saying something hard if it wasn't important, and it'll go a lot faster if we don't interrupt." Only I didn't use quite that many words. I boiled all of that down to "Fuck off, Morticia."

"Perhaps you and Sigourney do belong together." It didn't sound like a compliment.

Getting started had been hard enough; Choo didn't let himself get sidetracked. "And the boys I hung out with wanted me to thug it up. I joined the army to get away from all of 'em, but the army wanted to tell me who I was too."

He waited for me to say something, so I did. "That's kind of their job."

"Maybe so, but even my wife expected me to be all kinds of things that didn't come natural," Choo said. "She had all these ideas of what a husband was supposed to be, and it didn't feel like me. I didn't handle it right."

I waited. I feel qualified to talk about some things. Marriage isn't one of them.

"Then one day, a ghost tried to tell me who I was worse than anybody ever did," Choo went on. "It took me right over and made me into something I wasn't. You want to talk about not being right with Jesus? That thing messed me up. I'm still not all the way right."

I was listening, but I was starting to agree with Kasia just a little. "I know most of this already. I don't understand where you're going with it, Choo."

His answering smile wasn't amused. "I got into this business to show somebody something. Not sure who anymore. The universe, maybe."

"So, it was about control," I said.

"That's exactly it," he said. "I can't stand the idea of something sneaking up on me while I'm trying to do whatever it is normal people do again. But that thing with Simon back at that restaurant. This not telling us what's going on . . ." He stopped cold and tried to rephrase something or reexamine something. I'm not sure if he did or not. "The lady there said the knights will kill me if I try to walk away from this thing now. But I can't work like this."

"You're right," I said. "Maybe we can make Simon understand that."

We arrived at a small stone Catholic church somewhere between Omni Court and New City Gardens, carrying eleven large

177

pizzas between us. "Sanctified ground doesn't give you any problems?" I asked Kasia.

"It makes my ass twitch a little," she allowed.

Catholic churches have the same effect on me, but that's probably because Father Eric used to paddle us with a cricket bat. He'd brought it and a low tolerance for sarcasm straight from the old country.

There were a number of parishioners praying in the sanctuary even at eight o'clock. They all looked like normal working-class people, though maybe averaging a bit younger and fitter than I'd have expected, and if some of them weren't hiding knives and handguns under their clothes, I'm a disco diva. The altar boys there probably lit the candles with a flamethrower. I don't even want to think about what kind of armament the person hiding quietly in the small upper loft was aiming at us.

The priest who greeted us, Father Mendez, was trim and greying, and when he shook my hand, his palm felt like sandstone. Once we were out of the sanctuary, he took us to the basement where a knight made me set the pizza boxes on a table and open them one by one while his guard dog sniffed around them. We kept our weapons this time, but Father Mendez took a small needle and pricked my finger and held it until a small drop of blood welled up.

"That's an awful lot of pizza," the priest commented while he repeated the procedure with Kasia and Choo.

"I'm thinking of giving confession," I said. "It could take a while."

"It probably would." Father Mendez's smile and eyes were both hard, but he led us to where the others were waiting. The good father stayed on the balls of his feet the whole time, his hands loosely curled. I got the impression those hands were never very far away from being fists. Mendez had probably been a combat priest when he was younger, one of the specialists the Order trains up to accompany strike teams for exorcisms and blessings and wardings and such. Maybe he'd even been a paladin.

We went through a kitchen area and a gathering hall, past a honeycomb of very small rooms with wooden chairs and old-school blackboards rather than the large rooms of modern churches, the kind that can be sectioned off by rolling partitions and have aluminum folding chairs and rolling plastic whiteboards. Eventually, we wound up in an office that was a little larger and better furnished than I'd expected to find in a humble parish. The carpeting was a rich, thick red, and the oak furniture was stained a brown that looked natural. The icons were real gold, and I think the Italian-style paintings were really Italian too. One of the paintings was covered, a fact that I registered immediately but didn't comment on.

I also registered that Simon wasn't in the room. Sig and Molly were there, but the man waiting with them was pale-skinned and tall, at least six foot four, with straw-colored hair that had been cut conservatively to make him look like a young stockbroker or lawyer trying to be an older stockbroker or lawyer. His suit had been cut to achieve a similar effect. Basically, he looked like he had been born with a silver spoon in his mouth and a steel rod up his ass. The only thing awkward about him was his gangliness, which was more a result of his long limbs than a lack of coordination. It made him look ostrichlike, and the impression wasn't helped by the way his blue eyes focused completely on whatever caught his attention, his head moving with precise movements to track us as we came in.

"This is Woodrow Keeley." Sig's voice had a wry quality to it that suggested I was in for a treat.

I smiled at her. I couldn't help it. "Does this mean Simon isn't asking us to the prom?"

Keeley came over and offered me a hand, and, what the hell, I went ahead and took it. His handshake was crisp and formal. He shook hands with Choo too, but apparently, he and Kasia had met. "Mr. Travers is busy, as you well might imagine, given the grave nature of our current situation. Mr. Travers is grateful to you for suggesting that we focus more of our resources on individuals who went to Randy Prutko's high school, but rest assured, no one is going to be seeing the turcopolier in the near future unless there's a fire, famine, or flood."

I had to play back key words just to understand what he'd said. Was this guy for real? Choo apparently wondered that as well. "Fire, famine, and flood, huh? You forgot *plague*."

"I was being alliterative," Keeley responded stiffly. Ivy League school and wanted everyone to know it, I decided.

"You could just say fucking *plague*," I pointed out.

"My vocabulary and my resourcefulness are not so limited that I need to resort to crudity for clarification," he said. "For example, I could express my dissatisfaction with this conversation by just not having it any longer."

"I actually use crudity for emphasis and its cathartic effects," I said. "However, if it will expedite matters, I shall endeavor to formalize our discourse henceforth. I take it you are Simon's..." A lot of options came to mind, but most of them didn't go with the formal tone I was adopting. Stooge. Flunky. Lackey. Evil henchman. Apprentice. Suckass. Drone. Proxy. Protégé. Mini-me. Bath attendant. Minion. Finger puppet. Next funeral card...

"I am someone Mr. Travers trusts to deal with you. I am fully conversant with the background of the Book of Am, if that is your concern."

"Oh. Good." We walked around Keeley and took our pizzas to the large desk. I had to smile again. Sig was sitting in the big swiveling command chair at the center. She had probably claimed it just to piss Big Bird off.

I pulled a chair up close to her. Sig isn't much for public displays of affection, but she looked at me like something suddenly seemed right again, and it hit some chord deep inside me that I still wasn't used to handling. It made me feel exposed, which wouldn't have been a bad thing if other people hadn't been in the room. "Hey."

"Hey."

"Let's try to stop an apocalypse," I said. "Take two."

Keeley decided to remain standing. Squabbling over his chair probably would have been undignified, and he wasn't going to drag up a seat like some peasant, so he went for maintaining a superior altitude to go with his superior attitude. "Is all of that for you? Mr. Travers had some food prepared."

"We're good." Sig quickly cleared a large space on the desk for the pizza boxes and identified an anchovy pizza garnished with basil leaves, onions, and shiitake mushrooms. The place I'd gotten the pies from had advertised things like smoked mozzarella cheese and olive oil, maybe to justify their prices. It's one of the things I do like about New York City. Natives take their pizza seriously.

"You have to get used to watching them gorge themselves," Molly told Keeley, taking a slice of pizza covered with black olives and peppers for herself. "Their bodies burn more calories than ours do."

"Yeah," Choo muttered. He didn't sound happy about it. He hadn't said much since the overpass.

"If you want to get down to business, don't let this stop you," I said. "Start with this Book of Am that Simon neglected to tell us about."

"Whose secrecy Mr. Travers prudently chose to maintain," he corrected.

"Sure." I knew Simon really was busy, but I could see why he didn't want to have this conversation in person. Simon was probably the kind of guy who had his secretary cancel dates for him.

"Perhaps you should tell me what you know in order to save time?" Keeley suggested. "And I can fill in the blanks rather than reiterate."

"Perhaps I could introduce my foot to your ass," Choo replied.

Okay, that wasn't good. Choo was mad, hell, I was mad, but there were still lines to be respected. I had contemplated killing Simon or kicking his ass many times, but in all our interactions, I had never once threatened to do it. That's the sort of thing better done than said with truly dangerous people, and no matter how this Woodrow Keeley talked, any guy that Simon trusted could probably kill a man with a soft pretzel. Keeley's eyes went cold, Sig's eyes flared hot, and Choo's mouth stayed open, but before any of them could say or do something that would have been a lit match in a meth lab, Molly spoke up. "I think what Choo means is, you just want us to tell you what we know so that you won't have to worry about being caught if you lie or skip over stuff." She turned to Choo. "Is that right?"

"It'll do."

Keeley gave them both a tight smile. "Exactly."

Well, balls get you points sometimes. The tension went down a few notches, and Keeley refocused on me. I doubt he had any illusions about me being the leader of my group, but he probably assumed I would understand where he was coming from better because of our common background. "Mr. Travers is not going to apologize. He came to the same conclusions about this man you're calling Reader X that you did, but keeping the Book of Am a secret is incredibly important. He gave everyone, not just you, *everyone*, enough information to go after the right people with the right questions. No more than that. You would have done the same."

"I'm not so sure I would have," I said.

"Might I point out that you are not telling everyone everything either?" Keeley said with that strange politeness that is really condescension. "Such as who told you about the Book of Am? Somehow, you have gotten Kasia to keep quiet on that particular subject too."

"The difference is," I said, "I'm upfront about what I will and won't talk about. I'm trying to work with you as best I can. Your boss is trying to make me work *for* him."

Keeley acted like he was brushing that aside. He wasn't. "This is another reason Mr. Travers isn't here. We are in a crisis situation, and he doesn't have time to waste on finger-pointing and recriminations. Rule by committee is a fantasy. There has to be a chain of command."

Unexpectedly, it was Kasia who objected. "I agree. And if the first knight who interviewed Randy Prutko's grandfather had asked about Randy's football team, maybe your and Simon's minds would have gone down the same path ours did when you read the report later. But that would have been later, and you are reading a lot of reports while trying to deal with an escalating situation. There has to be a chain of command, but the one at the top has to delegate, too."

"Besides, how are knights supposed to ask the right questions when they don't have all the facts?" I asked. "If you wrote down the one hundred most important questions to ask a murder suspect, would the name of his high school football team be one of them? There's too little time and too much data to collect to screw around like this."

"Mr. Travers would do the same thing again," Keeley insisted. "He weighed the risks and tried to wrap the situation up quickly. He used himself as bait and tried to get the School of Night to attack him so that we could capture some of them, and it worked. He tried to enlist you so that Miss Norresdotter could cut some corners by talking to the dead, and it worked. Not telling people more than they need to know is standard procedure."

Sig put down her food, just for a moment. It's hard to be taken seriously behind a slice of pizza. "But the attack was made by mercenaries, and I came up with nada."

"Which is why it is called a calculated risk, not a calculated sure thing." Keeley almost lost his pretense of cool for a second. "That is why I have been sent to refocus your efforts when there are a thousand other things I need to be doing as well."

So, basically, Simon had taken two big swings and missed, and he couldn't afford to strike out. If I was reading the situation correctly—which was still a big if—Simon did need help, and knowing about the Book of Am let us in a very small circle, a circle that Simon wanted to make use of and keep tabs on at the same time. But he also knew that someone needed to finesse things personally because of the way he'd handled the situation, and that was one task he *was* willing to delegate.

"If only you had some flying monkeys," I said.

"This is more important than any of us. Argue later. Contribute now."

"Tell us more about this Book of Am," I repeated, "and we'll refocus."

Keeley obliged. "It sounds as if you know most of it. John Dee wrote a book intended to trigger a new age where magic could thrive openly. Most of the mythology around Enochian sigils—those are supposed to be fragments of angel language, if you don't know—is a byproduct of other works that Dee was writing at the time. Our organization tried to put a stop to the School of Night discreetly back in the sixteenth century, and we thought that we did. The book disappeared after we arranged for Dee to be imprisoned by the Church, and when it resurfaced, we took the book into our possession and tried to keep its existence a secret."

"But the Templars' central archives were compromised about half a year ago," Sig pressed. "Did someone steal this book?"

Keeley began monitoring his words more carefully. "Not... precisely. We believe one of the false Templars who infiltrated the archives smuggled part of the book out the only way she could—by memorizing it a page at a time."

"She?" Molly echoed.

Keeley was still addressing me. Maybe he was sexist. Maybe he was knightist. Maybe he just didn't want to get whiplash. "You killed her later, Mr. Charming. She was one of the chanters you shot when you caught the cultists trying to break into the central vault."

"That doesn't make any sense," I protested. "Those chanters weren't even the highest-ranked infiltrators there. And those guys weren't after a book... they were after the Sword of Truth. And why wasn't this book in the final vault with the Sword of Truth, if it's so dangerous?"

"The book was in the final vault," Keeley said. "It never left. And the infiltrator never got in."

This time, we all let our silence speak for us.

Keeley coughed. "Perhaps it will be easier if I just show you."

"The last time I heard that, we got attacked by a giant floating eyeball."

Keeley started walking to the painting that had been covered. "Do you wish to hear the whole story or not?"

"Fine," I said. "But if a giant nose materializes out of nowhere and starts blowing acid snot on us, I'm done."

Keeley winced, perhaps at the undignified nature of my words, but all he said was "No one but Mr. Charming and I should get too close to this painting. Our geas will protect us from being affected by it against our will. The rest of you might wish to stand back behind Miss Newman."

No one moved except Choo, who stood so far back behind Molly that he actually left the room. He closed the door behind him on the way out without a word.

Keeley looked at the door.

"He's waiting outside," Sig said confidently. "Choo has some poltergeist issues. Go ahead."

"Ah. That gives me an idea on how to illustrate my point." Keeley took a world almanac off one of the shelves built into the walls, opened the door Choo had just gone through, and tossed the book down the hallway before closing the door again. Then he went up to the painting and pulled the cover cloth off. Revealed was an exact portrait of the room we were in. Including little figures of us. All of us. I got up and went to examine the painting more closely, and the painted version of me moved forward.

I waved my palm over the painting experimentally. The pigments swirled slightly, and the painted version of my palm waved back at me.

"We used to keep this painting in a hall in the archives," Keeley said. "Anyone who is not protected by our geas or some other kind of ward will find themselves drawn toward it, and then their minds will be drawn into it. The Loremaster used it to trap would-be thieves."

That wasn't quite...I turned toward Keeley. "But the false knights weren't protected by a geas, and they were running around the archives."

"You are absolutely correct," Keeley said. "And this is what happened to one of them one day. Catch me."

Keeley fainted. I watched his body collapse to the floor with a heavy thud. His head bounced on the thick red carpet.

"John," Molly reprimanded.

"Oops," I said.

Sig, smiling wryly, pointed at the painting. "I think he saw that."

I looked at the painting, and the figure of Keeley in the portrait was no longer mirroring the physical Keeley. It was staring at me with a distinct attitude of angry disapproval. I gave the figure a small shrug, and it turned its back on me and walked toward the painted version of the same door that Choo had exited through. The painted Keeley opened the painted door, and there was a painted version of Choo standing motionless with its back to us, its painted hands in its painted pockets. I turned, half-expecting to see the real door opening, the real Choo standing there. But the real door was still closed.

When I turned back to the picture, the painted Keeley walked out through the painted door and closed it behind him. The painted Keeley was gone. A few seconds later, the painted door opened again and the painted Keeley came back with a painted book and got larger as he walked toward me. He held the book up so that I could see that it was a painted version of the almanac Keeley had thrown out into the hallway. He flipped the book open so that I could see that the tiny little painted pages had tinier little painted words. When I nodded, the painted version of Keeley fell to the floor. At my feet, the flesh-and-blood Keeley opened his eyes. "At some future date, assuming we all survive the current crisis, you are going to pay for that."

Letting Keeley fall hadn't just been an immature gesture. Simon had sprung stuff on us without warning so that we would react instinctively and do what he told us to do instead of arguing or questioning. If that approach kept working for the knights, the practice would become a habit. I was illustrating a point. But what I said was "What did any of that have to do with the Book of Am being copied?"

"We didn't know that the painting could duplicate any building it was in past the doors," Keeley said. "We think the infiltrator was pulled inside the painting, and while she was trying to find a way out, she went through that door and started exploring a painted representation of the entire central archives."

Simon always said "I" when he spoke for the knights. Keeley said "we." I wasn't sure why that was important, but it seemed worth noting.

Molly asked the next question while I draped the cloth back over the painting and Sig went to get Choo. He came back in, carrying the almanac. Something occurred to me too late; I peeked under the cloth, but the painted version of the almanac that had been on the floor was now in the painted Choo's hand. "Are you saying this person found a painted version of the Book of Am? Duplicated down to the print in the pages?"

"We believe so," Keeley said. "That is why she had to memorize it a page at a time. Nothing physical from our world can enter that painting, and nothing in that painting can physically cross over to our world. But information can be transferred."

"But if what you say is true, why weren't the painted vaults locked just like the real ones?" I asked. "And why did the painting let this woman back out, much less come and go as she pleased?"

"We're not certain. It may be that the painting just found a way to make trouble in a building full of people who were immune to its compulsions. Or it may be that the painting was co-opted. The Book of Am is one of the most powerful artifacts ever created, and it might be sentient. When Dee wrote that damnable book, we don't know if he created a series of magical system commands or a magical form of artificial intelligence."

"What *do* you know?" I asked.

Keeley grunted as if a tiny fist had punched him in the solar plexus. "We know the Book of Am is terrifying. The thoughts bristling around between its covers are like hungry snakes. As soon as one lets any part of them into their skull, the snakes begin eating. And the book does not depend entirely on being read to be interactive."

"Are you saying the book could have taken control of the painting when the painting duplicated its words?" Molly asked.

Keeley nodded. "The Book of Am wants to be read. That's why we're not keeping this painting in the archives any longer."

Apparently, Choo was caught up enough to reenter the conversation. "Why not just destroy the thing?"

"Because it is thaumaturgic magic," Keeley said. "We're not sure what would happen to the world the picture was mirroring when we did. We're not sure what would happen if we destroyed a book harnessing the power to manipulate atoms, either."

"Even if you are right about all of this, how did you figure out which infiltrator was responsible?" Kasia wanted to know.

"While we were investigating the background of the false Templars, we found a secret account the woman was using on the dark web. As far as we can tell, the School of Night didn't even know she was trying to duplicate the Book of Am. She was a peon, but she was an ambitious peon, and she knew her masters would try to take everything over if she told them what she was doing. And before you ask, I don't know if the book was influencing her or if she just had her own agenda. It looks like the only person she confided in was a secret lover. The individual you are calling Reader X."

"So, the reason the School of Night is sniffing around Simon is because they want to find this Book of Am 2.0 too," I said. "Any powerful magical artifact related to John Dee, this School of Night would be all over it."

"Yes," Keeley said.

"And the School of Night isn't responsible for these magical transformations," I went on. "Though they might want to control them."

The condescension became a little less subtle. "Are you going somewhere with this, or are we just summarizing?"

"Those ravens that were following us and then attacked us weren't any kind of shapechangers I've seen before... They were more like these magical transformations that have been happening than those mercenaries that attacked us at the restaurant."

Keeley had apparently already thought this through. "Yes. That wasn't the School of Night attacking you. That was Reader X, or perhaps the Book of Am itself. It does beg the question of which one is calling the shots, doesn't it?"

Sig had gone off on her own train of thought. "You said this Reader X was a secret lover. How secret?"

There was a stack of folders on the desk, in front of Sig because she'd taken the seat Keeley had planned to use. He leaned forward and selected one of them, then set the folder more evenly in the center of the desk. "So secret that all we know is that he's male and was using a variety of computers and burner phones in New York City. There's a printout of the text conversations from the woman's last burner phone in here. Even though some of the texts are very intimate, the two are very careful not to use any names or specific locations."

"If she was one of the infiltrators, she was trained to be a double agent from birth," I said.

"She was," Keeley agreed. "And she probably knew the School

of Night would have killed her and the lover if they knew such a potential security risk existed."

It was a lot to take in. "But you think our Reader X was keeping or copying the manuscript of a new Book of Am for his lover?"

"We do."

"Did I kill this lover before or after she was finished copying the book?" I asked.

"Before." Keeley didn't sound like that was a guess. "We suspect Reader X has started reading the manuscript his lover sent him and is trying to finish writing the book on his own. Or possibly the Book of Am has taken hold of him and is forcing him to do it."

"But you're sure the book wasn't finished," Choo said.

"Unless the lover's last texts were lying, yes. I'm not sure we would be here if the book had been finished. Or at least not this version of us."

"Maybe that's why this Reader X's imagination started out playing a much more direct role in the transformations than Dee ever intended," I suggested. "With more modern-day versions of the old magical stories. He's got more input than he was supposed to have. He's not just reading more and more of the book. He's adding to it."

Sig took that and went with it. "So, Reader X is probably a cunning man. A very powerful one."

"If he wasn't before he started reading the book, he is now." Keeley's expression was troubled. I thought it was just an appropriate reflection of the conversation, but then I realized that he was staring at an open pizza box with an element of longing.

"Go ahead and have a slice," I invited.

Keeley looked at me uncertainly for the first time since I'd met him.

"It's not going to hurt you." I felt a bit like a drug pusher. "Your dog's already sniffed the boxes for poisons or bombs."

"Dog," Keeley corrected absently. I don't think he could help himself. But he unbent enough to take a slice. Maybe the stick up his ass was fiberglass.

Keeley hadn't heard the contraction when I said "Dog's" and thought I meant *dog* plural instead of singular *dog has*. It was no big deal, but something was...Wait a minute. The place only had one guard dog? There were two different canine scents in the building, and both of them were fairly fresh, too. The two scents were very similar, but I had just assumed that both dogs had come from the same litter. "You mean only one dog on duty, right? Not just one dog?"

Keeley frowned. "I mean this place only has one guard dog assigned to it. It lives here. Father Mendez tells laypeople it's his pet."

"For how long?"

The frown got deeper. "For years, at least. What is this about?"

Kasia's sense of smell was almost as sharp as mine. "There are at least two dog smells in this church. And the beast that sniffed us does not smell like whatever dog has been in this office recently."

~21~

YOU SPIN MY HEAD RIGHT ROUND, RIGHT ROUND

Voicing our suspicions out loud turned out to be a bad idea, although to be fair, they were more like suspicions-to-be. The dog out in the community area who had sniffed us might have been a very questionable dog, but its hearing was still way beyond human. And it not only heard us, it understood us. It may have looked like a dog, but there was a human intelligence guiding it. There was a yell somewhere beyond the door to the office, noises made by frantically moving bodies, tearing flesh, something metal clattering to the floor.

Kasia and Sig and I were already scrambling for the door by that point, and I was wishing I hadn't left my weapons in Choo's van. Little fragments of thought were assembling in my head while I rushed. A dog spy. A dog that was smarter than a dog. A dog that smelled something like the original it was impersonating but not quite. A human intelligence duplicating the form of a real dog while it infiltrated a Templar facility for the School of Night. Add all that up and it didn't equal were-wolf or nix or ghost. Unless this was some other homemade monster cobbled together from God knows what, we were probably dealing with a skinwalker.

The human guard who had overseen the inspection of our pizza boxes was lying facedown on the floor of the meeting room at the center of the basement, and if he wasn't dead, he would be soon. His throat had been torn out. There were sounds upstairs where Father Mendez was apparently wrestling with something and yelling for help, but the dog, or rather the thing pretending to be a dog, wasn't growling or barking at all.

Kasia ran straight up the stairs without pausing, but I told Sig to hold on a second and headed for the half-submerged basement window covered in heavy curtains.

"What?"

I ripped one of the curtains off its hanger violently. "If it's a skinwalker, we'll have to restrain it."

A skinwalker's magical skin suit takes energy and distributes it down its body like the chassis of an automobile, dispersing the energy somewhere into the fourth dimension where the skin suit is anchored. Not just heat or electricity, but kinetic impact, too. In other words, a skinwalker is effectively invulnerable. The only way to hurt one is through cold, poison, or oxygen deprivation. They can be contained, though.

"I'll try to slow it down for you." Sig took off while I was still bundling the curtain into something manageable. By the time I made it to the entry hall, Father Mendez was sitting against a wall with a lot of small surface wounds, clamping a handkerchief down on a particularly nasty one on his right thigh and yelling at anyone and everyone not to shoot at anything but the dog. Kasia was rolling and scrambling to her feet in the middle of a small cloud of floating dog hair, her forearms bleeding from trying to put an indestructible mutt into a choke hold.

And Sig? There was a broken window where the skinwalker

had hurled its invulnerable body through the glass, and Sig was rushing out the front door after it. Me, Kasia, and two guards dressed like parishioners followed her out into the night in an uneven parade. None of us were shouting or firing guns; what would have been the point? There wasn't much activity on the street—it wasn't a residential area, and the scattered businesses weren't the kind that stayed open past six—but there was a woman walking some kind of lapdog down the sidewalk.

"Hypnotize the civilian," I told Kasia, and surprisingly, she didn't question me. Hell, I didn't even question me, and I have some real problems with supes trancing people. But if the choice was between making a woman forget the last two minutes, doping her with a drug that would mess with her brain chemistry and make her lose days, or killing her...well, hypnosis seemed like the lesser evil.

Kasia veered off while I ran after Sig. Normally, I would have overtaken her—Sig can out-arm-wrestle me every time, but I usually beat her in any kind of footrace—but the bundled curtain was throwing me off my stride. The skinwalker AKA Fido was on four legs and running close to the ground, moving over the paved street fast, but not faster than a normal dog. Sig and I were keeping pace with it as we followed it around a corner and down a side street, but then a dark green pickup truck that had parked on the curb ahead of us pulled out and slowly began driving away.

A tarp rose up out of the bed of the pickup truck, and the two men who had been hiding beneath it shrugged the thick rainproof covering off, although they obviously hadn't practiced the maneuver. Instead of watching two men working together like a well-oiled machine, it was more like seeing two cats scrabbling in a burlap sack. The tarp got caught on the barrel of one man's submachine gun, which was a very good thing, and his partner was preoccupied with fiddling with the pickup truck's tailgate. The one with the gun finally freed his weapon, but by that time, Sig had dropped into a firing position. She got off four shots fast. Normally, the shots would have had a tighter grouping, but all four bullets still hit the truck, and one of them hit the man with the submachine gun.

That didn't stop the skinwalker from jumping its dog form into the pickup truck's bed, and as soon as that happened, the truck began to accelerate. I veered to the side while I ran so that Sig would have a clear shot at the driver, but while I was doing that, the driver of the truck dropped something out of the front window. I heard pottery shattering, then the sound of compressed air being released. It was like the muffled noise an air rifle makes, only times a hundred. My ears popped and trash and dust began sifting and lifting off the pavement, but I didn't see anything when I ran into a wind that came out of nowhere and hit me like a linebacker. The curtain I was still carrying billowed up behind me like a parachute and then went flying out of my hands. I was picked up and hurled around and around and around and around and around, a roaring in my ears that was the sound of waves crashing without the wet. There was nothing to grab onto, nothing to hit.

Finally, I was released and hurled over a car, bouncing off its roof and into the brick side of some kind of bank. Seconds later, I heard Sig shrieking. Maybe she retained enough presence of mind to try to trace a rune or sigil in the air while she was inside that thing's area of effect, but if she did, she didn't have time to finish. There was a sound of breaking glass as Sig's body smashed against a car across the street. I staggered to my feet, lurching side to side while my equilibrium tried to get its composure back, and a line of white-hot pain with no clear beginning or end went off in my back. My spine was a piano key that had just been struck very hard, and it was badly out of tune. In the street was some kind of miniature whirlwind, not the grey mass that looks like a compressed slinky in movies and cartoons—the thing's radius was only visible by the dust and trash spiraling around in fast circles. The circular path they made was maybe six feet wide and eight feet tall.

Some asshat had bound a funnel ghost into a spirit jar. The biggest funnel ghost I'd ever heard of, what professional ghost hunters call a vortex phenomenon and Aussies call a whirly-whirly. The spirit wasn't intelligent enough to train, but it was seriously pissed off, and it didn't much care who it took its rage out on. Kasia came tearing around the corner at full speed and tried to dart past the funnel ghost by staying on the opposite sidewalk, but it veered to the right and swooped her up into a cursing whirl of arms and legs. It looked like a cartoon fight, only it was one-sided, and then the twister spit Kasia out as if she were a watermelon seed.

The pickup truck was almost gone from sight, but there wasn't anything I could do except count how many times Kasia's body skipped over the concrete. I had hit the brick wall wrong and pulled something serious in my back, or more likely several connected somethings, and my fast healing wasn't going to help me until I'd straightened and stretched and realigned whatever intact but twisted muscles were pinching my spine.

One of the knights who'd come running out of the church had apparently headed straight for his car. He came around the corner and tried to drive down the street after the van, but the funnel ghost veered again and caught the car under its right front side. The vehicle tilted sharply, continued forward on only its left tires, then went into a grinding skid on its side before flipping over on its roof in slow motion.

Momentarily bereft of moving targets, the funnel ghost

continued down the street, and Molly, Choo, and another knight came around the corner. The knight was no dummy. He took in the apparition at a glance and ran back for the church. I don't know if he wanted to get holy water or Father Mendez or if he just figured the funnel ghost wouldn't be able to cross over onto sanctified ground. Choo stopped uncertainly, and Molly kept moving forward, though she slowed down to a walk.

At some point in the last two years, Molly had begun making up her own banishing rituals on the spot. I don't know how she does it. Exorcism rites are important; they give people something tangible to hang their faith on, and saying a memorized prayer connects priests to whatever power resides in the echoes of all the exact same prayers said the exact same way by people of the same faith over the millennia. I like to think that all of those prayers are floating around in a place without time and building up a kind of spiritual static charge. But even then, rites aren't powerful in themselves; they help open up a channel to something I don't understand. Whatever that something is, Molly is on more familiar terms with it than I am. Or at least, she's dispensed with the formal introductions.

Molly took a deep breath as the funnel ghost approached her—so deep that I could tell that's what Molly was doing from the way she bent back and threw her arms out. And the wind effect came closer to Molly and simply...dispersed. As if Molly were in a Superman movie from the '80s, inhaling the whole damn mess. She stayed there, lips pressed together, cheeks puffed out, holding her breath until her body gradually relaxed. I don't know if she was having some kind of internal dialogue with the funnel ghost or not. All I know is that when Molly finally released her breath, it was a slow exhalation that took way longer than any breath should, and the funnel ghost was gone.

Of course, so was the pickup truck.

PART THE THIRD

A Faust Learner

~22~

YOU'VE GOT MALE

We weren't going to hang around a place that had clearly been compromised, but there were still details to take care of. I had to hobble back to the church and do some excruciatingly painful stretches before I could go anywhere, and Sig went back to get the folders Keeley had been planning to brief us with. From what I could hear, he wasn't giving them to her without an argument, and Keeley was discussing our next move with cold, condescending prick logic while Sig taught him a thing or two about stubborn intractability. Choo went to get his van, and Kasia went to take care of the pedestrian. Kasia hadn't taken the time to hypnotize the woman who had been walking her dog after all; she had knocked the woman out because she wanted to take time to mentally calm the barking dog instead of snapping its neck. Which was a little surprising but a good call on Kasia's part, because Molly loves dogs, and Molly can kick undead up and down the street and take their lunch money. I had no idea how a confrontation between Molly and a half-vampire would turn out, but I knew it wasn't a good time to experiment. Now Kasia was waking the woman up and trancing her.

Father Mendez had bandaged his wounds, and it quickly became evident that he was the real man in charge of the premises whether Keeley had been allowed to use his office or not. The priest had two knights going around giving everyone a skinwalker blood test, and I could hear Mendez outside on the street as he had his remaining knights, the ones dressed as parishioners, tip the overturned car back onto its wheels. Once they had done so, one of them was able to drive the car away. The only good thing about the funnel ghost was that it had probably kicked up so much energy distortion that nearby cell phones weren't working, and it bought Mendez some time.

Molly stuck around to watch the back that I was trying to stretch out. I braced my palms against a wall and leaned into it. My spine didn't like the idea of me stretching my arms out that far in front of me, and it wasn't too happy about the way I was ignoring its opinion on the subject, either. Molly seemed a little out of sorts herself. "You all right, Molly?"

"I'm fine."

"You don't smell fine."

"You realize that normally that remark would be incredibly offensive, right?"

I said something really intelligent and perceptive like "Uyyyarhhkkhh!" I was slowly tilting my torso left and right, and my spine had turned to barbed wire. Sweat was pouring down my body, the pain-stink kind of sweat. Fortunately, my whole life is one big deodorant commercial, and I had a couple changes of clothes in the personal gear I'd transferred to Choo's new ride.

"I don't like working with Kasia," Molly said. It was as if she had heard my thoughts about the dog. "I don't like the

Stanislav connection. Working with that jerk even though I didn't really trust him nearly got me killed."

"I know what you mean." Stopping to talk felt so good that I kept talking. "It's a little different, though. My instincts told me not to trust Stanislav the second I saw him. I ignored them because I didn't really give all that much of a shit whether I lived or died at the time, and I relied too much on his geas to keep him in line, because I didn't understand how a geas really worked back then. I really liked working with you and Sig and Choo, too. I needed it. But my instincts were going off like a fire alarm."

"And they're not now?"

"Not really. I think Kasia's dangerous but not treacherous. Besides, the kresniks had a vision with Sig and Kasia in it, and Sig's already on thin ice with those guys for killing Stanislav."

"That doesn't mean we have to go along with it. Or any of this."

"What do you think Kasia will do if her mission's to make sure Sig isn't a threat and she's not with us, Molly?"

"I don't know."

I pulled my shoulders forward and toward each other. "Me neither. But we're in a dangerous place, and Kasia's good in a fight. I'd rather have her where we can see her, working with us."

"Looks like I picked a bad time to stop sniffing glue."

If Molly was still playing our movie game, she was okay. "*Airplane*, right?"

"Leslie Nielsen. I love him."

I grunted and moved into a mountain pose and focused most of my energy on not whimpering. My range of motion had improved slightly.

"I'm not too happy about all of this talk about John Dee and angels, either," Molly confessed.

"The angel Dee claimed to talk to said it was the archangel Uriel. But Uriel's not canonical." A lot of my research on the School of Night had focused around John Dee by default. "I think Uriel came along with the Gnostics. And even if Uriel is real, we don't know that whatever Dee talked to was the real *real* Uriel. You see what I mean?"

I should have known better than to try to give Molly a lesson on theology. "That's what I've been thinking about. Uriel literally means *The Light of God*. As in, let there be light. Raw creation and destruction."

I brought my feet back together and let gravity pull my hands toward the ground in a slow forward hang. "Great."

Molly wasn't finished either. "Uriel's symbol was a book."

That was kind of a conversation-killer. From what I'd read, Uriel had a reputation for being as cold and pitiless as any demon. I tried a different tack. "It's not like God sent an angel out of the blue to visit Dee, the way it usually happens in the Bible. Dee was running around with a psychic named Edward Kelly and using crystal balls trying to contact beings from the other side."

"Hmmn." Molly's voice became more thoughtful. "You're right. I can't think of many instances in the Bible where someone went looking for an angel and found one."

I've spent a lot of time thinking about heaven and hell and God's will. Growing up a werewolf in a Catholic order of monster hunters will do that for you, or to you. "Yeah. God decided when and who got direct visions or visits from heavenly messengers, and the prophets never welcomed them. That kind of knowledge always demanded that people do something hard or dangerous. They'd have to sacrifice a son, or go visit the land of their enemies and save them, or get pregnant before they were married..."

"Don't forget King Saul." All the talk about angels and scripture and theory was tensing me up again, but it seemed to be relaxing Molly a little. "God wouldn't send Saul any messages, so he went to the Witch of Endor instead. That was blasphemy. Trying to do an end run around God by contacting angels with a psychic and a crystal ball doesn't sound any better."

"That's what I mean. It seems just as likely to me that Dee was talking to someone or something trying to cause trouble by pretending to be an angel. Or a fallen angel, if you believe in that sort of thing."

"It doesn't feel like we're going against God's will," Molly reflected. "I'll pray for enlightenment."

The Bible is also full of examples of God letting people know that they were going against the divine game plan in very unpleasant ways, but I really didn't think we were, and Molly smelled better, so I straightened up and decided to quit while I was ahead.

Choo rejoined us, and Keeley followed Sig up the stairs with his briefcase in tow shortly afterward. "I know of another place where we can finish this briefing."

"So do I," I said. "Get in the van with us."

"I think not."

Sig and Keeley were still in argue mode. She said, "We work out of moving vans all the time."

"As do pimps and people who abduct small children."

I could feel my quick healing moving through inflamed nerves now that they weren't being as actively constricted, but I was still in pain and crabby and too tired for any more heavy conversations. "Run, everyone! It's the attack of the fussy middle-aged white men!"

Keeley got stiffer, if that was possible. "I'm only thirty."

"Yeah, but that's fifty in entitled-prick years."

"I can see why Mr. Travers didn't want to spend any more time in your company than necessary."

Like I would view that as a minus. "Listen, the School of Night knows there's a strong chance that Reader X went to Randy Prutko's high school now," I said. "That means their next step is going to be getting a list of names, pictures, and addresses for those students."

"There's a thing called the Internet," Keeley said. "Perhaps you've heard of it."

I'd done some checking while we were driving around getting pizza. "You can get a list of the graduating classes from Randy Prutko's high school going all the way back to 1914," I said. "But their oldest online yearbook is from ten years ago. And if I was working for the School of Night, the first thing I'd want is a copy of Prutko's yearbook. You know: pictures, clubs, teams, awards, voted most likelys…"

"I'm sure Mr. Travers already has a copy of the yearbook by now."

"He probably does," I agreed. "But I don't, and the School of Night doesn't, assuming they're not already ahead of us. And this is a race, right? And the quickest place to go get a yearbook is the high school that sells them and stores them."

Whatever Keeley's official capacity in the Knights Templar was, I don't think he'd spent much time in the field. He seemed a lot more taken off guard by that observation than he should have been. "I…hmmn. You really think they'll go there?"

I shrugged. "It's worth a shot. We can argue about it in the van."

And we did. Choo's new van—actually, he was informally renting it from a friend of a friend—could comfortably sit eight, and we wound up sitting in three layers, Choo and Kasia up front, Keeley and Molly in the middle, and Sig and I in the back. As soon as Keeley was done talking to Simon on the phone, he began using a penlight to read to us from his folders. They were focused on the background information of the woman who had copied the Book of Am and sent it to Reader X a page at a time. The report was mostly nouns and numbers, not adjectives. Places the woman had lived, awards she'd gotten, job titles.

Her name had been Anna Hogan, and she had been born and raised in New York City. It sounded like Anna had been an academic by nature and by inclination, a voracious reader with a high IQ and consistently excellent grades. Anna had tried several times to become a merlin, one of the Templars' practitioners of defensive and investigative magic, but using magic requires a certain psychic sensitivity that can't be memorized or forced; Anna Hogan's psychic potential was apparently slightly lower than a turnip's.

Anna's lack of psychic potential made sense, in a way. The fake Templars hadn't been bound by a geas, but they also hadn't been protected by one. Working in the central archives would have been dicey for them. Even with tattooed wards and holy symbols and jewelry that disguised charms, any psychically sensitive person who worked in a complex full of haunted objects wouldn't have been able to function. The School of Night had probably hand-selected and groomed Anna for her career path once they realized what a magical dud she was. In any case, Anna had become an English major at New York University and then went on to Rutgers to get an MI degree for librarian training, then gotten a cover job at one of the Templar shell companies in Boston as a demographic researcher. Interestingly enough, she was the same age as Randy Prutko, though she had grown up on Staten Island.

Anna's lack of psychic sensitivity might also explain why she had been able to memorize and recopy pages of the Book of Am at a time without triggering its effects. Templar archivists learn all kinds of techniques for studying and transferring dangerous magical info, and the book hadn't been completely transcribed, either. Maybe there was some delicate tipping point, some percentage of the book that had to be read to be activated, and Reader X had finally crossed that line by trying to finish writing the book on his own, the way a composer might try to finish another long-dead composer's incomplete symphony. But still, the fact that Anna had almost zero magical aptitude must have helped.

That fact must also have seemed cruel. It must have been hard for someone who had wanted to be a merlin to be surrounded by magical objects she couldn't use. The equivalent of a tone-deaf person who had always wanted to be a singer, getting a job sweeping a concert hall.

Anna had been there when the knights finally realized what was going on and moved in to reclaim the archives. And I had shot her in the face. I can't say I enjoyed learning more about her under those circumstances. I didn't *want* to humanize her.

There was a little psychological profile tacked on to the end of Anna's background summary like a coda. According to the Templars' profilers, Anna had been introverted, heterosexual, a bit obsessive-compulsive about keeping things orderly, tended to compensate for low self-esteem with an inclination toward being self-centered, and was prone to a mono-focus that was both an asset and a weakness. The report had gone on to say that Anna had some anger issues that manifested in passive-aggressive behaviors and small acts of rebellion against authority. It also said that she'd had a series of unwise affairs with married men, direct superiors, and obvious players. The profiler theorized that Anna went for men who were unattainable, because knowing the relationship couldn't last made her feel safe to express her passion. Kind of like baring your soul to a stranger on an airplane.

"Or she just liked getting laid without a lot of complications," Kasia remarked. "I do not trust any opinion about female sexuality from a Catholic man in a country started by Puritans."

It was late and nobody else wanted to debate sexual politics. "The people putting this file together kind of missed the part where Anna was determined to betray them and bring their entire organization crashing down," Molly observed.

"They didn't even think that was a possibility," I said. "The fake line of Templars Anna was a part of convinced everyone they were geas-bound."

Next, we covered the texts that Anna had sent to Reader X, or at least the ones that the Templars had managed to recover. Keeley had been a teenager when the new millennium had arrived, and he was less cautious with his cell phone than Simon would have been. He had all texts of a non-magical nature on file, and he sent them to us over our individual phones so that we could comb through the messages in the van, picking out personal bits and favorites to read to Choo. There weren't a lot of texts, but the ones we had weren't made up of the typical terse sentences with emojis and cute misspellings either. They were more like love letters that had been sent in fragments.

Just as Keeley had said, the texts were extremely discreet when it came to omitting specific names, dates, and locations. That left a lot of room for graphic sex talk. "I can see why the knights are so convinced Reader X is a male," I commented.

Molly was apparently reading some fairly visceral texts too. "Either that or a really hardworking female plumber."

"Even then, I can't see Reader X being a woman unless this is actually a threesome and one of them is named Dick," Sig said.

"You guys are gonna make this black man blush," Choo warned from the driver's seat.

"Puritans," Kasia repeated.

Not all of the texts were sex talk, though. Kasia found one of the ones Simon had mentioned, a text referring to her field leader as one of the original members of the School of Night. She read it aloud: "I'm not sure that I'll have time to finish. Northumberland managed to get the wolves out of the archives, and the skinners are moving in fast."

"Getting the werewolves out of the central archives was a big part of breaking into them," Sig said. "And skinners are obviously skinwalkers."

"Who's this Northumberland?" Choo asked.

"He's another one of the original members of the School of Night," I commented. "He was the Earl of Northumberland, and people called him the wizard earl. It could be their field leaders take on the names of original members."

"Maybe it's the original Northumberland," Molly suggested. "You magic types don't always have the same kind of expiration date as us mere mortals."

"God, I hope not," I said. Cunning folk who've been around for centuries are the worst.

Sig had her own take: "This woman doesn't sound like a true believer. It sounds like she's wishing that the School of Night would have a harder time taking over the archive so that she could finish transcribing the Book of Am in secret."

I found another text written by Reader X that was kind of interesting.

Come back to me. I'm so tired of hiding who I really am from everyone. I want to be the real me with someone who knows me and loves me. I go to my meaningless job because you told me not to change my daily routine, and I go through the motions just like all of the puppets around me, but I just want to jump up in the middle of work and shout: "Look at me! No strings! You don't need this bullshit! That's not a safety net beneath you! It's a giant spider's web!"

I want to touch you again. I want to feel your beautiful ass in my hands and your heat against mine and taste the salty slick sweetness of you on my tongue.

And then the text got a lot more specific about how Reader X wanted the woman to touch him. If it was some kind of secret code, we were in trouble. The rest of the message was all about a buildup to a big explosion. Soon after, I found another text from Reader X that had the same type of impatience and contempt for society at large.

Do you remember that scene from *Alice in Wonderland* where Alice sees the sleeping Red King? Tweedledee and Tweedledum warn her that the Red King is dreaming them all, and that if Alice wakes the Red King up, bang! They'll all wink out of existence like a snuffed candle. I feel a little bit like the Red King. Only, I'm awake, and it's everyone else around me who's sleeping. And even that wouldn't be so bad, but their bodies are still walking around, and all they can dream about is their stupid fucking cars and cell phone plans and TV shows while they numb the despair with alcohol and two-day vacations from reality at the end of the week. I just want to wake them all up with one big bang! Let's get a NEW universe started! See MY dreams, bitches!

I frowned. The transition from feelings of powerlessness to feelings of omnipotence was pretty abrupt there. The woman, this Anna Hogan, seemed to think so too. At one point in her response, she said:

I'm scared that you've opened the book. You sound so desperate and impatient. I worry that you might do something impulsive just because you're so unhappy even if you know it's not a good idea. Or I worry that you sound that way because you've already started reading the book, and it's got a hold on you, and that's why you're urging me to send you the rest even though you know it's dangerous for me to rush. Please, please, please, let's not do anything too stupid and messed up and human and screw things up when we're so close. Don't be Orpheus turning to peek at the last moment, or Pandora opening the box. That's the world we want to leave behind. I want to make a new world with you, but I can't do that if I'm not *with* you. It would kill me if you wound up destroying yourself because of something I dragged you into. We are so close to having everything. Just wait a little longer and I will bring the final parts of the manuscript with me. I love you.

Bottom line: She wasn't about to trust Reader X with any more of the manuscript long-distance. "Has anybody read anything about how she's sending him the manuscript?"

"I've got a text here where she talks about his package," Molly said. "But I don't think it's what you're looking for."

We spent a little more time trying to glean something out of the texts, but they didn't tell us much, at least not from cursory inspection. Reader X was literate and male. Horny too, which might explain some of the predatory sexual undertones to some of the transformations that had been going on. Reader X worked for someone else along with a lot of other people and seemed to view capitalism with disdain. A lot of his fervor had a revolutionary undertone. He felt isolated and unfulfilled. He was both frustrated by and got off on having a big secret. And we knew he had played role-playing games at some point.

We took that sort of thing about as far as we could until Choo told us that we were getting near the high school's exit. We were on some kind of elevated bypass or interstate, and the thrum of wheels passing over concrete partitions was regular. By some mutual, unspoken consent, we switched our focus to the transformees again. Keeley had memorized the transformees' ages, locations, educations, and occupations, and he shared them willingly enough, though he assured us that he'd been over this stuff a hundred times himself, and that the data was being analyzed by mathematicians and demographic specialists and computer programmers and professional profilers. Even so, I could see why the knights were having a hard time tracing the magical transformations back to one source, even knowing about Reader X. That six-degrees-of-separation stuff works both ways, and there were too many possibilities.

Take the accountant who became a faceless being. Maybe Reader X worked at the same place the accountant did. Or maybe Reader X was a cousin or sibling. Maybe Reader X's contempt for capitalist flunkies came from his job, and he rode the same subway with the accountant to work every morning. Maybe the two had worked together at a previous place of employment. Maybe they worked together on a project because

Reader X had a job at another company with joined interests. Maybe Reader X had gone out with the accountant's sister at some point. Maybe the accountant was the new boyfriend of Reader X's ex-wife. Maybe they rode the same elevator going to different jobs in the same building, or maybe Reader X and the accountant had roomed together at college. There were too many possible points of contact. Simon had a lot of people at his disposal, but just trying to check out all of the possible overlaps for any one of the transformees was a huge undertaking, much less all of them, and then cross-referencing all of that combined information, looking for parallels with the others, was another massive task.

Too, Simon hadn't told all of the experts Keeley had so much faith in everything, any more than he'd told us everything. Knowing that it was a third party responsible for the transformations had shaken everything up, and assuming that Reader X had a high school connection changed things even further. And unlike the knight profilers, we hadn't been staring at the same data for weeks until we couldn't tell our assumptions from a hole in a theory. As if to prove this, Choo said, "I don't get the flute."

I could picture the way Sig was scrunching her face up by her voice. "You mean with the satyr? What's not to get? Satyrs have flutes. Or maybe reedpipes, I guess."

Choo wasn't buying something. "Back at that Chinese place, Simon said this guy—"

"Alex Holden," Keeley supplied.

"Sure," Choo said. "Simon said this guy became a satyr 'cause he hit on women and played a flute in high school."

"I wish you would call him Mr. Travers," Keeley complained.

We all ignored him. "But now we know this Alex dude became a goat pimp because it was Reader X who knew he hit on women and played a flute. You see? How did Reader X know this Alex dude was a flutist?"

"Flautist," Keeley corrected.

Choo's irritated tone said, *you say tomawto, I say what the hell is wrong with you*, but he didn't go there. "What I'm saying is, it don't sound like this Alex made a career out of playing the flute. Not everybody would know that about the man, and not too many people would give a damn."

"I played the clarinet in my high school band," Molly agreed. "It doesn't come up in conversation all that often."

Sig started to get excited. "You think Reader X might have known Alex while Alex was in his high school band?"

"Not just knew him at the time," Choo amended. "Maybe he knew the boy *because* he was in band. The thing about the flute stuck in his head."

"It's another stretch," I said. "But there's already a high school football connection. And football teams and bands come together a lot."

Keeley was dismissive. "You've been assuming that this Reader X went to high school with Randy Prutko and lived on the Lower East Side. Alex Holden didn't do either of those things." For all his attitude, though, he was texting something to someone while he spoke.

"That doesn't matter," Molly said excitedly. "Band is its own subculture. Band geeks from different high schools meet in all kinds of ways. The kids go to concerts, competitions, parades, camps, ceremonies...They see each other when their high school sports are competing. They form honors bands..."

I did my best to imitate a flaky young girl's voice: "I played a flute in band camp..."

Sig caught that reference and punched my arm before I could go any further with the *American Pie* quote. She didn't hit hard, just enough to function as a socially appropriate safety brake. I settled down, and we all thought about what Choo had said while we tried to poke holes in the theory that was emerging, or figure out how likely our assumptions truly were. It would drastically cut down on the number of possible suspects if Reader X knew Alex Holden because Reader X was in his own high school's band.

Just in case the punch hadn't been enough, Sig added something before I could. "Maybe we're getting the cart before the horse. Maybe it's the satyr part that's important, and the flute was just part of the myth that got pulled in. How many monsters that seduce women are there anyhow?"

"Lots," I said. "You should smell Simon's clothes."

Keeley sputtered.

"Plus, incubi, trauco, fossergrim, shokoys, gancanaghs, kapre, encantad…"

"Okay, now you're just showing off," Sig interrupted.

Molly wasn't giving up easily. "I hope this flute thing pans out, though. This is one of those trying-to-find-a-needle-in-a-haystack situations."

"I've never understood that saying," I grumbled. "If it's that big of a deal, just set the damn haystack on fire and pick the needle out of the ashes." Molly gave me a look over her shoulder. "What?"

Sig patted my forearm. "Let's try not to turn New York City into ashes."

Keeley smelled funny. Well, funnier. His pulse turned into a conga line. Sig started to say something else and I held my hand up to stop her. "What's going on, Keeley?"

"You mean besides a search for a book that warps reality?" His brisk little attempt at cheeriness sounded flat. "Assassination attempts, skin—"

"Yeah, besides that. Why did you get so upset just now?" I thought back. "When Sig said that thing about turning the city to ashes?"

The van's sudden drop in temperature had nothing to do with the AC.

What Keeley did wasn't a sigh. It was a deflation. "Don't assume for a moment that it's not an option."

Sig's voice became so tight it was painful to hear. "Turning the city to ashes?"

"The moment something appears that we can't fix...and I mean the exact second some dragon starts flaming everyone in Times Square, or some giant gorilla climbs a skyscraper with a blonde in his hand and starts swatting helicopters out of the sky, that part of the city is going up in the biggest explosion since Hiroshima." Keeley barely seemed to know what he was saying. "We have vehicles with bombs you can't make out of household items parked all over this city. Mr. Travers already has people laying out clues pointing to a new homeland terrorist group, if it comes to that."

"That's..." Choo stopped. I didn't blame him.

"Why are you telling us this?" Kasia asked.

"Mr. Travers told me I should break the news to you myself if it seemed you were about to begin speculating about it," Keeley said glumly. "He doesn't want you going off to investigate. He doesn't want to have you all killed or restrained while you can still be useful."

"That's so sweet," Molly managed.

"None of us wants to harm this city any more than it has already been harmed, and Mr. Travers says that your group has a way of finding unusual solutions while going off script."

"Back up," Sig commanded. "I'm not accepting this massive-bomb solution."

"Of course you're not." Keeley was way too young to be so matter-of-fact about it. "It's insane. And it won't be me making the decision, so please spare me the part where you strangle me or make any speeches about the humanity of it all. This isn't a James Bond movie. There is no one person to stop, no one secret code to halt a launch. We have to maintain the Pax by whatever means necessary. We have to. That's what our geas is. This isn't negotiable."

Sig looked at me. "John wouldn't blow up a city." I'd like to think there wasn't any uncertainty in her voice.

"Perhaps it's different for him because of his mixed breeding." There was definite bitterness in Keeley's voice. "I wouldn't know. But there will be knights who will be crying and fighting it with every ounce of willpower they have, but their fingers will still be pushing those buttons, even if they wind up killing friends and family. It's why I haven't slept in two days."

"You're actually being totally honest with us, aren't you?" I was operating under the kind of detachment that comes from shock. If Keeley had been talking about the death of one child with a name, I would have been fully engaged. The destruction of a whole city was too big to seem real. Out there, beyond the windows of the van, were millions of people whose lives seemed just as real to them as mine did to me. There were assholes and innocents and lovers and fuck-ups and people just getting along and people truly living their lives and people in pain. People hurting others, people helping others, people hiding their real selves, people looking for something they'd forgotten. And they could all be gone in the time it took to sneeze, like turning off a light switch or blowing on a dandelion.

It was obscene.

Keeley unbent a little further. I guess it was exhaustion and the probability that we were all going to die that was loosening him up a little. "You have to understand the situation. If you try to tell people what's going on and start a mass exodus, some higher-up will make the decision to blow everything up while Reader X is still in the city. The same thing happens if you contact Homeland Security and people start looking for bombs. The only way to prevent the deaths of millions of people is to help us find our man quickly."

"John was right," Choo said. "You're not the good guys."

That offended Keeley, but he didn't deny it. "I'm not enjoying this, if that makes you feel any better."

It didn't.

~23~

NURSE!

No one knew that life was fragile better than Merrit Dunsky. Miss a line on a chart and a patient might undergo an MRI while they had a metal valve in their heart, or wind up getting a medicine they were allergic to. Forget to check a box and the patient might not resume the life-maintaining medication that was temporarily halted while they were undergoing surgery. Get truly distracted and a patient might get someone else's medication altogether. Merrit had been a nurse for thirty years, and while she'd made her share of mistakes, she by God hadn't made more than her share, and none that were life-threatening. She was quite proud of that.

Not that it wasn't hard to stay focused in a place where there was so much pain and suffering. Especially a place where it would be so easy to get her hands on a little something extra to keep her going. But Merrit didn't get her reputation for being infallible playing about with that kind of malarkey. She didn't get her reputation for being a grim, humorless, old-fashioned martinet with no personal life that way either, but that was fine. Merrit had known who she was since she was twelve years old, hiding in the attic and pissing her panties while the thing that killed her parents slithered around making loud snuffing noises in the hallway beneath her. The knight who had rescued Merrit and arranged for her to be adopted by a Templar family took care of that. Merrit didn't need dances in the rain on warm nights in Paris. Merrit just needed a routine and a home that wasn't filled with personal weakness and chaos.

But in the three decades that Merrit had been working for the Templars, she'd never felt so poised on the brink of an abyss, not even during that vampire war at the turn of the new millennium that had forced her to treat so many knights off the record. Merrit had a sense for such things. All nurses did. Their fingers were on the pulse of more than just their patients. A city was like a person, full of different arteries and nerves and spasms and twitches, and hospitals were where cities showed the first signs of a breakdown.

So Merrit wasn't entirely surprised when Dianne Brandt came to her, Dianne's face as bleached of natural color as her hair. Dianne was still a party girl at thirty-four. Merrit had known other nurses who dealt with the death surrounding them by trying to hang on to their youth and experiencing life to the fullest every single moment of their off-hours. It worked for a time, but if the behavior was driven by fear or addiction, it eventually started to go badly. Dianne Brandt, in Merrit's opinion, was starting to go badly. And Dianne wanted Merrit to come see the patient in 4G, Chasney Shumate. Dianne wouldn't say why.

Merrit was expecting the worst, but when she got to room 4G, Chasney Shumate wasn't dead. It would have been far better if she were. Vines were coming out of her mouth. Green ropy vines entwining, hardening, forcing their way past the edges of the respirator that was keeping Chasney alive. Other vines were creeping from beneath the bottom covers of Chasney's bed, and Merrit had a horrible suspicion about where they were emerging from.

And the worst of it was that Chasney's chest was moving up and down at regular intervals.

For the first time in her thirty years in the hospital, Merrit almost fainted. It was impossible, and that wasn't fair. Merrit had already accepted the impossible. Merrit had spent her entire life accommodating the impossible, making sure that she never again felt like that twelve-year-old girl overwhelmed by the sheer shock and terror and unfairness of a world that everyone had lied about. There wasn't supposed to be an impossible impossible. There weren't supposed to be layers.

Merrit didn't know that Chasney Shumate had gone to a certain high school. Merrit didn't know that a certain role-playing game had a type of monstrous spore called a "Bad Seed" that put adventurers in a coma, then grew in their bodies, eventually animating them for its own savage, half-sentient purposes.

But Merrit knew her duty. There was a doctor who prescribed painkillers too liberally and profitably whom Merrit could blackmail to certify Chasney's time and cause of death. Another Templar lay servant who worked in the morgue. A number Merrit could call to finesse Chasney's parents and the funeral arrangements once Merrit took care of the immediate problem. She closed the door to the room, took a remote off the nightstand, and with a trembling hand turned the television mounted in an upper corner on. Dianne looked confused, and Merrit put a finger on her lips to indicate that she wanted to keep everything secret, then leaned forward to speak in Dianne's ear. "The Center for Disease Control is already on its way."

Dianne's face turned into a rush of confusion and relief. There was a logical explanation. Someone in authority knew what was happening and what to do. Dianne didn't see how that could be true, but she wanted to believe it, and she grasped that straw as if it were a life raft. "What's going on?"

Merrit pretended to take Chasney's pulse. "Shut that curtain and I'll tell you what I know."

As soon as Dianne turned, Merrit put her in a choke hold. If Dianne was lucky, Merrit would be able to dose her with Rohypnol, hide her, and tell everyone that Dianne had left for home sick, then later arrange for Dianne to be taken out of the hospital. If Dianne woke up the next day in her bed with no memory of the last forty-eight hours, she and everyone else would assume that Dianne had had an alcoholic blackout.

If Dianne was lucky. Luckier, anyhow.

~24~

GEAS, GIVE ME A HEART ATTACK, WHY DON'T YOU?

The radius effect of magic is never predictable. We went around the back side of the high school, and the parking lot lights—at least the section of them that we could see—were still going strong, but the lights inside the high school seemed to be off entirely. I couldn't even see vending machines glowing in the gym lobby, or the faint gleam of computers absentmindedly left on in classrooms on the upper floors. It seemed like a pretty good bet that we wouldn't have to worry about any security cameras or alarms.

"There's magic in the air," I said. "And I'm not talking about Christmas."

Keeley seemed more alarmed at the prospect of his cell phone not working than the idea that something was up. "We don't have a team in place yet."

They didn't? That didn't sound like the Simon Travers I knew. The Templars really must be keeping busy.

"See that ticket booth?" I pointed toward a small wooden shack set next to a practice field, right beside the driveway. "You can hide in there and be our contact person on the outside once we scout around a little."

Keeley protested, but only halfheartedly. Choo found a discreet place to park down the street, and he and Molly and Keeley focused on using their smartphones to find a map of the school and the name of the yearbook editor while Sig and Kasia and I looked around the outside of the high school for sentries or signs of an ambush. It was an even bet on whether it was Reader X's imagination or the School of Night's divination magic causing the supernatural static on the inside.

Normally, I would have taken several hours to scout the area properly, but, you know, magical monsters, nuclear bombs, nutjobs with the power of gods, clocks ticking. So, I did the best quick job I could, then found a house across a side street whose yard was almost completely in shadow. Once hidden, I tried to call Ben Lafontaine.

I say "tried" because my fingers wouldn't punch the buttons on the cell phone. The tendons in my wrist tightened up as if my shoulder were reeling them in, and the fingers of my hand were pulled into a painful claw. My heart started pounding painfully against my breastbone.

My geas was kicking in. I tried to stab the buttons with a knuckle and a choked sound came out of my mouth that made me realize I wouldn't be able to talk to Ben even if I did manage to call him. The wolf in me knew that the same city where my pack leader was sending a lot of werewolves had become a death trap, but the John Charming who thought in terms of tactics and strategy knew that Ben continuing to send more werewolves was the best chance to save the lives of the werewolves who were already there. And if all of the werewolves suddenly started fleeing the city, or even sending their families and friends out, there was no way it wouldn't be noticed by other members of the supernatural community, which would inevitably draw the attention of the people with their fingers on buttons.

And if that weren't complicated enough, the knight in me who was bound by a geas knew that if Ben found out about the Templars' nuclear option, it might irretrievably break the alliance between the werewolves and the knights once and for all. That wouldn't be good in terms of keeping magic a secret, and my geas wouldn't let me do anything that I honestly believed was in disservice to that cause.

I sank down to my knees and put my head on the ground. I wasn't being dramatic. My thudding heart was sending fight-or-flight chemicals through my body, and a bright, hot, sharp pain was starting to flare in my skull. The only way to get my body under control was to find a path that could make the wolf and the knight align with the man, or reason things out until I sincerely believed that what I was doing was the best way to serve the Pax Arcana.

The thing was, the knights couldn't keep going the way they were going. It wasn't just the specific circumstances; it was their mind-set. Even if I kept the nuclear scenario away from Ben and we managed to find Reader X and defuse this situation, no pun intended, the Templars and the Round Table would wind up going to war eventually. The knights thought of us wolves as disposable second-class citizens, and we wolves thought of the knights as fascists who couldn't be trusted, and that house divided against itself couldn't stand. I really believed that.

That was too abstract for my geas, though. The piercing pain in my head was still building.

Telling the truth to Sarah about the Book of Am had paid off because I trusted Sarah, and she was smart, and she had brought a whole new perspective to the problem that helped me make real progress. I trusted Ben. Ben was smart. Too smart to lie to or withhold truth from without him catching on sooner or later. And Ben might bring a whole new perspective to this problem. Ben didn't want war between the knights and the werewolves either.

Yeah, Simon's way might work, but it was a short-term solution, and it would definitely cause problems further down the road. I really believed that, too. Trusting Ben might backfire right now, but it might not, and it would be better in the long term. Simon's way might backfire right now too, and it would definitely lead to long-term disaster. Didn't that make trying to figure out a way to work with Ben a better option?

If the geas paralyzed me or made me pass out, Sig would call Ben anyhow. So, there was no point in my body shutting down.

The pain in my head suddenly stopped intensifying.

I was willing to try to keep magic a secret from the world at large; I really was. I didn't want scientists dissecting werewolves trying to cure cancer, or the military trying to turn monsters into super soldiers, or cults or religious crusades or fears of the apocalypse that the appearance of magic in the mundane world would certainly cause. I didn't want to discover what new kinds of racism might occur when beings that were actually different races instead of just ethnicities appeared on the scene, or find out what political platforms some ambitious prick might run on using fear of the supernatural as a focus, or have supernatural beings registered or questioned by Congress or put in camps until people felt safe again.

And maybe it wouldn't go down that way in some countries, but it would definitely turn to genocidal wars in others, and history wasn't very encouraging. I was willing to serve the Pax

Arcana, but to serve it to the best of my ability, I had to use my best judgment, and my best judgment was telling me that Simon was wrong.

I found a way.

The migraine started to dissolve, and my breathing slowed.

I called Simon, and wonder of wonders, the prick actually answered the number he'd given me. Keeley had probably been texting Simon that we'd figured out the nuclear scenario, and the tumblers in Simon's scheming mind would be whirling.

So, I didn't waste time. "You have to tell Ben."

Simon didn't waste time either. "That will cause the disaster you're trying to stop."

"No," I said. "It won't. Because nobody in the supernatural community will think it's suspicious when werewolf civilians start disappearing if they think there's another war between knights and werewolves brewing."

"What?"

"Ben's going to tell the Round Table that he's taking precautions because he's seeing signs that the knights are going to mount hostilities again when the current crisis is over. And you're going to spread signs of mounting tension among the supernatural community. Given our recent history, nobody will think it's weird when the werewolves start to duck and cover. The Round Table already has preparations in place to leave quickly and quietly if that situation occurs again, anyhow."

"You want to prevent a war between the Round Table and the Order by making everyone think there's going to be another war between the Round Table and the Order."

"I know it sounds crazy," I said. "But Ben can tell his wolves that he's just taking precautions. He can ask for some werewolves to volunteer to stay and keep working in the city so that the knights won't get suspicious while the Round Table is evacuating its civilians. Werewolves will go for that, and the families fleeing the city won't be calling every loved one they know to warn them about nuclear bombs, because they won't know about nuclear bombs. The werewolves who stay—and pack loyalty will have almost all of them stay—will know that they're volunteering for a messed-up situation they don't fully understand instead of being ordered into it. And Ben will know that you told him the truth. He'll know that you offered to look like the bad guy so that Ben could get the people he cares about out of harm's way. He won't like this nuclear craziness any more than I do—"

"Any more than I do," Simon interrupted.

"—but he'll understand that you're doing everything you can to avoid that possibility, and that you're respecting his needs and intelligence if nothing else. You'll be building a foundation we can work on in the future."

"He'll smell you all over this," Simon said.

"It doesn't matter," I said. "This is why he wanted me to work with you. Ben's smart, Simon. You don't know how smart. And you'll be telling the truth. We're going to make it the truth."

Simon went quiet for a time. Then he said, "If we spread that rumor around, I could have knights evacuate their families without raising suspicion, too."

Did it make Simon better or worse that he hadn't already done so?

"You could use the story to explain all kinds of unusual knight activity," I said. "The supernatural community has to know that something is going on. This story will have bystanders trying to get out of the crossfire instead of sniffing around."

Simon *hmm*ned. "Here's the problem. We can't have knights and werewolves thinking a war is coming very long without a war actually breaking out. The 'Hah-hah, just kidding' option has a short expiration date. And if me lying to Ben is bad, how is asking Ben to lie to some of his people any better?"

Was Simon saying "we" because he was trying to rope me in? Or was he doing it unconsciously? Either way was an improvement. "It's better because they're his people. And we're desperately trying to buy time no matter what we do. That's why we're going to find this asshole and his Book of Am before the sun rises."

"We are?"

"Of course we are," I said. "We don't have a choice."

There were other things to say, but ultimately Simon went for it.

I called Ben. "I don't have much time. Simon's about to give you some bad news. But he wants to work with you, and we can use this."

Ben caught the urgency in my voice immediately. "What bad news? Use it how?"

"When this situation is over, we're going to leverage it to demand that some of our most promising young wolves start getting put through knight training alongside human geas-bound," I said. "Things like that."

Ben swore. "Exactly how bad is this news?"

"Just keep what I said in mind when you listen to him," I said. "This is either a disaster none of us are going to recover from, or it's our biggest opportunity. You have to think that way or we're all screwed, Ben. I'm trusting you."

Ben wanted more information, but I said, "Simon has to tell you himself, or it doesn't mean anything. We can compare notes later." And I hung up. Ben and Simon were going to have to work out the details themselves. I had just told Simon that this would all work out because I was going to find Reader X before another day went by.

No pressure.

∾25∾

I WASN'T EXPECTING THE
SPANISH INQUISITION[1]

When we weren't ready to go, Choo dropped us off anyway. He found a small courtyard hidden between the protruding high school gymnasium and the library and parked there. We were hidden from the rest of the world, which was a good thing because the rest of the world might have wondered why four adults were prowling around a high school, two of them openly wearing Japanese swords and another carrying a spear.

Choo stayed with the van and kept it running. I wish I'd said a proper good-bye. But life isn't kind like that. I had no idea I was seeing Choo for the last time.

No, just kidding.

The school was large but old. The windowsills were wood and white and peeling, and instead of being a tasteful montage of light crimson and brown and white hues, the bricks were an unusually dark red, even faded as they were. Newer additions to the campus, like a digital signpost that wasn't working

---

1. With all due respect to *Monty Python's Flying Circus*.

and the recently paved parking lot, seemed like expensive wigs stuck on a corpse. It had been a prosperous-looking place once. Now the high school was just trying to hang on to its dignity.

"Do you remember the drill?" Kasia asked Sig. As far as I could recall, it was the first direct word either had spoken to the other since the Chinese restaurant.

"It doesn't matter," Sig said. "It's just like the other places I went to today. I'm not picking up any kind of spirit activity at all."

We found a single glass door, and Sig cracked a chem stick. We were at the bottom of a stairwell: Cheap but sturdy pinkish-peach siding with a brick design traveled up about five feet of the walls before exposing cream-colored cinderblocks. The entrance's lock looked tough, but it was actually a push-over. Once inside, there was a modern alarm with a keypad next to the door, but we didn't have to worry about it. When Sig held the chem stick up to the small square glass screen, the alarm wasn't functioning.

Kasia went up the stairs first. She had sharp senses and moved quietly and regenerated just like I did, so if she wanted to put herself in the line of fire, I wasn't going to argue. Chivalry be damned.

Ten steps led to the landing of a first floor whose darkness was nearly impenetrable. Kasia slipped silently against one side of the open doorway. At some point, she had started holding her gun. I moved and took the other side, my knife in hand. I wasn't picking up any sounds or smells that indicated intelligent life, but from what I understand, that's fairly typical of modern high schools. From a crouching position halfway up the stairs, Sig threw a chem stick through the opening.

The gleaming cylinder bounced off a stone wall and landed on a grey floor. What was weird was that the floor surface looked like linoleum, but the print was made to unconvincingly resemble a surface made of cobblestones. The walls, on the other hand, were made out of real stones shaped just like modern cinderblocks, but the rock seemed old and organic and unpainted. In the faint borders of green chemical light, manacles were set into the opposite wall by dark thick chains. It was like an art deco version of a medieval dungeon. Andy Warhell.

I took out my flashlight and shone it eastward through the opening. I could see a door made of bars, but beyond it were the smooth matte-black counters and cheap metal stools of a modern high school science class. Beyond the cell door I could see modern fluorescent lights set into the ceiling, but next to the cell door, in the hallway, was an old-fashioned torch mounted on brackets. But what really caught my attention was the greyish-brown metal door frame next to me where a stairwell door had once been emplaced and later removed. On one side of the doorframe, the wall was grey stone. On the other, cream-colored cinderblock. But the division wasn't quite equal. The grey rock seemed to be slightly extended past the metal door frame on my side, as if the cinderblocks were being infected by it. I held a penlight right next to the door frame and the penlight went out.

To hell with it. I went back and had a brief whispered conference with the others. It's not like there was any point trying to be completely silent. Molly, God bless her, is not ninja material. "It's not just people and animals changing…it's places now. But I don't think there were any people in this building to transform."

"So, there's no ogre guarding this castle?" Molly didn't quite succeed in sounding nonchalant.

"I'm not smelling or hearing anything like that. But it's not a castle," I said. "This place is becoming a dungeon."

"Wow," Sig said. "I guess Reader X really did go to this high school. And he didn't like it much."

"I saw a torch," I said. "I'm going to go light it."

I took out my World War II lighter and moved across the hallway to light the torch, but then something weird happened. When the torch ignited, it was followed by another whoosh of air and burst of light, and then a third as torches farther down the hallway lit one after the other, the effect traveling down both walls until they reached two iron doors on the north side of the hall and a lobby with a visible cafeteria beyond it to the south. By the time the effect was finished, I was back in the stairwell with a gun in one hand, a knife in the other, and a heart going pitter-patter like a rabbit's instead of a wolf's.

"What did you do?" Kasia hissed.

"You caught me," I hissed back. "I'm secretly the bastard son of the god of cigarette lighters."

"Ease up," Sig said soothingly. "There's a lot of active magic in the air, John. You probably activated some law of sympathy or contagion by accident."

I had seen Sarah White do a similar trick with candles once, but on a much smaller scale.

Kasia peered at me suspiciously. "Are you some kind of cunning man?"

"No. Maybe the molecules in this place are just getting used to being shoved around." I stepped out into the hallway. It wasn't brightly lit, but there were six torches, three on each side, covering roughly a fourth of a mile, with deep swells and patches of shadows in between. The overall effect was of a dark tunnel sporadically lit by flames.

"This is pretty much how I remember high school," Molly commented.

"Come on," Sig said. "The contents of the classrooms don't seem to have changed yet. Let's go look for a yearbook."

Molly sighed. "The Spanish class should be the second-to-last room on the right." The Spanish teacher was the yearbook editor.

"Okay." I took a torch off the wall and addressed Kasia. "One of us should guard the rear."

"Enjoy it." Kasia took a torch for herself and began walking down the hall, slowly, looking through the barred doors of the classrooms. Sig and Molly followed her. I trailed behind.

We went by what had probably been a trophy case built into the wall, but instead of bronze or brass trophies and pictures, the shelves were full of gold gem-encrusted chalices and old-fashioned paintings of kids in modern uniforms. Pennants with medieval script unfurled from the ceiling, but instead of announcing jousting tournaments or royal proclamations, they listed past victories in football, basketball, and baseball, most of the events from ye olde twentieth century.

"Hold on." I broke the glass display window open with the hilt of my knife. "These chalices look like real gold."

"You want to steal them?" Molly asked.

"The Templars are going to burn down or blow up this building anyway," I said. "We might as well take some of this stuff to study, and it might as well be stuff that has a profit margin."

"I want a cut," Kasia called back.

Well, fair was fair. Sig had a backpack on her shoulders for gathering yearbooks. It was considerably fuller when we moved on.

We passed what was clearly a teacher's lounge, with a modern bathroom and a bulletin board and a copying machine, but in the corner, there was a huge keg. Braces of garlic cloves and figs and candied apples hung from the ceiling. Probably where the vending machines used to be.

We reached the Spanish class without further incident, and Sig threw her chem stick into the room and grabbed the barred door. She had to brace her feet against the wall, but she tore the door open with a loud snap of metal from the lock, then steadied herself by hanging on to the bars when she stumbled backward.

There was a series of old lockers built into the back wall of the classroom—I have no idea why—and we lucked out. The yearbook staff did keep copies of past yearbooks in the room. There was only one copy for each year, but they dated all the way back to the 1920s, jammed side by side and taking up two of the deep lockers. They were even organized chronologically.

"Yay," Molly said after Sig removed six of the books. "Let's get out of here."

"We should go out through the windows." I was standing guard in the doorway. "I don't want to risk those books getting turned into scrolls or something." Not to mention I wanted to get out of that creepy-ass building as soon as possible. The active changes going on made it feel as if the building was alive, and I didn't much like being in the belly of a beast.

"Uhm, John?"

I was already following Sig's upward gaze. The Spanish class was only sporadically lit by torchlight and moonlight and chem sticks, and the corners of the room were in dark shadow. Spiders the size of tennis balls were crawling down the wall from those areas, pitch-black spiders flickering in and out of three dimensions. Shadows of spiders. Or spiders of shadows.

I don't know what made me glance down. The ink-black rats that were creeping out of the dark corners on the floor weren't making any noise. Or the silhouettes of rats, if silhouettes can have width and breadth and length and dimension.

"Come on!" Kasia dropped her torch, grabbed a classroom desk, and held it in front of her while she ran and jumped through a window. The window was maybe six feet tall and three feet wide, and the entire pane shattered and fell, either outward or in large shards that dropped and cracked flat on the floor.

Unfortunately, the rest of us didn't move like a finely honed unit. There was no way I was charging past Molly and leaving her behind, so I moved closer to her and slashed my torch at a shadow rat that was darting toward us ahead of the others. The dark thing melted in half and dissolved. Sig had the same idea that I did. She picked up the torch that Kasia had dropped and thrust it upward at a shadow spider that was dropping down from the ceiling on a black silky strand. The spider shriveled in on itself and disappeared. We both backed away from a wave of shadow rats that were coming at us from several different angles, swishing our torches in front of our feet in awkward scuttling crouches as we knocked desks aside.

The problem was, Molly wasn't taking advantage of our actions and making a break for it. I could hear the faintest suggestion of a prayer on her breath as Molly stared transfixed at the spider and rat forms emerging from the upper and lower corners of the room. The vermin didn't seem to have a finite limit. My torch wasn't built for swinging around like a katana, and the rows of desks filling the classroom didn't offer a lot of freedom of movement. Shadow rats were darting between the chair and desk legs. Our margin for reaching the window before it was blocked was extremely limited. I kicked over a desk to give myself some room, but the desk didn't squish the shadow rat it landed on. The thing slipped right under, and I brought my torch down on it. "Molly! Move!"

Molly snapped out of it and began taking jerky steps toward the window, running, but running as if her legs had fallen asleep. A pair of headlights appeared in the windows outside the classroom and turned Molly into a profile. The shadow things paused, only for a moment, but it was a precious moment. Kasia yanked Molly through the large open frame that used to be a window, and Sig and I backed after her side by side, trying to protect each other's flanks.

It didn't work. We got swarmed before we reached the opening. I lost track of everything else for a moment and went into some high-kicking, whirling seizure. None of the shadow rats crawling over me were dislodged by the momentum. I sliced a shadow rat on my thigh with my silver steel knife, but it was like slicing through pudding. The shadow rat moved on without even a squeal and took a needled nibble out of my waist. Burning two rats off me left portions of singed skin, but in the time it took me to do so, several more rats climbed on me from below and at least two spiders dropped on me from above. Sharp pains were multiplying all over my body, and death by a thousand small bites moved right up to the top of my personal nightmare list.

Then everything went bright and blinding as Choo tossed a magnesium flare through the broken window from outside. The shadow vermin on and around me dissolved, leaving the world as silently as they'd come into it. My infravision had kicked in at some point, and I was entirely blinded, but I followed the air current and hurled myself through the window frame. Shattered glass crunched beneath me on the ground, but all of it was lying flat in fragmented sheets, not sticking up like shards of a bottle would have.

Choo lit and tossed two more magnesium flares into the room, spacing them so that the entire room was filled with a pale, fierce light. Forget the Batman crack I'd made to Simon; maybe I needed a utility belt.

Several other vehicles' headlights came wheeling around the library section of the high school, and Woodrow Keeley's voice began yelling not to shoot. I'm not sure if he was addressing us or the knights who had arrived. A knight who didn't bother to give his name came running over, covering the Spanish class with an M4 carbine and covering his apprehension with attitude.

He moved fast for such a broad man, built for power like a football player rather than for show like a bodybuilder. "What the hell's going on in there?"

"Shadow creatures," I gasped out. "We're going to have to burn this school down."

He didn't like that. But he wasn't pumping me full of silver bullets either, which meant that Simon had decided to go along with the plan and not try to have Ben and me assassinated before news of the knights' nuclear scenario spread any further. So...yay. His attitude was all ice cream cake and candy sprinkles, as far as I was concerned. "Shadow creatures? You mean shades or umbra sprites?"

"I mean shadow rats and spiders." A thought flashed through my head—there was a fairy tale called "The Boy Who Went Forth to Learn What Fear Was," and in it, shadowy animals had kept pouring out of the dark corners of a room that was supposed to be haunted. "And that whole building is transforming into some kind of dungeon."

I don't know what kinds of things that knight had been seeing in the last few weeks, but he'd seen something. He asked me for more details, but he didn't question my honesty or sanity once.

~26~

LOOKING FOR GUIDANCE

We didn't stay for Operation School's Out or whatever the knights called the latest pain-in-the-ass cover-up we'd dumped in their laps, and Keeley didn't stay with my group. He informed us, and not with any particular regret, that he had a lot of tasks to organize and was jumping off our merry-go-round. Or *scary-go-round* might be more accurate. I couldn't say that I was sorry to see Keeley go, but I did say, "And Simon is okay with that?"

"Mr. Travers's exact words were *Charming's a pain in the ass, but he finds trouble the way a hog roots out truffles. The best thing to do for now is let him loose and follow the trail of bodies.*"

"It always feels good to be appreciated." There was no way Simon wasn't still spending all of his own resources on finding Reader X without our help, but if he wanted to give me some autonomy, he could phrase it any way he wanted to.

Keeley did agree to set up a meeting with the high school's old guidance counselor, though I'm pretty sure he only did so because Simon was already covering that base for himself. When we got to Pamela Nelson's modest town house at way o'clock at night, one of Simon's agents answered the door for us. Agent Dickerson—we never found out her first name—was a geas-bound who worked for the FBI. She was cocoa-skinned, short, and had a large presence. Agent Dickerson had already been questioning the former high school guidance counselor about anyone who might be connected to the still officially missing Randy Prutko.

Choo and Molly stayed in the van because everyone couldn't go. Sig went because she was able to speak to the dead, Kasia went because she could hypnotize Pamela Nelson if necessary, and I went because I wasn't leaving the two of them alone together.

Agent Dickerson informed us that Miss Nelson's daughter and two grandchildren were living with her, and that the grandchildren were sleeping. We quietly followed her through the house.

Miss Nelson was in a small, mostly green kitchen in the back, sitting at a proportionately small table and drinking coffee from a pot that she had just made. I smelled the coffee, and my entire body puckered. Fortunately, I don't think anyone noticed. Miss Nelson was a gnomish-looking woman in her late sixties, complete with grey hair tied back in a bun and thick spectacles, wearing a soft pink bathrobe and fuzzy slippers. She was either just that confident and comfortable around company, or she was making a passive-aggressive statement about how late it was. If the latter, it was a very passive statement; she greeted us warmly and offered us some of the coffee. I managed to keep myself from bowling her over on the way to the coffeepot or kneeling down and slobbering kisses on her feet, but it was a near thing.

We spread the yearbooks out on the table and got down to business, asking Miss Nelson if she could look at the pictures of male students that we'd circled and tell us if any of them might have been bullied by Randy Prutko. It was a daunting proposition. Randy Prutko had gone to a large high school, and the band had had around two hundred members on any given year. Randy had been at the high school for three years, so that included another hundred and fifty band members who had come and gone during that time. Once we narrowed the number down to males, we had one hundred and eighty-nine candidates, one hundred and thirteen of whom had been in the band while Prutko was a football player.

"There were a lot of boys who might have been bullied by Randy," she stalled. "He had a difficult time of it."

I took that as guidance counselor–speak for Randy being a violent young sociopath with a low IQ and not much charisma. If he'd grown up in certain Eskimo tribes, a couple of tribal elders would have taken young Randy out on a canoe to go fishing, and he wouldn't have come back. "Still," I said, slathering on a little butter, "this was back when guidance counselors actually counseled. You must have some ideas."

Behind that soft voice and those professionally warm and friendly eyes, Patricia Nelson was a cagey customer used to covering her own ass. I had a very random impulse to introduce her to Randy's grandfather, Alek Prutko. "I'm afraid my interactions with Randy were limited."

I played along. "Why? It sounds like he was troubled."

Miss Nelson pursed her lips regretfully. "Most of my interactions with Randy were about him trying to get into the special education program."

"Why?" I repeated.

"Honestly?"

I was momentarily paralyzed while my mouth struggled to say something smartass and my mind clamped down and refused to let my lips move. Sig filled in the pause by smiling supportively and giving the correct answer, which was "Please."

"Randy only wanted to graduate high school so that he could go into the military." Miss Nelson sounded regretful. "And he thought getting into the special education program was an easy way to do that. Don't tell anyone I said this, but a lot of students who don't have good study habits or much support from their family try to play the system."

I'm not sure that this was as groundbreaking a revelation as Miss Nelson seemed to think it was.

"But Randy was one of those low-borderline students who don't actually have a learning disability," Miss Nelson continued. "He dropped out of high school soon after he was rejected from the program. The real failure is, I don't think Randy could picture a world where he actually came to school regularly and did the minimal work he would have to do to pass his classes with a D average. I saw that more than I liked with children who didn't have any structure at home. Do you think Randy is a threat to one of these boys you're asking about?"

She was good. She had slipped that question into the conversation almost organically.

"We found some disturbing references on his cell phone," Sig said. "We really can't go into more detail than that, Miss Nelson."

"Of course." She continued to waffle. "But that was a long time ago. The person you should really talk to is the class president, Lexi Coleman. These would have been her peers, and Lexi will be the one in charge of staying in touch with students and organizing reunions. Or maybe Mister Spraglin. I know a lot of boys who didn't want to eat lunch in the cafeteria ate lunch in his room. It was a high school tradition."

I guess she knew the band director had died. And despite Miss Nelson's claims to a fuzzy memory, she had also known who Randy Prutko's class president was. "Those are good suggestions; thank you." I wrote down the names in my pocket notebook.

Miss Nelson eyed the notebook. "Gracious, I don't see those very often anymore. It's all cell phones these days."

"Agent Graham's a bit old-fashioned," Sig said. I was a Graham? "But still, since we're already here…"

"Miss Nelson, I am a professional hypnotist," Kasia interrupted. "If you do not mind, I could put you under. You might remember more than you think."

Miss Nelson laughed a little nervously. "Oh, my. You could try, I suppose, but I'm one of those people who can't be—"

She stopped because she was already in a light trance. Again, I'm opposed to the way vampires and dhampirs can mess with people's minds on general principle…often violently opposed. But it beats having to dispose of witnesses like the dog walker, and Miss Nelson had sort of given her permission, and things went a lot faster after that. Miss Nelson looked at the pictures in the yearbooks while Kasia prompted her into a running commentary. I listened carefully. Upstairs, someone was pacing restlessly above our heads. At a guess, Miss Nelson's daughter was waiting up, ready to pounce on her mother the moment the FBI left. She was probably tweeting all of her friends about it.

Agent Dickerson got a phone call somewhere in the middle of all that and left the room, then came back in a few minutes later. "We just found out that Mitzi Unger went to Randy Prutko's high school too."

We'd had a lot of information thrown at us fast, but I was used to that. Mitzi Unger was the woman who had been transformed into a siren and then forced her sons to kill their father.

"She's not in any of the alumni sites," I said.

Still in a trance, Miss Nelson chimed in helpfully. "Mitzi was only at our school for a few months. She transferred in after her mother left her father, but the mother went back to the man a short time later."

"Was Mitzi in the high school band?" Kasia asked.

"She was, but I don't think she actually learned to play anything. I used to see her helping the pit crew during the football games."

Kasia kept speaking in the same calm voice. "What was Mitzi like?"

"Oh, she was a sad little tramp," Miss Nelson said without a filter. "Sexualized very early. She liked to corrupt boys who were younger than her."

"Corrupt them how?" Kasia asked.

"She liked to take their virginity," Miss Nelson droned on with no hesitancy or tact. "She hung around students who were younger than her and got them to do things like drink or take drugs for the first time. It was a power issue with Mitzi. I don't think she felt like she had any power at home."

Kasia said, "How do you know all of this?"

"The mother of one of the boys complained. It's why Mitzi wound up leaving our school."

Sig cleared her throat. "Do you remember the boy's name?"

"Robert Peet."

That was one of the high school students who had been in the band. Agent Dickerson left the room to talk on her phone again.

～27～

NO, YOU DO THE CAVITY SEARCH

Luis Rodriguez stopped at the edge of the platform, right at the mouth of the subway tunnel. His face was rigid and his chest was moving up and down a little too rapidly.

"I'm not getting any closer than this."

Luke Pritchett had never worked with Luis before, but any Templar who became a transit cop in New York City wasn't likely to frighten easily. It was commonly held wisdom among knights that any lay sergeant who worked the subways had a strong heart, and any lay sergeant who worked the sewers had a strong stomach. The city only got worse the farther down you went. For Luis to resist his geas and embarrass himself like this, he must have been truly terrified.

Luke looked at his partner, Matt Petrucelli. The big paladin shrugged. Like most of Matt's motions, the shrug seemed more expressive for coming off a six-foot-six frame. That was good because Matt didn't like to talk much. It was bad because Luke was six feet one and spent most of his life feeling short. "All right," Luke said kindly, and left it at that.

The two warrior priests proceeded down into the tunnel,

stepping around a forest of iron girders that had been propped between the ground and ceiling like mine supports. They carefully avoided the third rail of the subway tracks even though they had been assured that it had been turned off. Luke didn't know what pretext was being used to shut the tunnel down, or how high up the Templars' operative in the Transit Authority was. All he knew was that a lot of knights were pouring into New York City from the surrounding states, and that he and Matt had been told to hurry it up. Few things generated as much pressure and public distress in New York City as having modes of transport disrupted.

At least the tunnel was fairly well lit. Lamps burning sacramental oils were hung about the tunnel, and blocks of dry ice made out of frozen holy water were coating the floor with a roiling mist. If those precautions weren't having any effect, Luke privately suspected that any exorcisms he and Matt performed wouldn't do much good either, but he kept those doubts to himself.

Even knowing what to expect, Luke's heartbeat speeded up when he spotted the protrusions. Roughly the size of steamer trunks, grey-white and emerging from both the ground and ceiling, the irregularities looked like nothing so much as the tips of teeth coming in.

The mouth of the subway tunnel was growing fangs.

～28～

TROUBLE AND DIM SUM

I couldn't get ahold of Keeley immediately, but Kasia got Simon on the phone with an ease that again made me wonder what kind of deal he'd made with the kresniks before all of this started, and why he trusted her to keep an eye on us. So much bullshit, so little time. I could hear Simon assure Kasia that Templars of various job descriptions would soon be swarming all over one Robert Peet before our team could do anything useful, and he further insisted that the Templars didn't need assistance checking out other male band members who had graduated from Prutko's high school.

"You could help us by coming in and working with one of our crisis response teams," Simon said. "But if Charming wants to keep looking on his own, let him. He made me a promise, and he has insane luck."

Well, it hadn't really been a promise.

"Good luck or bad?" Kasia asked.

"Both," Simon said. "And I can't tell how much of it is karma or instinct."

Another mental flicker: Sarah insisting I had psychic leanings that I was repressing because of my Catholic upbringing. And doing a damn good job, too. I repressed the thought.

"It was the same with Sig when I worked with her." Kasia didn't try to sound neutral. "Perhaps it is the company he keeps."

Kasia filled the others in on the pertinent parts of the conversation when we were back in the van, and we talked about finding a place where we could get some more coffee and figure out our next move.

"Are you sure we should stop at a public place?" The new van seat squeaked as Molly shifted nervously. "I don't want to drag any innocent bystanders into it if we get attacked."

"We're the ones doing the hunting this time," Choo said.

"Are you sure about that?" Molly asked. "Didn't John say something about bird people following and attacking him and Kasia?"

"But no one has attacked us while we were here," Kasia pointed out.

"Those raven things didn't attack us until they knew we were onto them," I said. "And there's a lot of dark sky up there above us."

"I could use some caffeine," Choo put in. "And I'm driving."

"Maybe we should compromise," Sig said. "Let's not go to any crowded places or busy streets. What do you think, John?"

I thought Molly had a good point. We didn't know enough about how Reader X and his Book of Am connection worked to know what to expect. Those ravens that had manifested didn't seem to match the other transformations. They exhibited a degree of conscious intent and calculation and control that was unsettling. Was the Book of Am really becoming increasingly sentient and beginning to cause spies and obstacles to manifest in places that might lead to it without Reader X being conscious of the process? Was Reader X slumped over the book, knocked out and dreaming all of this with his forehead pressed against the pages, or was he standing around in a bathrobe, listening to opera music and wildly waving his hands around like a mad conductor while he caused more creations to transform his past into magical monsters? Was the guy a terrorist, a master criminal, a pawn, or a schizophrenic? How much did he know about us? How much did he want to know?

"If we want to make sure we're not being magically followed, I think we should get Kevin or Sarah to meet us someplace," I said. "Kevin's mojo picked up on the ravens last time."

Which is how I wound up getting on the phone. It wasn't a fun or friction-free conversation, because I didn't tell Sarah about the knights' nuclear scenario. That would have been betraying the pact I'd entered into with Simon and Ben, but Sarah could tell there were things I wasn't telling her, because she's as sharp and quick as a diamond-toothed chain saw blade.

"All I can tell you is that we're dancing on a tightrope made of barbed wire stretched out over a bottomless pit," I finally said. "There might be another war between the knights and the werewolves on top of everything else if I don't step carefully."

Every word of which was absolutely true. If it helped spread the idea that the knights and the wolves were preparing for a throwdown without explaining why they were preparing for one or why I wanted to spread that idea...well...was I really deceiving Sarah? Even if I was pretty sure she'd be okay with that if she understood my obligations and the stakes involved?

Sarah seemed to think so. I wound up owing her a favor.

I also wound up going to one of those mostly empty concrete stretches that stitch together the patchwork quilt of counties, districts, neighborhoods, islands, municipalities, slums, and industrial areas that form New York City. It was a poorly lit street on the edges of a neighborhood and not quite in a business area. There was virtually no visible traffic, foot or otherwise, and only two brightly lit buildings, a convenience store two blocks down, and some kind of restaurant in the middle of a small, otherwise-deserted strip mall.

The restaurant itself was a fast food operation set up to sell dumplings: pork dumplings, chicken dumplings, and beef dumplings to go. The only concessions to variety were two choices of soup that were basically tasty broth, and fried rice. It was a grimy little place that was almost all red counter, and everything was served in foam bowls and cups or paper plates. The place wasn't quite as deserted as it looked, though. I could hear muted voices from a back room, mostly male. Some of the voices were angry, some excited, some exultant, but they were all speaking Chinese, a fact I was only aware of because I know some Chinese curse words. I'm pretty sure I heard the click and rattle of dice as well. I guess the high customer volume wasn't why the place was staying open into the wee hours.

Kevin was waiting for us at one of the red tables.

"Number one son!" Molly hugged Kevin. Charlie Chan was Chinese, not Japanese, but Kevin didn't seem to mind. I don't know if that's because he was too young to get the reference or because Molly is one of those people who can get away with anything. She and Kevin had spent a lot of time together in a van the last time we were in New York.

Kevin wasn't able to reassure us or warn us about any specific spies or threats, though. When we asked him if he had any intuitions with extra cheese, he said, "I'm not a Ouija board, you know."

"Of course not." Molly pointed at Sig. "She's the Ouija board. You're the Magic 8 Ball."

"I'm not a Magic 8 Ball either."

Molly wasn't having any of Kevin's attitude. "Are you sure?

Maybe I just didn't shake you hard enough." She grabbed Kevin by the collar and shook him back and forth with exaggerated motions until he started to laugh reluctantly.

"The reply is hazy," Kevin told Molly. "Try again later."

Sig intervened. "So, is no news good news, Kevin?"

He wrinkled his forehead—maybe that's the way psychics scrunch their nose—and said, "It maybe feels like something's missing, but I don't know why. The last time I was with you, we were being followed. Maybe it just feels different because we're not being followed now."

I would have liked that better without the *maybe*.

The establishment sold both coffee and tea, but the coffee was burnt and the tea smelled fresh and excellent. I drank the coffee. The six of us scrunched uncomfortably around two high round red tables we'd pulled together, but the place did meet our other needs: There were no other customers in our immediate vicinity, the acoustics were horrible, and we had a clear view of an empty street. I was also at least eighty percent convinced that the expressionless young Asian man running the joint really did have limited English skills. We spoke quietly anyhow. It didn't take long to realize that we needed more information before we could even figure out how to get more information.

I finally managed to get Keeley on the phone, though he wasn't happy when he found out that I was requesting further data rather than providing some. "You seem to be under the impression that I am your secretary."

"Don't be ridiculous," I said. "I'm always polite to secretaries." I am too. Any halfway intelligent person who's ever spent any time researching or investigating anything develops that habit pretty damned quick. After a little bit more back-and-forth of that nature, Keeley sent me a list of the high school graduates that the Templars had managed to eliminate as potential suspects so far. They were working fast. "You'd think I was asking him to invest in a Ponzi scheme," I grumbled as I prepared to forward the list to the others. It took a little longer for me and my flip phone than it would have the average modern citizen.

"He's under a lot of stress." Sig was feeling charitable for some reason. "And Simon's assistants do have a way of dying horribly."

"You're right," I replied. "There's hope."

She punched me in the arm lightly. "That's not what I meant."

I finally managed to send the text, and everyone got their phones out and looked over the lists that Keeley had sent me while we waited for our dumplings to cook.

"It looks like one out of ten of the band members have died before the age of fifty," Kevin noted. "Isn't that number a little high for normal people?"

Molly paused to blow on her broth. "I'm not sure the people in my high school band would have counted as normal. And proud of it, too."

"Yeah, what do you mean by *normal*?" Choo asked. "White people? Asian people? Middle-class people?"

Kevin sounded mildly offended when he said, "I mean people who aren't freaks like us. But statistically, I think it holds up across the board. The last time I took a social studies class, the average life expectancy for an American black male was seventy-one years of age. The life expectancy of a white male was seven years longer. And women tended to live longer than males no matter what their ethnicity."

"One of the rare cases of social justice," Sig interjected.

Kevin looked at her and added, "Asian-American females had the best life expectancy of anyone in the US."

I was too tired to dwell on all the weird friction and subtexts. "Okay, so unless somebody knows the average life expectancy of high school band members on the Lower East Side, could we just assume that what we have here is a pretty high number of deaths?"

"We should check out all of the dead people's obits," Sig said.

Choo nodded. "I get you. Some of 'em might have meant something to Reader X, and people who mean something to this dude have been getting the short end of the stick."

"More like the sharp end," I said. "Those texts we read made it sound like Anna Hogan spent a lot of time coaching our guy to hide his tracks. If he wasn't good at it, Simon would have found him by now. I'll bet you whatever you want that some of those names on the dead list died because they knew our guy in the present, and they died in the last year."

Molly spoke up in a brisk, cheery voice: "Or maybe we'll get a text in five minutes saying someone found Reader X and this is all over."

I studied her for a moment. That voice had sounded forced, and Molly didn't usually sound fake. She hadn't been acting entirely present since freezing in the Spanish room back at the high school. Not that my nerves weren't a little tight too. "Sure," I said.

Molly stuck her tongue out at me. "Pessimist."

"Realist," I corrected.

"I can remember when realists didn't talk about magic books and monsters," Choo said. "Man, I miss that time."

"Maybe I'm a surrealist." The kid at the counter gave me a nod that seemed surly from the sheer lack of being anything else, and Choo and I got up to get the dumplings. Sig always does the actual looking on lookout duty because she has the best eyesight, and in this case, it paid off. She spotted something through the window and said, "Trouble."

Three large humanoid shapes were shuffling down the middle

of the dark street toward us. I couldn't make out their features, but they looked to be somewhere around twelve to fifteen feet tall. A blue Ford Escalade passed the restaurant and drove down the street, and bizarrely, the car slowed and carefully made its way to the left, taking its time while it navigated around one of the monsters as if edging past roadkill. The Pax Arcana at work again. The couple inside the car were probably still talking about the merits of whatever place they were coming from, or arguing about a TV show, or complaining about their jobs, or discussing friends who were going to break up, hook up, or screw up.

The monstrous form paused and looked down at the car invading its space the same way I would look at a tumbleweed or a dog that didn't smell unfriendly, but it didn't otherwise react, and I got a better look at it in the car's headlights. The thing was basically human except in scale, but its skin was a greenish grey and its clothes were a hodgepodge of several outfits. The thing's feet and legs were bare, and a pair of normal-sized grey sweatpants were tied around its waist like a loincloth. Its torso was covered by three different T-shirts, although I couldn't tell if they were sewn together or just melded, and the sleeve covering its massive right arm was made out of a medium-sized tan hoody, the hood flapping loosely, the metal seam of a zipper glinting in the headlights. Then the car went past.

Sig began moving with purpose toward the exit. She had a lot of pent-up frustration to take out on something. "Let's go."

Worked for me. The guy behind the counter probably wouldn't even notice anything as long as the fighting didn't get near him, and even if he did, I kind of doubted he would try to contact the police. I handed Molly several white, greasy bags as I went past, speaking over my shoulder and trying to sound offhand: "Don't drop the dumplings."

"That better not be a metaphor!" she called after me, her

voice only a little shaky. I was already out the door, and I could hear the others coming close behind me. Kasia joined Sig and me, walking on my other side, and Kevin trailed us. Choo moved toward the back of his van while Molly headed for the driver's door.

I could smell the shapes coming toward us now. We had crossed a bridge to get to the area, and these things had the distinct smell of fetid mud and a slight tang of salt permeating the odor of unwashed... something. It was human flesh, but somehow the scent was more intense than usual. I was pretty sure they had come from under the bridge. Trolls, I suppose. More specifically, trolls cobbled together from the flesh and garments of several human bodies.

Sig kicked the base of a speed limit sign to loosen the pavement's hold over it, then pulled the metal signpost out of the ground. It sounded like rock being shredded with the world's toughest cheese grater. As if the noise were a signal, the three trolls began picking up speed, lumbering toward us with strides that covered a lot of ground.

Kasia moved to put a parked grey Volkswagen Passat between her and the foremost troll, aiming her pistol carefully and firing three rounds into its huge, misshapen face. She shot out at least one of those bulbous eyes, and the other eye must have been blinded by sprays of blood and a loose flap of flesh, but the troll put a large forearm over its face and kept coming. Kasia jumped onto the trunk of the Passat, then ran over the top of the car before the troll could push the vehicle aside. She leaped toward the troll's head in a front kick, but if she was counting on the troll's impeded vision to make it helpless, she miscalculated. It reacted to the sound of her feet denting nearby metal and swung its long, heavily muscled arm outward, smashing Kasia out of the air like it was aiming for the stands. I was focused on my own problems, but I heard bones crack, and when Kasia's body hit concrete, it sounded like it was a long ways off in the darkness.

Sig ripped the flat, painted sheet metal off her signpost and tossed the small square aside like a Frisbee. She caught the advance of the troll charging her by thrusting the signpost up under its breastbone. The troll impaled itself but kept moving down and forward. Large grey-green hands with fingers the size of bratwursts grabbed Sig's shoulders as the troll forced itself down the length of the sign and over her. Sig anchored the bottom of the sign post against the ground like a pike and dropped to her back, curling her legs up to get her feet between herself and the descending mass, her body scrunching up like an accordion.

I saw the problem when I feinted right and darted left as soon as my troll committed itself to a lunge that its own gigantic mass wouldn't let it pull out of. My shoulders were roughly at the level of the thing's hips, and as I passed the troll's left leg, I barely had to bend to slash an Achilles tendon with my knife. One Achilles tendon. The thing had several. I could see them pulled taut beneath its skin, cables straining beneath a sheet of leathery lime flesh.

These things really were multiple bodies hastily crammed into one organism. Sig had probably stabbed her troll through its heart, but if what I was seeing was any indication, it might have several. Likewise, Kasia had probably put a bullet in her troll's brain, but only one of them.

It took my troll longer than me to halt and change directions, the same way it takes a truck longer than a car to hit the brakes. By the time it lurched to a slightly off-balance stop, I was already charging it from behind, catching its rear end with my shoulder while it was still leaning forward and teetering on the balls of its feet. The troll went sprawling, and I ran down its descending back, hacking with my knife and severing at least one spinal cord in the deep valley between its shoulder blades and the base of its neck. When the troll tilted and lifted its right arm to throw me off, it was a relatively weak gesture, but "relatively" means that I only went rolling six feet to the side instead of twelve.

I came to a crouch and was almost flattened by the troll that Sig had finally managed to kick off her. I slammed my knife into an eardrum the size of a mouse hole, but it was pure reflex. I had to throw myself backward in an ungainly sprawl to avoid getting grabbed.

At least the troll that had knocked Kasia aside wasn't jumping in to stomp me to death. Kevin had turned the damn thing into a candelabra. The monster's hands, head, and crotch were on fire, and Kevin was dancing back and waving his burning beechwood cane while the thing stampeded blindly around him. Some twenty yards away, Choo was firing paintballs full of gasoline at the troll to fuel the fire. There were several bigger guns lying in the back of the van that he could have chosen, but Choo wasn't about to go spraying rounds into open civilization in the dark. He didn't have to. When all of the tiny streams of gasoline leaking down the troll's body connected and made contact with flame, the thing went up in a funeral pyre.

I had made some smartass crack while Choo was patiently using a hypodermic needle to alternately drain and fill paintballs with gasoline slightly watered down with holy water. I couldn't remember what I had said exactly, but I was pretty sure Choo was going to remind me later.

Sig's troll quit groping backward and sat up, and Sig stepped forward and swung the gore-covered signpost that was still in her fists two-handed, smacking her improvised club off his skull. The troll fell back. Sig did not. Her next swing was downward, still aimed at the troll's head. However many brains it had, they were all going to get sloshed around and scrambled until it passed out.

My troll was propping itself up on one arm and dragging itself to its feet to face me when Kasia leaped onto its back from behind. I could tell she was hurt—her expression was as much agony as anger—but her fangs were bared and she was tearing at the troll's throat like a wolverine while she held on. Only one of the troll's arms was working, and the thing was visibly weakening while blood spurted from its neck, a leak in a very large water hose with more than one pump. The troll went back down to its knees and never stood up again.

Kevin and Choo's troll was still and imitating a roasted marshmallow. When I looked at Sig, her troll was lying flat on the ground, and she was trying to tear its head off by using the signpost as a crowbar. I felt kind of redundant, but that was okay. I could get used to it.

The real problem was that our current van didn't have enough room in the back for transporting the bodies. I began to walk away from the carnage, looking for a manhole lid or a Dumpster, any place where we could stash the corpses until the Templars could send a cleanup crew along. Molly had started the van and turned it around by this point, probably so that she could use it to ram one of the trolls if needed, and she was sticking her head out of the driver's window. "Is everything okay?" she called out.

"We're all good," I said.

"Speak for yourself," Molly told me. "I think I dropped some dumplings."

∾29∾

PETER PANIC

All of us had at least one change of clothes and basic medical supplies in the van except for Kevin, and he didn't need either. Given our last experiment with whether or not we were being tracked, we went back to the bridge we'd crossed, and I climbed down an embankment and quickly buried the gold I'd taken from the high school with a loose layer of dirt just in case that was how those trolls had found us. It was, in fact, the same area where the trolls had come from. There were homemade fishing lines dangling over the riverbank and warm embers and charcoal grey sticks from a campfire. Homemade mattresses had been dragged high up the concrete slope of the bridge foundation to hide them from overhead passersby. The men had probably formed a rough community to protect themselves against the kind of shitheads who like to go bum-hunting for fun, hiding the kips where they kept precious items they couldn't carry on their person. Not much of a life, maybe, by some criteria, but it had been theirs, and whatever had changed them against their will was evil by any definition.

This Book of Am was a kind of magical life rape. No God,

assuming there was a God, who allowed so much suffering for the sake of free will would have endorsed it. It was just another case of men trying to assume Godlike power when they were nowhere near Godlike enough to handle it, not much different from cloning or artificial intelligence or nuclear missiles or bio-plagues except in degree.

When we were done, we drove until we found an automated car-cleaning center. The place was a series of big red drive-through boxes that featured coin-operated vacuums and water hoses. More importantly, it was brightly lit and deserted.

I wanted to start checking those obits; I could feel the need to make some kind of progress pressing against the backs of my eyeballs, but it was important to make sure we weren't being tracked too, even if our race with time was turning into a bumper car ride. We were hunting a man with the power of a god, small g, and if he knew exactly when and where we were coming, there were only two possible outcomes. We would never find him, or he would find us.

Accordingly, Choo was going over the van with some fairly sophisticated anti-surveillance equipment. Kevin was doing some wards. I was smelling everyone. Molly was blessing everyone and praying. And Sig and Kasia were scanning the sky and surrounding distances with eyes that could see long distances and infrared heat sources respectively. We had taken the batteries out of all our phones except a fresh burner that Choo had bought that afternoon, and the only people who had its number were Sarah and Ben and Simon; it didn't seem likely that a magic-type loner was tracking us that way, anyhow. Saying the situation was a conundrum didn't quite cover it. Saying it was a stick of dynamite with a lit fuse jammed up our collective rear end might be a little more on point, and my group was having trouble finding its own ass with its own hands.

I was still thinking about that when I was smelling Molly, and as I crouched down and put my nose near her knees beneath the bright lot lights, I saw something that hit me like a plunge into icy water.

Molly didn't have a shadow.

I screamed, and my knife was in my hands before my lunge was finished, plunging under her sternum and up.

No, of course it wasn't. What am I, insane?

"Molly," I whispered. "You don't have a shadow."

"What?" She sounded dazed. "What does that mean?"

"I don't know." I took her hand. "But I swear I'll find out."

Yeah, right. Like I'd really do that, either. I guess I just don't have the drama gene. What I did was force myself to keep going through the motions of smelling her even while my movements felt stiff and my skin went cold. I was going to keep doing it until my brain started working again.

There were scent traces of the green peppers Molly had put in her omelet that morning where they had sweated out and dried on her skin.

"It's not my fault if I need a shower," she said.

"I'm not here to judge your life choices," I heard myself saying. Then I forced myself to stand up and start walking toward Sig, who was the farthest away. I needed time to think. I wasn't going to do or say anything until I had some clue about what the right thing to do or say was. Kasia would hear any words I spoke, and God only knew how she or Simon and the knights would react if they found out.

Training kicked in. Calm down. Keep walking. Work the problem. I could always kill Molly (I wasn't going to kill Molly!) later. This was too important to get wrong.

I wasn't aware of any shapechangers whose scent would match Molly down to the meals she'd been digesting all day, and it seemed unlikely that any had taken her place before we even got to New York. There are certain kinds of ghosts and undead that don't cast a shadow, but there was no way that Molly had been possessed by one of them. For one thing, her holy mojo would have fried any ghost who tried it. It would be like a bug trying to infiltrate a bug zapper. For another, Sig would have picked up on any ghost activity even if a spirit had succeeded.

Molly usually repelled any curses that came her way, too.

What did that leave?

The only other thing weird about Molly was that she'd been acting maybe just a little distant or distracted ever since the high school, where she'd frozen up in the Spanish classroom for a minute. Frozen in that room where shadows were animating. And now her shadow was missing.

Okay.

Work the problem. I didn't have a choice. It was the only thing keeping the ball of panic and anger that was welling up in my chest from bursting up out of my throat. What else did I know? We were being spied on or tracked. Molly's shadow was missing. Assume those two things were related. The last time magic had been used to track us, the person doing it had transformed ravens into something out of an old fairy tale. Could the same person have transformed Molly's shadow into something else? Were there any monsters from old fairy tales or fables that stole people's shadows?

Peter Pan lost his shadow. Okay, that probably wasn't helpful.

What if this was something out of those role-playing game books? I wouldn't have a clue. Why hadn't I taken a few hours to memorize that Nightcrawlers' Guide?! No, dammit, forget that. I hadn't had a few hours, and it was too late and not helpful. Focus on the known and the doable. What was that?

Fairy tales about people losing shadows. There was the one about the man who sold his shadow to the devil, but that didn't really apply here either. Molly would never sell her shadow, much less to the devil. And in that story, everyone had started irrationally hating the man until his life became unbearable, and nobody was reacting that way toward Molly.

And they weren't going to, either.

There was that fairy tale by Hans Christian Anderson about a man whose shadow separated from him and grew a life of its own. The man in that story had been wise and kind and virtuous. It was even sort of implied that the reason the shadow had separated was that the man was too good for this world, that he'd been denying his darker side, and the shadow got impatient and left to get its needs fulfilled.

Molly might be vulnerable to something like that. If the parameters of that kind of magic included finding someone who was almost too virtuous, Molly would be the one from our group who most fit that criteria. But how did the rest of the fairy tale go? How did that fit us being spied on?

The shadow in the story had gone off and lived its own life, and the man had gotten weaker and poorer and sicklier while the shadow got richer and stronger and more substantial. Later, the shadow appeared before the man and made an offer. The shadow would pay for the man's medical care if the man would follow the shadow around and be the shadow's servant instead of the other way around. The man reluctantly agreed, and events predictably went downhill from there. The shadow continued to get stronger and more influential, and the man got weaker and more socially ostracized. The evil shadow eventually got engaged to a rich princess, and by the time the alarmed man tried to tell the world the truth, he was so physically and mentally deteriorated that he was unrecognizable. The shadow had its original owner locked up and then executed.

The fable was a riff on a lot of Russian and Germanic and Celtic stories about doubles who spring into existence and try to kill the original person who inspired them. It was also a cynical parable about how the wicked prosper and the good get screwed.

Who cared?!? Focus! Did the shadow in the story know what the man was doing? Could it spy on the man through some kind of psychic link? That had never been spelled out one way or the other, but it had at least been implied. The shadow never had a problem finding the man, and it always seemed to be one step ahead of him and know what he was thinking.

Was some shadow version of Molly working for the enemy to destroy us now? And how the hell did this Reader X even know we existed? Again, how was he going from pinballing between seemingly random incidents pulled from fantasy war games and his own psyche to creating magical spies with agency from old fables and legends? If it wasn't random, I couldn't see the connection.

Focus. What did I know? It seemed highly likely that someone was using Molly as a spy or a tracking device, either because she'd been replaced by something that cast no shadow, or because some version of her shadow was being used like a psychic tuning fork. And if someone was looking through Molly's eyes or listening through Molly's ears, I could leverage that to get Kasia and Simon to cooperate and not kill Molly by convincing them that this was a chance to feed our unseen enemy disinformation. I'd gotten Simon to go along with the Round Table stratagem by putting it in terms of feints and ploys. Simon lived for that kind of thing.

That meant I couldn't let Molly know what was going on, or let the thing behind her know I knew.

But who could help Molly while I stalled everyone else? Probably not a priest. If this was a matter of holiness, Molly wouldn't have gotten targeted in the first place. A cunning person, then. And the most competent one that I trusted was Sarah.

"John?"

I'd been thinking so intently that I hadn't realized I was drifting into Sig's orbit. But that was okay. By the time I reached her, I would know what to say to Sig and the scary-ass dhampir byatch who would be listening in.

I would.

Yep. Any second now.

∽30∾

AND FOR MY NEXT TRICK,
I WILL PULL ANOTHER PLAN
OUT OF MY ASS

Three rushed and half-coherent phone calls later, to Sarah White, Ben Lafontaine, and Simon Travers respectively, and everyone but Kevin was back in the van and headed for Central Park. The knights had increased their presence there, and the park was still closed for a few hours. It seemed like as good a place as any to have my worst fears blow up in my face.

I had told everyone that Sarah White wanted to meet me there because she'd found someone who could help, which was close enough to the truth that I wasn't likely to trip over any glaring contradictions.

"Did Sarah say what was so important?" Molly wondered from where she was sitting alone in the middle.

"She says she thinks she's figured out a way to locate Reader X." It was weird, dangling bait for Reader X while talking to Molly. "But she wouldn't get too specific over the phone."

"Of course not." Sig lifted her own head and kissed my

cheek. "Then we might know what we're doing. But it must be dangerous or she wouldn't have sent Kevin away." She didn't quite succeed in keeping it light. Sig had been a bit pale ever since I'd told her what was going on.

"I always know what I am doing," Kasia said from the front of the van. She seemed unruffled by what she'd overheard, though she'd spent some time arguing with me at a frequency no one with normal hearing could pick up on. "The only times I have had this kind of chaos and confusion in my life were when I was working with you, Sigourney. You seem to breed it."

What the hell was Kasia doing? Was she venting her pent-up hostility, or was she trying to take Sig's mind off Molly before she gave away that something was up, or was Kasia giving whoever might be watching through Molly a show to keep them distracted? That was the sort of thing I would normally do if I weren't a little distracted myself. I had a sudden memory of Kasia's index finger stabbing the dashboard repeatedly while she said, "Poke, poke, poke."

Sig took it reasonably well, maybe because she had more important things than Kasia on her mind. "I was at the lowest point in my life and caught between two control freaks back then," she replied. "Those old times got really old. That's why I don't appreciate you showing up and trying to drag me back into them."

Choo, who did not have enhanced hearing and was perforce clueless, turned on the radio. Some slickly produced dance song about working it cranked out of the speakers. "New York has more radio stations than Clayburg. We ought to listen to them while we got the chance."

Kasia turned the volume down. "Appreciating things never was your strong suit, Sigourney. I know someone who saved your life. He helped you stop drinking. He trained you and gave you a purpose. And you killed him."

The van went silent. Sig took her head off my shoulder and looked away into the warm, dark night through the window on her left. For a moment, it was like we were in a Tracy Chapman song. Then Sig began saying emotional things in an emotionless voice. "I wish I *had* been the one to kill Stanislav."

"You might as well have been. You are sleeping with the man who killed him," Kasia said. "And he killed Stanislav because of you. Betrayal does not go much deeper than that."

"Are we there yet?" I asked plaintively.

Sig and Kasia didn't seem to hear anyone but each other. "Stanislav betrayed me first," Sig said. "I stayed with him a lot longer than I should have because he convinced me that it was the *loyal* thing to do. I was just too scared to see what was going on."

Kasia flickered a glance over her shoulder at us. I thought about Kasia's statement that she and Stanislav had cheated on Sig, but Sig and I hadn't had time to talk about that, and I sure as hell wasn't going to set off that string of firecrackers when we had bigger explosions to worry about.

On the other hand, if Kasia really was trying to keep us all distracted from thinking about what was going on with Molly too much, she was maybe doing too good a job.

"A part of me always felt like the new person I was trying to be was a fake." Sig went on in that same bleak monotone. "Sometimes, I still feel that way. Like I'm really the person you're trying to make me feel like right now."

If she brought up one more person and one more verb tense, I was going to get confused, but Sig restrained herself. "I thought Stanislav really knew me. The real me. I thought if he hated me, I must be somebody who deserved it. He had to actually shoot me full of drugs and leave me and my friends as fang candy for vampires for me to admit how messed-up that was."

"That was how we found you in the first place." Kasia sounded thoughtful.

"That's what Stanislav said." Some real emotion crept back into Sig's voice. "Since I didn't appreciate all he'd done for me, he decided to take it all away and leave me back at square one again."

"That does sound like him." Kasia's voice seemed to hold a certain grudging admiration.

"He betrayed you too, didn't he?" Sig asked. "I didn't see it at the time. All I could see was what a bitch you were."

"Everyone betrays everyone sooner or later." Which meant Kasia didn't want to talk about herself. "We just have to decide when such things are forgivable and when they demand vengeance."

"Okay, way to clear the air, everybody," I said briskly. "But maybe you two should try talking to each other using cute hand puppets."

Molly reached back around her seat and patted my knee. Was it odd that she hadn't tried to intermediate? It was hard not to overthink everything about her.

"Why did you really come to the US, Kasia?" Sig asked. "What do you want from me?"

"I did not expect Stanislav's death to make me feel sad, but it did," Kasia said. "I do not like feeling sad. When the kresniks asked me to come here because one of them had seen us in a vision, it seemed like fate in more ways than one."

"What do you want from me?" Sig repeated.

"I do not have an evil plan," Kasia said. "I wanted to observe you for a time and satisfy my curiosity. If you want to know the truth, I did not expect your new lover to spot me."

"I didn't expect him to find me, either." For just a moment, Sig's voice warmed.

Kasia's voice grew chillier in response. "Be that as it may, Stanislav and I had a bond. I did not like him at the end, and I could not work with him. But there was a time when he saved me the same way he saved you. I may owe the man he used to be some gesture."

"Even if it's an empty one?" Molly asked.

Kasia gave an eloquent shrug. At least she didn't trot out one of her stock responses about all gestures being empty.

I kind of understood. Stanislav had been Kasia's family. I've never actually had a family myself, but I know that for some people, it goes deeper than like or dislike. Maybe even deeper than love or hate. The knights had been my closest thing to a family, and I still had ties to them even if I fought them, even if there was no logical reason behind the feeling.

Central Park covers about nine hundred acres, and it wasn't difficult to find an off-avenue entrance with low traffic and some tree cover. We had three beings with greater-than-human strength in the van—even if that strength was only slightly greater in my case—and we were able to manually lift the van sideways over a two-and-a-half-foot-tall whitewashed retaining wall. The park is mostly flat terrain, and in theory, the van would be able to move over and through the wooded area as long as it avoided the densest patches. Simon could have easily had some of his people let us through an avenue entrance, but I didn't want whoever might be listening through Molly to know how much the knights were involved.

Something began to manifest on the avenue behind us. I

don't know how I knew it, but the knowledge was bristling in my scalp. I looked, but the only unusual thing I saw was a small dog with no sign of an owner. It was prancing hurriedly down the sidewalk from the north. Then a large dog on the opposite side of the street appeared, trailing a leash and moving toward us from the south. Across the way, the silhouettes of two dogs moving through a side alley became visible.

I couldn't immediately think of any fairy tales where there was some kind of Pied Piper for dogs. I also still didn't really understand how this Reader X thing worked. Was it the book or Reader X causing these things to happen, or some kind of hive mind between the two of them? Was Reader X still fever-ishly researching John Dee and writing his thoughts down while some disembodied presence became more and more real, acting without his knowledge? And if Molly's shadow really was somewhere else, taking on substance and being used to keep tabs on us, who was using it? How were the shadow and its summoner communicating?

I didn't actually articulate all that in my head; the thoughts flitted just beneath the surface of my mind like minnows dart-ing beneath a fast moving stream. The thoughts probably would have been forgotten, except one of them suddenly gal-vanized and jolted me hard. The idea of Reader X feverishly researching John Dee. The guy had to be reading a lot of John Dee if he was trying to finish Dee's book, and not many people outside of academics and occultists did. New York had some of the best libraries in the world, and I hadn't even thought of looking to see who was checking out John Dee–related works that you couldn't find on the Internet. For that matter, while I was trying to research the School of Night, I'd had to jump through some hoops to join the Folger Library in Washing-ton DC. The Folger Library was one of the best sources of historical documents from the Elizabethan era in the United States, so Reader X had probably had to become a member. Surely, Simon or one of the kajillion knights he supposedly had working this thing had covered that angle? Except Simon hadn't researched the School of Night personally—he'd had other people doing it for him—so he might not know about the Folger. And book researchers think differently from skip tracers and bounty hunters, and Simon wasn't telling all of his left tentacles what his right tentacles were doing. Why the hell had this idea waited to occur to me until a moment when there was absolutely nothing I could do about it?

We got in the van and drove through the park, and maybe a hundred yards in, I glanced over while Choo made a turn. To the left, I caught a glimpse through the trees, a silhouette briefly highlighted by a street lamp as it jumped over the retaining wall. Whatever the thing was, it was bigger than any of the dogs I had seen. I remembered how the trolls we'd fought had apparently been made out of the merged bodies of vagrants. Were those dogs I'd spotted meeting and converging into some rough beast? Whatever the being was, it still had four legs, but it was as high to the ground as a horse, and it didn't have a long arching neck, either.

I'd been hoping to put a little distance between us and whatever magic was brewing back on that street, but I returned the cell phone's battery and tried to text Simon, both to warn him of what I'd seen and tell him about the library angle. I'd already told him to have knights check the obits from Randy Prutko's high school classes, but the library thing might be useful too, and I didn't want it to go unexplored if I died. But of course, the phone wasn't working. I didn't say anything to the others. No, let's be honest here: I didn't say anything to Molly. One more item on the to-do list.

Make time to memorize the contents of those Nightcrawlers'
   Guild books.
Tell Simon about the Folger Library connection.
Get Molly's shadow back where it belonged.
Kill Reader X.
Change underwear.

If someone was conjuring up spies and messing with my
friends just to keep me too busy to get my act together, they
were doing a pretty good job of it. But if I'd made a mistake, it
was too late to do anything but try to survive it.

∾31∾

STUCK IN PARK

I know Central Park pretty well. I try to avoid New York City whenever possible, but I also try to go to Central Park when avoiding New York City proves impossible. Being in the big city always makes me a bit crowd-crazy, and going to the park helps. It's like breathing through a straw when you're submerged underwater. Looked at one way, those little breaths aren't much. Looked at another way, they're everything.

So, I navigated from the back of the van and we found our way to a paved trail fairly quickly. I was taking us to a small stone bridge called the Ramble Arch, and we parked the van before we got there. It was dark and leaves were thick on the trees and the smell of wolf was in the air. Lots of wolves, but hopefully that just meant that Ben had come through.

We had chosen the Ramble Arch because it was in the park's bird-watching territory and easy to find, a tiny bridge wedged tightly between the cleft of two rock outcrops. The Ramble Arch was made of stone, maybe fifteen feet high and not very wide. Only two people could stand beside each other on the top and still maintain some swinging distance. As for the *arch* part of the name, it came from the narrow domed opening beneath the rock foundation of the bridge itself, a walkway for hikers on a lower trail. The tunnel was so skinny that adults couldn't stand in it and fully stretch their arms all the way out.

In other words, the Ramble Arch was hidden from view and easy to defend: high enough to protect from most ground creatures, narrow enough to guard against hordes, and low enough that we could jump down and cram into the narrow passageway below if any flying monkeys showed up. Hopefully, whatever was coming after us wouldn't get past Simon and Ben's forces, but if it did, I wanted to have some options.

For once, we had our favorite crowd-inappropriate weapons with us. My katana was strapped to a quiver of arrows slung over my shoulder. I'd swapped out my short sword for a black composite longbow that I know how to use but rarely do. Sig was using the butt of her favorite spear like a walking stick, and a custom-designed sword with a weighted tip was sheathed between her shoulder blades. Choo had a bandolier of sheathed clips he was wearing across his chest and back. He was carrying a highly illegal assault rifle with a sound suppressor that he swore halfway worked. A working crossbow mount had been welded to the rifle's barrel, and a hip sheath with six quarrels was on Choo's left side. The quarrels were odd-looking—they had sharp points, but beneath the metal tips were white plastic cylinders wrapped around the shaft. Kasia had both of her Japanese swords crossed over her back and pistols on each hip, with knives on the outside of her boots. Molly had her hands in her pockets.

Sarah White came into smell before she came into view, and unfortunately, human language doesn't have a comfortable way of expressing that. Sarah occasionally left her bakery, but her bakery never entirely left her; its scents were melded into her skin, a buttery musk of vanilla and honey and cinnamon. Sarah also smelled scared, but she didn't show it while she waited in the middle of the bridge, dressed in a white summer dress and holding her staff. With her were four people who smelled like half-elves and a tall Latina woman in a yellow tank top and tight shorts. The Latina began to look more like a girl as I got closer, maybe in her midteens despite her long-legged height. She had a lot of thick black hair going on, and her two long braids had been tied off with white ribbons whose ends made bunny ears. Black eyes and a line of a mouth had been drawn on the ribbons' knotted bodies to make bunny faces. I have no idea why. Bunny Girl smelled entirely human, but the smile on her face was more elfin than the grim expressions of the half-fae around her.

The half-fae, two males and two females, were dressed somewhat formally in light dresses and leisure suits, though their shoes were only as fashionable as shoes that don't preclude running can be. The men wore rich, bright-colored dress shirts beneath jackets without vests. Like me, the half-elves had longbows and swords, but I could tell from the way the men's zippers were tugged upward to the left or right that small, heavy objects were holstered at their backs. It's almost impossible to keep pants' zippers from revealing that kind of thing—they're right there around the center of gravity.

Three of the fae had the look of professionally violent people. Despite their elegance, their fingernails were blunt, their jewelry limited to the occasional non-dangling earring, their eyes fully engaged, and their hair barely long enough to cover the tips of their ears. They were poised on the balls of their feet rather than just poised. Their leader was the exception. His long red hair was unbound and went past his shoulders, and his posture was languid. I knew him, a gambler and professional pleasure-seeker named Aubrey Dunne. We weren't exactly friends, but we weren't strangers, and we weren't enemies.

It was entirely like Aubrey to step forward before Sarah could say anything. "Hello, Mark. Or I suppose I should call you John now. John Charming, indeed."

I ignored him and addressed Sarah. "Is this a neon red enema tango situation?"

She looked at me as if I was insane for a moment, then her expression cleared as she remembered our conversation earlier that morning. Had it really been just that morning? I felt a lot older. "No, we invited them here."

"Good," Sig said beside me. "I'd almost regret having to kill Aubrey."

"Almost?" Aubrey was only playing at being offended. Very little got through Aubrey's pleasure in being Aubrey.

"Guests should wait their turn, Aubrey." Sarah gestured to the girl she had brought along. "This is the person I told you about, the Fisher King of New York City."

The girl mock-curtsied, although I think that was our job, technically. "If *majesty* seems awkward, you may call me Marisol." She didn't sound Latina at all. Her only accent was that precisely clipped, over-enunciated, weird, grand, non-regional, pseudo-British manner of speaking that Americans use when they're trying to imitate classically trained stage actors. Her theatrical air said she was half-goofing, but maybe only half.

"New York City? Wouldn't that make you a fisher mayor?" I wondered.

The girl made a face and her accent took on a Brooklyn undertone. "Oh, gawd, I hope not."

Just a little background here: A Fisher King is a supernatural and/or holy being who both reflects and is a reflection of the land he or she lives in. If the Fisher King gets a venereal disease, crops wither. If the Fisher King is happy, the day is sunny and a feeling of contentment lingers in the air. Or something like that. The most famous stories of a Fisher King are in legends of King Arthur and the Holy Grail. By some accounts, the Fisher King was King Arthur himself, and the Holy Grail was the only hope of healing Arthur of a mysterious illness. By curing King Arthur, his knights hoped to heal all Britain, which had a bad case of the Dark Ages.

In other stories, the Fisher King is a lame old beggar who is mystically attuned to his country. These accounts are largely influenced by the old tales of gods walking the earth disguised as humble folk, particularly Odin. In reality, "Fisher Kings" are psychics who are so powerful that they can't help becoming mentally and emotionally attuned to whatever area they're living in. There isn't just one per country like in the old tales, and I don't know if that's because populations were a lot smaller back then or if the old tales were just full of it. What matters is that when a Fisher King has a bad dream, native residents around Fisher Kings start having bad dreams too. When lots of locals die in a fire, a Fisher King feels hot and flushed and gets a fever. Basically, Fisher Kings can't help being living, breathing police scanners on crack. I could see why Sarah had thought one might be useful; in fact, the speed with which she'd set up this meeting suggested that the reason Sarah hadn't been around was that she'd been busy tracking this girl down because of her psychosynonymous connection to NYC.

And yes, I just made the word *psychosynonymous* up.

"Seriously, though, would you prefer to be called a fisher queen?" Sig asked curiously.

"I would not." Again, the girl made it sound like a regal proclamation, but it was so over the top that I hoped she was funning. Marisol seemed hungry for attention but not adept at handling it; it's not an uncommon attitude among intelligent young people who have realized that they're never going to fit in and have decided to embrace it. "At least most people have heard of a Fisher King. *Fisher Queen* makes me think of a frozen food brand."

"Marisol is a cosplayer in her spare time," Sarah said as if that explained everything. Maybe it did.

Marisol gestured grandly toward the elves. "Our companions are Aubrey Dunne, Caitlin Flint, Alannah Brady, and Darian of no last name. And you, sirrah, would be the knight Sarah has been telling me about?"

I almost said *I wouldst*, but, you know, Molly. Missing shadows. Imminent attacks. Nuclear devices. Still, our world has rules. "I'm John Charming. This lovely battle goddess is Sig Norresdotter. The dhampir goes by Kasia, the grumpy-looking man with the weird-looking rifle is Choo, and Molly Newman is our holy person."

Marisol glowered at us with that same overly dramatic air that was impossible to take entirely seriously. "I am not pleased to meet you. This is one highly messed-up situation."

"It really is," Sig agreed. "Can you help us with it?"

Something calculating and ruthless flickered behind those brown eyes. Whatever this girl's story was, she was no stranger to pain and cruelty and pointlessness. I suppose, given what a Fisher King was, there was no way she could be. "I have no choice, and that really pisses me off. But first, my companions have something they would like to say to the knight."

Ticking clocks or no, I couldn't help myself. "I'm not a knight. Maybe knight-ish."

Marisol crossed her arms. "Don't give me that. I can't feel you. And when you looked us over, you had that nasty-ass, knighty *look at me wrong and I'll stab you* attitude."

"It's possible I'm a little tense," I admitted.

"You need to look closer," Sarah told Marisol gently. "We're used to being able to cheat. Don't just look at the little he shows you. Look at what's not there."

Marisol leaned forward and squinted at me owlishly. Then she turned to Sarah. "I don't see what's not there."

Sarah smiled. "Hate."

"Hmmph." But Marisol's expression became a little more thoughtful.

"May I speak now?" Aubrey's bland tone suggested that Marisol really wasn't any kind of royalty and that he was perhaps getting just a tiny bit bored humoring her. Marisol flapped a hand at him, and Aubrey took it as permission. "My mother wanted me to talk to you." Aubrey's mother is a nymph who writes bestselling paranormal romances. She is also a fairly big deal in the New York City half-fae community, or at least one of the half-fae communities. Maybe that's why Aubrey stopped and waited for me to comment.

"She's a lovely woman," I said.

Aubrey gave me the kind of pitying look that only a child whose parent has been complimented can deliver, no matter how old all concerned are. But what he said was: "There's a group of fae who want to go back to the Faerie realm, and they don't plan on getting turned away at the door. They have visions of raising armies of magical beings and charmed human slaves with modern weapons."

I knew a little about the half-fae in question; they couldn't go *back* to the Faerie realm because they had never been to it in the first place. As far as I know, the only fae left stranded on earth when the Fae, capital F, went back home centuries and centuries ago, were the poor half-fae bastards who had been born here. I don't pretend to understand fae attitudes toward racial purity, but I know they're as screwed-up as any other ideas about racial purity. "I've heard of them."

"These idiots have supposedly allied themselves with some secret group of cunning folk who want to tear down the knights," Aubrey said. "And mind you, I understand how that could be inconvenient."

"Maybe just a tad," I allowed.

"But the knights have gone *insane*," Aubrey said. "They're acting as if all fae are involved in this idiocy. Some of us have been brutally beaten. They even held my mother in semi-captivity while they questioned her for two days."

I tried to consider what Aubrey wasn't saying, but it wasn't like we were sitting across from a fireplace, sipping hot toddies at our leisure while we reflected on past loves, philosophical quandaries, and the folly of man. I knew the knights had been looking for the School of Night hard, and knights don't have to worry about search warrants or Miranda rights. It wasn't surprising to hear that they'd been making the lives of a lot of half-elves stressful while they did so. "Okay."

"It is not okay," Aubrey insisted. It was the most serious I'd ever seen him. "It is about as far from okay as possible."

"I meant I'm listening," I said. "I could say *no-kay* if that would make you more comfortable."

"The knights are acting like we're Japanese-American citizens in World War II," Aubrey said. "It's the same kind of paranoid-thug mentality that almost started a war with the werewolves."

Uh-oh. I had that first real inkling of where all this was going, and it was a fissure appearing in concrete. "Aubrey..." I began.

"My mother wants you to talk to them," Aubrey said. "She wants you to tell the Templars that they can't just go around lumping all fae together in one basket."

"Aubrey," I protested. "I have no pull with the knights."

Aubrey raised both eyebrows in that kind of snide pretend-shock that people use to imply that others are being a liar or a fool. "You arranged this meeting, didn't you?"

Shit. I hadn't told Molly that knights were involved, because I didn't want Reader X to wonder about that too much. "There are a lot of knights in the park right now, and I got permission to use it," I said. "That's all."

"That doesn't seem like such a small thing to me." Aubrey threw his hands out in a helpless what-am-I-supposed-to-think gesture. "Not with all of this talk about tension between knights and werewolves building. And you're the one who brokered some kind of peace treaty between the knights and the werewolves in the first place, aren't you?"

There is only a small, no, make that a *microscopic* group of werewolves who know the full story about why and how the largest pack of lycanthropes in North America became the Round Table. In the resulting information vacuum, a lot of rumors have gotten started and distorted. "It's not that simple."

Aubrey sniffed dismissively. "It's not that complicated, either."

"Things seem complicated enough to me," I told him.

"If the werewolves and the Knights Templar do go to war, there are a lot of us who might be tempted to throw our weight behind the werewolves," Aubrey said. "Especially with the knights going around, antagonizing everyone."

I saw what he was saying. The most numerous supernatural species in North America are vampires and werewolves, mostly because birth rates among immortals are low, and vampires and werewolves don't have to give birth to reproduce. But that statistic only counts if you don't consider all of the various fae offshoots that can pass for human as one group. Or if you don't count cunning folk as a species separate from humanity.

Aubrey was suggesting that some half-fae were trying to use the Templars as a common enemy to unite lots of the different supernatural creatures that knights had spent centuries keeping apart.

"Will you get involved or not?" he asked me.

Hell, no. Between Molly and the Round Table and the Book of Am, I was already juggling too many live hand grenades as it was. The world Aubrey wanted me to get even more deeply mired in was a lying, crying, dying kind of a world, lurching backward and forward on the edge of a cliff. No. No, and fuck no. Nyet. Nein. Nahi. Non. Nunca.

"All right," I said a little dazedly. Shit! I could hear the words coming out of my mouth, but I couldn't recall forming them. "I'll see what I can do. No promises."

This new, serious Aubrey accepted that. "In that case, my mother wanted me to tell you something. Something she refused to tell the knights who tried to intimidate her. Consider it an offering of goodwill."

"All right."

"The person trying to rally elves together to take back the Faerie Realm...he's claiming to be a full-blooded fae who stayed behind when the rest of them went back home all those centuries ago. He says it was because he refused to abandon us, his children, to this shithole of a world."

"Doubtful," I said. "Even if he is a full-blooded fae, it's more likely he's a spiteful exile than an idealistic revolutionary."

Aubrey's mouth made a smile his heart couldn't keep. "I said it was a claim."

"Does this individual have a name?"

"He's calling himself Uriel."

I put one hell of a pin in that one. It was more like a harpoon. But we really didn't have time to do much else. At the mention of that name, somewhere behind us, in the direction we'd come from, a wolf howled, followed by the call of another wolf. The distinct muffled sneezes of suppressed gunfire followed, but they came from the other side of the bridge. Whatever was out there, there was more than one of it, and while we'd been talking, things had been entering the park from multiple directions to surround us.

"Oh, dear," Marisol said. She wasn't entirely dropping her act, but she suddenly sounded very young. "There are bad things coming."

~32~

RAGNARUCKUS

An awkward shuffle ensued while our small party worked out how to spread itself out along the bridge. I was really pissed-off that Aubrey had wasted our time before we'd gotten to Molly, but there was no point indulging it. "Can you use that bow, Aubrey?" He'd never struck me as much of a warrior when I'd met him at a kind of supernatural fight club. Aubrey had just been there to get in on the betting.

"All fae can use bows," he said with breezy assurance.

"Sure," I said. "And all Irish people can hold their drink, all Native Americans can track, and all black people can play basketball."

He tried to look earnest. It wasn't an expression that came naturally. "Don't judge us by human standards, John Charming."

Huh. It was the second time someone had hinted that fae had some kind of racial memory that was way more extensive than a human's. Yet another something I wanted to hear more about. But not at the moment. "Then how about you guys guard your side of the bridge, and we'll guard ours." I returned my attention to Marisol and Sarah. "And...Marisol? Maybe you and Molly should stay in the middle."

Marisol clasped her hands and squeezed them together over her heart, beaming. "That's my favorite place to be!"

Yeah, well, she obviously hadn't spent a lot of time in crossfires. I turned and found that Choo and Kasia were already facing outward. The side walls of stacked rock around us weren't uniform, and Choo and Kasia were kneeling by parts of the walls that were particularly high so that the bridge would give them some protection against side attacks. Both of them had their respective firearms pointed out, and Choo was lighting flares from a small pile on the ground and Kasia was throwing them out in all directions, forming a rough perimeter of light. She knew what she was doing. The flares were far enough out that we were still in shadow, hot enough to keep creatures with infrared from being able to see past them clearly, and bright enough to keep anything sketchy from creeping up on us too close. The only drawback was that the flares would draw in creatures from a distance, but then, we hadn't come to the park to hide.

Sig and I got behind Choo and Kasia, looking over opposite sides of the bridge at the trail below. "If anything gets too close, move back behind John and me," Sig whispered. "We'll give you time to switch to short-range weapons."

But we actually had a little more time than we thought. We crouched there in half-darkness for three years. I mean, three minutes. Give or take a lifetime. The live radio show we were listening to was pretty violent. Marisol had moved so that she was behind Molly, crouching in the place where Molly's shadow should have been. From the way Marisol was steadying herself with a hand on the bridge's side wall, her head tilted back, I didn't think this was an accident.

At least one thing was going according to our half-assed plan.

I set my bow flat on the side wall beside me in easy reach. I wanted my hands free to draw my katana if the battle went that way.

It was actually a relief when the danger finally presented itself. It was a wolf, stepping out from the woods onto the paved trail beneath me. The creature froze, sniffing, trying to peer past the visual confusion created by the flares. At first I thought it was a werewolf, that some optical illusion was playing tricks with scale. But it wasn't a werewolf. It was a giant wolf, taller than I was by a good foot and a half, wider than a bear or buffalo.

Another giant wolf appeared on the upper trail, facing Choo and Kasia, just visible at the edge of flare light, followed by the shadow of another. I heard a slight intake of breath from one of the half-fae that suggested they had spotted something on their side of the bridge too.

Giant wolves? Trolls. Giant wolves. Somehow, the back of my mind added those things together and came up with *Fenris wolf.* Maybe realizing that Sig was a Valkyrie had made Reader X start thinking in terms of Norse mythology? Or maybe it was feeling like we were at the death of one age and the birth of another. The Fenris wolf was a sign of Ragnarok, the Norse apocalypse.

But...hey. "There was only one Fenris wolf, you know!" I called out. That's actually a subject of some scholarly debate, but I'd had a weird idea. If obeying book logic was important, and if this stuff was coming out of Reader X's mind...if he could hear me on any level, and if I could create some doubt...well, I wouldn't lose anything trying. "This many shouldn't exist!"

But not all ideas came to something. None of the wolves started fading or winking out.

"Try using logic to convince them that they're vegetarians," Sig stage-whispered.

Choo made a sound that was half-amused and half an admonition to stop fooling around, and then one of the silhouettes facing him on the upper trail charged the bridge. Choo didn't have his weapon set for single bursts—his assault rifle ripped into and around the wolf, some bullets burying themselves, some tearing off bits of hair and flesh, but none to much effect. Thick fur, dense muscle, and lots of motion kept the thing moving forward at an alarming clip. Choo would have been better off with an elephant gun. But then Choo shot a quarrel from his crossbow mount, and something strange happened. The bolt sank into the giant wolf's chest, and there was a muffled explosion. Bits of flesh came flying out of the wolf's mouth. The beast couldn't stop, but it veered off the path, and then the sound of a heavy body falling could be heard.

Choo had rigged up some kind of economy-sized compressed CO_2 dart for his crossbow. The kind deep-sea divers put on spear guns to kill sharks. He must have hit one of those oversized lungs.

I didn't have much chance to think about it. Two more wolves came charging down the upper path like very fast rhinos, and Kasia and Choo both came running back—her handgun was about as useful as a straw shooting paper wads. Sig and I ran forward, me unsheathing my katana, Sig holding her spear two-handed before her like a battering ram.

There was no way I was going to be able to meet my wolf head-on, and no way I could stop it cold, so I charged past the bridge and shoulder-feinted at the wolf as if I were going to leap high and right. The wolf went for it, moving its head to snap at the point where I was headed, and I let gravity take me back down and went left. I took half of the wolf's right paw with me as I went past, unleashing my katana in a sweeping motion.

It was a bit like being a matador, but here's a dirty little secret: Matadors sever muscles in their bulls' necks before every bull fight so that the animals can't swing their heads with a full range of motion. The wolf I was fighting didn't have that problem. Even while it was falling and lunging down, it managed to convulse and whirl around and bring its head back at me, reaching so far so fast that it seemed a bit like cheating. Maybe it had been getting some practice in by licking its own genitals.

My sword was on the wrong side to deal with the jaws coming at my spine, so I had to whirl my body to get out of range and try another swing. My katana removed a fang the size of a trumpet, but my body still hadn't finished charging when I changed direction, and I lost my footing.

I mean, I strategically dived off the path.

Only the thick brush slowing my fall kept me from slicing myself with my sword. The multitude of small branches that I rolled off snapped back, and maybe some of them whipped into the pursuing wolf's mouth and eyes, or maybe adjusting to using three paws slowed it down. Something kept me from losing both of my feet.

Scrambling upright, charging through the brush with the wolf's breath on my neck, I darted behind a midsized tree. The wolf tried to follow me, but its crippled leg and massive body worked against it. I went all the way around the tree while the wolf was still trying to negotiate with physics, and brought my katana into the side of the wolf's neck from behind. The blade sank deep, severing muscle on the way, and I shouldered in and used the katana like a crowbar to rip out the wolf's throat.

The wolf was still moving when it toppled down on its side, but it didn't get up again, and I headed back toward the bridge.

Two other giant wolves appeared on the trail behind me. I passed another dead wolf on the ground as I ran from them, the point of Sig's spear sticking out the back of the corpse's head. There never was an expression that went, "Up your nose with a Norse battle spear," and there's a good reason for that.

My katana was a mess. I didn't have time to wipe it down, and I wasn't going to sheathe it the way it was because I only had one sheath, so I committed blasphemy and threw my katana at the closest wolf. I needed time to grab the haft of the spear. I actually had to plant my foot on the dead wolf's skull and kick off, but I pulled the spear free before the two pursuing wolves were completely upon me. The one closest had the hilt of my katana sticking out of its cheek. I whirled the spear like a bo staff to distract it, and its eyes were on the wrong end when I spun the spear tip under its lunging jaw and slid under the wolf's torso. The wolf instinctively tried to bring its head down to snap at me and wound up driving the spear through its chin and up into its brain.

The wolf also wound up collapsing on me. I'd underestimated how heavy the damn things were. The remaining wolf half-dragged its partner off me, and I was still rolling and trying to reach for either my katana or the spear when giant jaws clamped onto the quiver on my back. I don't know if the quiver saved my spine or made me vulnerable, but the wolf yanked me free and then shook my body around viciously in the air as if it were a dog and I was its new chew toy. Canines do that to snap smaller animals' necks, but the wolf's fangs weren't sunk into my shoulder, and I knew enough to go limp.

The wolf paused when I fell out of the quiver strap and landed on my hands and feet. I managed to lurch upward and slice at its nose with a backswing of my knife. The wolf tottered back awkwardly. It didn't have a choice. There's a reason elephants look like elephants and horses look like horses, and wolves weren't meant to be that high above the ground. I would have taken advantage of the moment, but all of that shaking had done something to my inner ear or cranial fluid, and I fell, sprawling.

It was another moment when I should have died, would have died if left to my own devices. The wolf prepared to leap on me, and a mass of feathers and claws came hurtling down from the night sky. The flock was made of hundreds of birds of different species, few of them nocturnal. Sarah's doing, or maybe Marisol's. The birds swarmed over the wolf like feathered locusts, tearing at its eyes and ripping out tufts of fur. Distracted, the wolf swallowed two to three birds at a time in frantic snaps, but it was blinded, its nose clogged with feathers, its ears filled with bird screams and the flapping of wings. I came back with my katana. Japanese longswords aren't really meant to be used like lances, but over the decades, I've worked out moves that no swordsman fighting traditional human opponents ever considered. It wasn't pretty, but my body weight was behind the blade when it went through the corner of the wolf's left eye and into its brain.

The wolf died, but somehow I wound up several feet away and on my back again. The wolf's skull had headbutted me, probably. I think maybe I passed out for a few seconds. I wasn't hearing properly because of a dull roaring sound in my ear canals. Oxygen deprivation, maybe, or some kind of aftereffect of all that shaking. That was fine. I staggered back up, shoved the quiver back on, flicked a lot of blood and viscera off my katana, then ran stumbling back to the bridge, gaining momentum and coordination as I leaped over a flare. If I'd been thinking clearly, I would have picked up Sig's spear instead, but by the time that occurred to me, I'd gone too far to waste time turning back. A giant wolf was yelping on the lower trail, on fire and running away. Sarah's work. I passed another wolf corpse that had wet flesh dripping out of its ears—Choo must have literally blown its brains out with another of those crossbow quarrels—and right at the bridge, I saw another dead wolf with the tip of a katana sticking through its economy-sized skull. There were also tendons and part of a wrist in the wolf's mouth.

Then I was back on the bridge and my eyes began adjusting to the darkness again. There was a half-fae corpse on the bridge, and another half-fae, the one called Caitlin Flint, was kneeling beside it, bleeding and sobbing. Most of the action seemed to be occurring on the lower trail now. The survivors had barricaded themselves in the narrow tunnel that ran beneath the bridge's solid foundation. Flames were shooting out from the left side of the bridge below, keeping two giant wolves at bay, and I could make out Sig's voice yelling from the right side. I peered over the edge on the right and saw three giant wolves snapping and darting around the narrow archway opening while Sig guarded the tunnel entrance with her sword. Sig couldn't swing inside the arch, and darting out made her vulnerable. Only the wolves' size and the way they were crowding and interfering with each other were keeping Sig from being dragged out or decapitated.

Part of the rock wall on top of the bridge's right side had been torn loose, but my bow was still right where I left it, though at a different angle. I set my katana down and picked up the longbow. There were only three arrows left in my quiver, though perhaps, given the vicious shaking the quiver had undergone, I should say that there was a miraculous fortune of three arrows left in it.

I was already nocking the second arrow when the first one bounced off a giant wolf's skull. You try using a longbow to shoot a darting target from an elevated position at a sharp angle in the dark, then judge. The second arrow went into the side of a different wolf's head. It didn't kill the wolf, but it disabled it. The wolf lurched off, staggering in disjointed near-circles for all the world as if it were drunk. I didn't shoot the third arrow. The wolf in the middle came leaping upward at me, its opening mouth impossibly wide, its breath meaty and hot. Giant fangs seized the end of my bow and tore it out of my hands as I leapt back. The wolf's chest bumped against the bridge and dislodged more stones, and then it dropped down. I lunged forward and used my foot to push one of the teetering tie stones over the edge of the bridge after it. When the wolf landed on its front paws, a stone the size of a breadbox thumped off its skull, and Sig chopped through the leg above its left ankle.

The last intact wolf shouldered its wounded brother aside, sending it tumbling and gagging, and Sig leapt back into the entrance just in time. A snapping motion, and Sig's sword went flying. She moved farther back, and the unharmed wolf rammed its snout into the archway entrance, trying to force its broad shoulders through to reach Sig. It looked bizarrely like a dog that had just chased a small animal into a burrow. The rest was pure instinct. I dropped down, swinging my katana overhead, and by the time I landed in a crouch, I'd already sliced through the side of the wolf's throat. The wolf tried to bite me with its last red-bubbling breaths, but when it backed out of the archway and turned its head sideways, Sig came after it, driving her shoulder up under its jaw so that the wolf couldn't snap at either of us effectively. The giant shook its muzzle violently back and forth, trying to dislodge her, but one of Sig's hands was clenching fur at the edge of the slash I'd made, and when the beast flung her off, it also tore the wound open further. A half-second later, the wolf collapsed.

The wolf that Sig had amputated had risen unsteadily to three legs, but Kasia came out of the surrounding woods then and drove her short sword through its eardrum. I could smell burned flesh where Kasia had cauterized her missing hand with a flare, and she was swaying slightly. Kasia regenerated just like me, but she could still get weak from blood loss.

Another giant wolf appeared from the woods on the lower trail, but this one had three werewolves in lupine form running after it, ripping at its back legs even if they did look like bizarrely savage puppies next to that damned thing. When the giant wolf tried to round on the weres, they began circling it, playing the age-old game of bait and bite. As soon as the giant wolf snapped at one, another werewolf would attack it from behind, and the giant wolf was already bleeding from a dozen wounds. Two other werewolves darted in from the opposite side of the trail to join in.

The last giant wolf's death wasn't pretty to hear, and I didn't care.

"You all right, bright eyes?" I asked Sig.

She squeezed my arm in answer while she looked over her shoulder and called, "How's Molly?"

It was Marisol who answered. She and Aubrey dragged Molly out of the archway. "I dropped a rock in front of her and then knocked her out from behind so anyone seeing through her would think part of the archway came down on us. It's for the best. Trust me."

"So, you know what you're doing?" I asked.

"Of course not." Tears were streaking Marisol's cheeks, and all the playfulness had gone from her voice. "But nobody else is here to help."

God, did I know that feeling.

"That's all of the doggies," Marisol said sadly. "Poor things." Choo came hobbling behind her, leaning on Sarah.

"Are you okay, Marisol?" I took Molly from them and half-laid, half-cradled her on the ground while I inspected her head wound. There was an ugly little gouge mark where something heavy had clipped the back of her skull.

Marisol kept her face aimed at the ground, refusing to look at me. "I'm sharing Caitlin Flint's pain."

That's not all Marisol was doing. I'm very good at smelling moisture in the air, and there was something going on in the atmosphere that wasn't natural. It started to rain, a light summer rain, but still building. I looked at the tears on Marisol's cheeks. Felt the rain hitting my own. Was it possible?

"I have to put out the fires this stupid fight caused," Marisol sobbed.

Being me, I couldn't help wondering what happened when Marisol got gas. Earth tremors? Sarah came and knelt by us and took a small metal flask from her side. For a second, I thought she was going to take a quick shot of whiskey, but Sarah unscrewed the lid and forced some of the flask's contents down Molly's throat. Sarah noticed when I tensed, and she promised the draught would help heal Molly and keep her unconscious. That's not all it would do. I'd smelled that stuff before. Mugwort. Wormwood. Dream herb. Unwashed ass. It was the same stuff Sarah had given me the first time I went to the Dreamtime.

Then Sarah offered the flask to me.

Oh, shit.

~33~

DREAM ME UP, SCOTTY

No, see," I said. "The plan was that *you* would try to trace this shadow connection back to whoever is doing this."

"I tried," Marisol said. "But whatever is going on with your friend doesn't feel like the work of the Foolish Man."

I could practically hear the capital letters. "Who's this Foolish Man?"

"Whoever's kicking up a fuss, trying to make my city a better place."

Huh. "Why is trying to make the city a better place foolish?"

"You can't *make* the city anything." Marisol seemed to think that answer was obvious. Maybe they teach that kind of thing in Fisher King 101.

"We're improvising, John," Sarah said. "We need someone who has an emotional connection to Molly to follow her in the Dreamtime. Someone who psychics won't be able to detect. And it has to be now."

So I didn't argue. I didn't protest about all the things I couldn't do, or ask Sarah what she expected me to do. I didn't try to come up with alternatives or accuse them of springing this on me. There was no way I was going to let what had happened to Molly stand, and even if I hadn't wasted a lot of time making speeches or hitting anything or making a point out of telling everyone how steely and resolved I was, I was all in. If Sarah thought she could help, well, that was what we'd come here for. All I said was "Am I looking for anything in specific when I get there?"

"You won't have to try to do anything if Marisol has this figured out right." Sarah took the flask back. "You should be shadowing Molly."

"Is that a bad pun?" Sig demanded.

Sarah answered her while patting my forearm. "Molly doesn't have a shadow right now, and nature abhors a vacuum. In the Dreamtime, John is going to be her shadow for her."

"Oh, God," I said. "I mean, good. Oh, good." But I was already assuming the position that Sarah had made me take the last time I'd done this. Bent over. Hands around my ankles. Pants down.

"Whoever's doing this to Molly might be able to travel the Dreamtime too," Sarah continued while she smeared some ointment above my upper lip, directly under my nostrils. It smelled like lemongrass. "We don't want them to know if we find anything out."

I just nodded.

"Hurry up." Marisol was already crouched next to Molly. "I'm keeping her tethered, but she's strong-willed. Her soul knows something's wrong, and it wants to go into the Dreamtime and find out why."

So I took Molly's hand, and light and shadow coalesced around us, enveloping us in a living chiaroscuro of luminescence and darkness until I seemed to be looking at the world around me through some twilight realm.

Okay, that was a total lie. Sorry. We just sat there. Marisol was holding Sarah's right hand, Sarah was holding Molly's, and I was holding Molly's left. Not in a circle—in a line, as if we were trying to ground lightning. But that doesn't quite convey the tension of the moment, and besides, I've always wanted to use the word *chiaroscuro*.

In actuality, the world didn't cooperate with giving us a quiet meditation space. I was sore and looked and felt like someone had scrubbed me with a giant Brillo pad, and shutting that out was a bit of a chore. Choo was loudly demanding to know what was going on, and Aubrey was taking stock of the half-fae wounded. The only other fae survivor, Caitlin Flint, had a gut wound, and she wasn't being quiet about it. But if half-elves don't regenerate, they're still a lot more resilient than humans, and they have healers among their kind who can work miracles.

No healers were going to be able to help the half-elf called Darian, though. His body was headless and lying on the ground next to the archway entrance, a fact that I'd noticed but hadn't really thought about while the battle was still going on. "What happened up there?" I heard Sig ask Aubrey quietly.

Aubrey responded bitterly: "As soon as I got wounded, Mother's bodyguards began tripping all over each other, trying to put themselves between me and the wolves. I think they wound up putting us all in more danger than if they'd stayed in position. I didn't ask them to."

"We know." It sounded like Sig really did know, too. She has that gift, sometimes.

"This is why I don't like being around Mother and her followers." I was trying to focus on entering a meditative state, holding Molly's hand, matching the rate and depth of my breathing to hers, feeling her pulse, but maybe a part of me was resisting it too, and a few things about Aubrey made more sense to me. Aubrey had always struck me as reckless, oddly reckless for someone who claimed to enjoy living a long life, but if he had spent most of his eternal youth resenting feeling overprotected, I could see how that mentality might have evolved. How sad would it be, to be a couple hundred years old and still have a mother who never let you grow up?

"So, why are you?" Sig asked curiously. "Hanging around them, I mean."

"I'm in Mother's debt. You know that."

The last time I'd seen Aubrey, his mother had helped Sig and me bail Aubrey out of a huge mess. Maybe rebelling against his parent also kept him dependent on her long after he shouldn't be. It's weird how it works out that way so often.

"Could you people take it somewhere else?" Sarah snapped with uncharacteristic peevishness.

Then a bigger surprise, one of the werewolves showing up turned out to be my pack leader, Ben Lafontaine. I smelled Ben and peeked. Ben is a solid and craggy Chippewa whose movements are a lot younger and leaner than he is, which is even more evident when he's naked. The werewolves who'd come with Ben were still busy ripping the giant wolves into pieces— not for dinner but so that the corpses would be easier to drag off into the woods—but Ben stepped away from the frenzy and began to transform in front of our eyes. It wasn't seamless or pretty, and it jarred me out of my trance again. That was me over there. I did that sometimes. Gross. My body's muscles and joints twinged sympathetically.

Ben walked up to Sig as soon as he'd shifted, and she took the bloody jacket off Darian's headless corpse and threw it at Ben. "Tie this around yourself. There's a minor present."

Ben obligingly made a loincloth out of the jacket, tying its long sleeves behind his waist. He looked at where Choo was bandaging Sig's head, then looked at Kasia, his face expression-less. "This is your stalker?" There was a calm contemplation of violence in the question. Ben likes Sig.

"We are past that," Kasia told him.

"That's news to me," Ben said.

It was news to me, too.

"Take it somewhere farther away than that!" Sarah urged. "We've only got one chance at this, and you're distracting John. He has werewolf hearing, you know."

"One chance at what?" Ben asked, but Sig was already pull-ing him off.

"John, you'd better come back," she called as she led the rest of the group away. It sounded more like a threat than an endear-ment, but not too long before, she wouldn't have said that much with so many other people with sensitive hearing around.

I wasn't my body. I was in my body. Following my breathing down into my chest. Staying there while the breathing went away again. I was in my hand, the hand over Molly's hand, in Molly's hand, listening to her breathe. Feeling her blood throb against my skin. Molly. *I love you, Molly. You're not going any-where without me.*

Merging. Breathing. Sinking. Blurring.

Suddenly, heavy wet clothes are pulling me down into dark water. I thrash around, upward, frantically. I am in a swim-ming pool in a backyard, at night. Fifteen feet away from me is the brightly lit family room of a house. My parents are inside it, my friends, the man I am supposed to marry. They are all laughing and enjoying each other's company.

"I'm out here!" I scream. "Help me." But they can't hear me. They're talking to another Molly standing there in the room. The only me they care to know. I am dragged down into the water by the weight of my outfit, a heavy overcoat. Down,

down. My breath is getting tighter in my chest, swelling in my cheeks. My limbs are getting heavier as I try to thrash frantically. NO! I WILL NOT DIE THIS WAY!

The world shatters like a mirror, and I am standing in the middle of a pencil sketch. The drawing of a classroom around me is a thing of straight lines and empty spaces. Pictures of dark black rats and spiders are crawling out of the corners of my sketch world, moving like stop animation, covering the intervening grey shaded spaces between us in blanks. No. This is not where I am.

I walk through them, and the world passes me like a flipping page, leaving a small pencil picture of a restaurant in its wake. The sketch window has figures moving, becoming larger, three of them. No. This is not where I am. I walk through the window and the world flips again

into a sketch of a bridge in the middle of pencil woods. Cartoon wolves begin to emerge from the trees and NO!

I am no longer in a drawing. I am in dark, lightless suburbs surrounding a brightly lit city by water. There are forgotten things moving through silent streets around me, but I ignore them and take a step that goes far farther than a step should.

I am in a lit street in the city between tall buildings, some of them darkened, broken-windowed, in decay.

Another step and I am in front of a tower. It is some kind of corporate building that looks half modern industrial and half medieval; the edifice is tall and has large, long reflective windows, but the foundation is wider than most skyscrapers, and a part of me that is not Molly notes how the building scapes inward every three floors. At each of these plateaus, there are small crenellated walls surrounding the edges—defensible firing positions—and the top levels of the building become circular instead of rectangular, ending in a large dome with a small steeple. I

step into a marble lobby where there are statues. I can feel them watching me. There are wide lobby stairs between two sets of elevators, and I walk up them, past men in dark robes, taking entire staircases at a time. I walk until

I am in a dark room. A short, portly man with curly, receding grey hair and a big beard and seamed skin and too-bright eyes behind big glasses is staring at me in a light that is not light, a book open before him. Behind him is me. I am standing in front of my own open coffin, staring at a body that has no soul, staring at myself staring at myself with insect eyes. I—

—came out of it gasping like I'd been holding my breath for a long time. My God. My God. I was sitting on gravel, just inside the archway. It was dark. Soft rainfall was smacking the ground around me.

"Are you all right?" Sarah asked me.

I didn't answer her. I wasn't all right. Not at all. None of us were. I had been to the city in Molly's dream before.

It wasn't New York. It was Detroit.

∽34∾

NOW LET'S SEE, WHERE DID THAT SOAP LAND…

Our little circus had broken down into a series of necessary tasks. Sarah is a good artist, and she always carries something to write on in a weird purse that looks like an oversized shaman's pouch, so I had her draw a sketch of the man I'd seen in the vision while the memory was still fresh. There were distances to be walked so that phone calls could be made, crude splints and stretchers to be fashioned, dressings to be applied, spears to be fetched, mists to be conjured so that Fisher Kings and half-elves could get Caitlin Flint out of the park without being spotted, and so on.

At least we didn't have to take care of all those giant wolf corpses. It was one of the plus sides to working with larger organizations—I didn't have to do all of the cleaning up. Sig took advantage of that and cornered me, taking my hand as if she wanted to make sure I was really there. "What's up with that picture Sarah drew? Did you find anything out about Molly?"

I squeezed her hand. "Sort of." Over Sig's shoulder, Ben was nodding curtly to indicate that I should follow him. "Can you wait a second so I can tell Ben and Simon at the same time? It's complicated."

"Sure," Sig said. "I love waiting to find out about whether my best friend is going to live or die or not."

"If we have anything to do with it, she's going to live. That hasn't changed." I kissed her hand briefly, and then my girl-friend and I walked through fallen bodies and giant wolf corpses and the sounds of tearing meat. Sig and I have a lot of romantic moments like that. Sometimes, I wonder what Dr. Phil would have to say about our relationship. I didn't protest when Kasia followed us. Simon had said the kresniks had sent her because of a vision of Sig and Kasia in a dark tower, and I'd just seen a dark tower. Sarah and Choo stayed behind, but only because Sarah was looking after Molly and Caitlin Flint, and Choo couldn't put any weight on his left knee.

"You didn't tell me you were coming to New York," I told Ben when I caught up to him.

Another werewolf named Louis Martine, one of Ben's higher-ups and a member of Ben's original tribe, followed along. Louis had never liked me much, but that was fine. I didn't have any strong feelings about him one way or the other; Louis rarely spoke, and when he did, Ben's words came out of his mouth.

"Did you really think I'd send wolves here and stay behind while all of this was going on?" Ben asked.

That would have been the rational thing to do, maybe even the responsible thing, but werewolves aren't like humans in all respects. I mean, werewolves are humans, but... Well, let me put it this way: A werewolf leader who sends other wolves out on the front lines and never takes any risks won't be a werewolf leader for long. Maybe that's a bad thing, because a lot of competent werewolf leaders get lost that way, but on the other hand, werewolf leaders don't send their young into battle to fight for oil-field rights while they stay behind collecting campaign donations from lobbyists, either.

"I didn't think about it at all," I admitted. "I've been a little busy."

Ben grunted. "Me too. This going to war alert status but not really going to war and still working with the knights is tricky. I'm getting so turned around, I tried to scratch my chin and wound up scratching my behind."

We made our way through a tree line and found ourselves next to the lake when my cell phone finally came back on. "Is it okay if I include Simon in on this?"

Ben thought about that. "Do you have to?"

"I never talk to Simon unless I have to," I said. "But this isn't a geas thing, if that's what you mean."

"Answer one question first," Ben said. "Would it help things if I killed Simon?"

Things as in dirty-bomb scenarios and species friction. "I don't think so," I said. "The knights' geas is defined by how they see the world. The only way to keep them from coming up with cures that are worse than the disease is to change the way they think about things long-term. I mean, even if you could commit genocide and destroy all knights, would you? You going to kill their kids, too? And all the lay servants who aren't geas-bound who work with them? And do you really want to live in a world without them when all is said and done? There are a lot of bad things out there. Simon is a prick, but he's a smart prick."

"If it comes to killing Simon, you should let me do it," Sig said. "John and I could go on the run without dragging the Round Table into it."

I wasn't sure if I was worried that Sig had already been thinking along those lines, or reassured.

Ben sighed. "What a mess."

No argument from me on that score: "I'll brief you first if you want, but if we're ever going to do this right, we all need to start acting like real allies."

"Honoring a treaty with white men," Louis said. "What could go wrong?"

Nobody commented.

"Go ahead and call him," Ben said.

"And hurry up about it," Sig added. "I want to hear this."

There was an electronic series of hums and clicks as my call was transferred to Keeley. "We're getting close to finding Reader X. Can this wait?"

"There are two copies of the Book of Am out there," I told him. "Two Reader X's."

Silence. Keeley didn't say anything. Ben and Sig and Kasia and Louis didn't say anything. I didn't say anything.

"I'll go get Mr. Travers."

"What the hell are you talking about?" Simon greeted me after Keeley had arranged some kind of party line where we could all talk to each other.

"We've been suckered," I said.

"Explain."

"Imagine you're some higher-up in the School of Night," I said. "You're trying to break into the Templar Archives, and a chance to steal a book that warps reality falls right into your lap."

"Could we just skip the sales pitch?"

"No. Pretend you're that higher-up in the School of Night. Your problem is," I said, "nobody knows exactly how the book works. The book may be some kind of demon that possesses the reader, or it might be a highly addictive drug. All anybody really knows is that the book is supposed to have its own agenda and that it causes magic creatures to start appearing out of the reader's imagination. Are you going to read that book?"

"Probably not," Simon said. "I'm going to test it first."

"Sure," I said. "But you can't use rats or rabbits or monkeys for this. The test subject has to be able to read."

A pause. Then Ben said, "So, if you're a bad guy, you have someone else read the book for you. Someone you have control over."

"Normally, sure," I said. "But there are problems there, too. The Book of Am was discovered when the School of Night was trying to infiltrate the Templar Archives. We didn't even know the School of Night existed, and they were doing everything they could to keep it that way. The last thing they wanted was to have magical creatures start appearing in Boston and sending up signal flags that something huge was going on."

"The book transforms people and places the reader knows, too," Sig said. "You wouldn't want to give it to anyone who knew you or anything you cared about, because that reader might wind up turning you into something just because they know you. You might wind up getting turned into leprechauns or snails."

"Exactly," I said.

"You're saying they set up the man we've been calling Reader X," Simon said. "Anna Hogan made him think he was going to be the father of a new age, but he's really a fall guy."

"I think Anna Hogan seduced him as part of a cover story the School of Night created," I said. "They began sending

Reader X a partial manuscript, a page at a time, long-distance, as a way of controlling the terms of the experiment. The School of Night wanted to observe the gradual effects the book had on Reader X and what effects Reader X had on the book. They wanted to develop strategies for controlling the process. But if Reader X kicked up a hell of a fuss while he was being their crash test dummy, it was a bonus. The School of Night would get to study how the Knights Templar responded to magical manifestations appearing out of nowhere, and they'd also get to see how we'd try to track down the persons responsible. You know... for when they were ready to make their own move on a big scale."

"It was a test run in a lot of ways," Ben said.

"That's why the School of Night has been trying so hard to spy on us?" Sig asked.

Simon was following right along. Hell, as devious as his mind was, he might have been getting ahead of us. "And they keep turning up because the School of Night wants to keep us convinced that they're still looking for the book too. That's assuming you're right. Where are you getting all of this from, Charming?"

I wasn't inclined to get too specific about me dream walking. "We found someone who knew how to trace the psychic connection between Molly and her shadow back through the School of Night's wards and magical defenses. The guy who used a book to create Molly's shadow is older than our Reader X would be, and he's in a skyscraper in Detroit."

Apparently, Keeley was listening in too. "That's all? You derived all of the rest of it from that?"

"It's a lot of guesswork," I admitted. "For example, I don't know if the School of Night has a completed copy of the Book of Am or not. Maybe I really killed Anna Hogan before she finished copying the book, or maybe I just killed her before she was done feeding Reader X a page at a time. I don't know if Anna Hogan knew Reader X from before, or how she picked him. But I'll bet I've got the gist of it."

"You said this man was in a skyscraper," Kasia pointed out. "And the kresniks had a vision of Sigourney and me in a tower."

I didn't much like that. "Yeah."

"The School of Night has mostly been working from a distance," Simon mused. "Except for one skinwalker, they've been using mercenaries and drones and creatures that were magically summoned."

"Those creatures are another thing," I said. "All along, I've been having a hard time seeing a connection between these fantasy role-playing creatures that Reader X has been conjuring up, and the classical story creatures that have been spying on us. One Reader X seemed to be some random dude on a magical power acid trip using the Book of Am as his own personal therapy session. The other Reader X seemed to think in terms of traditional fables and fairy tales and seemed to know what was going on. The second Reader X also seemed to have more control over his creations and was focused on monitoring our progress. I was even wondering if the book itself was operating apart from its reader, but it makes more sense if there really are two readers."

Simon got to the point: "Can you identify this skyscraper?"

"Give me a good computer and a phone line to someone who knows Detroit," I said. "It won't take long."

"A few things still don't fit," Sig said. "The last few fairy-tale creatures weren't just trying to spy on us. They were trying to kill us. That's what really gave Molly away."

"Yeah, they started trying to kill us when we started getting close to finding Reader X." I remembered what Aubrey had told me. "I don't know if the School of Night planned it this way or not, but having the knights tear New York City apart looking for the book has been paying off for them. The knights have been acting like thugs, and they're pissing off a lot of the supernatural species that the School of Night likes to recruit. I think the School of Night wants to keep our Reader X in play for as long as possible."

"About that..." Simon said.

∾35∾

CRACKPOT! I MEAN, JACKPOT!

Working for the New York City Office of Chief Medical Examiner sucked. Working for the Knights Templar at the same time was extra trimming on the suck sandwich. But there was no getting around it. If Brendan Bowman hadn't had Templar blood in his veins, he wouldn't have gotten a job for the Office of Chief Medical Examiner in the first place. Left to his own devices, Brendan would be a plastic surgeon, spending his life looking at live women's breasts and butts in a way that wouldn't be cheating. Or maybe a pediatrician or veterinarian. Kids and animals didn't suck. But Brendan was what he was, and when he got a phone call at five fifteen in the morning, he took it even though it was a Sunday.

Brendan listened to the voice on the other end of the line, then told it to hold on and got out of bed. The absence of Brendan's weight made the mattress sway like the deck of a ship—the extra twenty pounds Brendan was carrying around didn't help—and Brendan's wife, Angie, protested with a soft little grunt, but she didn't wake up even after he leaned over and gave her a little smooch on the shoulder. Netflix had turned out to be pretty hard on Angie's sleeping schedule. Brendan's wife was the kind of person who couldn't put down a book until she finished reading it, and now that binge watching was a thing, she had to be careful not to start any new TV shows until the weekend.

Brendan padded downstairs to make some coffee while his computer booted up, and to hell with his geas. Caffeine would make him more efficient, though he made it half-caff because of his asthma. That sucked too. But at least Brendan's asthma had kept him from becoming a knight. Those guys were assholes, most of them, but Brendan saw what knights had to deal with up close. Sometimes, he had to dissect or cremate what knights dealt with up close. They were welcome to their lives and their deaths and their attitudes, thank you very much. Looking up the names of some people who had gone to the same high school and died in the last year was much more Brendan's speed.

Thinking about knights made Brendan think about Denver, and these days, Brendan couldn't think about his eight-year-old son without a rush of love and sadness and fear tensing up high in his left breastbone until he felt weak. Denver was so goddamned athletic and fearless. Brendan was terrified that one day, the kid was going to qualify for advanced squire training and get inducted into one of the private schools that transformed young men into killing machines. He had actually contemplated trying to sabotage Denver's health on more than one occasion, but whenever Brendan considered it too seriously, his heart started to flutter and his pulse started to speed up.

He knew Angie felt the same way, but they weren't talking about it yet. That conversation was waiting out there in dark waters on the horizon, the tip of it occasionally popping up like a shark fin. Maybe there was more than one reason Angie was having trouble sleeping lately.

Okay, wait, there it was. Brendan hadn't needed to write down any names—that part of squire training had never given him any problems—and he was looking for signs of anything unusual, and one of the names Brendan had been given had never been officially examined by anybody. Cameron Shaw. Several eyewitnesses had seen Cameron jump off the George Washington Bridge at night. It had been in a blind spot as far as camera footage went, but since a Ford Focus in Cameron Shaw's name had been abandoned at the same location, there was no reason to doubt anyone. The body hadn't been recovered.

Scuba-diving for corpses in freezing water didn't always take top priority in New York City. Sometimes, it was easier to just wait for the temperatures to rise and let decomposing gases do the rest. Spring didn't just bring rainbows and roses; when the waters warmed up, the harbor patrols usually spent a couple of weeks fishing out the corpses that were popping back up to the surface like corks.

But Cameron Shaw's body had never been officially identified.

"It's good to see you again, Cristian," Gloria Waterhouse said pleasantly. The last time Gloria had seen Cristian Ortiz, she'd been riding along with an ambulance staffed by geas-bound, and Cristian had just been bitten by a Mongolian Death Worm. Gloria had placed him under a small enchantment before moving on to the next paramedic crew—there had been too many wounded and too many witnesses and too much confusion to quarantine everyone or question them properly, so Gloria had asked the basic questions and then implanted a command for Cristian to find her at this closed-down South American café at five o'clock the next morning, and here he was.

Cristian sat down in the wooden booth, and Gloria arched her sixty-year-old back in a way that she probably wouldn't have if she'd been thinking of Cristian as a person. Her breasts were a little bit large for her long spine, and they hadn't gotten easier to bear with age. Black might not crack, but Gloria's body had started making popping sounds lately. "How is your niece, Cristian? Noemi, wasn't it?"

"She's okay."

And with that last pleasantry out of the way, Gloria led Cristian through it. He talked about having to watch Noemi carefully because she liked to put pebbles in her mouth. Talked about how many people were there, then started with the woman who'd been next to him, the divorced lady with the stack of papers who sounded like a teacher. Talked about their conversation, how the woman's kids were playing that game where they couldn't touch the ground because there were big snakes in it.

Gloria had been idly jotting down notes in a legal yellow pad, but she went from idle to overdrive in the space of a second. "What?!"

"What?" Cristian repeated.

Hold the breath in. Pause and reflect. "Tell me more about the children who were playing a game about snakes coming out of the ground."

Cristian began talking again, but now that slow monotone was suddenly maddening. If Gloria'd had a fast-forward button, she would have been holding it down. Under constant prompting, Cristian told Gloria about the woman's ex-husband, how the woman had said that the husband used to take the kids to the park and play this make-believe game where they had to cross the whole playground without touching the ground because there were big snakes under the pebbles.

"Do you know the woman's name?" Gloria forced her voice to stay even.

"No," Cristian said.

"But she was divorced and had two children? What were their genders?"

"Their what?"

"Were they boys or girls?"

"Two boys."

"Did she mention their names?"

"Rafe and Jude."

Anything Gloria wrote down, she remembered. She had been that way even before she went through merlin training. It was one of the reasons she went through merlin training. The woman's name was Mary Keaton. She had sat across from Gloria in that same wooden booth three hours earlier, and somehow, the fact that her boys had been playing a game involving snakes hadn't surfaced.

But the ex-husband's name had. It was Cameron Shaw.

"I got a hit."

I'll give you a hit, Anson thought, and not for the first time. Wheelchair or no wheelchair, Anson could turn Jojo Huffman into a blood pudding anytime he felt like it. The kid's forearms wouldn't have any definition at all if it weren't for gaming consoles and whacking off.

Jojo'd had the misfortune of being the first member of the hack factory that Anson had met, and some explosion had gone off inside Anson's gut at first sight. He'd hated Jojo's soft belly roll, the T-shirt that said some bullshit about some TV show that Anson had never seen, the weird unfocused way the kid peered around behind those big glasses, how Jojo couldn't keep track of his keys but could call up all kinds of trivial nonsense that meant absolutely nothing to anybody who mattered. Anson looked at Jojo, and all Anson saw was how he'd lost so much more than the use of his legs to that motherfucking abaasy back in Arizona. Kids like this Jojo were Anson's peers now. This soft, slug-fleshed twelve-year-old in a twenty-five-year-old's body who had never actually risked anything for anybody and looked down on people who had. Who had no real understanding of how lives could hang on the information they were digging up.

"What kind of hit?" Anson asked.

"A palpable hit." Jojo beamed muzzily through the haze of too many power drinks.

Anson looked at him and pictured driving his knuckles into a spot that would rupture Jojo's liver and send toxins pouring into his bloodstream.

"You know, like in *Hamlet.*" Jojo faltered. "It's that Shakespeare library, the Folger place. One of the people on that list you gave me is a member. Cameron Shaw."

PART THE FOURTH

The Write Stuff

∾36∾

A PLANE-DEALING VILLAIN

It didn't take long to identify the building as the Rockwall Tower West—those crenellated scapings and the steeple top were pretty distinctive—and our party had shrunk by the time we met Simon at a private airfield. Choo had messed his knee up pretty badly when he jumped off the side of the Ramble Arch, and Molly would soon be waking up in a hotel room where Sarah would explain that Molly had a concussion and was going to have to stay off her feet for a while. It wasn't perfect, but the alternative was having three farmhands who looked like me, Sig, and Choo explaining that Molly had hit her head during the tornado and that it had all been a dream. So it was Sig, Kasia, and I who wound up going through a small Templar-owned airport with Ben and a half-dozen hard cases that he'd handpicked from the werewolves at the park.

The airport looked like the sort of place where former military pilots go to die. You know, the kind of grizzled guys who look like they're ready to drop everything and go fishing at any moment and don't take anything seriously unless it involves antiaircraft fire or engine failure. The ceiling was made of Styrofoam tiles laid out in an aluminum grid, and the once-white floor was laminated in a thin sheen of grime. The fading and cracked neon plastic seats had probably been around since the nineteen seventies, and a horizontal freezer full of ice cream treats was set by the long window overlooking the airstrip, a sheet of notebook paper with handwriting on it taped to the sliding glass doors. The ice cream treats were a dollar apiece, and I grabbed a couple of Nutty Buddies.

I say the airport *looked* that way, but I don't mean to imply that it really had a secret underground hangar with high-tech stealth jets or surface-to-air missiles or anything like that.

The airport probably did run legit charter flights and banner-towing services and tourist rides around the Big Apple or whatever; I just mean that these weren't the only kinds of flights it ran, and at wee o'clock in the morning, we didn't have to hide the weapons we were carrying with us. The cameras were off, and it was on.

We were escorted to where Simon and his own matching set of a half-dozen handpicked killers were loading the largest plane in the hangar with air-drop bags and green footlockers that probably didn't hold I HEART NY T-shirts or little statues of the Empire State Building. We had been told that the plane would seat eighteen people if one of them sat in the copilot's seat.

"Load your gear," Simon called out. "We're leaving in five."

Ben cleared his throat and addressed the group. "Hold on a moment; this is worth saying. The people we're after have been killing us, impersonating us, targeting innocent civilians, and trying to get us to turn on each other. They tried to get both our peoples to kill each other because we're the only ones who can stop them. I'm not saying we don't have legitimate grievances on both sides. Werewolves and knights don't have to like each other. All we have to agree on is that we don't want our children killing each other. We have to agree not to be fools."

To Simon's credit, he didn't say "Leaving in three." Nobody looked like they disagreed with Ben. If they had been the kind of people who didn't know when to set aside kneejerk emotions, Ben and Simon wouldn't have chosen them. But nobody was applauding, either.

Sig whispered in my ear. "If some magical whatzis appears on the plane, won't all the electricity shut off?"

"Sig wants to know what the in-flight movie is," I called out to Simon, just to fill the awkward silence in a little.

"I do not." Sig gave my arm a halfhearted punch. She was tired.

Kasia seemed distantly amused. "Sigourney just mentioned that if another magical manifestation occurs, the engines might shut down. It is a good point."

"The next person who speaks for Sig other than Sig is going to get Sig's foot up their ass," Sig announced. "That's what Sig says."

"It's a good point regardless of who said it," Simon responded. "But nobody should know we're coming if we did this right, and we can't spare the ten hours it would take to drive to Detroit. Besides, this plane is as hardwired against magic as we can make it. It uses sacred-tree formation circuits instead of loops, and it has Zener diodes and induction shielding and gold wiring and other things I can't even begin to understand."

"Don't ever tell people that everything is so state-of-the-art that nothing can go wrong, Simon," I said. "That's the beginning of every disaster movie ever."

"Leaving in two," Simon said.

"Makes me glad this is my last flight before I retire," the pilot told me with a wink.

I pretended to be upset, looking out among the assembled knights and werewolves, all of whom probably picked their teeth with machetes. "Okay, seriously, am I the only one here who understands how jinxes work?"

"Don't worry; nothing bad's going to happen to me today." This from a big werewolf who had a lot of hard muscle sheathed in body fat and whose long hair was bound in a samurai knot. "I just bought my girlfriend an engagement ring."

Another werewolf who really liked tattoos said, "And I haven't scratched the lottery ticket I just bought yet."

The lone female knight, a hard, fit, dark-haired young woman who was packing a disassembled crossbow into something that looked like a large jeweler's box, looked up at me. "I'm pregnant."

All of the knights around her went quiet. She went back to her packing without ever cracking a smile. "What are you, my mothers? It was a joke."

As it turned out, there was no in-flight movie. For entertainment, Sig and I talked about Molly and her missing shadow. If I'd been by myself, I would have grabbed a power nap like most of the knights on the plane, and I probably would have accomplished something more tangible by doing so. But it was good, having someone to emotionally vent with a little, even if it was a little strange knowing that seven werewolves and a dhampir were listening in. How did werewolves who stayed with their pack all of the time stand it?

"Do we know that killing this shadow thing won't hurt Molly?" The side of Sig's head was resting against my shoulder, and the side of my head was propped against the top of her skull.

"This is all I know," I said. "In the fairy tale, the shadow gradually weakened the man it separated from. The man got sicker and sicker, and the shadow turned the tables and made the man act like its shadow. Then it killed the man, and when it did, the shadow didn't vanish. It was like, the shadow was free to live its own life once the man was finally gone."

"But it did it in stages," Sig said.

I squeezed her hand. "Yeah. Still, once the shadow separated from the man, it went from being a symbiont to a parasite." Symbionts live off another organism, but it's a mutually beneficial relationship, like birds that perch on a rhino's back and feed off the insects trying to burrow into the rhino's skin. Parasites just take and take and take, gradually infecting or weakening the host if nothing is done about them. Like ticks. Or bad spouses.

Sig burrowed in closer, but she was definitely a symbiont. It was comforting. "Do you think this thing has taken some of Molly's darker emotions with it?"

"It's hard to tell," I said. "She seemed a little listless, maybe, but it's not like Molly goes around being a raving byatch, anyhow."

"Hmmmn."

"In the story, the shadow and the man were in a struggle to the death, and the man didn't know it." I was repeating myself a little, thinking aloud more than delivering a conclusion. "He was too nice. He didn't realize that he had to destroy the shadow until it was too late."

"We should still try to capture this thing instead of kill it," Sig said. "We can take it to some cunning folk. Or take it to Molly."

I shifted so that I could kiss the top of her head. "Just don't get killed holding back."

And then we had the same conversation again two or three

times using slightly different sentences without arriving at any new conclusions. I was only half-involved in the recycled conversations, though. Part of me was also listening to Simon and Ben as they talked quietly to their people on the ground in Detroit.

At one point I heard Simon say to someone on the phone, "Forget computers. They probably have websites that will trigger a warning if anyone searches them. It's a Sunday morning. Break into the city records."

A little later, Ben said to his own phone, "It's too early to have anybody with weapons walk by for at least a mile out. We don't know what kind of magic defenses they've set up."

At which point, Simon paused in the middle of his own conversation and responded, "We have some legit cabdrivers there, Ben. One of them could drive your scout by the tower with the window open. The driver's geas would turn away any scrying magic, and your scout could at least smell some smells."

Later still, Ben was telling someone, "Stay off the roofs. Detroit is supposed to be full of abandoned buildings. There's got to be at least one with an eyeball view of this place."

And then Simon: "Don't have them move out until you get some of our real municipal workers down there in the sewer with them. Sabotage some pipes if you have to."

To which Ben added, "Take some of my people along. We do really well in the dark."

Apparently, Rockwall Tower West wasn't responding well to long-distance scouting. The windows were thick security glass with reflective surfaces glazed over them, and it sounded like neither technological nor magical spying was doing much good, not heat imaging or scrying or bouncing soundwaves off the windows. None of the phones listed under the businesses in the building were actually in the building when Simon tracked them and turned them into directional microphones, and there didn't seem to be any security cameras in the building that anyone could hack into. Which begged the question of what kind of security measures the tower did have in place.

I wasn't directly involved until a printer Simon had brought on board whirred, and I heard him tell Ben, "Pass this to Charming."

"This" turned out to be the copy of a newspaper article about the efforts to revitalize downtown Detroit. The main focus was on some investment group that had bought Rockwall Tower West and was renting the floors out to small businesses that depended heavily on Internet sales. A man was talking to Detroit's mayor at some kind of ceremony. He was grey and slim, somewhere between gaunt and fit. His name, or at least the one he used publically, was Evan Gilbert, and he was responding to the mayor's smile and handshake with a glance so distantly polite that I'm surprised the camera lens hadn't frosted over.

"What am I looking at?"

"This is the man who owns that tower, to the extent that any one person owns that tower."

"He's not the man who was holding a book in Molly's dream."

"You sound pretty certain for just seeing a sketch."

"I didn't just see a sketch. The people I met with conjured up a vision." Which was true as far as it went.

"It would be helpful if I could meet these people myself."

I was still reading the article, but responding to that didn't take much thought. "You keep bringing me into stuff like this because I can talk to people who don't want to talk to you. If I start going back on my word to them, I won't be able to do that any longer."

Simon let that go, at least for the moment.

"It says here this Gilbert guy's investment firm is named Banner Rally Investments," I said.

"So?"

"So, what banner is this investment company supposed to be rallying around?"

"We've known about these people in Detroit for two hours," Simon said. "Hopefully, they'll be dead before we figure it all out."

～37～

ABRIDGED TOO FAR

It was sad how small Cameron Shaw's life had become. The hot showers he rented at the truck stop were the highlight of his week. It wasn't that he was filthy—Cameron wiped himself down with baby wipes and toweled himself off every day, and he washed his clothes at a laundromat every two weeks, but life in the storage silo Anna had rented under an alias was a fairly grim affair nonetheless. Cameron didn't mind living off the canned goods he'd stocked before faking his own death—food had always been more fuel than fun to Cameron. He didn't mind reading and writing by candlelight and sitting on the air-filled plastic furniture that he had inflated with a bicycle pump either, though the air mattress he used as a bed made annoying sounds when he shifted. It was the day-to-day biological demands that were a problem.

Even a minimal lifestyle accumulated an amazing amount of byproducts, especially when there was no running water. No matter how many trash walks Cameron took, there always seemed to be used Gatorade bottles full of piss and toothpaste spit in the corner, next to the truck stop magazines that

Cameron masturbated to because he was afraid to use the Internet. There were times late at night when Cameron couldn't hold it in that he had to squat over the newspapers he kept scouring for signs that his grand work was having some effect, had to pull his pants down around his ankles and grunt like an animal while he relieved himself, later crumpling the newspaper around his own waste and used toilet paper, careful to only touch the edges. The smell of air-freshening spray and disinfectant was probably permanently soaked into the storage silo's walls.

But maybe it was good that changing the world wasn't the glamorous, godlike affair Cameron had envisioned. All births were messy, and none came without suffering. Cameron remembered the birth of his first son, Rafe. None of those pregnancy videos had warned Cameron that his baby's skull would be so soft and flexible; Cameron had been terrified when Rafe emerged from the womb screaming and looking like a tiny alien, blue-skinned and blood-covered, his little head elongated and shaped like a banana. How much uglier and more intense and oddly beautiful should the birth of a new world be?

Memories of Cameron's ex-wife continued to move through him, sliding off and pouring down him with the soap foam, draining away at his feet. A lot of his most primal memories had been doing that lately. It was one of the side effects of being alone without distractions for extended periods of time, this turning inward. Maybe that was fitting too. Most holy people isolated themselves when they wanted to achieve a vision, monks and shamans and even Christ . . . what had it been, forty days and nights in the desert? Maybe they were detoxing their minds the same way dieters went on a juice cleanse.

An image of Mary, pregnant, saying that Cameron couldn't take care of a child when he was still a child himself. The catalyst for this particular criticism being that Cameron still read comic books and played video games. Then a ticker tape parade of similar memories with the same theme. The bitch had gone to college and two grad programs on her daddy's credit card, hating her family but not hating them enough to cut the purse strings and get a part-time job or student aid, and somehow letting her parents pay for everything made Mary an authority on how to be an adult. Cameron was the one who actually supported himself and their family as best he could, taking out student loans and teaching a few side English classes at a community college and working in writing centers and tutoring athletes to pay for the same college and master's program that Mary's daddy paid for, and she had still spent most of their marriage lecturing Cameron on being responsible while she passed their children off from one university-provided day care program to another and studied new ways to argue that she was nurturing and oppressed by virtue of having a vagina.

To Mary, being an adult meant dressing fashionably and using socially appropriate keywords and passing blame and parroting the same bullshit that everyone else in the English department was repeating, talking knowledgeably about academic articles whose abstracts she had skimmed. Maybe she even had a point. Mary had gotten into a PhD program and Cameron hadn't. That had been when the fissure cracks in Cameron's marriage had started to widen into gaping pits, when Cameron became a social liability in Mary's ongoing campaign to further her career. Increasingly rare tenure-track positions had become the Holy Grail of academia. Nobody in English literary circles wanted to speculate about Christopher Marlowe's clandestine life or how it might have informed his writings anymore, not unless Marlowe was racist or sexist or homosexual or, better yet, bisexual or pansexual and secretly writing the plays of William Shakespeare. Well, no one except

Anna. The first time Anna had contacted him because of his posts as Napalm451, Cameron had gotten an erection so hard and hot that just remembering it made his penis feel like rebar. Anna had reached a part of him that Mary had spent seven years eroding.

Cameron had no idea that across the city, Mary Keaton was turning into a literal harpy, the rough edges of feathers emerging from her skin, her feet hardening and extending into callused claws, her screams turning into caws. He did not understand that the knight team staking out her apartment was the only thing that might keep the children sleeping in the adjacent room alive, or that this was the second time his imagination had almost destroyed his own flesh and blood.

"The fucking bitch." Cameron said the words so loudly that he startled himself. It was another of the side effects of being alone so much; he'd been talking to himself at a normal level of conversation more and more frequently. Fortunately, the sound of cascading water kept the cretin who was sharing the truck stop shower area with Cameron from hearing him, or if he did overhear, he didn't mention it. Mouth breathers or not, truckers probably understood something about loneliness.

Tilting his head back so that hot spray would hit his hairline, Cameron stared up at the ceiling and let water seep down through the roots of the thick, greasy hair he'd been growing out since faking his own death. He should probably get out of the shower now; it was less depressing to exit before the timer turned the water off and left Cameron standing there. Cameron never felt secure being apart from the book very long anyhow, much less leaving it in the rental locker that the truck stop provided. He knew the fear was irrational—the last thing any of the idiots in this place would steal was a book—but if fears had to be rational, mankind would be a much different animal.

Cameron was so close. He could feel it. There were times when Cameron was jotting his own thoughts down on the pages next to the words of John Dee that his skin prickled and his body heated. Like he was coming back to life. Or at least, the part of him that had been numb since Anna stopped texting him.

Cameron knew Anna was dead. When he had met her, the covert nature of the magical world Anna had shown him was thrilling. It had given the days Cameron spent grinding out ad copy that went straight from people's mailboxes to their trashcans an underlying excitement. But now Cameron was terrified. He had moved through the stages of Anna's backup plan feeling as if his entire body was one big pulled muscle. Why wasn't anything happening? Why were the newspapers still talking about the same old world of credit cards and tenure committees and racism and global warming and politics as usual?

The rustle of the plastic shower curtain, the draft of cool air, and the sharp, piercing pain between the two uppermost tendons at the base of Cameron's skull were almost simultaneous. His head was forced down even while he swayed on his feet, barely able to process what was happening. An arm wrapped around Cameron's chest from behind, holding him up. His body felt so light. His eyes down, he noted how pale and emaciated he had gotten with almost clinical detachment, as if it were someone else's bony arm and white belly and skinny legs that he was staring at. Drops of blood were dripping down between Cameron's feet and staining the water near the shower drain, and who did that other pair of shoes belong to and then Cameron Shaw was

∽38∽

DYSFUNCTION, FUNCTION, WHAT'S THAT JUNCTION?

Pretty car. I want to drive it," Kasia said to the knight behind the steering wheel of the Jaguar XE, a burly squat knot of bearded muscle with angry eyes. I recognized him. His name was Stuart, and the last time I'd seen him, he'd been riding in the backseat of a vehicle being driven by the Templar Grandmaster. "Move."

"You don't know where we're going." Stuart's eyes were measuring Kasia for a coffin, but he had a better handle on his temper than the last time I'd met him. He was at that early- to mid-twenties stage where people do a lot of growing up in a few years. Or giving in. Stuart must have belonged to some powerful family within the Templars, was maybe someone Emil Lamplighter had known since Stuart's childhood. He seemed to be someone who Emil trusted implicitly and was grooming for better things at any rate; every time I saw Stuart, he was functioning as some kind of aide to a mover or shaker. Geas or no geas, the Templars aren't immune to nepotism and trading favors. The only difference is that their old-boy network goes back the better part of a millennium.

"I take directions well," Kasia said, all evidence to the contrary. "And it may be that we are all going to die soon. It is important to take what little pleasures we can."

"Let her drive, Stuart," Simon had instructed, which had ended the discussion. Stuart wound up giving directions from the backseat with me and Sig, while Simon took shotgun.

It was a pretty slick-looking car, dark and expensive but not corporate or government make. I had leaned forward and whispered to Kasia sotto voce, "Whatever you do, don't touch the cigarette lighter," then settled back in my seat.

I hadn't been to Detroit very often since the American auto industry shit their bed, and every time I did, I wound up in a different city. Over half of Detroit's population was gone now, and even though we didn't really need the polite gesture of dim streetlights in the early-morning haze, it was obvious that many of the city lights, maybe most of them, weren't working. We drove by entire blocks that had been razed to the ground to create firewalls between relatively intact neighborhoods and abandoned buildings, and I couldn't figure out if that was a sign of desolation or renewal. The few early-morning pedestrians we did see as we passed a downtown district didn't seem depressed or scared, and there were non-franchise-type restaurants and small businesses among empty storefronts.

I saw gardens growing on the rooftops of dilapidated buildings and wondered if Detroit was like one of those old western towns now, or Australia when England first began exporting its criminals and its desperate to a new shore. A place that was lawless and wild, but with energy and opportunity and life as well as danger and darkness. Maybe that was why the School of Night had made some kind of headquarters there.

If Detroit had become a pioneer town, I wondered what it was a pioneer of.

Simon hadn't looked up from his phone the entire drive. "The man you've been calling Reader X is dead," he announced. "We've secured the book he was using."

"Does that mean those bombs you mentioned are being dismantled?" Sig asked.

"It does," Simon agreed. "But the people Cameron Shaw transformed into monsters aren't transforming back."

"They're not?" Sig was thinking of Molly. I know because I was thinking of Molly.

"It's early days," Simon said, almost kindly. "And we haven't destroyed the book itself yet."

Kasia wasn't thinking of Molly, or else she didn't want anyone dwelling on it. "Let us just hope that there are not fifty more copies of the book out there. Now that we know there is at least one."

"I don't think there will be," Sig said. When had she and Kasia started talking without turning the words into chain saw blades? "Something that magical would have to be copied by hand, and it sounds like it's hard to do that without causing weird things to pop up."

"The book confers power, too," Simon chipped in. "Even if it's hard to predict. The people in charge of this School of Night wouldn't want to let something like that out of their control by mass-producing it. At least not while they're still figuring out how to use it."

"Are you sure about that?" Stuart asked. "We don't know much about them."

Simon dismissed the question. "People in power are the same everywhere."

I don't know if I agreed with that or not, or at least not to that extent.

Simon turned around and looked at us. "Speaking of powerful

people, I've been hearing rumors of a Fisher King in New York City."

"It's possible." I kept my voice neutral. "Places with dense populations are where those guys are supposed to form."

"If it is true, someone like that could be a big help in preventing messes like the one we're trying to clean up."

I didn't say anything.

"I'm only mentioning this because you apparently located a cunning person who was powerful enough to put Kasia under some kind of charm that prevents her from telling me everything."

"Do not flatter yourself," Kasia interjected. "I never tell anyone everything."

Simon went on. "And this someone was apparently able to psychically locate an enemy that our best merlins can't get a whiff of."

"I see where you're going with this," I said. "And you're welcome."

Simon's voice got a shade tauter. "You're pretty fond of lecturing people on which allies they should share information with. You don't seem to practice what you preach, though."

"Fuck off," I said diplomatically. Well, it was more diplomatic than stabbing him in the side of the neck, anyway. I like to think that these things are relative.

Stuart made an angry grunt on the other side of Sig. As I recalled, he hadn't liked it when I'd spoken disrespectfully to Emil Lamplighter, either. Sig patted his arm and he visibly startled. I don't know why he got so worked up about a patted arm—she usually punched mine. "What John means is, maybe we should shelve this particular discussion until after we've dealt with the people who've been magically messing with my best friend."

The tension in Simon's voice eased off a bit and he settled back into his seat. "You're probably right about that."

"Also," Sig said, ignoring her own advice, "fuck off. Whether you've admitted it to yourself or not, John was the one who took the first real step in turning this thing around, and he did it by ignoring the way you were trying to parcel out information. Letting some air in between you and Ben might just keep this whole mess from backfiring in your face, too."

"I've never said that John wasn't useful." Simon crossed his legs, I think because crossing his arms would have made him look like a little kid. "That's why he's still alive."

I raised a palm. "I'm right here."

"And I admit it, I'm still learning how to do my new job," Simon continued. "But Ben and I aren't the only ones who need to change the way we work together. You two can't keep hiding in Clayburg after this is all over. Times are changing, and Charming seems to have an intuitive understanding of them that most of us don't."

I hadn't been expecting that. "You and I both know how to do what we have to do if it comes to that."

"We do," Simon agreed.

"But I'm not going to turn in the names of all the supernaturals I know to the knights," I said. "I don't see that ever changing. Not so long as I'm protecting people and you're protecting a status quo."

Simon didn't like that. "You spend so much time being crass. It still takes me off guard when you make your pretty speeches."

"Sure," I said. "But you and your cronies keep talking about how it's weird that I can defy you in spite of my geas. The thing is, I honestly believe that me being someone people outside the knights can trust is the best way to maintain the Pax Arcana. It's paid off so far, hasn't it? I'm not resisting my geas. My geas wouldn't let me be your informant even if I wanted to."

That seemed to get through to Simon in a way that nothing

else I'd said had. He and I were occasionally making eye contact in the rearview mirror, and he even pursed his lips, the drama queen. I didn't know if what I'd said was true or not, but it felt true, and it might keep Simon from dwelling on fantasies of having me in an interrogation room.

"Do you really mean that?" Unexpectedly, it was Stuart, and even more unexpectedly, he sounded thoughtful.

"He might." Simon didn't sound happy about that. "You'll figure out what Charming will lie about and what he won't, if you spend any time around him. This is a grey area."

Okay, there was an undercurrent to this conversation that I really wasn't getting. Maybe I'd gotten it wrong. Maybe Stuart was some kind of assassin in training, and I was someone he was supposed to study. He didn't seem like a particularly promising assassin, but then, a promising assassin wouldn't.

When Simon spoke again, it was a non sequitur of sorts. "You know, Charming, back when you were a fugitive and I was the Grandmaster's personal troubleshooter, I used to wish that he would set me on your trail. I always wanted to see how long you'd last if I was hunting you."

"Well, you know what I always say about wishes and assholes."

Simon's lips curled. "Everyone has them?"

"No," I said. "I just wish you weren't such an asshole."

～39～

RALEIGH AROUND THE FLAG

Finding a place to gather discreetly wasn't an issue in Detroit. I was a little concerned about the volume of people we were assembling and the quality of the car we were traveling in, but Simon told me, "It's all right. People will just assume we're doing something illegal."

I guess Detroit still hadn't recovered that much.

We wound up meeting in a downtown tower of our own. The Order had claimed the property years earlier by the simple expedient of having merlins post Turn Away wards all around the building and its two neighbors. The charms kept homeless people and predators and photographers and urban-renewal types out, kept out everyone but the knights, who aren't affected by such things. We did have to carry Sig and Kasia into the building, Stuart piggybacking Kasia, me princess-carrying Sig as if I were taking her across a wedding threshold, but once we were about ten feet past the wards, they were fine.

"I realize this sort of thing is in your genetic code," Sig said. "But you can put me down now."

I looked into her blue eyes. "What if I don't want to?"

"Then maybe I should carry you around like this in a room full of people that you want to take you seriously." But she was smiling, and she wasn't looking away.

I set her down.

Even with Simon present, we still had to get frisked, pricked, scanned, smelled, and blessed, and we rejoined Ben and his entourage simply by virtue of the fact that they had gotten bottlenecked at the checkpoint. It wasn't as bad as it had been at the hack factory, though. The guards stopped before anyone got legally married.

There were two elevators in the lobby, but they were mostly for show. Even though the electricity was probably working fine, no Templars will willingly put themselves in a small box that's likely to stop the first time strong magic appears, and as a knight led us up to the third floor, the wide, unlit stairwell was crowded with fit, heavily armed people. It reminded me of my time as a squire, of those nights when we were pulled out of bed without warning and forced to run up and down dark stairs until only one of us was left stumbling along, usually me. It was the exact wrong way to try to convince people that I didn't have a werewolf taint, but I've always had a stubborn streak and a high pain threshold.

We wound up in a small auditorium that seated maybe two hundred people in ascending concrete rows, and Simon left us to find our own seats while he went up on the stage to join a man who was so fat that he had to be really good at his job in the fitness-obsessed Templar culture. Most of the seats were filled with knights and lay sergeants in full battle gear, but there were also a few people in police, paramedic, or firemen uniforms, and a number of werewolves dressed in loose, light clothing that they could shed easily. I felt like I was at a seminar where someone was going to teach me how to sell real estate in hell. A group of local wolves near the front had saved seats for Ben and his following, and we slipped in among them.

The obese man—who committed another sin in Simon's eyes by being unshaven and having his white oxford shirttails untucked—had curly brown-grey hair and ruddy cheeks and big honking glasses that had to be at least partly for dramatic effect. I later found out that his name was Franklin Tobin, and Tobin was giving a running commentary on the images on the huge screens that dominated the room. One of the screens illustrated a maze of sewer lines, heating ducts, air vents, utility tunnels, access corridors, and an abandoned section of subway, all of which had apparently been built on top of and around each other until they resembled a huge helping of oddly angular spaghetti.

Another screen showed an overhead view of a particular patch of downtown Detroit, with streets and alleys clearly marked. But the screen Tobin was focusing on showed an image of a fit, short-haired man in a naval uniform. I recognized him from the newspaper printout I'd seen, though this was a younger version: Evan Gilbert. He was staring at the camera as if someone had ordered him to do so, his face the same cold, humorless granite that it had been in the newspaper photo. If he wore any expression at all, it was a look that said, "Take your damned photo and hurry up about it before I have my manservant kill you."

It turned out that Evan Gilbert really was the spearhead of Banner Rally Investments; he'd created the company seven years earlier, a tent pole holding up a hodgepodge of several small businesses who hardly seemed worth Gilbert's time. He came from old North Carolina money and held the reins of a family whose financial assets included interests in Big Tobacco, shipping, real estate, and full-time lobbying. Gilbert had served in the navy for twelve years and made the rank of lieutenant, which didn't mean quite the same thing that it did in other branches of the armed forces (the ripple effect created by a naval captain being a much higher position than other captains had translated downward to lieutenants as well), and Gilbert had supposedly been a brilliant officer. His promising military career had been cut short, however, when he was discovered to be the author of a book on naval history that discussed the modern military in an unflattering light.

Gilbert wasn't drummed out of the service, but he was given one of those commissions that basically amount to being put on hold, and when he resigned at the end of his term of enlistment, no one protested, despite the need for proven veteran officers in the Persian Gulf at the time. Then things got interesting.

"We've been assuming that the name Banner Rally meant that the investment company was having several businesses rally around a flag, presumably on a crusade to revitalize Detroit. But rally doesn't have to rhyme with Sally. It could rhyme with trolley." Several knights and werewolves around me began to shift restlessly while Tobin was talking. They didn't want the tease or the slow buildup. They just wanted the facts. But they obviously hadn't spent the last several months reading up on what little there was to read about the School of Night.

Tobin seemed oblivious to any signs of restlessness among his audience. "When the School of Night tried to break into our central archives, the attempt was spearheaded by a man operating under the codename Northumberland. Henry Percy, the wizard earl of Northumberland, was one of the members of the original School of Night. And one of the highest-placed double agents we found when we were purging our ranks of skinwalkers and the false Templar family was a woman named Marlo Davis. She was a screenplay writer in Los Angeles, and she was a contact point for several skinwalker cells."

This was news to me.

"And Christopher Marlowe the playwright was another member of the School of Night. Marlowe's activities as a spy have been written about and speculated on. You see? Marlo. Marlowe."

"Get to the point," Simon said crisply.

"Now we have a man operating under the name Rally, and he has interests in big tobacco in North Carolina... a naval career... real estate development... authorship... political manipulation..."

"You're saying he's supposed to be Walter Raleigh," Simon interceded, both to hurry Tobin along and to catch the rest of the audience up. "Another of the School of Night's original members. But the Order got King James the first to execute Raleigh, and it seems very unlikely that our ancestors wouldn't have made sure of it."

"I'm not saying that he's the original Walter Raleigh," Tobin said. "Some occult rituals are created by having participants reenact key events using similar actors under the same names in the same basic pattern of events. Truly significant historical developments echo in the collective unconscious that forms the fabric of our reality. They carve lines on the fourth dimension like sigils. I think this School of Night has been grooming certain individuals or families to take the place of its key original members so that it can complete some occult undertaking that our brotherhood interrupted back in the beginning of the seventeenth century."

I got a chill, but the audience started getting restless again. The words *magical bullshit* were practically floating above everyone's heads in a big connected thought bubble. Even Sig didn't seem to sense all the implications branching off from Tobin's words, and I know how smart she is from losing so many arguments to her. But then, Molly. I was a little better than Sig at locking the screaming, howling part of me in a mental cellar while I focused on the best tactical way to kill somebody, because I'd spent most of my long life doing it, but as soon as my surface thoughts ran across Molly, I almost growled. "So, they're taking the names of dead men," Sig said grimly. "Seems appropriate to me."

A lot of the werewolves around us grunted approval. I guess Sig wasn't just popular with Ben. When had that happened?

I tried to help Tobin out. "Walter Raleigh had a half-brother whose last name was Gilbert. Has anybody traced this Gilbert guy's family all the way back to the early sixteen hundreds?"

Tobin's face brightened. He was obviously one of the Order's merlins, and if he was like every other cunning man I'd ever met, Tobin would probably greet the sudden appearance of a long-extinct manticore by studying the complex webwork of its wings for any signs of how it managed to keep its lion's body airborne while the monster was tearing Tobin to pieces. "Not yet."

Simon spoke up again. "We haven't had time to analyze Gilbert's book, either. In fact, if we make a list of all the intelligence we haven't gathered yet, we're going to get depressed. But I'd rather hit these bastards now, while we still have the initiative, then wait for them to ferret out what we're doing. We know they're our enemy, and we know that they're terrifyingly good at spying on our Order."

The room resonated with grunts of approval.

"We also know they use skinwalkers—men and women who have to eat human flesh and kill someone they love just to be able to use their powers—to replace knights and werewolves and do horrible things wearing their faces," Ben said by way of support. "This School of Night has been staging supernatural attacks in the middle of crowds—not to make the world see magic, but to make it see monsters. We all have a stake in seeing these bastards dead, whatever they call themselves."

"Do you have anything else of importance to add before we get down to the logistics?" Simon asked Tobin.

Simon still wasn't telling everyone about the Book of Am, which meant he wasn't telling everyone about the man who was reading the School of Night's version. But I understood now—even if the knights hadn't identified the squat, balding man with the bushy beard and big glasses yet, he would likely be operating under the name Dee in some form or other. John Dee, the original scholar, author, or translator of the Book of Am.

"I have found something else you should know," Tobin said. "One of the business groups in that tower is a small firm that basically connects small companies and manufacturers. Almost like a business dating service. And one of the people on its board of investors used to be Gregory Apraxin."

Sig and Ben straightened as if someone had pulled their spines like zip cords, but no one else but Simon seemed to grasp the significance of that name. Simon explained it to the room at large. "Greg Apraxin was the Day Horseman, the servant of the Baba Yaga who worked with Bernard Wright."

The entire auditorium went motionless and quiet. Everyone recognized the name Bernard Wright. The werewolf who had tried so hard to start a war with the Knights Templar. The man who had confined and tortured werewolves in his attempts to start a werewolf plague. The man who had captured and impregnated female knights because he wanted to create a strain of hybrid werewolves who could resist their curse enough to have children. He was the closest thing to a big bad wolf that the Order and the Round Table had. If any name could unite both sides against a common enemy, it was Bernard Wright.

"And if you recall, we got into a war with a coalition of several vampire hives because they were violating the terms of the Pax Arcana and converting key political figures into vampires," Tobin said. "I've been examining the positions those political figures held, and most of them are under the influence of Gilbert's lobbyists now. These are tenuous connections, but we've only had a few hours to scratch the surface."

"What you're saying is, this School of Night has been working behind the scenes to start an all-out war between the Knights Templar and the supernatural world for decades," Simon said.

"I think the School of Night has been trying to have the most powerful organized groups in our world destroy each other before the School made its presence known." Tobin adjusted his glasses. Yeah, they were at least partly props. "But again, I need more time…"

"Time works both ways," Simon said. "These people have been sitting back and using pawns and puppets to mess with us at their leisure for at least seventy years. That's over as of now."

And then the discussion got serious. Not that it had been a lighthearted romantic comedy before, but we came close to just blowing the whole damn tower up outright. We talked it over, and the only things that made Simon decide against it were: (A) No matter how we covered it up or what strings we pulled, Homeland Security would get involved, and Simon hadn't had time to prepare a false narrative in Detroit; (B) Simon wanted to get his hands on any records and clues to the School of Night's organization and history that were in that tower; (C) we weren't entirely sure if we could destroy a magical artifact that way, or what would happen if we did. The last thing anybody wanted was a massive pile of rubble and ash and a lingering question about whether we had actually destroyed the Book of Am or not.

We were going in.

⚘40⚘

TOWER OUTAGE

At first, the attack went exactly according to plan, rarely a good sign in my experience.

Several knight teams had invaded the homes of people who worked for the businesses—or business fronts—that occupied that tower, and Simon had gotten his hands on more than a few individuals who had some intelligence on what went on inside it. The prisoners had a tendency to die if they said keywords like School of Night, but the interrogators had gotten used to that while rounding up the School's double agents inside the Templars. There was a risk that one of those abductions might send up a flag as someone who was supposed to go somewhere or call someone else didn't check in, but it was worth the risk for the intelligence we'd gained.

For instance, we knew that a mysterious cunning man was staying at the top of the tower and hadn't come out of the building for weeks.

Teams of knights moved through the various underground tunnels surrounding Rockwall Tower West and placed a series of Turn Away ward stones at precise locations that had been mapped out by merlins. It wasn't really one massive spell but a system of many tiny enchantments overlapping and meshing together, kind of like small rings forming an entire set of chain mail. Once the stones were set, a number of apprentice merlins moved behind the knights, performing the rituals that would key them.

The end result was that Rockwall Tower West was encased in a sphere of magic. I pictured it like one of those snow globes with a cheap plastic building immersed in a transparent dome. Passersby simply stopped looking at Rockwall Tower and went out of their way to avoid walking near it without consciously thinking about it. Naked supermodels and pro wrestlers could have rushed into the pavilion at the base of the tower and started up a game of touch football using live cats for footballs, and no one would notice.

Unfortunately, magic on this scale disrupted a power conduit beneath the ground and caused a major power outage for several blocks. Rockwall West wasn't using electricity anyway, presumably because its own magicks were already messing with the atmosphere, but another team of knights had to plausibly and severely sabotage another conduit farther away in order to conceal the real reason behind the outage from the rest of the city. This created an even larger power outage, but from a purely strategic point of view, any looting or riots would actually divert attention away from us, and the worst of them wouldn't start until the sun went down.

And then things stopped going to plan.

There really was a second Reader X in that tower—our John Dee—and despite our efforts to be subtle, his imagination kicked in soon after the last Turn Away charm was placed. It got foggy around the tower, real foggy and real quick. In fact, it wasn't fog so much as a descending cloud, and any plans of sending in a lone assassin through the sewer tunnels and up the air ducts went out the window, as did any backup plans of dropping knights onto the top of the tower via helicopter. Our ersatz John Dee could have walked out of the building with the book and gone past a knight four feet away without being seen.

But he didn't. Knights and werewolves rushed out to form a ring around the tower the way peasant fiefdoms used to form giant rings to trap woodland creatures on hunt days. The guards came out of cars, out of shops, out of sewers, off sidewalks, out of alleys, and they didn't draw their weapons until they were inside the boundary of the Turn Away wards. Some of them were dressed in full field armor, some of them as pedestrians, and more knights began driving toward the area from outlying posts.

Then things got ugly. Something very large materialized in that unnaturally dense fog. If I had to guess, it was the kind of large that went *fee fi fo fum* and smelled the blood of Englishmen. Whatever it was kicked one knight like a soccer ball, stepped on another, and uprooted a small tree planted in the pavilion to use like a club.

The giant was practically invisible in the fog. Its skin was horny and thick, its muscles were dense, and its bones were harder than any human's in order to support that much weight. The giant took hits from a lot of bullets, but it was going to take lots of armor-piercing ammo chewing away at one spot or something explosive to take it down, and the knights were too disciplined to fire blindly when stray shots might hit surrounding buildings outside the Turn Away ward.

It was on.

∾41∾

SHOOTING HIMSELF IN
THE FOOTNOTE

Unlike the cunning man who represented John Dee, Evan Gilbert was not living in Rockwall Tower West, toiling away on the School of Night's copy of the Book of Am. Perhaps that would have been a little too much like the real Walter Raleigh, who had spent several years confined in the Tower of London. Or perhaps Evan was just a sociopath and understood that self-sacrifice was for weaker people and fools.

No, Evan and his wife were in one of the remaining mansions in Detroit, eating filet mignon and ostrich eggs and crepes for breakfast in their bedroom. Evan was still in his pajamas when he heard the strange plants in his garden being burned with flamethrower units and salted with blessed salt. While a poison gas made with cyanide extracted from elderberry seeds began dropping his bodyguards downstairs, Evan took the time to cut his wife's throat with a letter opener, then took a handgun out of his nightstand and made his way to an honest-to-God secret passage that connected to the back of his closet. The mansion, like a lot of mansions in Detroit, had been built during Prohibition because of Prohibition, and the original occupant had wanted a secret means to a secret cellar.

The School of Night had taken that secret cellar and expanded on it, making an escape tunnel that led to one of the nearby abandoned manors in Brush Park.

Once inside the secret passage, Evan continued to indulge in clichés. There was a bomb with a nonelectrical timer that was powerful enough to destroy the entire manor directly beyond the door, and Evan set it to detonate in ten minutes before making his way inside the walls of his house, abandoning his two children.

Unfortunately for Evan, one of his supernatural bodyguards, a golem made of stone, did not need to breathe. Golems are nasty customers. Animated statues with no vital organs, the only way to kill golems is to destroy the animating word that is somewhere inside their body, either inscribed in their unliving flesh or written on a small parchment.

Lacking any feasible alternatives, the invading knights opened fire on the golem with armor-piercing rounds, chipping away at him, so to speak, and the golem happened to be in front of the wall that Evan was walking behind. Modern safe rooms and passageways are designed to be bulletproof, but there weren't a whole lot of modern mansions being built in Detroit when Evan had taken residency. Call it dumb luck or poetic justice, but Evan was shot several times, and even though none of the wounds were immediately fatal, he wasn't going anywhere fast, either. Several knights noticed the passageway peeking at them through torn sections of wall, and when they stepped around the rubble they'd made of Evan's golem and began knocking larger openings in the wall, Evan Gilbert took the handgun he'd brought along and ended his own life.

The knights found the bomb with three minutes to spare.

❧42❧

RAT RACE

Nothing resembling a phone or radio was working in the sewer tunnels beneath Rockwall Tower West, so I heard about the strange cloud outside of it through an ad hoc telegraph system. Werewolf observers were spread out in a line aboveground and below—it didn't take many wolves—and they relayed information verbally, relying on each other's sensitive hearing. The only difficulty was the human tendency to reinterpret. Psychologists have done studies where a group of people will pass a single sentence down a row by having each person whisper in their neighbor's ear, and the sentence will almost always get distorted by the time it reaches the end of the line, usually in minor ways, sometimes to the point where meaning is drastically altered or open to interpretation. With twenty people, "The roof of my house caved in" might become "The top of my house collapsed." With forty people, it becomes "I lost my house when the stocks collapsed." With sixty people, it becomes "I lost everything in the stock market crash." With a hundred people, it becomes "Some loser died in a stock car crash."

We only had eight werewolves relaying information, and the sentences I heard coming from farther back down the sewer tunnel were simple and straightforward.

"Some kind of fog just sprang up. The snipers can't see anything."

Long pause.

"We can't see nothing either. The B team is going in."

Long pause.

"It's cold."

Brief pause.

"Helicopters won't work."

Much longer pause.

"Some kind of giant thing is in the fog."

That was enough for Ben. Simon had been forced to stay behind to coordinate all of the different teams moving on the tower above- and underground, and Ben had taken charge of the underground efforts simply because that's where the most werewolves were concentrated. Wolves do well in the dark, technology or no technology, but we don't do so well in organized formations once the blood starts spraying. Ben could keep a large group of wolves in line when no one else could. Kasia and I were scouts, and Sig was behind us in case we met something spooky. We were going in, and I don't know if it was the right decision, but I don't know that there was a right decision. It was Ben's call, and he made it.

I put on my helmet. Its base had pressure-sensitive tabs that locked into small openings in the iron collar that was sheathed in my body armor. The openings showed through vents in the Kevlar, and when the helmet was engaged, little studs stuck out of my neck Frankenstein-style. The setup protected my carotid artery and made it harder for beings stronger than me to snap my neck. I also had a katana sheathed on my back, a sawed-off shotgun in my hands, a Ruger Blackhawk on my right hip, two silver steel knives in sheaths built into the outside of my boots, and some shotgun shells and chem sticks in various easy-to-reach loops, pouches, and pockets. I was more loaded down than I liked, and I still didn't feel prepared.

A safe distance ahead of me was a mismatched brick wall that covered up an access point to the tower's central air system. If by some miracle the industrial-sized fans were working, we would flood the building with nerve gas; otherwise, forget it. A low-explosive charge took the wall out.

The resulting dust cloud provided some cover, but it also meant that Kasia and I were partially deaf, mostly blind, and unable to smell much when some things cloaked in dust mess and darkness gagged and hacked loudly in front of me. They were distinctly animal sounds. I had a feeling that whatever was making that noise wasn't there to confer with me about the possibility of setting up a social engagement, so I discharged one of the barrels of my shotgun on general principle.

More than one creature screamed in response, high-pitched shrieks of rage and agony that cut through the ringing in my ears. I discharged my other barrel, and Kasia's handgun, a Desert Eagle without a suppressor, began sparking and roaring beside me. It gave me enough time to reload, but then Kasia gave a surprised grunt, and her gunfire ceased. I discharged both barrels of my shotgun at once, dropped the weapon, and drew a knife in each hand. Sharp claws made several small slices in the armor over my left forearm, and I disemboweled whatever large furry thing was behind them. I know I disemboweled it because...well...never mind.

Something else tried to skitter past my left side on clawed feet, and I tripped it and stabbed down into a writhing and squealing mass. A chem stick flew over my head from behind, and by the time it landed, the dust was clearing enough for me to get partial glimpses of bodies: fast-moving furry bodies in a square tunnel maybe eight feet wide. There were at least a hundred of the things. They were humanoid and clambering over their dead, some of them clinging to the sidewalls on all fours. Not werewolves. Rats. Man-shaped, human-sized rats. I tore out a throat and then went down beneath a biting, squirming avalanche, still holding on to my knives in that mosh pit of the damned.

It actually could have been worse. I'm stronger and heal faster than your average idiot, and my throat, eyes, wrists, groin, and stomach were protected from sharp edges by Kevlar and dense plastic plates, or reasonably so. I managed to kill the rat thing that was most directly on top of me, then killed the next ratling that tore the corpse away, then the next. Slice, rinse, and repeat. Doing this helped me keep a barrier of dead flesh between them and my most vital organs. Most of the damage I took was minor, claw slashes and fang punctures to my calves, forearms, and shoulders. The immediate danger was a slash on the femoral arteries in my thighs or the veins in my wrists, or a hard blow to the side of my head. Something tried to take the time to gnaw through my right boot, and I kicked its teeth down its throat in a way that probably broke its neck in the bargain. A bullet or its ricochet fired by a knight behind me slammed into the top of my helmet, a real bell-ringer, but the bullet had passed through some meat to get to me and the helmet held up. So did I. I managed to hang on to my knives and stab something next to me in the groin. Sig was somewhere behind me, firing tracer bullets so that other knights and members of the Round Table could fire effectively into the mass that had buried me.

There was a flash and a bang and new heights of squealing, and the weight on top of me lessened slightly. Then my dark new world crumpled and bucked with an explosion that didn't impact anything but air. A pressurized whispering sound filled my ears, and a hissing mist obscured my glimpses through the dim light of the chem stick. Teams made up of knights and werewolves from four different access points were flooding the tunnels with the nerve gas we'd brought along in case of skinwalkers. It was a crude, dense gas. It had to be. My helmet had a breathing filter built into it that scrubbed the contaminants out of the air before I breathed them in, and more subtle gases would have at least partially made it through or demanded a more sophisticated breathing apparatus. It was the only reason we Round Table members had agreed to wear knight armor and helmets. Wolves don't like being muzzled.

The rat things around me stopped focusing on attacking, though their unfocused thrashing was almost as bad. They screamed and scurried off me in all directions, some of them charging the mass of knights and werewolves behind me with their last breaths, some of them trying to flee. Soon the rat things began convulsing violently, and the convulsions didn't last for long. The dust had dispersed enough that I had a clear view of the proceedings. I kind of wished I didn't. There was ichor and just plain ick everywhere. I was covered in small cuts and punctures and felt like I'd just been in a dodgeball tournament played with baseballs, but I could move.

The one bright side—other than me not being dead, I mean—was that the rat things reverted to just plain rats upon their death, though each body seemed to fall apart into multiple rat corpses. No wonder there were so many of the damn things. It might be that they were based on some kind of Nutcracker or Cinderella tangent, but more likely they were inspired by Gallic stories about loup-garou, evil spirits that fashioned humanoid bodies out of possessed animals.

I heard Kasia grunting to my left and looked over. She was sprawled against the remains of the brick wall we had passed through, tugging at a jagged piece of pipe that was embedded in the plastic plate over her heart. Her efforts were hampered by the fact that her right hand was still a nub, and a bloody nub at that. Some rat things had been chewing on it.

Somewhere fairly far off I heard a door shut. I almost took off running to pursue the sound right there, but in the last two minutes my function had shifted from scout to perimeter guard. The knights and werewolves behind me were performing basic first aid on the severely wounded and sorting out the injured. There was the unharmed group, the defenseless group, the ones who could still hold a weapon and maintain a line until reinforcements arrived, and werewolves who would regenerate enough to function on the go. The knights who could still continue on were already reloading, reorienting, and reorganizing, in that order, but they needed a sentry. I don't know if it was deeply ingrained training or pack instinct that made me walk over to Kasia and grab the pipe by its shaft, grounding her with a foot on her thigh.

"Can I pull it out?" I didn't want to yank the pipe if it was the only thing holding Kasia together.

"It is only in up to the tip." I could hear the smirk behind her helmet. If Kasia was still up for sexual innuendo, she was fine. The pipe came out cleanly, and I didn't hear any wet sounds or sense any fluid resistance. If the sharp point really had made it through the thick plastic plate and Kasia's body armor, it hadn't done so by much.

"Yo," I called out. This was the call word that meant I wasn't reporting something urgent, like an imminent attack or tunnel collapse or the smell of explosives. Ben was busy passing information to a werewolf further down the relay system, but he immediately stopped and listened to me. "What?"

"Those rats were conjured up just like the monsters in New York."

"And?"

"So someone who can conjure monsters out of thin air knows we're here. We need to make a mad dash for the finish line."

༄43༄

KUMBAYAHHHHHH!

Thank God for the gas attack, and how many times does a man think that during his life? The tunnel we were in led to a higher and wider throughway made of smooth concrete. The area was filled with underground storage warrens protected by security fencing, and it was large enough to accommodate shipping and receiving. I didn't want to take the hours necessary to check and clear each of those chambers out thoroughly, and what would have been the point? A monster could appear in an area after we'd already checked it thoroughly, anyway. We didn't want to leave our rear completely unsecured for the same reason, though, so we sprinkled lookouts behind us like salt to keep bad things from growing up out of the ground behind us.

Large square pillars at least ten feet wide ran through the area at twenty-foot intervals, and Kasia and I made our way by weaving around them in alternating order, directly across from each other. We threw three glowing chem sticks in a wide pattern, and the one farthest in front went out. Not instantly—it was like the chem stick was a soda straw, and the light was being sucked through it by an invisible mouth.

I knew what that meant: ghost. More specifically, a ghost drawing on the energy from the room in order to manifest, despite what Sig had said about the Book of Am and spirits competing for the same resources. "Geist!" I yelled, or tried to yell. The sound didn't carry anywhere near as far as it should have. The temperature dropped several degrees, so cold that my breath was probably misting, though I couldn't see it, and the other two chem sticks went out even more rapidly than the first. There was something wrong in the darkness that followed. Something heavy was in the air, vibrating like a struck piano key whose presence is still lingering even though it isn't making an audible sound any longer.

We had passed a baling machine and three large squares of compressed cardboard about the circumference of a kiddy pool, and after Ben rapped out an order, a knight behind us set the bales on fire. It was a good thing. It was the one good thing. The reddish light revealed close to a dozen silent silhouettes. Kasia and I were in the middle of a small forest of dark human-shaped outlines that had silently sprouted up around us somewhere in the last ten seconds.

I didn't think this was the Book of Am in action, or at least not directly. I could smell Molly. More accurately, I could smell the thing that was the antithesis of Molly. I suppose it followed that if Molly helped stranded spirits move on to the other side, her shadow would summon them. The towers in this area had been built when most construction companies in Detroit were in the mob's pocket if they weren't owned by mobs outright. Because of this, mobs liked to use cement beds that hadn't finished hardening to get rid of bodies, and a lot of the biggest buildings in Detroit have bones mixed into concrete foundations that can go several hundred feet down. There had probably been plenty of violent, restless souls for Molly's shadow to draw on.

A wind that wasn't a wind began hurling debris around the room even though my own body was unaffected. There was a silver cross hanging under my armor, but I hadn't worn it visibly because I hadn't wanted it to glint. Dust coated the visor of my helmet, and while I was trying to wipe it off with my forearm, a fallen carpenter's nail embedded in the back of my right calf. My armor was tough, but even natural winds can drive straw into trees, and this was no natural wind. A shard of glass tore past my shoulder at the same angle that thin rocks skip across water, and the glass took some of my blood with it. My shotgun's barrels popped open and down, and two shells smashed past my fingers as I tried to reclose the breach. Then giant invisible fingers grabbed my helmet and tried to rip it off. Instead, my body was lifted off its feet and flung backward.

As soon as I was finished skidding, I rolled over to my elbows and knees and pulled myself into a crouch, but something was keeping me from standing up. The visor of my helmet was made of bulletproof glass, but I heard it begin to crack, and I had no idea if the nerve gas we'd used had dispersed yet. Then the pressure was suddenly gone.

"Come on, John." It was Sig's voice. Clear. Easy to hear. Unafraid. She took my hand, and the pressure around me disappeared as if it had never existed. I stood up. "Don't be silly," Sig was saying firmly, but she wasn't saying it to me. "You can't find peace by attacking people. Don't you know that?"

There was such love in Sig's voice, so much raw compassion, that it made my throat tight. Sig was more guarded with the living than the dead. Me, I would never have the courage to speak to anyone that way except maybe Sig or Molly or a hurt child, and there was probably something to that. Maybe ghosts are more like hurt children than anything else. Sig led me through the room by my hand as if she were walking an exceptionally large toddler, and I followed her meekly.

The spirits began to fade out as we walked across the room. I would like to compare them to candles being blown out, but they were the opposite of that, really. They were more like those trick candles whose black burnt wicks reignite, patches of light being restored.

We came across Kasia huddled and shivering on the ground in a fetal position. I let go of Sig's hand and picked up Kasia's Desert Eagle. It was missing its magazine, so I took one of the spare clips attached to her outer armor and slammed it into place. Then I reholstered Kasia's gun and slung her body over my shoulder, ignoring her faint stuttering curses. Better me than Sig.

"John," Sig said tersely in a voice I'd never heard before.

I was already looking around for whatever the hell had gone wrong now. "What?"

"Something's changed. The air is different."

"You mean through your breathing filter?"

"I...can't explain it. It's like a shadow passing over the sun."

Since we couldn't see the sun, I didn't find that comparison particularly helpful.

~44~

THOSE MOUNTAINS DON'T LOOK
LIKE BIG ROCK CANDY

What we didn't know...what we couldn't know...was that those spirits hadn't come to us. We had gone to them. The knights who had either been headed for the tower or were trying to see through that dense fog with sniper scopes suddenly saw the fog disperse, but when the mist was gone, the concrete courtyards at the base of the tower were empty. All sounds of combat or destruction had vanished, and as to the tower itself...well, have you ever seen a dead body? Have you ever stood across a funeral casket and seen something that looked like someone you used to know, but somehow you understood that what you were staring at was just a body-shaped mass of nothing? Apparently, staring at the building was like that. Everyone who saw the tower understood immediately that it was...not just empty but devoid.

I don't know if that tower was another kind of shadow being, or the ghost of the one that went somewhere else.

What I do know is that the people who had vanished were having the opposite experience. The knights who had been directly outside the tower saw their entire world change. The mist was gone, and so were the sounds of Detroit streets behind them. The smooth concrete of the tower's pavilions suddenly merged into barren fields of ash and patches of pale white grass. On the distant horizon were surrounding mountains of brown glass glinting in the light of a dying red sun.

There are a lot of Eastern European fables and folktales about a land with mountains made of brown glass. A few of them even made their way into the Brothers Grimm collection. It was a place somewhere on the borders between the land of the living and the land of the dead, sometimes a shadow of one, sometimes a shadow of the other, never completely a place of life or death.

Basically, our John Dee's imagination had just found one hell of an emergency exit. If you think of our reality as an airplane, he had just punched out of the cockpit and taken everyone in or around the tower with him.

~45~

BEST BE NIMBLE, BEST BE QUICK, IF YOU GO BENEATH THE LIMBO STICK

Not knowing what the hell else to do, Sig escorted me to the far side of the storage bay, where another narrow tunnel ramped upward. I set Kasia down beside the entranceway and took another chem stick, this one off Sig's hip. I cracked the stick and tossed it upward. The glowing cylinder landed and briefly revealed a freight elevator and a door, then rolled back halfway down the sloping hallway before the cylinder's path curved inward for reasons known only to it and mathematicians. The chem stick traveled in a semicircle and wound up nestled against a wall.

I moved forward while Kasia pulled herself to her feet and Sig urged on those who were still waiting on the other side of the storage bay. They were knights and werewolves, ferocious fighters every one, and there was still a long, reluctant pause before they obeyed her.

The door at the end of the hall had a window the size of a

small picture frame centered in its upper half, and beyond it I could make out a stairwell going up. I stepped to the side and broke the window with the butt of my shotgun and was rewarded with a burst of flame that set the forearm of my armor on fire and blew the door off its hinges. There was no point waving and running about—it was the fresh rush of oxygen that had caused the fire to ignite—so I bent down and folded myself over my forearm until the flames were smothered by my fire-resistant armor.

Sig and Kasia moved up to cover the door from the side while I composed myself. "Molly's shadow did this," I told Sig.

It was Kasia who responded. "Why do you say so?"

"Smell that?" I asked. The air was full of a potent blend of cleaning products, lighter fluid, and concentrated amyl nitrates whose presence I won't explain further because they're really not the kind of thing anybody should play around with. But somewhere on the other side of that used-to-be door was a container whose lid had been lifted when Molly's shadow walked past. "I was the one who taught Molly how to make that trap out of cleaning supplies and a few odds and ends."

"Hmmn." Kasia nodded at the freight elevator. "Which do you prefer, then? The elevator shaft or the stairwell?"

"The stairwell." More practical or not, I was following Molly's shadow, but I didn't feel like admitting to a sentimental streak right then.

Ben's voice came from where he was standing down the hall, behind the corner of the entranceway. "Hold up. I want to bounce something off you."

Bounce was another code word. It could mean that Ben had just gotten word through the werewolf telegraph system, or it could mean that one of the knight teams had managed to enter the building through the access tunnels and ventilation ducts or lobby. If that were the case, the forces aboveground could flush out any nearby ambushers or trap them between our two forces.

"Sure," I called back to Ben. "I was just thinking the other day that you and I never really have a chance to chat anymore. What's up?"

"I'm having a little problem."

"I told you to go before we left," I said. "We're not stopping to look for a bathroom now."

"I'm not getting word from Simon anymore. Somewhere down the line, our telegraph system got cut."

My first thought was that we'd been flanked, that some kind of butt-uglies had cropped up behind us and were rolling our forces up like a carpet. "Anybody hearing any signs of attack?"

"No."

"There wasn't an attack," Sig said. "They're just not there anymore. Or we're not."

"What do you mean?"

She shook her head in a way that could have meant anything and didn't mean anything. "I don't know what I mean. But it's true. It feels like the whole world is a ghost."

"We're not in hell," I said. "Trust me. I once worked at a fast food restaurant in Cleveland where the milk shake machine was always breaking down."

Sig's helmet stilled as she gave me a look.

"We might be on the spirit paths," Ben said.

One part of my brain was rapidly thumbing through mental index cards of every fairy tale and fable involving spirit worlds and alternate dimensions that I'd ever read, but there were so many that I gave up fairly quickly. Another part of my brain was tallying how many people we had in or around the tower. There were probably at least a hundred knights at the tower lobby.

Three other underground teams had been moving through ducts, service tunnels, and ventilation shafts, with at least forty fighters trailing them. "So, what I hear everybody saying is, we're screwed, and there's nowhere to go but forward, so we'd better stop talking and go there fast." I speak Fucked fluently.

Ben didn't take more than three seconds to think that over. "Yeah."

At least this John Dee didn't seem any more capable of using his Book without limits than Reader X had. The ground would have swallowed us whole. The air would have turned to fire. Hell, the bowels of the building might have turned into actual bowels and farted us out the sewer system.

The sounds of gunfire and breaking glass and the smacks of shattering concrete were breaking out in the stairwell above us. Ben had one more thing to say, though: "The traps this Molly shadow thing is setting are bad news too. Molly knows how you work. You might want to keep that in mind."

"Got it," I said.

I still wasn't used to working with people in helmets again, and when four knights and four werewolves emerged from the shadows, I couldn't stop myself from taking the time to identify them by smell and size and movement. One of them was Ben's right hand, Louis. Another was Stuart, the young, stocky knight who kept showing up and smelling pissed-off about it. I used sign language to split us into two teams.

Louis took control of the second team, and they began to noisily unload climbing gear in front of the elevator doors. The sounds of fighting upstairs had only gotten louder, and I moved into the stairwell and inhaled deeply. It was still difficult to smell anything other than burnt air and ammonia.

"There's something worse waiting for us in this stairwell," I told Kasia.

"How do you know?"

I knew because I had taught that fire trap to Molly to keep werewolves or vampires from sensing anything else. The explosion temporarily damaged enhanced hearing, the heat from the fire interfered with infrared vision, and the dispersed ammonia disrupted scent trails. "Trust me."

There were faint hints of illumination coming from the stairwell landings above. The light was shining through the small square windows in the upper frame of each stairwell door, but it wasn't much. Each set of staggered staircases was separated by three-and-a-half-feet-high metal rails, but the bars had a solid wall of thick red sheet metal welded over them, with the words ROCKWALL TOWER WEST painted on them in white swirly letters. There was a slanted crack shaped like a triangle where the stairs on the left and the stairs on the right met and passed each other, so that you could only peer through the rails for half of the steps.

I risked a peek upward into the vertical crack, half expecting something nasty to come dropping down. Molly's double had already proven that she could make homemade combustibles, and that wasn't even accounting for magical nasties. But all I saw was a dark stairwell that went fourteen floors up. I felt like I was at the bottom of a huge gullet.

I began to creep up the stairs, negotiating the deep shadows cast by the scant lighting. Kasia trailed one flight behind me, and Sig was a good eight feet behind her. A paladin named Miguel who I didn't know was our anchor, and after him, Stuart took charge of the larger group that would be following us. Below, I could hear the second scouting group begin to pry open the freight elevator doors. Thankfully, there were no explosions from that direction, but there were yells coming from the ground-floor lobby above. No, not yells. Screams.

Each separate set of stairs was twelve steps between landings, one middle landing between each floor, and I kept creeping my way up to ground level. The screams and gunshots were coming through the first-floor landing, and I tried to look through the small square window, but the window was coated in blood and fleshy bits. "Watch the first-floor door until I get back," I whispered to Kasia. There was no way I was going to bypass that door without at least peeking through it—I'm just not wired that way—but I was still convinced that something nasty was waiting for us farther up the stairwell, and I at least wanted to secure the landing directly above us before we stuck our noses in any other wood chippers.

That turned out to be the worst good decision I ever made.

As I cautiously moved up to the stairs that led to the second-floor landing, something big moved. It was reptilian and scaled and long-bodied and flexible and cold-blooded and apparently capable of staying completely still for long periods of time, and did I mention that it was big? A head the size of an armchair came lunging around the landing from the adjacent stairs above me, and I fired both barrels of my shotgun. I think the loads ripped into the thing's eyes. The head did stop moving forward, in any case, but a jaw opened and revealed fangs that seemed a lot larger than that head should have been able to contain. I saw those fangs clearly because fire built up at the base of the thing's throat right before a solid sheet of flame came roaring out of its mouth.

It was a dragon. A live dragon. No, bigger than life, and blacker than sin, and the dragon had its own opinion on how likely it was that a man called Charming could ever really win a fight with such a thing.

Later, I would decide that the dragon had been a number of security guards. Later, I would wonder if the security guards had been particularly fierce, or if John Dee 2.0 just associated dragons with beings who guard precious treasures. At the moment, though, I was too busy throwing myself over the rail to my right with no thought of dignity or how I was going to land. My upper torso hit the adjacent metal rail, and Kasia hooked her arm around my neck and pulled me over before I slipped and caught in the crack in between. Unfortunately, Kasia only had one working hand, and that hand was full of Desert Eagle. She shunted me aside, and I landed painfully and slid farther down the stairs as flames hit the landing wall above us and rebounded.

When I tumbled down to the next landing, I lost track of what was happening for a few seconds. There's a sound that a very heavy, very sinuous body makes when it moves over a hard surface on clawed feet, its legs built low to the ground. I have no idea how to describe that sound, though. I don't think the English language was designed with that kind of sound in mind, and I doubt many people who ever heard the sound lived to describe it. So I'll make up my own word. *Sklurrphlitle.* There was a *sklurrphlitl*ing sound.

The paladin, Miguel, passed me while I lay on the ground silently reevaluating the decisions that had led me to this point in my life. He was unslinging a carbine of some kind from his back. Sig had stopped to pull me to my feet, and Kasia's handgun came clattering down the stairs as I let go of Sig's arm. I heard the distinctive hiss of a katana being unsheathed even with all of the background noise. Then I couldn't hear anything but an impossibly loud roar. Something wet and fleshy hit the wall above me—I think it was a large piece of dragon tongue—and then Kasia's sword and Kasia's body followed it, her torso smashing into the same wall so hard that Kasia actually crushed a thin layer of stone and showered me with dust.

I'm not sure, but I think the dragon had used its own skull and powerful neck muscles like a club.

Miguel's carbine began chattering, and I didn't wait to see how that was going to turn out. Naptime was over. I screamed at Sig to back up and grabbed Kasia by the scruff of something and hauled her body to the side, down three or four of the next set of steps, and a few seconds later, another rush of flame came pouring down from above and filled the landing we had just vacated. The sound of large teeth and tearing flesh followed. Miguel. I guess the dragon liked its meat well done. I eased Kasia's body farther down the stairs, staying low behind the sheet metal that covered the stairway rail.

Below me, Stuart yelled some question and Sig yelled something back at him, but I was focused on what was going to hell above me. And I mean directly above me. A huge reptilian snout was peeking out over the stairway railing directly over my head, crossing over the vertical crack between adjacent staircases. The dragon sniffed loudly, its eyes gouged out by shotgun pellets, and then it started to open its big mouth again, probably to bathe the entire staircase in fire. I really wasn't in favor of this idea, and I strongly expressed my disapproval by grabbing Kasia's katana off the top of the landing and stabbing its blade upward into the underside of the dragon's jaw.

The dragon recoiled violently, banging its head on the stair rails above it. I hope it bit more of its tongue off too, the bastard. The dragon roared again, and if it had been able to throw its entire body in the crack between overlapping staircases, it would have killed me for sure. Instead, it began *sklurrphlitl*ing down the stairs across and above me, preparing to sinuously twist around the landing so that we could meet face-to-face. I wasn't too enthusiastic about that idea, either.

I had no clue where my shotgun was, and it would have been

empty if I did, so I held on to Kasia's katana and stepped up on a handrail, then vaulted over the sheet metal separating the staircases. The top of the adjacent metal rail caught me in the chest again, and if it hadn't been sharply tilted, I wouldn't have scraped over it. But it was, and I did, and I landed on the moving scaly back of a beast that was at least eighteen feet long and four feet off the ground. Like most dragons from the old tales, it was wingless.

The dragon was suddenly in an odd position. Its forefront was now on the landing below me, its head just peeking around to the lower levels where I was supposed to be. Its hind legs were on the landing above me. And I was right on top of its middle. The dragon's spine was too long for it to buck, and its mass was too great for it to ripple, so it just writhed. Fast. The metal railing lurched and half tore loose from the concrete stairs, but my foot still managed to kick off it so that I bounced back and stayed on the dragon's spine, at least until the dragon veered in the opposite direction. Then I slid over the ridged, sandpapery surface of the dragon's back before I could find any kind of handhold, and when I fell, I got pinned between the far stairwell wall and a massive torso that slammed into me like a tidal wave made of meat.

But that torso also impaled itself on the katana whose hilt I had managed to brace against the wall. The dragon's scales only covered the upper half of its body. I couldn't move anything but the forearm holding Kasia's sword, but move that forearm I did, slicing the blade deeper so that I could lean into the wound.

The dragon screamed. Then there was a loud impact sound and the dragon died. Yeah, I know. Anticlimactic much? Unfortunately, the dragon didn't stop moving. The dragon's body kept convulsing from side to side and pounding me against the wall while I tried to free the sword and climb up over its back again. I'd grab a breath, have it knocked out of me, grab a smaller breath, and have my torso squeezed. I was having a Lamaze lesson from hell.

Somewhere in there, the cracked visor of my helmet turned into a spiderweb of fractured glass.

I'm not sure how long I spent like that before Sig came walking over the top of the dragon as if it wasn't shuddering from left to right. She grabbed the shaft of the spear that was emerging from the back of the dragon's skull a few inches beneath the sharp tip and pulled. I guess the spear had traveled between the dragon's open jaws, up into the roof of its mouth, through its brain, and out the back of its skull. Once Sig had freed her spear, she held out her right hand so that she could grab my left. "Come on."

Like I was just taking time to sightsee. To our left, we have stinking scratchy blood-splattered dragon scale that smells like bad aftershave and fish tank. To our right, we have profusely bleeding dragon flank that smells like burnt brass. Don't be alarmed, folks; the blood may or may not be poison, but it isn't acidic.

I could hear the second team that Stuart was leading moving around. The dislodged rail and its sheet metal covering had turned the lower stairs into a kind of crawlspace. Then Sig pulled my hand as soon as the dragon's body shifted again. It gave me enough purchase to free myself and clamber up. I lay there on top of the dragon's back for a few seconds, trying to regain my breath while its corpse shuddered beneath me. It was as if the dragon and I had just finished a particularly vigorous bout of lovemaking. The thought was so obscene that it almost got me moving again, but not quite.

"Good job." By this time Sig was on the landing above me,

guarding us. "You got it to open its mouth wide enough for me to throw my spear up its nasal cavity."

"Just like I planned," I gasped. The glass visor on my helmet was so splintered that I could barely see through it, so I took it off.

"Your pants are on fire."

I thought Sig was just calling me a liar, but there really were small flames flickering on my left calf. I patted them out. Knight field armor is serious stuff. "Is Kasia okay?"

"She is. She won't be moving for a while." Sig didn't sound too upset about that, but she didn't sound too upset about Kasia still breathing, either.

"What are those sounds coming from the subbasement?" Now that my mind wasn't going *dragon dragon dragon dragon dragon*, I was registering that the screams from the lobby had stopped, but there were new and weird noises down there.

Ben's voice traveled up the stairwell from wherever he was crouching. "There are flying things in the elevator shaft." He said this way too matter-of-factly. "Louis is handling it."

Okay, then. I leaned Kasia's sword against the wall. "Hey, Kasia," I said in a normal tone of voice. "I'm leaving your sword on the landing right above the ground floor."

Somewhere down below, I heard her voice, faint and ragged but alert. "Thank you."

"Have you picked up Molly's scent again?" Sig asked.

"No," I said. "But I'll find it."

And I would.

∾46∾

HIGH GROUND: IT'S NOT JUST USEFUL MORALLY

A brown-haired werewolf named Jay who looked like a high school wrestler came up and helped Stuart try to clear an access point on the landing behind us. Said landing was blocked by a couple tons of dragon carcass, but Stuart shot out the small viewing window in the door and peeked through. I could hear the urgent, quiet conversation that he had with another knight in Latin. It wasn't smooth because the Romans had some kind of stick up their butts about prepositions, but their hurried conference translated something like this:

"What lobby danger troubles you?"

"Living statues. But that is the lesser vexation."

"What mean you?"

"We occupy some strange dimension. Detroit is gone, brown glass mountains surround us, and the sun is red."

"Incestuous mother lover! Do you require our immediate aid?"

"Only one living statue visually remains."

Then Stuart yelped, and he didn't even have being a werewolf as an excuse. What he did have was a heavy fragment of reception counter caving in the top of the stairwell door where he'd just been standing.

I sluffed up the steps. I wasn't there to lead a slow careful expedition that cleared the tower floor by floor; I was there to move into enemy territory and play capture the flag, and now that I knew a dragon had been guarding the upper stairwell, I kind of doubted anything else was. I wanted to take advantage of the dragon's absence before anyone or anything else stepped in to fill the void.

I didn't run all out, though. Oxygen and I were just barely on speaking terms again, and I wanted to retain the option of shrieking hysterically. I was also finding and reloading a shotgun as I moved. Everybody's life has given them certain skill sets, whether that be making omelets or shooting foul shots or texting one-handed without looking, and I could probably thumb shells into a shotgun while skateboarding down an escalator.

At the next floor landing, I took a shuffling peek through the viewing window built into the door. There wasn't any electricity working, but it was day outside even if it had turned into a foggy day in a dead dimension, and most of the long hallway I saw was traveling between glass offices and conference rooms. I didn't see anything moving, not even shadows. Especially not shadows.

The next two floor landings yielded similar experiences. It was the fifth-floor landing that sucked. I took my glance, and it's a damn good thing my body was moving because some kind of javelin came straight through the small square viewing window faster than any major league baseball. I think the sharp point took a millimeter off my neck hair.

The door flew open and I discharged a shotgun barrel into

it just as bad things came boiling out. They were men, sort of, but they had an extra pair of arms coming out of their torso, and most of their four hands were clutching short swords, daggers, shields, or spears. Red eyes had emerged from every side of their skulls, and insect mandibles had sprouted from their humanish cheekbones. Their skin wasn't completely chitinous, but it was harder and more polished-looking than normal flesh, and their muscles were bulging and oddly segmented.

Ant men. As far as I know, the few remaining real ant men live in networks of underground tunnels beneath the surface of Greek islands, but there are still myths about how Zeus created them from ants to replace an island's population after a plague wiped out all of the humans. Whatever the case, these versions were strong. The one I shot and killed was pushed forward violently, and I barely moved my arm aside before the next ant men used their brother's corpse to pin me against the opposite landing wall. I did move my arm aside, though, and I angled the shotgun around the dead body and discharged a second barrel into the ant men who were using their dead brother as a battering ram.

The flesh under the ant men's jaws was soft and vulnerable for some reason—I guess it had to do with neck mobility or swallowing—and two more of them had their throats torn out by the load. Hundreds of tiny ants went flying out of their bodies when they were wounded, splattered against the wall like dead flies on a fly strip. Some tiny ants that were still alive began crawling out of the exposed wounds, but I didn't really register that at the time because Sig's spear flew out over the railing from the stairs below me and struck another ant man through the side of its head. I shoved the corpses around me back and drew my katana.

The next ant man had short swords in each fist, which was

actually good, because I kicked the body of the ant man Sig had killed and impaled the corpse on the blades in its left hands, making an impromptu kebab. God help me if something that strong with that many limbs started getting handsy. I ran around the left side while the ant man was still freeing its fouled blades and cut its head off with a katsugi-waza strike from my shoulder; then I was past it and smashing another set of left blades down. The uchi otoshi strike smacked my blade back up from the impact in a way that would have horrified a lot of kendo instructors and let me impale the katana under the jaw of another ant man in the doorway. I spun away and used a stiff forearm to push the dying body off my blade in the same motion, and then I was running up the next set of stairs and Sig was following me with her handgun roaring in my ears.

We made it past the choke point, and several ant men tried to follow us through the landing door and up the stairs, but they were stepping over bodies and slipping on gore, and a burly werewolf, Jay, was suddenly on the landing and swinging a fire axe.

Stuart was on the stairs right beneath the landing, and he braced the barrel of a riot gun on the stairway rail, ready to begin firing the moment Jay was out of the way. Jay's hands were changing into claws around the haft of his fire axe, and his voice was a lot more ragged behind his helmet. "GO!" he roared, and I'm not using that verb figuratively. It's not like Jay needed to be loud for my sake.

"Go for their throats!" I tossed over my shoulder. Something about those tiny ants I'd seen reminded me of the trolls that had still been assimilating out of vagrants when we'd killed them. It gave me a very strong feeling that we really had caught the School of Night off guard, that John Dee 2.0's mind was frantically calling up things to protect him. If he was like most cunning folk, he probably didn't like capitalism all that much, and he'd been confined in this office building for weeks. Maybe the rat men represented the corporate rat race on some level. Maybe the ant men were office drones. If the world of myth and magic envisioned by John Dee really was colliding violently with workplace reality, I'd better hurry the hell up before I found out what kind of monster an office manager would inspire.

The stairs of the next few floors were caked in dead bodies. They weren't human or inhuman, but too much human. The corpses looked as if their skin had been turned into candle wax that was melting off their bodies. In some cases, agonized faces were trying to emerge from chests or shoulders that were sliding off their frames like a loose tarp, while above those chests and shoulders a head flopped like a loose hood.

"The hell?" I muttered to Sig as we rounded a stairwell toward floor seven.

"Skinwalkers." I didn't ask how Sig knew. Apparently, dragging psychically sensitive magic users who had killed their loved ones and turned cannibal to a place where vengeful ghosts were more active hadn't been entirely in the School of Night's favor.

Floor eight went great. Nine was fine. Then came ten and sucked again.

The door on ten opened while I was still moving up from the landing on floor nine. "Sig? John?" a voice called out from above. Molly's voice.

∾47∾

SO MOLLY'S SHADOW ACTUALLY TURNED OUT TO BE PRETTY AMAZING...

Hey, shadow bitch," I called up while I reloaded my shotgun.

"John, it's me!" Molly's voice said, and said it just the way Molly would, too. "I know what you're thinking, but you've got this all wrong. I'm not some shadow thing. The shadow thing took my place—you left it back in New York."

"We know; that's why we're here to rescue you," Sig said. "Come on down here and give us a hug."

"I'm serious, Sig!"

Seriously trying to mess with our heads, maybe. It didn't matter how unlikely what the shadow thing was saying was; if it could insert the tiniest little doubt in the backs of our minds, we might hesitate or freeze up at a critical moment. "So, you're alone?" I asked, wishing I'd brought some grenades. The shadow bitch was probably wishing the same thing.

"Some skinwalkers were holding me prisoner, but then they started pulling some *Help me, I'm melting!* number."

The Wizard of Oz. She was even referencing movies the way Molly and I did.

"Some four-armed things ran past me too," the shadow bitch continued. "But they weren't very bright."

Apparently, she thought we weren't either. I had made a connection with the real Molly and followed her in a dream. Even if I hadn't, there was no way Sarah and a Fisher King would have been fooled by some kind of wraith. I angled the shotgun up between the cracks in the railing and fired blind. Something metal rang off a stairway rail while the shadow bitch uttered a profanity I'm pretty sure Molly never would have. Then the Uzi it had been aiming downward while hoping to get me to peek upward bounced off another rail and clattered to the stairs below me. I was already up and moving around the next bend in the staircase before the echoes had died down.

Molly...I mean, her shadow, darted through the stairwell door to floor ten even while she yelled my name. She wasn't dressed like Molly had been. She was wearing a mask made out of a bull's skull and dark robes. Don't ask me what religion or anti-religion that was supposed to represent. That whole thing about the Devil having horns isn't biblical. It came about while the early Christian church was trying to convert the Greeks and Romans and Celts by demonizing gods like Pan and Mithras and at least half a dozen others whose avatars or ceremonies involved goats or bulls.

The shadow bitch was bleeding.

We followed Molly's double, shadowing the shadow. I suppose all the small aches and pains were still there, but I wasn't feeling them through the adrenaline spike. When we reached the landing of floor ten, we saw that floors eleven and up had become somewhat problematic. Ice was everywhere. The individual stairs of the stairwell were gone, obscured by a thick slope of ice. The walls were covered in ice. The next landing was covered in ice. A mist that seemed to be moving around a little too much to be lifeless filled the space between the floor and ceiling, and there was an unnatural absence of sound.

More ghosts, probably. Drawing on energy, including heat and sound, to manifest something unpleasant. And don't ask me if we were really in a land of the dead, or a book version of the land of the dead, or if the book had created some shunt that allowed real ghosts easier access to our plane, or replicated those effects, or what the practical difference between any of those options would be, because I never did manage to figure that one out, or care.

I decided to follow Molly's shadow, at least until I found the adjacent stairwell on the other side of the building or another set of elevator doors or a window. Trying to fight whatever was in that stairwell while making my way up a steep slope of ice didn't seem like it would end well. The sound of Molly's shadow retreating was in my ears while I thrust the door open and angled the shotgun sharply to the left and fired to clear the doorway.

"I thought we were going to try to take her alive," Sig said while I held the door open with my foot and thumbed two more shells into my shotgun. I could smell blood coming from floor ten. Lots of blood, fae blood, iron-rich and fresh. I could smell fear stink too, and pain sweat, and voided bowels and bladders. What had been going on in there?

"These particular shells are loaded with blessed salt," I said. "They won't kill a normal human being, and anything else they do to that thing, I'm pretty sure it needs to be done."

The sound of the shadow thing's footsteps was getting farther away, and there was something odd about their quality, muffled and resonant at the same time. I kicked the door open and peeked around the entrance, but you know that saying about being ready for anything? It's a crock.

I was facing the walls of a maze. Said walls were made of thin white stone the color of office cubicles, and those walls reached from the floor to the ceiling. Maybe the maze went with those rat associations that John Dee 2.0's mind had made earlier, or maybe the son of a bitch's imagination had conjured up a literal corporate labyrinth.

"This feels different," Sig said. "Like something's keeping the spirits out on this floor."

Well, she would know. I went in, trusting Sig's words and trusting her to keep me in her line of sight. I had it in my head that I would follow the Molly smell straight to the shadow thing, but the shadow must have been over each twist and turn and path of the maze several times, confusing the scent trail like a fox. I inhaled deeply, and the air was so dry that it stung my sinuses. Could you make stone walls out of moisture molecules and dust motes if you sucked enough of them out of the air? I could hear Molly farther ahead, but that didn't mean there weren't wrong turns and dead ends between us, and the multiple bends and angles were messing with echoes.

The shadow thing spoke to me low enough that Sig couldn't hear it, and it had given up on trying to convince me that it was the real Molly. *She doesn't love you, you know. Sig. She's never gotten over feeling guilt for the way her parents died. She only picks men that it won't hurt too much to lose. Her lovers are a way of punishing herself.*

I found a dead body at the first fork. It smelled like a half-elf. The half-elf's ears looked human, probably because of plastic surgery, and it was dressed like an ordinary office worker. The body was lying facedown in a pool of congealed blood that had poured down from a slit throat. Normally, I would have suspected it of being some kind of undead, but Sig had said there were no restless spirits in there. And hell, I probably would have had a similar reaction to an office job myself.

She went straight from a loser like Stanislav Dvornik to you, Molly's voice continued. *Doesn't that tell you something? She doesn't love you; she just doesn't want to be alone, and you're the kind of train wreck she thinks she deserves.*

My body was covered in a lot of cuts and slices, and I rubbed my left forearm hard enough to leave a spot of dried blood on the white wall. I didn't have a ball of thread to unwind if I took wrong turns and confused my own scent trail, or bread crumbs to drop, but bloodspots five and a half feet off the floor that smelled like me would do. A horizontal smear to indicate I'd come this way unimpeded. Two drabs or dots to indicate the passage led to a dead end.

The other me doesn't love you either, Molly's voice whispered. *She's the kind of idiot who can't help picking up any kind of wounded animal she finds along the road, even if taking care of them is gross and inconvenient. You're one more burden to her.*

I didn't respond. The shadow thing's hearing probably wasn't as good as mine, and I didn't want to give away my location. Instead, I retraced from a dead end and went west and found part of a collapsed desk with a laptop and printer dumped on the floor. A big yellow coffee mug had shattered when it dropped.

It was almost possible to visualize how the maze walls had sprung up. The desk was in fragments, but it wasn't as if it had been shattered. Most of it was just gone, not cleanly sliced, not missing bite-shaped chunks, just…gone. The same held true for the office equipment that had spilled out of partial drawers. Half a stapler. An anonymous black stub of plastic. The desk's molecules must have converted while the level was reassembling. There was a picture of an awkwardly smiling family of three still taped to the maze wall where a cubicle slat must have transformed or expanded beneath it, the woman holding a small girl in a way that suggested forcible restraint as much as a hug.

Choo and I talk about you as if you were a mad dog; did you know that? Deep down, we wonder if you're going to turn on us someday or get us killed.

Had the people who worked on this floor been normal people who had no idea where they were working? Or was it just that even minions had families, mortgages...wait a minute... the knights hadn't gotten up there yet. Who had killed these people? And why?

I found another body whose throat had been slit. This time, the sleeves of its suit had been hiked up enough that I could see ligature marks on its left wrist. It had been bound before it had died, and it had struggled against those bindings hard. But why remove bindings after killing someone? Was it that important to cross their arms over their chest so that they made an *X*? A junction or a crossroads? To spread its feet so that the entire body made a *Y*. An *X* and a *Y*. Male and female symbols together?

We know you don't really care about us, any more than you care about Sig. You're just in love with the idea of being in love. You'd convince yourself that you loved cardboard cutouts of people if they'd let you call them your friends.

Why was the shadow trying so hard to distract me and get me to go after it in a blind rage? What had Ben said? Molly knew how I thought, and her shadow knew that I was the one who was the most familiar with lots of different kinds of lore. What was it that it didn't want me to think about?

You're just a dog that's been kicked too many times, and when you're not biting, you're crawling around, whimpering for someone to love you. Anybody who takes you in does so out of pity.

That was the second time it had compared me to a dog. No, don't think about that. That first body... I tried to track back mentally and figure out where it had been in position to this new body. Two bodies, and I could smell that there were more in the maze ahead. Both bodies I'd found had slit throats. Like sacrifices. At least one had been bound, then untied, then positioned here. Had it been carefully positioned? I was pretty sure John Dee 2.0 was a cunning man, and the shadow thing had been here long enough to get some instructions. If the shadow's unholy mojo was as strong as Molly's holy mojo...

The person you call Molly is the one that isn't real. She's a fake that you project all of your need onto. It kills her inside because she feels like that's who she has to be for your sake. I'm who she really is, and I can't stand you. You're as alone as you ever were. It's just pathetic that you don't know it.

If her unholy mojo...oh, hell. I whispered to Sig, "Watch that left path for me."

"What's going on?"

"I think these bodies are making some kind of pentagram that we can't see because of these maze walls. They're sacrifices, and she's trying to draw us in toward the center of them." That's why Sig couldn't sense any spirits around us. A pentagram is basically a Star of David with a twist, a Solomon's seal, a protective barrier designed to keep things out or keep things in. If they're placed in a spot where the boundaries between dimensions are thin, things can be summoned inside them and contained there.

And if these bodies had been placed at specific points by

Molly's shadow for a specific reason, I didn't want to leave them there. I grabbed the body by its ankles and pulled it back the way I'd come while Sig guarded my back.

I'd dragged the body maybe twelve feet when it began to thrash, a meat puppet being animated. The occult design that the bodies had been placed in really had kept the spirits from that place from messing with them, animating them. The same spirits probably would have been animating all of the knights and werewolves who had died, if knight armor didn't have holy symbols stitched into its threadwork or encased in the plastic plates covering vital organs. Would have been animating the monsters we'd killed if those conjurations didn't use up the same kind of energy that spirits use to manifest physical presences.

I dropped the corpse's leg and my shotgun and drew my katana. It wasn't all one motion, but it was so fast that it probably looked like it. I cut the body's head off with a blessed blade, and it suddenly remembered that it was dead and stopped moving. Somewhere farther in the maze, Molly's shadow started screaming. Not screaming words. Not screaming in pain. Just screaming out pure frustrated hatred.

I really had ruined some big occult surprise she'd been preparing for us. Maybe it would have made a better story if I hadn't, assuming I would have survived to tell it. Maybe Sig could have sacrificed her life so that we could defeat whatever big boss the shadow had in mind. Then Sig could have made a nice speech right before dying. I could even eventually find somebody new to sleep with, and then Sig could come back from death in some contrived bullshit way, and we could wind up in a romantic triangle later.

But screw that. It was my life. I'd do what I wanted with it.

Now that the rite was broken, the first body I'd passed came running around the corner, but it was making noise and I wasn't, and it wasn't used to having a physical form again yet. I was waiting around a wall with my katana poised, and I took off part of its left shoulder and all of its head with one stroke. Then I was running back the way I'd come.

Sig was already removing a spear from another dead body that had animated and come her way. The runes carved into the haft of her battle spear were glowing. I smeared some of my blood on the corner of a turn and went past her, turned again, and wound up bouncing off a dead end when I couldn't stop in time because I'd been moving too fast.

Stone walls might not a prison make, but they don't care if they ruin dramatic moments either. And screw you, Richard Lovelace. Another two dots of dried blood, two turns, and suddenly, I saw something that changed everything.

A stairwell exit. Meanwhile, Molly's shadow was still making noise farther in the maze. Pure evil or not, shadowlike or not, it had also inherited Molly's lack of stealth. I turned to Sig and nodded at the exit. Mimed reading a book. Killing whoever was conjuring up all kinds of fresh hell out of nothing took top priority. There was no point capturing Molly's shadow if we were killed by the next wave of made-up monsters. On one level, Molly's shadow was the most important thing, but on another, it was a distraction.

Sig's mouth tightened, and then she nodded toward the interior of the maze. She was going to make sure the thing that was part of her best friend didn't get away first. That was probably for the best, tactically; Sig could handle any spirits that Molly's shadow whipped into a frenzy and keep them off my back. Whether it was for the best or not, I wasn't going to change Sig's mind, and she wasn't going to change mine.

So I listened carefully, made sure I didn't hear or smell

anything nearby, then handed Sig the shotgun with shells full of blessed salt, took her helmet off, and kissed her. I kissed Sig harder than I've ever kissed anyone in my life. I held on to her like I was trying to mash our bodies into one being. I kissed her like I was trying to drink her through my mouth.

Then I left her there.

Ꮽ48Ꮽ

VIVA THE RESOLUTION

The adjacent stairwell was not full of ice. It was full of yells and the sounds of gunfire, and the stairs were vibrating beneath my feet from the impact of heavy treads, but most of that seemed to be coming from below. The other thing coming from below was Kasia. Her fully functioning hand was holding her katana; her nub of a hand was braced against the wall as if she needed it. She was a mess, her armor ripped in several places, her exposed skin covered in blood and grease and things I couldn't identify and didn't want to. Kasia's helmet was gone, and a hunk of her hair was missing, and she still looked oddly beautiful and I still didn't care. She was dressed appropriately for the kind of party we were about to crash.

"What's going on down there?" I asked when our faces were closer.

"The dragon's teeth began popping out of its mouth and turning into swordsmen," she said with a straight face. Oh, wait. That was from the story of Jason and the Argonauts. One of Medea's magicks. "They are like human-sized enamel golems."

Got it. I began moving up the stairs again.

For the record, I never saw the spinnerets that were giving holy hell to the teams who were trying to crawl up the ventilation ducts. I never saw the Cherufe either, the man-shaped lava being from South American stories that usually only crawls out of volcanoes but this time appeared in a furnace room. I was just one piece of a puzzle, and I never saw the whole picture.

Damned if I wasn't going to be one of the last pieces that went in at the center, though.

Wonder of wonders, we made it up two more floors without incident, and then I had a decision to make. The tower was fourteen floors high. Would John Dee 2.0 be holed up in the highest floor, or would he go for cheap symbolism and take floor thirteen? If he had faked everyone out and was hiding in a small storage closet on floor nine, we were screwed, but I didn't think so. This version of John Dee struck me as an intuitive, symbolic thinker, not a tactician. The School of Night member who had been coming up with complicated feints and double feints and coldly sacrificing people like pawns was probably the one who was supposed to represent Walter Raleigh.

I gave the thirteenth floor a glance and a sniff just to make sure nothing was going to pop out two hot seconds after I passed it, but I didn't search it. The original John Dee hadn't been a Satanist, so that whole thing about thirteen being the number of people at the Last Supper probably didn't amount to much. There were modern short stories and movies where a thirteenth floor was some kind of dimensional suck hole of evil, but this guy didn't seem to do modern, and he didn't think of himself as evil. He thought I was the one who was evil; he was some kind of liberator. He seemed to be fixated on fairy tales, and in fairy tales, the top floor of the tower was always where the action was.

Kasia gave me a look but followed. Maybe she thought I knew what I was doing because of the dream.

Floor fourteen was all one big huge red-carpeted circular space. Maybe it had been separate offices once, but it had been converted into a library. The wooden bookcases were around seven feet tall and filled the four corners of the room with neat rows, all of them forming around the large center of the room, which was essentially a loft apartment. There was a bed, some writing desks, some storage cabinets, an old-fashioned crank phonograph, lots of candles, and some comfortable-looking armchairs. Like most of the rooms in the building, this one was lit by the light from long windows, though several kerosene lamps had also been lit.

There was a wide aisle between bookcases leading from our door straight to the center, and I could clearly see the man from my dream sitting at the writing desk. He was portly, short, bespectacled, balding, wearing a blue bathrobe over green flannel pajamas, and surrounded by open books. Books on the desk. Books on the floor around him. And one particular book that he was drawing a picture in.

I realized something then. The reason this John Dee wannabe had more control over his creations than Reader X was that he'd sussed out some kind of ritual or magical air brakes. He wasn't just conjuring stuff out of his imagination. Sarah... or maybe it was Kevin... had said that the book drew power from a place that was like an ocean made up of different minds that were individual drops of water. The drops of water didn't know what they were doing or where they were going, but they were still powering dams and water wheels, sometimes forming tidal waves. That's what the Book of Am was: a way to channel those imaginations from that place where they all connected.

And the Book of Am was sympathetic magic. This guy wasn't

just standing around, thinking hard about something he'd read, and waving his hand and boom! Alakazam, presto amazo, butt-uglies appear! When this Book of Am tapped into a place of archetypes, of stories that existed in the imaginations of millions of minds, it started with a small part representing the bigger whole. More specifically, the spell started with a literal book that was inspiring the act of creation, and it had to be a story that had been read by lots of people. Forget that metaphor of waterwheels; the storybook was like a diamond drill, being used to bore through a dam and creating a specific-shaped hole that water shot through and spilled over into our world.

Bottom line, as part of the summoning ritual, this reader was sitting down and reading a book, then writing about it and drawing sketches in the Book of Am. Instead of using his own memories or passions as a filter, he was trying to draw clearer boundaries as he encapsulated the stories he wanted to tap into. If that contempt-for-capitalism theme I'd been picking up on in the transformations was real, he hadn't been entirely successful, but it seemed to me that he was trying to keep his connection to his Book of Am from being so intimate that he didn't know where he ended and the book began, to keep those thoughts of the original John Dee's from resonating so intensely that they seemed like his own. Even if I was wrong, whatever this guy was doing took time and concentration, and we'd been pressing him hard.

The windows beyond that center area revealed that the fog I'd heard about was gone. Maybe it was back in Detroit. All I could see were mountains of brown glass glinting in a crimson sun and birds. Lots of birds.

Kasia didn't waste time sussing that or anything else out. She started firing at the man that I was thinking of as John Dee 2.0. Unfortunately, the bullets stopped roughly six feet away from him, sparking off some invisible barrier and caroming around. Was it a ward or something that the book he was transcribing had conjured up? The man startled, did a kind of sitting jump in his chair, and looked up at us, but then he ducked his head and went back to focusing on his book.

Whatever the barrier was, Kasia stopped firing and ran through the rows of books without pausing, counting on her speed to carry her past anything that might be hiding in them. I followed her more cautiously, scanning the aisles and a few book titles as I went. I might have to burn this place down, and I was hoping I'd see books like *How to Commit Ritual Sacrifice* or *Cannibalism for Dummies* as opposed to *White Oleander* or *Cat's Cradle*. But the few titles I could read didn't tell me anything except that the authors were short on clarity and very impressed with themselves. Kasia slammed into the barrier as if it were a transparent steel wall and dropped to the floor. It took her a little longer than it normally would have to pick herself up again. She was still healing, and that adrenaline surge had cost her.

"You're John Dee, right?" I called out. What the hell. I'm not normally one for trying to have a conversation with someone before I kill him, but I didn't have anything better to do at the moment, and maybe I could distract him or get him to reveal some weakness. "The zirconium version, I mean."

The man glanced up again, ignored me, went back to his writing, and then suddenly looked up again as if realizing something. "You're him."

"No, I'm me. Him's on first."

"You're the Charming fellow who killed Northumberland and Aine."

"Oh, that *him*. Yeah."

"And now you're here to kill me, too."

"You make it sound like I murdered them in cold blood. Your friends tortured me because I pissed off a dalaketnon they were sucking up to. The dalaketnon brought a picnic basket so she could watch."

He ignored that. I expect he was good at ignoring inconvenient things that conflicted with his version of events. The Book of Am seemed like an endeavor that encouraged mono-focus.

I reached the invisible barrier with my palm held out and stopped. I had been hoping that my geas might let me pass through it, but no such luck. While I was pressing against it, the room darkened as something huge appeared in the window behind me, blocking out the faint red sun. I half-turned and saw a giant bird's eye the size of a trampoline staring at me through the window. Then I caught the feathered crown of a giant bird's head and the beginning of a giant bird's beak as it bobbed up and down on giant wings and air currents.

"Is that a roc?" I managed to keep my voice steady.

"I thought some of you might try to scale up the side of the building." Dee was still reading one book while scratching something in another. I could vaguely make out winged shapes. He seemed distracted more than hostile, but some of the most evil and horrifying deeds are engineered by people in labs who don't quite get that other people are real. I thought about that giant bird beak snatching men off the side of the building, the knights' scaling ropes trailing them like fishing line, and I had to repress a shudder.

I was close enough now to see that the second book, the one Dee was reading from as he wrote, was in Chinese. I couldn't read it, but I knew enough to know that the characters weren't Japanese. There were all sorts of Chinese legends about places protected by magic barriers. I was pretty sure there was a city of dragons beneath the ocean protected by some kind of magic bubble or dome that could be impenetrable or permeable as the inhabitants wished. There was Shambhala too, the fabled city that inspired Shangri-La, though I couldn't remember if that city was magically shielded by something like this. Or maybe the barrier had come from one of the other books around Dee, and he had moved on.

Kasia had pulled herself up and was moving across the span of the room, trying to find a weak spot or opening in the barrier. I don't mean to give the impression that I was just taking my leisure with a spot of calm conversation. My mind was humming busily while I talked. Sound and light could obviously get through the barrier. Could I work with that? Unfortunately, I didn't have any screamers or flash-bang grenades. Oxygen could pass through it too, probably, unless he just had a lot of air to work with in there. Would a non-dense gas work? Could we smoke him out? What if explosives brought the floor around us down?

So when I asked, "What are you reading there?" I was busily thinking of ways to murder and create even if I didn't sound particularly threatening.

He ignored the question, and when he spoke, it was with the fussy, semi-hostile, impersonal preoccupation of a kid who's trying to concentrate on his video game while people keep bothering him. "Names have power, and so does blood. I won't deny it. But you're not the hero here. You realize that, don't you?"

I went with it. "And you are?"

He ignored my question again, his speech coming out sounding like disjointed mutterings even though the words had a theme. "Your geas enslaves people. You kept us from destroying the geas. That means you're on the side of slavery. You're no different from the blacks who fought with the Confederates, or Jews who cooperated with the Nazis."

I'd actually had doubts about what I'd done at the central archives myself, though I hadn't really been trying to stop the intruders from destroying the geas. I'd just been trying to stop the intruders, period. There had been no guarantee that they were telling the truth, and even if they were, any good deed that someone tries to accomplish through kidnapping a baby, employing skinwalkers, murder, lies, torture, and dark magic can't be right on some level. Screw any greater good that assumes people have to be killed and misled and terrified in order to be cattle driven to the side of righteousness. That's operating straight out of a terrorist's playbook.

That said, the Templars had been ready to set off a dirty bomb in New York City.

"The School of Night just wants to come out of the shadows." Dee didn't even glance up from the book this time. "We want to live in a world where we can tell people who we are without the Pax Arcana keeping them from believing us, or people like you from killing us. You've left us no choice but to destroy the geas the hard way."

"You mean by creating so many big, magical threats that the Pax overloads on its own." The needs of raw survival are one of the few things powerful enough to break the Pax's spell.

He didn't deny it. "When we're ready. Cameron Shaw was just a trial run."

"So you're going to kill lots of innocent people in the process and justify it by saying the world left you no choice. Isn't that what you hate about the knights?"

John Dee continued reading and scribbling. "No, I hate people who are so afraid of hard choices that they complain about the status quo but never do anything to change it. There is no change without chaos and sacrifice."

"And somehow, the people who talk that way the loudest

always mean sacrificing *other* people." What if I set the room on fire? Would the flames travel through the floor and to the other side of the barrier? "I have done something to change the status quo, you know. The knights and the werewolves are working together now. That's a positive change, and for all your talk, your organization has done nothing but try to tear that change down and go back to the old way."

John Dee's voice remained emotionless, whether he really hated me or not. "Getting werewolves to help the knights be better fascists was not a positive change."

"Oh, so you get to decide what's a positive change and what isn't? How is that chaos or sacrifice?" I demanded. "The truth is, you don't want to try to change the knights. You need them to be fascist for your own agenda. You're trying to rally supernaturals to your cause by making knights the bad guys they should band together against, and everything you do is designed to bait the knights into playing along. It's the same mentality that leads to blowing up school buses in Ireland, or bombing plazas in Israel, or causing planes to crash into towers. You sent Cameron Shaw a copy of the Book of Am, knowing it would cause innocent people to die. And you hoped it would cause the knights to act like shits."

For a moment, he smiled a sly smile. "Cause them? I thought you said everyone had a choice. But that's the rub, isn't it? The knights don't really have a choice. They have a geas. We aren't trying to bring out the worst in you Templars. We're trying to expose it."

"That's like unleashing a bio-plague and killing lots of innocent people," I said, "then blaming the government for nuking the area because it was the only way to contain the plague. How are you any better than the thing you're trying to do away with?"

That made John Dee look up. "Magic is not a plague."

"That's why it's called a simile, dumb-ass. The magic you've been unleashing is killing innocent people." That made him flush. Insults about ruthlessness or hypocrisy he could handle, but he didn't like having his raw intelligence challenged. "And why are you so sure making magic public is such a good thing? The Templars didn't create the tens of thousands of werewolf trials in the official records of France. They didn't start the Inquisition in Europe, or the witch trials, or the Dark Ages that made the Fae leave our world and create the Pax Arcana in the first place. Dragging the worst examples of magic out into the light the way you're trying to do is just going to create the same environment of fear and paranoia and jealousy and mistrust. Even if you succeed, you won't change anything. You'll just go back to an even worse status quo. How many violent revolutions weren't replaced by something worse?"

"Well, I can only pray you're wrong about that." He didn't sound particularly reverent or regretful. If anything, he sounded condescending. That's why I have a problem with a lot of cunning folk. Most of them talk as if they're spiritual or enlightened, but too many of them have devoted so much of their intellect to re-envisioning reality, or escaping it, or rationalizing it away, that they never make whatever basic connection with humanity that breeds real compassion and humility. I understand that you can't kill as many people or things as I've killed and still be a good person. I came to terms with that a long time ago. But trying is still important. Maybe even more important. And I've never killed anyone or anything for something as stupid as a political belief.

Kasia, meanwhile, was taking a signal flare and setting fire to a pile of books that she'd made on the floor. I decided to try a little harder in distracting him.

"If you pray for anything," I said, "pray for a fast death."

"Finally," he said, "the thug comes out."

"Your organization was responsible for killing Nick Arbiter, the closest thing to a father I ever had," I said. "Then you kidnapped my goddaughter. Now you've turned my best friend's shadow into some kind of life-sucking parasite, and it's trying to kill the woman I love. I could agree with everything you've said, and I'd still kill you. Screw philosophy. You asswipes keep coming after my family."

But Dee wasn't listening to me anymore. He'd smelled the smoke coming from the books Kasia was burning, and that got to him on a level that went deeper than anything I'd managed.

"YOU BITCH!" he screamed. Rather than distracting him, the rage seemed to provide some kind of extra push. In the far window on the other side of the tower, behind John Dee Junior and his barrier, I could see birds gathering. Not the roc. Flocks of normal-sized birds: crows and ravens and pigeons and purple-colored birds the size of eagles. In one case, I saw three smaller birds meet in midflight and emerge as one of the purple-colored birds, barely making a ripple in reality.

The merged bird crashed through the window and flew straight toward me. I drew my katana and waited, half-expecting the bird to crash into the barrier between us and fall, but neither of us was that lucky. The zhenniao—and I knew that's what it was because of its coloring and the Chinese book that had apparently summoned it—flew straight through the barrier unimpeded, and my sword cut through its extended right foreleg and neck.

Zhenniao are extremely poisonous, and I don't mean that their claws have been dipped in venom. The whole bird is toxic. Just dipping one of its feathers in a glass will poison whatever drink is inside it, and its claws and beak will infect the blood beneath any skin they break. They smell so rancid that cutting into one almost made me gag, and that with the little matter of my own survival distracting me.

The zhenniao's blood landed on a slash in my field armor and made my skin burn.

More of the poisonous purple birds came crashing through windows behind me and to the side, gliding toward us in smooth arcs. I took one hand off my katana and drew my Ruger and started firing at them, but I counted my bullets carefully. "I'll take the right!" I yelled to Kasia. But there were already too many of the things, six in the room and no sign that the pressure was going to let up.

Dee was scrambling for another book, sifting through a pile of unopened ones on the floor, until he finally found what he was looking for—probably something that would put out fires—and went back to the Book of Am.

The blood that had dripped on the open cut in my left arm was a thin slice of fire. My katana dropped from my hand with no prompting on my part. I shot two zhenniao that were coming at me from the east, and I could hear Kasia's Desert Eagle firing behind me, but more and more of the poisonous birds were gathering and merging outside the windows of the tower. Another came soaring through the broken window behind Dee, and I jumped up on an office table stranded on my side of the barrier to get the right angle and aimed, shot two bullets against the barrier to make certain of its location, then fired my last two bullets into the zhenniao's mass.

The bullets passed through the bird's body while it was intersecting the barrier and thudded into John Dee's back on the other side. Small geysers of blood erupted from between and below his shoulders, and he toppled over. "That's how you use a story, dumbass," I said, though I doubt he could hear me.

"*Ill Met in Lankhmar* by Fritz Leiber. Suck it." The climax from that book wasn't an exact parallel to what I'd just done, but it was certainly close enough to count as an inspiration. The cunning man landed on the Book of Am and began bleeding on its open pages. You can't buy that kind of cheesy symbolism.

I think it was the blood destroying the writing on the parchment that made the zhenniao on my back suddenly drop away into three smaller, relatively harmless birds.

I dropped away myself, falling down to my knees, suddenly dizzy. I didn't think the poison was going to kill me, but I was in for a rough time while it worked its way out of my system. My right hand released the Ruger and my face hit the desk I'd been standing on, and then I fell off it and landed on the floor on my back. Another poisonous bird that was flying toward me split into two birds that went in opposite directions.

Molly. What was happening to Molly?

Kasia came up and stood over me. The poison that was paralyzing me didn't seem to be affecting her undead body at all, but vampires and dhampirs have a pretty rudimentary nervous system, and their version of converted blood passes through their body a lot slower. "Well done," she said, and then she leveled the Desert Eagle directly between my eyes. "The kresniks send their regards. This is for Stanislav Dvornik."

I went ahead and tried to move but couldn't. I knew for a fact that her gun was loaded with silver bullets. I tried to say something and wound up spitting foam. What a damned stupid way to die. Then Kasia lowered the handgun and smiled. "Just messing with you."

～49～

GUESS I'LL NEED A FAMILY PLAN

Everything that happened after that is a feverish blur. Sig came around and was pretty upset at finding me in that kind of condition again. "Molly?" I asked.

Sig told me that she'd captured Molly's shadow, and then her lips were moving but I kept losing the words as I slipped in and out of consciousness. At one point, I gestured for her to bend closer, and I whispered what might be my last words to her: "Loot this place."

I guess I'm just a romantic at heart.

Stuart showed up too, or maybe I was the one who showed up, since they were carrying me past him on an improvised stretcher by that point. Stuart motioned for the people carrying the stretcher to slow down and then looked at me for a long moment. "We've never formally met," he said.

I tried to say something flip and couldn't make words.

"My name is Charming," he said. "Stuart Charming."

I was pretty sure the poison had me hallucinating.

The next thing I remember is waking up in a hospital bed, but I wasn't in a hospital. The Templars have a lot of rooms like that. Sig was sitting in an armchair that was way more comfortable than anything an ordinary hospital provides, and a woman was standing next to my bed. The woman was middle-aged, but it was a smooth-skinned, hair-dyed, bright-eyed, and slender middle age. She had been pretty once. Now she had a kind of severe beauty, and she dressed it well.

Sig smiled. "Welcome back, sleeping beauty."

"Who's this woman, Sig?"

"I'm Laurel Charming. I see you're as tough to kill as everyone says you are." She sounded a little disappointed.

Well, I wasn't overjoyed myself. "No offense, but if this is the part where you say you're my daughter, I'm going to need some pretty compelling evidence."

She smiled a meaningless smile. "It's not like that."

"Okay," I said. "But first, what happened with the Book of Am? Or books?"

"I set John Dee Junior's Book of Am on fire," Sig said. "We'd been stuck in that dead place for a day, and I was sick of it. I almost gave some merlin a heart attack, but it worked. Molly's shadow disappeared too. We went back to Detroit, and the things that had been transformed started changing back, even if a lot of them were broken or dead."

"A day? How long have I been out?"

"The doctors wanted to break it to you in stages, but I told them you'd want the truth as soon as you woke up." Sig came over and took my hand. "John, it's been ten years."

"You've got bruises you picked up in the tower."

"Oh. Maybe it's only been two days, then." That's one of the problems with being a smartass. What goes around comes around.

"Did we set Reader X's copy of the Book of Am on fire, too?" I asked.

Laurel answered for her. "Yes. We're debating whether or not to do the same to the original." *We?* Laurel spoke like someone fairly high up in the Templar power structure, or at least like someone with connections.

"What about the people that book transformed?" I asked.

"They've changed back as well," Laurel said crisply. "Simon's dealing with them."

That probably wasn't as ominous as it sounded. Probably.

"So, how is your last name Charming?" I asked. "I thought I was the last one."

Her face made that empty shell of a smile again. "That's what I'm here to talk about. Would you ask your Valkyrie to leave the room?"

"My Valkyrie can stay if she wants to," I said. "But if it's going to be that kind of a discussion, I need to pee first."

Biology doesn't pay much attention to dignity. When I made it to the bathroom, and I made it on my own after a few wobbly moments, I discovered that I was wearing a diaper. Finally, we got it all settled. I was sitting on my bed fully dressed in clothes that didn't have blood and God knows what else on them, drinking some orange juice. Sig was back in the armchair. Laurel remained standing.

"My mother, Emily Dunn, was married to a knight. He died after you became an exile in the sixties, and my mother went back to her maiden name. Charming."

I couldn't remember any cousins or second or third cousins named Emily, but I had grown up in an orphanage. "And she changed your name back, too?" I asked.

"No," Laurel said. "My mother was determined to keep our family name alive. She was forty years old, but she had three more children after that without marrying. It was quite the scandal at the time. We grew up illegitimate, but we still had a last name. Your last name. It just made us more determined to earn respect."

It was a lot to take in, and I was still a bit out of it. "And you went forth and multiplied?"

"My four children are legitimate, but I made my husband take my last name." Something about the glint in her blue eyes... my blue eyes... made me believe it. "You've met Stuart and Janine."

"Janine?"

"The female knight who carries a crossbow around with her like some sort of absurd good luck charm," Laurel said. "She hasn't shown much interest in assuming her part of making sure our family survives yet."

"You all took your time introducing yourselves," Sig observed from the corner.

Laurel answered her but spoke to me. "I'd still be taking my time if Stuart hadn't taken matters into his own hands. I'm only here to clarify my position: I've spent my entire life being tainted by you just through association. I've been trying to make the name Charming something to be proud of again, and you've spent most of that time not having the decency to commit suicide or get killed. Do you know that Bernard Wright was committing atrocities and making the knights think that you were responsible?"

"I found out about that later," I said. "Before I killed him."

That made her nod. "You've made strides in restoring your honor despite your..." She hesitated.

"Lycanthropy?" I suggested. It sounded more clinical than *hell-spawned infection.*

"Yes. And God knows you're not the first Charming to be cursed." This was true. We'd been blinded, turned to statues, had our memories stolen, and been transformed into at least three different kinds of were-beings if half the stories were true. Or even true-ish.

"So what now?" I asked. "Should I buy an ugly sweater and bring a casserole for Thanksgiving?"

"No." At least she wasn't pretending to smile. "But regaining our influence and completely avoiding you might not be practical any longer. Simon seems intent on bringing you closer to the center of things."

"Batten down the hatches," I said. "Tie down the loose cannons."

"I suppose so," she agreed. "So I won't forbid my children to interact with you." That was big of her. I hadn't really gotten to know Stuart or this Janine, but I had the impression that forbidding things wasn't the right tactic to take with them anyhow. "But I have no intention of sending you a Christmas card. If it's all the same to you, I think I'll just quietly stand aside and hope you die while you're still barely in the plus column."

"It better be damned quietly," Sig said. "And you'd better not do more than hope. John isn't alone anymore."

Laurel gave Sig a look as if she were humoring her. That wasn't going anyplace good, and I was too tired to deal with it. "You've given me a lot to think about and gotten a few cheap shots in, Laurel. You should probably go while I'm still on medication."

"Then I'll take my leave." And she did.

"Sorry about that," I told Sig. "If I'd known she was going to get all weepy and sentimental, I would have asked you to leave after all."

She took my hand again. "We're family now."

I raised Sig's hand to my lips and kissed her knuckles gently. I didn't trust myself to say anything else.

Epilogue

DAMN YOU, WINDMILL!
PREPARE YOURSELF!

So that's it? We can go home?" The crutch that Choo would be using for a few weeks was leaned against the table next to him. Choo and Molly and Sig and Sarah and Kevin and Ben and I were gathered on the third floor of Food Gallery 32, a place in Manhattan crammed full of independently owned Korean food stalls. The ambiance reminded me of an IKEA cafeteria in Charlotte, North Carolina, that Sig is always dragging me to. The two places weren't really all that alike—the IKEA didn't have videos of Korean pop stars playing in the background for example—but they did both have the same weird combination of bright walls and traditional foods and big rooms with big views.

"Yes," Ben said. I was too busy chewing. The spicy pork teppanyaki was excellent.

We were waiting for Kasia. She was going back to some place that she wouldn't specify, but I was pretty sure it was one of those Eastern European places whose name ends in the letters *ia* and whose language has a lot of sharp *K*s and hard vowels.

We had a last bit of business with her. Sig had found several rare books in John Dee Junior's private library that Sarah had assured us didn't reek of black magic, and we'd gotten two hundred and twenty-nine thousand dollars for them at a shop that Sarah knew about. Kasia was entitled to a split. It wasn't much after being divided seven ways, not after Choo's expenses and the purchase of some outrageously high-priced tickets to the play *Hamilton* to celebrate Molly being all Molly again, but it was something. The gold I'd buried had changed back to trophies and plaques made out of cheaper metals and gold paint.

"Are you sure you want to go home?" Sarah asked Molly. "You would be welcome to stay with me again for a few weeks."

"Thanks, but I need to see my pup, and I don't think I'm suffering any side effects from whatever happened to me." Then Molly shifted the fork she was using so that she held it in her fist. She raised the fork over her head and stared at me with a glazed, wide-eyed maniacal look.

"Cut that out," I told her.

"Sorry." Molly didn't sound particularly apologetic. She smelled more relaxed than she had since I'd met her, not that I recommend having your negative emotions literally sucked out of you and stuffed back in by a homicidal grimoire. Still, it seemed like the experience had been some kind of soul enema or something.

"That wasn't funny," Sig scolded, but she was smiling. Sig was still just a little tentative around Molly. She hadn't talked too much about her experience with Molly's shadow, so I imagine the shadow bitch had dumped a lot of the same kind of toxic waste in Sig's ear that it had dumped in mine. The kind that has just enough truth to burn, but never the whole truth, or even the most truth. Life is what you choose to emphasize.

"About home." Choo looked down at his plate. "I'm moving to Charlottesville to be with Chantelle. Near her, I mean. We aren't ready for more than that."

"Are you telling us good-bye, or are you asking us to move with you?" Molly asked.

For some reason, Choo was surprised. "Would y'all be willing to do that?"

Sig looked at me. I shrugged. "We've been thinking about moving someplace closer to Washington DC and New York anyhow, and there's no way I'm living in a city. Besides, that's only half an hour away from the Blackfriars Playhouse in Staunton."

"Why are you thinking of moving closer?" Sarah sounded suspicious rather than pleased.

"I'm going to have to be more active with the Templars now."

That didn't exactly reassure her. "Active how?"

I didn't have a specific answer yet. "John Dee Junior wasn't wrong about everything."

"That's so sad." Molly was working on a Red Mango frozen yogurt.

"Which part?" I asked.

"That you and this John Dee person wanted so many of the same things, and you had to kill him anyhow. It makes me wonder what he'd think if he could hear us now."

I wasn't in the mood to dwell on how tragic that particular cunning man's fate had been. Our brief meeting had given me a lot to think about, and think about it I would whether I wanted to or not, but at the moment, I was in healing mode, not feeling mode. "It just makes me think of that old joke: What's the last thing to go through a bug's mind when it hits a windshield?"

Choo obliged me. "What?"

"Its butthole."

Molly spooned a small portion of froyo onto her tongue. "Sig, would you punch him for me?"

Sig obligingly punched me in my upper arm, but she didn't put any effort into it. She gets sophomoric gallows humor. I leaned over to kiss her cheek, and she turned her face so that our lips met briefly. We'd both been maybe a little clingy since the tower. Not constantly asking for emotional updates or anything, but not letting each other out of our sight, touching each other on the flimsiest pretext as if just to make sure the other was still there. I expected we'd start to get over it once we were out of New York, and for now, neither of us seemed to mind.

"But are you sure that it was really him?" Kevin was staring at his spicy noodles dubiously. I think the vendor had maybe gone light on the spice to suit American palates, and Kevin liked his spicy noodles flamethrower-hot. "How do we know this School of Night didn't pull some complicated switch again? They seem really good at it."

"I talked to his ghost." Sig didn't quite manage to say it casually.

Sarah raised her eyebrows. "After John killed him?"

"It was a lot easier in that dead place we were stuck in, and I wanted to find a way out. He had a lot to say." Sig's tone and expression discouraged any requests for elaboration. "None of it was useful."

Sounded like the saddest epitaph ever: *He had a lot to say. None of it was useful.*

And speaking of useful information, we had finally found a lot of it in regards to the School of Night. The companies that had been working in that tower were mostly shells, conducting their legitimate business over the Internet from other locations where technology worked, but we had found our first real records of property holdings, financial transactions, and communications with people who had to be members or minions. The Templars were busily rooting out connections leading to bigger connections, which was part of the reason we hadn't invited Simon to lunch despite my resolve to start doing things differently. The other reason being I was still recovering my appetite.

Nothing is ever really over like in fairy tales and movies. There is no happily ever after. Real life goes on after people say "I love you," and credits don't roll when someone dies. I hadn't forgotten that Aubrey had mentioned some elf renegade calling himself Uriel, for example, but even if it really was the same being calling itself Uriel that had communicated with the original John Dee, it was a being that was really good at hiding and whose plans took centuries to crystallize. And we had just ruined its latest one.

I hadn't forgotten that the Templars had dirty bombs and were willing to use them under the right (or wrong) circumstances, either. The thing was, I knew from personal experience that the only way to work around the knights' geas was to change the terms they were thinking in, and there was no easy, short-term way to do that. I had a feeling that I was done with rushing around in crisis mode with a critical deadline and insane consequences hanging over me for a while. I had some long-term one-step-at-a-time groundwork to start building, in both my personal and professional life, if you can call what I do a profession.

"I have some ideas on how John might get more involved," Ben announced.

I stopped eating. "I'm not passing out any fliers."

"You're the one who suggested having werewolves and squires train together," Ben reminded me, without explaining why he was reminding me.

"So?"

"I was thinking about that orphanage that Simon came out of," Ben said. "The one for kids who grow up with knights' blood without knowing they're geas-born. Those kids can see all the things that the Pax Arcana usually screens out, and they don't know why, and they don't understand why they can't talk about it, right?"

"That's what I heard. Those places are supposed to be pretty hard-core because not many people know about them, and the kids don't have any connections or sponsors to protest how they're trained. A lot of the deadliest knights are supposed to come out of them."

"Sounds perfect. It wouldn't raise a lot of opposition, then, and those kids would be on the track to be knights, but they wouldn't have a lot of the attitude against werewolves drilled into them yet."

"You're thinking of a test school," I said.

"Magnet schools were test schools once," Ben said. "And now they're some of the best schools around. But a school that trained young geas-born and werewolves would have to have good teachers. People who knew what it took to be a knight and a functional werewolf and weren't irrationally prejudiced against either."

"I've got all kinds of issues with both."

"I never noticed." Ben's eyes crinkled. "I said *irrationally prejudiced.*"

Sig seemed intrigued. "Starting small might be good. You said you wanted to change the way knights think. This would give you a chance to mold some minds."

"You want me to be an authority figure." I started eating again. "I hate authority figures."

Ben's smile was pure evil. "Revenge."

"Revenge for what?"

Ben didn't even have to think about it. "For making me do all the hard work while you went around killing things. For being so damned hard to lead. Have you ever heard the expression *don't piss off a Chippewa*?"

"No," I said.

"Well, I just made it up," Ben admitted. "But it's still good advice."

"I don't care what you call it. Me being an instructor is the single worst idea I've ever heard."

Molly clapped her hands.

"What?" I asked.

"That means you're going to do it."

"It absolutely does not."

Sarah smiled gently. "How many worst ideas have you heard that you wound up *not* doing?"

I opened my mouth and realized that I didn't have a ready rejoinder to that.

Sig smirked. "I thought you understood how jinxes worked."

"If you're right about me and worst ideas, it explains how I wound up hanging around you bums," I grumbled.

"Speaking of bad ideas and people you hang around, what's taking Kasia so long?" Kevin wondered.

I was glad to get the opportunity to shift the attention off me for a while. "Why are you so interested? Did her flirting get under your skin, Kevin?"

He reddened. "She just didn't strike me as the kind of person who's late. Ever."

"Uh-huh. Methinks the laddie doth protest too much."

Choo had his own concerns. "Are we sure she isn't lining us up in her rifle sights right now?" He only sounded a little uneasy, but then, he was on painkillers.

"She said she'd decided not to kill any of us." Sig almost sounded disappointed. "She wouldn't lie about that unless somebody was paying her to."

"Well, that's a relief," Sarah said caustically.

"You can all relax," I said. "She got stuck in a food line downstairs."

"How do you know that?" Sarah was still a little hung up on establishing that I had a little psychic something extra.

"Because she's coming up the escalator." And she was. Kasia had recovered from her wounds, and I didn't even want to know how she was getting her blood transfusions. She was in one piece now, but that one piece was still moving stiffly compared to her usual panther's grace.

Sig reached over and squeezed my hand. "Whatever we decide, I guess we won't be taking any more trips to Iceland for a while."

"I hope that's not how you guys refer to having sex." Was that a joke from Kevin? Maybe he was loosening up because he'd almost been killed a few times, or maybe he was just getting me back for teasing him about Kasia, but it still seemed like a good sign.

"Sig and I took a vacation in Iceland a few months ago," I explained, then took it a little further because Kevin seemed embarrassed that he'd spoken up, and I didn't want him shutting down again. "We call making love *taking the night train to Valhalla*."

"We do not," Sig said firmly.

"You mean I never said that out loud?"

"You did not." Sig addressed the rest of the table then. "And just so everybody knows, anybody who makes any jokes about my caboose is going to wake up regretting it."

I started to say something—nothing bad, honest—but Sig

cut me off. "If I even see you thinking it, I'll throw you out the nearest window."

"Sig, I love you," I said. "But if you start seeing my thoughts, I'll throw myself out the nearest window." She rolled her eyes, but the corners of her mouth twitched up, and I kissed her cheek, then her lips again. We stared at each other, our eyes maybe four inches apart. *Hey, you. We're still here.*

"Please stop." Kasia had arrived. "I was planning to eat." And she was, too. She'd brought enough food to stay awhile. Huh. She sat down next to Kevin, and we got back to the business of being happy to be alive.

extras

orbit

meet the author

An army brat and gypsy scholar, ELLIOTT JAMES is currently living in the Blue Ridge Mountains of southwest Virginia. An avid reader since the age of three (or that's what his family swears, anyhow), he has an abiding interest in mythology, martial arts, live music, hiking, and used bookstores.

introducing

If you enjoyed
LEGEND HAS IT
look out for

STRANGE PRACTICE

A Dr. Greta Helsing Novel

by Vivian Shaw

Meet Greta Helsing, fast-talking doctor to the undead. Keeping the supernatural community not-alive and well in London has been her family's specialty for generations.

Greta Helsing has inherited the family's specialized medical practice, and she can barely make ends meet with her entropy treatments for local mummies. Normally, her biggest problem is making sure her ancient Mini still runs.

But when a sect of murderous monks begins to scour the city's underbelly, intent on killing her supernatural friends (and nearly succeeding), Greta must team up with her undead clients to keep them—and the rest of London—safe.

extras

The sky was fading to ultramarine in the east by the time a battered Mini pulled up in front of Ruthven's house. Here and there in the maples lining the Embankment itself, sparrows had begun to sing.

A woman got out of the car and shut the door, swore, put down her bags, and shut the door again with more concentration; something had bashed into the panel at some time in the past and bent it sufficiently to make this a production every damn time. It was really time to replace the Mini, but even with her inherited Harley Street consulting rooms, Greta Helsing was not exactly drowning in cash.

She glowered at the car and then at the world in general, picked up her bag, and went to ring the bell. Ruthven lived in one of a row of magnificent old buildings separating Temple Gardens from the Victoria Embankment near Blackfriars Bridge, mostly taken over by hotels and high-priced art galleries these days. It was something of a testament to the vampire's powers of persuasion that nobody had bought the house out from under him and turned it into a trendy little wine bar, she thought, and then had to stifle a laugh at the idea of anybody dislodging Ruthven from the lair he'd inhabited these two hundred years or more, even if he'd had to sublet it from time to time when, for various reasons, it became advisable for him to disappear. He was as much a fixture of London as Lord Nelson on his pillar, albeit less encrusted with birdlime.

"Greta," said the fixture, opening the door. "Thanks for coming out on a Sunday. I know it's late."

She was just about as tall as he was, five foot five and a bit, which made it easy to look right into his eyes and be struck every single time by the fact that they were very large, so pale a grey they looked silver except for the dark ring at the edge of the iris, and fringed with soot-black lashes of the sort you saw in close-up mascara advert photos. He looked tired, she thought. Tired, and older than the fortyish he usually appeared.

"It's not Sunday night; it's Monday morning," she said. "No worries, Ruthven. I couldn't possibly *not* come after a call like that. You'd better go into more detail than you did on the phone."

"Of course." He offered to take her coat. "There's coffee. Black, two sugars?"

"Make it three. I didn't get to eat dinner." She rubbed at the back of her neck. "Thanks."

The entryway of the Embankment house was floored in black-and-white-checkered marble, and a large bronze ibis stood on a little side table where the mail and car keys and shopping lists were to be found. The mirror behind this reflected Greta dimly and greenly, like a woman underwater, and as she waited for Ruthven and coffee, she made a face at herself and tucked back her hair. It was pale Scandinavian blond and cut like Liszt's in an off-the-shoulder bob, and fine enough to slither free of whatever she used to pull it back; today, it was in the process of escaping from a thoroughly childish headband. She kept meaning to have the lot chopped off and be done with it, but never seemed to find the time.

Greta Helsing was thirty-four, unmarried, and had taken over her late father's medical practice after a brief stint as an internist at King's College Hospital. For the past five years, she had run a bare-bones clinic out of Wilfert Helsing's old rooms on Harley Street, treating a patient base that to the majority of the population did not, technically, when you got right down to it, exist. It was a family thing. Really, once she'd gone into medicine, there wasn't a lot of mystery about which subspecialty she would pursue: treating the differently alive was not only more interesting than catering to the ordinary human population; it was in many ways a great deal more rewarding. Greta's patients could largely be classified under the heading of *monstrous*—in its descriptive, rather than pejorative, sense: vampires, were-creatures, mummies, banshees, bogeymen, and the occasional ghoul.

She herself was solidly and entirely human, with no noticeable eldritch qualities or powers whatsoever, not even a flicker of metaphysical sensitivity. Some of her patients found it difficult to trust a human physician at first, but Greta had built up an extremely good reputation over the five years she had been practicing supernatural medicine, largely by word of mouth: *go to Helsing; she's reliable.*

And discreet. That was the first and fundamental tenet, after all: keeping her patients safe meant keeping them secret, and Greta was good with secrets. She made sure the magical wards around her doorway in Harley Street were kept up properly, protecting anyone who approached from prying eyes—she had a witch colleague of hers come round every month and touch up anything that was fading—and regularly tested how they worked herself to make sure. Passersby were able to see the door perfectly well, but ordinary humans watching it would inexplicably fail to notice anything *odd* about the people who came and went, or in fact to recall with any clarity what they had looked like.

Ruthven emerged from the kitchen with a large pottery mug. She recognized it as one of the set he generally used for blood, and had to grin. The coffee was both strong and good, with a kick to it that nudged away several of the accumulated hours of fatigue sitting on her brainstem, and he'd put in quite a lot of sugar. "That's better," she said, straightening up a little. "All right, tell me more about your visitor. He's one of the big names?"

Ruthven led her to the drawing-room doorway. He'd lit a fire, despite the mildness of the night, and the creature lying on the sofa was covered with two throw rugs and a fluffy blanket. Greta could make out a beaklike nose and a shock of greying hair and not a lot else. "He's sleeping," Ruthven said, quietly. "That's Sir Francis Varney. I don't know if you would've read the penny dreadful—"

"*Varney the Vampyre, or The Feast of Blood*?" Greta said, the italics audible. Ruthven looked relieved.

"That's the one. You may have twigged that the bit where he throws himself into Mount Vesuvius was by way of being artistic license, but I do believe some of the other stuff actually is true. But I called you because he's been wounded by something I don't recognize and he isn't even beginning to heal, and he's warm to the touch."

"Warm to *your* touch?"

"Exactly. The attack itself doesn't make any sense to me either; he was apparently set upon by three people dressed up like *monks*, if you can imagine. Who first had a go at him with garlic, going on about unclean creatures of darkness, and then stabbed him with a peculiar sort of knife. Well, I *say* knife. It must have been more of a four-bladed spike. The wound is... cross-shaped."

Greta stared at him. *That's a hell of a coincidence, isn't it?* she thought.

There had been a series of high-profile murders in London over the past month and a half—six people stabbed to death, four of them prostitutes, all found with a cheap plastic rosary stuffed into their mouths. The modus operandi didn't exactly match how Ruthven had described this attack—monks, a strange-shaped knife—but it was close, and for the first time, Greta wondered if it wasn't just one person behind the murders.

If, in fact, there were more than one: a *group* of people doing the killing.

Unclean, she thought. *Creatures of darkness.* The murder victims had been perfectly ordinary humans, as far as Greta knew. So far.

So far, the police hadn't been able to do much of anything either, and a rising fear had suffused the city: people were paying more attention to the news than they had in years, checking the BBC website every morning in a kind of dreadful anticipation of the next Rosary Ripper case. Conspiracy theories abounded, none of them making much sense.

"There was nothing on the news about the murders that mentioned weird-shaped wounds," she said out loud. "Although I suppose the police might be keeping that to themselves."

Ruthven made a face. "I have a hard time thinking of serial killers dressed up as monks," he said. "But you're right; it's too near the mark. I think I'm going to call Cranswell and see if he can do a bit of research for me. Varney didn't say anything about a rosary, though."

"Maybe they keep that for humans," she said. There hadn't been anything in the supernatural community to indicate the Ripper was branching out into other species, but then again, Greta was not privy to the goings-on of the entire London underworld: she got her news from her patients.

Her patients, she thought, including the one she'd been summoned to attend. "I'd better get on with it," she said, handing back the empty mug, and went through to the drawing room.

In the years Greta had been in practice, she had become familiar with the physiologies of at least a dozen different creatures, none of whom were covered in the standard medical-school curriculum: she'd relied on her father's books and the small but intense community of supernatural-medicine practitioners, both there and on the Continent, to continue her professional education. As a child, she'd shadowed Wilfert Helsing as much as possible, knowing even at the age of ten what she wanted to do with her life.

Most of the species she saw were divided into discrete sub-types, including the sanguivores. If she remembered the text of *The Feast of Blood* correctly, Varney *was* a vampyre with a *Y*, a lunar sensitive, not a classic draculine like Ruthven and the few other vampires in London. (You barely ever saw the nosferatu this side of the Channel, and she herself had never encountered one.) Which meant that Polidori had managed to get his tax-onomy dead wrong in *The Vampyre*, on top of everything else.

Vampyres with a *Y* were less common than the draculine vampires for a number of reasons, mostly due to the fact that they were violently allergic to the blood of anyone but vir-gins, which made life rather complicated in modern society. They did have the handy characteristic of being resurrected by moonlight every time they got themselves killed, which Greta thought probably didn't come as much of a comfort while expir-ing in the throes of acute gastric distress brought on by dietary indiscretion. This one was pale grey and sheened with sweat, cadaverously thin. Shadows stood out under his sharp-edged cheekbones; the delicate skin beneath the eyes was stained bruise-black. Something was terribly, profoundly wrong with him, much more than could be explained by a simple flesh wound, and she had no idea what it could be.

She pulled on a pair of nitrile gloves and began her examina-tion.

A few minutes later, she came through into the kitchen, where Ruthven was tiredly going over a newsletter manuscript in red pen, and began to rummage in cupboards. He watched her for a moment. "Is there something I can help you with?"

"There's something still *in* there," Greta threw over her shoulder, and pulled out a large Pyrex mixing bowl from one of the cupboards. "It needs to come out right now. He's pushing eighty-seven degrees and his pulse rate's approaching living human baseline. Can you put on a kettle? I need boiling water." She set a small shagreen case on his countertop and took out a series of tweezers and probes that would have fit right aboard a ship of Nelson's navy.

He got up and filled the kettle. "What is it, then? Whatever got him was poisoned, that's obvious, but what the hell kind of poison can do that to a vampire?" Their normal body temperature hovered around eighty. Eighty-seven was . . . frightening.

"Vampyre," Greta said, tucking hair behind her ears. Ruthven could hear the subtle difference in pronunciation, but only because he was paying attention. "It's possible there's a different physiological response to some kinds of toxin in the lunar sensitives than with your type. Short answer: I don't know. Long answer: I intend to call in a few favors and find out."

VISIT THE ORBIT BLOG AT

www.orbitbooks.net

FEATURING

BREAKING NEWS
FORTHCOMING RELEASES
LINKS TO AUTHOR SITES
EXCLUSIVE INTERVIEWS
EARLY EXTRACTS

AND COMMENTARY FROM OUR EDITORS

WITH REGULAR UPDATES FROM OUR TEAM,
ORBITBOOKS.NET IS YOUR SOURCE
FOR ALL THINGS ORBITAL.

WHILE YOU'RE THERE, JOIN OUR E-MAIL LIST
TO RECEIVE INFORMATION ON SPECIAL OFFERS,
GIVEAWAYS, AND MORE.

imagine. explore. engage.